DECOLONIZATION AGONISTICS IN POSTCOLONIAL FICTION

Decolonization Agonistics in Postcolonial Fiction

Chidi Okonkwo

First published in Great Britain 1999 by
MACMILLAN PRESS LTD
Houndmills, Basingstoke, Hampshire RG21 6XS and London
Companies and representatives throughout the world

A catalogue record for this book is available from the British Library.

ISBN 0–333–63869–7

First published in the United States of America 1999 by
ST. MARTIN'S PRESS, INC.,
Scholarly and Reference Division,
175 Fifth Avenue, New York, N.Y. 10010

ISBN 0–312–22068–5

Library of Congress Cataloging-in-Publication Data
Okonkwo, Chidi, 1952–
Decolonization agonistics in postcolonial fiction / Chidi Okonkwo.
p. cm.
Includes bibliographical references and index.
ISBN 0–312–22068–5 (cloth)
1. Commonwealth fiction (English)—History and criticism.
2. Literature and society—English-speaking countries—History—20th
century. 3. English fiction—20th century—History and criticism.
4. Decolonization in literature. 5. Colonies in literature.
I. Title.
PR9084.O46   1999
823'.914099171241—dc21   98–53052
                                                             CIP

This book is printed on paper suitable for recycling and made from fully managed and
sustained forest sources.

10   9   8   7   6   5   4   3   2   1
08   07   06   05   04   03   02   01   00   99

Printed and bound in Great Britain by
Antony Rowe Ltd, Chippenham, Wiltshire

To Njide, Ije and Ugo
With love and gratitude

Contents

Preface

The last two decades of the twentieth century have seen a proliferation of various 'postcolonial' cultural and literary theories under the aegis of postmodernism and poststructuralism, a direct concomitant to the globally homogenizing forces that have been loosed in the New World Order. Under these totalizing discourses, the literatures created by ex-colonized peoples to combat the material and psychological effects of colonialism past and present are increasingly assimilated into the discourses of (neo)colonialism, within the rubrics of a political concept of 'postcoloniality' that seeks to erase the contradictions between the colonizer and the colonized. 'Postcolonial literature' has accordingly been defined as a catch-all category for the literatures of all the world's peoples (including the United States of America) outside the male-authored texts of the dominant European imperial powers.

The present book seeks to refocus attention on the literatures of formerly colonized peoples through a close study of the decolonization tradition as it has developed over the past half-century in three regions of the Third World – Anglophone Africa, Polynesia and the West Indies – between the late 1940s and early 1990s as a historically determined cultural product. Its main focus is on how the nationalist impulse behind this fictive tradition has shaped various aspects of the novel form and the internal relationships among these aspects. In the course of this, it attempts to offer an alternative postcolonial mode of critique to the current practice which is severely handicapped by its derivation from, and servile imitation of, academic postmodernism in the West. Its concentration on the literatures of Africa, Polynesia and the West Indies is based primarily on the fact that, in addition to their shared experience of British colonization, these are cultures that acquired the technology of writing in the course of the colonial experience, and it is hoped that a serious investigation of the interaction between oral conventions of aesthetic representation and inherited written forms will contribute substantially to the development of comparative studies of such literatures. The selection is also governed by the realization that the ragbag approach favoured by homogenizing postcolonial theories compelled eliding major distinctive features of decolonization literatures for the purpose of assimilating the literatures within the universal broth, or infiltrating the literatures with issues derived from European cultural history and social conflicts.

The term 'agonistics' is used here to mean 'result-oriented action' directed against an identified antagonist. Hence 'decolonization agonistics' means actions and strategies designed to engage the psychological and material effects of (neo)colonialism with a view to reversing them, even while offering critiques of postcolonial society. My definition of 'postcolonial society' is quite specific. It means a *society* that directly experienced European colonization. The emphasis here is on 'society' rather than country, for in a country where a European Diaspora has installed itself in permanent occupation through conquest – as in Australia, Canada, New Zealand, the United States of America and the Latin American countries – its relationship with the conquered indigenous populations is that of colonizer and colonized. Such a paracolonial country comprises two different societies, with the conquered population existing as the Third World underbelly of the dominant European society. Postcolonial literature is therefore used interchangeably with decolonization literature to refer to the literature created by the people of paracolonial or ex-colonial societies in direct response to the experience of (neo)colonialism, with a view to challenging (neo)colonialist assumptions and combating the psychological and material effects of (neo) colonialism.

I have employed the term 'Third World' throughout this book without any pejorative connotation to refer to those countries or societies that have experienced or are experiencing European (neo) colonialism, in preference to the meaningless cosmetic designation of 'Less Developed Countries'. The term therefore precludes countries like China and Japan, although during the Cold War the former found it ideologically expedient to apply the designation to itself. In the same vein, 'European' is used to designate both the people of present-day Europe and the European Diaspora of North and South America, Australia and New Zealand. When 'America' as a distinctive manifestation of Europe is intended, it is designated as such, and the West is specified when dealing with phenomena that are specifically Western rather than European. The literature of Europe, as here defined to include that of the United States of America, is thus generally referred to as European literature while that of the European Diaspora is designated as 'imperial outpost' literature in recognition of the Diaspora's self-perception and historical reality as the extension of Europe.

Engagement of decolonization issues and a serious concern with aesthetic forms are the major criteria governing my choice of authors or novels. I have avoided the practice, common in postcolonial discourse, of shoe-horning into this discourse fashionable but unrelated issues, usually specific to Europe or manifested outside European society in distinctive ways that discourage generalizing them as universal. Application of the two criteria also means that I have not let myself be bound by any misconceived principle of balancing either by region or by gender. Thus, while I have selected a few African and Polynesian writers and treated a large selection of their novels, I have discussed only a representative sample each of the work of some West Indian writers, with the exception of V.S. Naipaul who is represented with several novels. Selection, here, is guided by the fact that only Naipaul's novels offer an equivalent of an indigenous or pre-European culture in conflict with the European, as found in African and Polynesian novels. In contrast, neither politics nor the colonial experience has featured prominently in African women's novels, with the notable exception of those of Grace Ogot. Only Ogot has therefore received extended treatment. Nevertheless, the need to keep the study manageable while striving after representative depth and breadth has meant that many writers or novels that meet the criteria have been left out.

Another departure from prevailing practice is the importance given to criticism of actual literary texts rather than using the texts as points of departure into endless recycling of so-called cultural theories which often have little relevance to any postcolonial culture. The approach adopted is to use theory primarily as a guide to critical analysis, and in doing so contribute to the development of a genuine postcolonial mode of critique that is consonant with the 'ideology' and mood of the literature itself. A sociological-historical approach, literary stylistics and myth criticism are integrated in pursuit of an understanding of the literatures in their cultural distinctiveness even while responding to fundamental transformations in their socio-historical contexts. Particular attention is given to cultural psychodynamics and the codes or conventions of aesthetic representation which nationalistic novelists exploit as strategies of political assertion and cultural resistance. By implication, therefore, prominence is given to authorial purpose and ideology, in conscious rejection of the minimization of the author and exaltation of the theorist and critic in post-structuralist and postmodernist cultural/literary theory. Finally, an attempt has been made to avoid the shamanistic language of much contemporary cultural/literary theory and criticism, bearing in mind the study's primary audience of undergraduate and postgraduate students of culture and literature.

The first three chapters engage the theoretical and critical issues that preoccupy mainstream postcolonial discourse, and through extended discussion of a variety of novels attempt to establish alternative approaches to these literatures as well as rejuvenate effective approaches that have been smothered by the 'first past the post' scramble for pre-eminence among leading theorists of postcoloniality. Chapter 1 thus examines the identity crisis which has hampered the development of a genuine postcolonial discourse, tracing it to the neocolonialist origins of the discipline. The historical and ideological origination of decolonization literature is also explored, to demonstrate both the distinctiveness of the literature and the impossibility of developing genuine cross-cultural studies from mainstream postcolonial discourse whose parameters, frames of reference and fundamental cultural assumptions are all European-originated and defined. From a starting position that the literary form has been developing along an orality–literacy continuum in tandem with transformations within the socio-cultural context, Chapter 2 relates the development to novelists' nationalistic strategies for engaging the interlocking forces of (neo)colonialism and internal self-violations. Drawing upon insights developed in various fields of linguistics and cultural studies, the chapter further attempts to account for novelists' handling of the constitutive elements of the novel in their continuous search for adequate formal embodiment for their aesthetic and ideological visions. Appropriation and transformation of the colonizer's language into an agency of self-reintegration and anti-colonialist resistance is discussed in Chapter 3, which goes beyond ephemeral issues of style to seek out other significant relationships between decolonization ideology and language strategies.

Attention shifts to themes in Chapters 4 and 5, the former focusing on strategies of self-affirmation in the first generation of decolonization novels, while the latter discusses the responses to neocolonialism and post-independence failures. Both chapters stress thematic aspects that have received inadequate attention both in traditional criticism and the postcolonial mode of critique, notably the creation of counter-histories, the exploration of society in motion, and the formal embodiment of these concerns. It is hoped that these and the preceding chapters will together give the reader new insights into the development of the fictive traditions that form the subject of this book.

For various forms of assistance in the conception and execution of this book project, I wish to thank: the Vice-Chancellor's Office and the Department of English, University of Auckland, the Postgraduate Board and Clare Hall of Cambridge University, England, and the Validation Board of the University of Wales. I am also grateful to various people: Professor Chimere Ikoku, former Vice-Chancellor, University of Nigeria, Nsukka; my teachers Professors Chinua Achebe and E.N. Obiechnina; Professors D.I.B. Smith, Michael Neill and W.H. Pearson of the University of Auckland; the writers Witi Ihimaera and Albert Wendt; Professor Kate Belsey of the Centre for Critical and Cultural Theory, Cardiff University of Wales; Professor Roger Fowler of the University of East Anglia; Dr Robert Fraser and Tim Cribb of the Faculty of English, Cambridge University; Joseph V. Landy, SJ; Lee Nichols of the Voice of America; Rev. Canon E.V. Binks and Mrs Julie Dagnall, former Principal and the Personnel Director, respectively, of University College Chester; Gyles Brandreth, former MP for Chester; Beryl Reubens of Cardiff; and Sydney, Joan and Trudy Swan of Auckland.

To my wife Njideka and my children Ijeoma and Ugochukwu, I owe the greatest debt of all for their unflagging support at all times.

CHIDI OKONKWO
University College Chester

List of Abbreviations

When page numbers of novels used in this study are cited, the novels are identified by abbreviated forms of their titles within the text. Single-word titles, including those with an article, are identified in full, the article being omitted in the latter case. Many novels are also referred to by shorter forms of their titles throughout the text. All dates are those of the editions used for the study rather than dates of first publication. The following abbreviations are used:

AMOP	A Man of the People
AOG	Arrow of God
AS	Anthills of the Savannah
BR	A Bend in the River
BS	A Brighter Sun
CCM	Crick Crack, Monkey
DOC	Devil on the Cross
FR	The Famished Road
GOW	A Grain of Wheat
IFS/'IFS'	In a Free State/'In a Free State'
LBT	Leaves of the Banyan Tree
NLAE	No Longer at Ease
PL	The Promised Land
POB	Petals of Blood
PWD	The Palm-Wine Drinkard
RB	The River Between
SOA	Season of Anomy
TFA	Things Fall Apart
WAWSB	Why Are We So Blest?
WNC	Weep Not, Child

1

Crisis and Politics in Postcolonial Discourse

we black Africans have been blandly invited to submit ourselves to a second epoch of colonisation – this time by a universal-humanoid abstraction defined and conducted by individuals whose theories and prescriptions are derived from the apprehension of *their* world and *their* history, *their* social neuroses and *their* value systems. It is time, clearly, to respond to this new threat, each in his own field.[1]

THE CRISIS OF POSTCOLONIALITY

The development of a 'postcolonial' mode of discourse as a direct derivative of postmodernist theories of knowledge and culture creates a historic crisis for the study of decolonization literatures – those literatures created to combat European colonialism in the past and neocolonialism in the present – by subverting its purpose with a universalist, homogenizing discourse that denies the very essence of the subject matter of the study. Many major exponents of the term 'postcolonial discourse' justify the use of the concept on such grounds as:

(i)   the need to liberate the discourse from the hegemonic connotations and neocolonialist entanglements of such terms as 'Commonwealth literature', 'New English Literatures', 'New Literatures in English', or 'Third World Literature';
(ii) the advantage of a field of intellectual inquiry that embraces all europhone writing from formerly colonized peoples, rather than merely anglophone writing;
(iii) the need to end the marginalization of the literatures and cultures of the vast majority of the worlds' peoples who have hitherto been subordinated to Europe, the imperial centre, and to strengthen the oppositional role of the majority's discourse; and

1

(iv)   the empowerment of those marginalized peoples and cultures by asserting the validity of their historical experience, cultural products, and world views in opposition to the universalist claims of imperial Europe.

There is a superficial attractiveness in this argument, for, as Rajeswari Mohan has rightly argued, 'whether a text is read as a Commonwealth, third world, or postcolonial text makes all the difference to its meaning and status, the prefixes activating different genealogies, emphases, and, inevitably, politics'.[2] In the particular case of postcolonial literature, however, the terminological change is purely cosmetic, for it has deviously consolidated the old negations under a new rubric that submerges the experiences and concerns of the ex-colonized peoples in a welter of Western ideological or strategic priorities.

All prevailing definitions of 'postcolonial literatures' are variations on the formula offered by the Australian trio of Bill Ashcroft, Gareth Griffiths and Helen Tiffin, and each variation has merely served to entrench the theorist's or critic's priorities as a member of a social, political, ideological, or racial group. Ashcroft et al. define 'postcolonial cultures' as 'all the cultures affected by the imperial process from the moment of colonization to the present day', and 'postcolonial literatures' as all those literatures that 'emerged in their present form out of the experience of colonization and asserted themselves by foregrounding the tension with the imperial power, and by emphasizing their differences from the assumptions of the imperial centre'.[3] There is a fundamental conflict between these definitions. Whereas the definition of the literatures properly applies to those that foreground colonizer–colonized contradictions, the definition of postcolonial cultures overwrites this distinction and proceeds to reformulate postcoloniality as a universal condition of 'the world as it exists during and after the period of European imperial domination and the effects of this on contemporary literatures'.[4] The crucial terms of the definitions are therefore too vague and self-contradictory to be useful. It comes as no surprise that Ashcroft and partners finally assimilate postcolonial discourse into neocolonialist political theory which actually de-emphasizes colonialism by postulating a misleading analogy 'between the power relationship of the colonizer to the colonized and that of men to women, the upper classes to the lower, or men to the landscape'.[5]

An intriguing aspect of Ashcroft and partners' concept of post-coloniality is that while it includes African, Asian and South Pacific ex-colonies as well as the English-speaking European Diaspora-dominated countries of Australia, Canada (excluding the French-speaking part), New Zealand and the United States of America as postcolonial societies, it insistently excludes all non-English-speaking European Diaspora countries. Suspicion is thus raised that the major concern of this revisionist conceptualization of postcoloniality is not the illumination of the historical phenomenon but the advantageous repositioning of the English-speaking European Diaspora within this history. The inclusion of the United States of America is justified with the spurious argument that '[despite] its current position of power, and the neo-colonising role it has played,... its relationship with the metropolitan centre as it evolved over the last two centuries has been paradigmatic for post-colonial literatures everywhere'.[6]

The first casualty of Ashcroft and partners' casuistry is historical truth. An unwary reader may be seduced into forgetting that the so-called 'Americans' combating the 'metropolitan centre' of European imperialism/colonialism were actually European colonizers engaged in the grim task of exterminating the real Americans, celebrating the atrocities in their literature (a pattern re-enacted in Australia and Latin America), and literally creating their wealth from the lifeblood of millions of enslaved Africans. It is significant that Ashcroft and partners do not specify the 'two centuries' they refer to, or when that period ended and the era of 'neo-colonising role' began. But it is an indisputable fact of American literary history that American literature, like its Australian, Canadian and New Zealand counterparts, began as overseas transplants of European literatures, and even subsequent attempts to infuse the literature with a sense of national identity were done within the tradition of imperial triumphalism.

Ashcroft and partners' brand of postcoloniality, therefore, represents a denial of history through linguistic disruption of the concepts through which that history could be discussed, for, as Edward Sapir has noted, 'concept does not attain to individual and independent life until it has found a distinctive linguistic embodiment'.[7] *The Empire Writes Back* must therefore be interpreted as a neocolonialist work inspired by Australia's strategic need to reposition itself in the post-Cold War global geopolitics of the New World Order. Properly speaking, the Australians are merely deploying cultural theory in a manner analogous to Third World writers' practice in their struggles against (neo)colonialism. In all societies and all periods of history, intellectuals have played the role of theoretically rationalizing those developments that are reshaping the society, and redefining reality from desired ideological perspectives. What makes it peculiar is two-fold: first, its deviousness, and next, its connection to the larger Western designs for the New World Order.

THE EMPEROR RIDES BACK: POSTCOLONIALITY IN THE NEW WORLD ORDER

With the West's defeat of the Communist Bloc in the late 1980s, and the 1991 disintegration of the Soviet Union itself, the West is poised to resume its quest of remaking the world in its own image, for triumph has reinvested (neo)colonialism with an aura of manifest destiny. The emperor rides back after a retreat forced by the Cold War, and reprocessing of history through various reality-denying discourses constitutes the ideological evangelism necessary for con-solidating the new order. At the same time, however, the Western powers' shift from Cold War priorities to accommodation with the rising economic powers of Asia has generated new anxieties for the smaller European Diaspora countries like Australia and New Zea-land, who must reinvent and ideologically reposition themselves in the new order. Even the United States, disposed as it is to play global sheriff, needs a reorganization of historical knowledge to erase the sordid realities of its origins and historically imperialist role.

These needs are served by the new internationalist discourses whose major objective is the blurring of colonizer–colonized con-tradictions by homogenizing all histories and social conflicts. Just as reality-distorting propaganda has effectively established a mythical 'international community' as a euphemism for America's State Department and its foreign policy objectives, these new discourses are concerned with the construction of a universal postcolonial cul-ture within which the self-serving policies could be legitimized in the name of humanity. Edward Said has pointed out the role such aesthetic theorists as Carlyle and Ruskin as well as 'the great Euro-pean realistic novel' played in justifying imperial aggression and in 'sustaining the society's consent in overseas expansion'.[8]

Australia presents an interesting case study. Up to the 1960s, it shared with several South American countries a whites-only immig-ration policy while pursuing its own programme of exterminating the Aborigines. It is still a member of the Australia–New Zealand–United States (ANZUS) military alliance and had been proudly proclaiming its role as the brave outpost of European civilization. The end of the Cold War has, however, compelled it to recognize that it is neighbour to Asia rather than Europe. It is in this context that one can understand the strange spectacle of European Australians endlessly inveighing against 'the atrocities of European imperialism', or the universalist zeal of works like *The Empire Writes Back*, Brydon and Tiffin's *Decolonising Fictions* (1993) and a flood of 'postcolonial literatures' readers produced through Australian initiative.

Brydon and Tiffin's work is quite illuminating. Here is a supposedly 'cross-cultural' study of the 'postcolonial literatures' of Australia, Canada and the Caribbean which, by selecting its samples through the sole criterion of possession of English as mother tongue, eliminates the indigenous writers of Australia and Canada who offer a counter-discourse to the European Diaspora, in order to homogenize non-white West Indians (including some whose mother tongue is not English) with white Australians and Canadians. Such enterprise must be seen in the same light as related attempts to rewrite colonialism as a men-only enterprise in which European women played no part, as Elleke Boehmer tries to do in her *Colonial & Postcolonial Literature*,[9] at a time when Western women are joining the armed forces in masses to play in the New World Order the military roles denied to them in the past. Again, Edward Said provides a timely reminder that, embarrassing as it is today, European 'women's as well as the working-class movement was pro-empire'.[10]

Many political observers were surprised in June 1997 when the Australian government publicly spurned British and American pressure to join their boycott of the swearing-in ceremony for the Hong Kong Provisional Legislature upon the territory's reversion to China on 1 July. Australia 'was determined to use its position on the edge of Asia to build itself up as a centre for trade and business within Asia', *The Times* of 14 June 1997 reported the Foreign Minister as declaring. 'Gone are the days when we would wait to see what Britain and the US did before deciding our own agenda...We are an Asia-Pacific country. Britain is a European country. Our future, our destiny, is in the Asia-Pacific.' About the same period, however, the *Sunday Telegraph Magazine* featured the rearguard fight by parliamentarian Pauline Hanson and her One Nation Party for 'a return to a cherished Australia of the past'. Hanson rallies European Australians to her banner with the spectre of Australia being 'swamped by Asians' and a call to 'extinguish all "native title" [to land]'. Her image of the Aborigines comes straight from European-Australian colonialist anthropology and literature: 'They just sit around all day, doing nothing, with their hands out...If they're so in tune with the land, why are they so dirty?'[11] As Bill Pearson has noted, the settler-Australian writer Henry Lawson similarly used the adjective 'Maori' as 'an epithet of contempt' and represented Maoris as dirty, stinking and lazy animals.[12]

European Diaspora literature of the colonial experience is therefore best designated as 'imperial outpost literature', a category that also effectively embraces such genres as 'Westerns' and kindred frontier literature that arose with European expansion. For this Diaspora, nationalism can only mean consolidating the gains of conquest, whereas, as the Maori feminist Atareta Poananga has observed, nationalism for the colonized 'is about reclaiming their heritage, subsumed under the invader culture – inspiring a colonized people to realise their political potential and regain power as *tangata whenua*, the first and only authentic people of the land'.[13] With the explosion of computer culture and technology in the 1990s, the frontier tradition is expanding into the new genre of computer games. In the 'exploration and conquest' and the 'guarding civilisation against evil forces' variety of computer game, the forces of light and civilization are invariably American or the Western Alliance while the villains are Third World peoples, reflecting the reality that African and Asian countries are replacing the Soviet Union as targets for America's nuclear and other weapons of annihilation.

The real postcolonial literatures of Australia, New Zealand, Canada, the United States of America and the Latin American countries, therefore, are those of Aboriginal and other minorities. Two years before the publication of *The Empire Writes Back*, the Australian Aboriginal writer Kath Walker renounced her British name and MBE and adopted the Aboriginal name of Oodgeroo Noonuccal in a gesture 'to strike a blow in the interest of the cruelty that was inflicted upon the Aboriginals'.[14]

Four years before Oodgeroo, another Aborigine, Colin Johnson, had disrupted Australian complacency with his novel *Doctor Wooreddy's Prescription for Enduring the End of the World* (1983), portraying the European invader–Aborigine collision on Bruny Island, and the invaders' extermination of Tasmanian Aborigines. He, too, has renounced his European name in protest against colonialist atrocities, and renamed himself Mudrooroo Narogin. His more recent work, such as *Master of the Ghost Dreaming* (1991), bears the same relation to European Australian writing as the works of Maori writers bear to those of the Pakeha in New Zealand. Mudrooroo maintains that:

> Aboriginal Australian literature is a literature of the Fourth World, that is, of the indigenous minorities submerged in a surrounding majority, and governed by them. It must and does deal with the problems inherent in this position and it must be compared to similar literatures, for example the American Indian, for the correspondences and contradictions to be seen it should not be compared to the majority literature.[15]

PITFALLS OF MULTICULTURALISM AND CROSS-CULTURAL CRITIQUES

'Cross-cultural studies' and 'multiculturalism' are frequently invoked as the unique selling points of postcolonial discourse. The claim is untenable. Cross-cultural studies have been conducted for decades before the advent of postcolonial discourse, and with more intellectually fruitful results too. Furthermore, whereas one can properly speak of multiculturalism in New Zealand, Nigeria, Great Britain, or any other country comprised of different ethnic cultures that may or may not evolve towards a national culture, it is inappropriate to apply the term to interactions across national territories. In cultural exchanges between separate countries, assimilation of what is received makes it part of the existing whole while lack of assimilation leaves it as an alien obtrusion.

Desirable as cross-cultural studies are, they can hardly be rewarding in the present climate of conflicting political priorities, nebulous concepts of postcoloniality, and ignorance or false assumptions about European cultural history. Any dispassionate scrutiny of theories of culture formulated within postcolonial discourse reveals that they have their roots in nineteenth-century theories of race inherited from colonialist anthropology and social Darwinism, continuously elaborated to incorporate all aspects of contemporary society, and sometimes rephrased to reflect prevalent political sensibilities, but always within a closed system of thought. It is this fundamentally unchanging character of racial profiling that accounts for many of the enduring controversies surrounding European writing about Third World cultures, typified by Margaret Mead's *Coming of Age in Samoa* (1928) and Joseph Conrad's *Heart of Darkness* (1902).

Coming of Age in Samoa, Margaret Mead's 'study' of sexual behaviour among Samoans, established her as an oracular figure in Western academia, and for six decades shaped the representation of South Pacific cultures in European literature and criticism, gender theory, films and tourists' fantasies. Yet as Professor Derek Freeman has now proved (1996) and many Samoans have always known, Mead's book and her Ph.D. 'research' from which it originated are based on a hoax played upon her by two Samoan travelling companions whom she had embarrassed with her desperate questioning about Samoan sexual mores in the last days of her stay in Samoa, after neglecting her research until the very end.[16] The Samoan novelist Albert Wendt has always known this, and ridicules Mead and her book in a series of essays and novels.[17] The heroine of Wendt's novel *Ola* (1991) scornfully asserts:

> If you mean free love as described by the matriarch Margaret Mead in her *Coming of Age in Samoa*, then I've again not met one genuine free lover, not even in Samoa. Mead lied, was misled, wanted to believe in the romantic myth of a South Seas paradise. And became famous because of it. (*Ola* p. 135)

On another occasion, she concludes a description of her own dressing with a contemptuous: 'so much for the Hollywood/Margaret Mead myth of easy nakedness in Paradise' (*Ola* p. 321).

By his own account, Professor Freeman's exposure of Mead's hoax incurred his vilification by members of the American Anthropological Association, who voted 'by a tribal show of hands' to denounce him as 'unscientific' – proof, he points out, of 'the kind of fanatical behaviour that is released in the zealots of a closed system of thought when one of their principal certainties has been effectively challenged'.[18]

For its part, the Conrad quarrel was rekindled in 1975 with Chinua Achebe's denunciation of the Polish novelist Joseph Conrad as a racist on the basis of his portrayal of Africa in his grossly overrated novella *Heart of Darkness*. Achebe charges that European scholars have ignored Conrad's racism because it represents a quintessentially European attitude to Africa, 'the desire – one might indeed say the need – in Western psychology to set Africa up as a foil to Europe, as a place of negations at once remote and vaguely familiar, in comparison with which Europe's own state of spiritual grace will be manifest'.[19] Most defences of Conrad have been based on various questionable theories about the human condition. Thus, dismissing Achebe's attack as a 'tendentious' product of 'passionate misreading', Terry Collits predictably invokes 'the post-structuralist concern with the instability of the text and the relative insignificance of authorial control'. Achebe's error, he contends, was that 'he took *Heart of Darkness* for a stable and unproblematic embodiment of its author's beliefs in the first place', rather than 'a text so slippery that it can never be pinned down, locked into the play of an inconclusive ironic meditation which leads no more to the need for political action than to a quietist awareness of the philosophical absurd'.[20]

Such fashionable academic quibbles contrast sharply with the unanimous certainty of the West's denunciation of Michael Jackson's thoughtless use of the word 'Jew' in his 1995 song 'Black and White', or Microsoft Corporation's mindless offer of 'savage' and 'cannibal' as synonyms for 'Indian', with 'Aryan', 'civilized' and 'Christian' as synonyms for 'Western', in the thesaurus for the Mexican-Spanish language version of the Microsoft Office software suite released in mid-1996. In other words, the principle of slipperiness and indeterminacy of language is scandalously selective in its application to peoples of different colours and economic power. For many of Conrad's defenders, indeed, appeals to post-structuralism mask a thesis that Conrad's portrayal of Africa cannot properly be characterized as 'racist' because despite its negativity it is true and therefore justified. Bruce Fleming states as much in his 'Brothers under the Skin: Achebe on *Heart of Darkness*':

> Yet perhaps we may get a sense of the choice involved in such formulations by asking ourselves whether we would choose to express the Ibo practice of throwing away twins as religion, or merely inhumanity. Or whether we are willing to refer to the so-called female circumcision (that is, clitoridectomy) still prevalent in Black and White Africa as an initiation rite, or whether it should instead be described as sexist barbarism.[21]

It is instructive that though Conrad portrays no African social organization or customs, Fleming hastens to update the novella for him, in that tradition of collaborative reading which imperial outpost writers confidently expect from a European audience.

Genuine cross-cultural studies must be based on knowledge – intimate knowledge of one's own culture as well as the foreign culture one is interested in, rather than smug assumptions, conference hall gossip, travellers' tales, or racist anthropology. It must also take all cultural practices and lifestyles as its province, not just those that, for self-enhancing reasons, a coterie of middle-class academics define as the most urgent task facing humanity. Unfortunately, few postcolonial cultural theorists have seriously probed the realities of Europe's cultural history or challenged the selective righteousness which encourages Bruce Fleming's concept of civilization. Such probing would reveal that the image of Europeanness or Westernness as an eternal structure of rationality, refinement and Christian godliness has been fostered over the past five hundred years by treating European social history as a palimpsest that is constantly wiped clean and written over, so that past reality is endlessly realigned with present priorities. Such rewrites of history are often presented as results of fresh insights gained from more rigorous scholarship or new evidence, and are in no way restricted to minor works or the numerous works of 'cultural studies' that have proliferated since the 1980s. In two massive publications posted on the Internet in the first half of 1997, Joseph McCabe has documented hundreds of what he charges are extensive mutilations introduced into *The Encyclopaedia Britannica* (from the 14th edition of 1929) and *The Columbia Encyclopaedia* (from the 2nd edition of 1950) to purge out unsavoury accounts of European history recorded in previous editions.[22] The Australian-originated theory of postcoloniality falls within this practice of treating history as a palimpsest.

THE POLITICS OF GENDER

Nowhere has palimpsest historiography been more effectively applied than in the gendering of postcolonial cultural studies. Though gender conflicts exist in most cultures, what is peculiar and suspect about postcolonial gender theory is the dual-track approach which enables it to codify European conflicts as a universal paradigm even as it reformulates them as characteristics of non-European cultures. It has thus become an article of faith that Third World women need leadership from European people (men and women together) in a gender war against Third World men, while questions of European women's contribution to the misery of Third World women have yet to be recognized within the purview of gender theory.

To rid postcolonial literary and cultural studies of the crippling baggage of ethnocentrism, and counter the use of faddish gender shibboleths to mask neocolonialist aggression, it is important to put European culture itself under the searchlight. The question of clitoridectomy, raised by Bruce Fleming, provides a good starting point. This practice is usually presented in European postcolonial gender theory as a sexual mutilation of women in patriarchal Third World cultures. Yet Oliver Bennett has recently written a reminder that European cultures considered the clitoris as 'too dangerous to exist', and 'during the last century female genital surgery [that is, clitoridectomy] was fairly common in the UK, the US and other western nations . . . as a therapy for women who seemed to be more interested in sex than was then considered healthy'.[23]

Perception of the ritual act of circumcision as mere excision of the clitoris results from a cultural fixation which cannot see the clitoris or women in any other context than commodities for sexual consumption, and arrogantly pretends that its obsessions are universal. The difference between the European practice and the African raises a major question for gender studies. Whereas genital mutilation in Europe was practised exclusively on women, for the sole purpose of crippling their sex drives, African circumcision was applied equally to both sexes as part of a serious (albeit misguided) quest for ritual wholeness, in which control of sex drives had no part. Even the throwing away of twins in some parts of Igboland in the past must be seen against Europe's current annual slaughter of millions of unborn babies through abortion, often for purely cosmetic reasons, with the United States alone accounting for some 32 million cases in the 21 years ending in 1994, according to a reliable recent study.[24]

Evidence from historical records, law archives, artistic/literary representation, myth and legend, public standards of taste, and language (English terms like 'spinster', 'old maid' and 'dumb blonde', for example) is equally illuminating. Gender theorists have yet to explain why it is almost invariably women who are sacrificed to monsters in European myths like that of St George and the Dragon. Such stereotypes of women as 'femmes fatales', 'la belle dame sans merci', 'cherchez la femme', 'the woman scorned' and 'the devil in disguise' are all European, not universal.

In the domain of cultural tastes, one notes that whereas many non-European cultures traditionally enhance bodily comeliness, irrespective of sex, with clothes and ornament, European cultures tend to strip the woman naked for men's visual ravishment. From sports to advertising, commercial pornography and the strip-tease show, European cultures design women's costumes to bare as much of the body as possible to the male gaze. In political life, several nations of the Indian sub-continent had women as prime ministers decades before any European country. Among the Igbos of Nigeria, who until British conquest had had democratic institutions older than the United States of America's existence as a nation, women traditionally enjoyed political power that European women are only beginning to achieve in the late twentieth century. Pre-European Maori women were similarly empowered, as Maori feminists Atareta Poananga, Mana Wahine and Te Ahi Kaa have convincingly demonstrated:

> Pakeha colonists, political, religious and military, came from a patriarchal society where women's lives were defined by men, and were part of their property. The status of Maori women was *different* – we shared political, spiritual and cultural leadership in our tribes, and one *not* derived from male power. In most tribes female ancestry was as equally valued as male ancestry. Gender did not determine leadership and the possession of *mana*, but whether you were *turkana* (senior) or *teina* (junior) line.[25]

In questions of love and marriage, traditional European cultures (and present Indian culture) considered women so worthless that eligible bachelors had to be bribed with a large dowry of worldly goods, as amply illustrated in European Mediaeval romances, Shakespearean drama, British Restoration comedy, and many Victorian novels. Conversely, African cultures made men pay a bride-wealth from a recognition of the woman's worth. But by a curious logic, Europeans consider their custom 'civilized' and the African barbaric. Even more overwhelming evidence for European man's literal proprietorship over woman is provided by the 'chastity belt', an infernal machine used in the recent past by European men to literally lock up their women's genitalia whilst they themselves romped through the land in search of virgins.

It is important, therefore, to distinguish between the career-promoting, frequently neocolonialist, practice of gender theory from either political feminism or feminist scholarship. Political feminism is a historically inevitable equal rights movement to end women's marginalization in patriarchal cultures, and occasionally assumes the role of social conscience to intervene in major international debates where morality has been drowned by financial or strategic calculations. At its best, feminist scholarship involves serious inquiry into cultural practices, institutions and artefacts (such as literature), though in the West it is still tainted with ethnocentrism. By contrast, postcolonial gender studies originated in the strategic calculations of government think-tanks, with United Nations agencies as its main vectors. Theoretically rooted in the discourse of nineteenth-century anthropology and colonialist messianism, it has neither the sense of social responsibility found in feminist activism nor a concern for Third World women in European societies, but readily adopts and propagates the doctrines of oppressive institutions like the International Monetary Fund (IMF). Thus, the IMF's argument that ex-colonial societies' poverty is entirely rooted in their patriarchal cultures, in which neither (neo)colonialism nor the IMF's own predatory debt-relief programmes play any part, has become a central pillar of gender theories about the political economy of such societies. Academics scrambling to distinguish themselves in what they see as a career-friendly field rarely recognize their real role as cogs in the machinery of neocolonialism. At the same time, the legacy of nineteenth-century colonialist rationalizations emerges in ritualistic claims of bringing light to the benighted, giving voice to the voiceless, and blazing trails in an academic jungle. Yet neocolonialist gender theory is rarely concerned with new or unknown writers. In African literature, for example, extravagant generalizations are based on the work of five established female writers – Flora Nwapa, Buchi Emecheta, Ama Ata Aidoo, Mariama Bâ and, sometimes, Grace Ogot – who have received critical attention since they started publishing, and enjoy international reputations that tower above those of the enterprising 'messiahs'.

Alison Donnell's 'Writing for Resistance: Nationalism and Narratives of Liberation' and Katherine Frank's 'Women without Men: the Feminist Novel in Africa' illustrate the obsession with fashionable phrases at the expense of serious investigation. Donnell claims that her reading of Caribbean Creole women's poetry written during the 1930s and 1940s as well as Jamaica Kincaid's *A Small Place* (1980) 'has alerted [her] to how unstable the signifiers of nationalism are, and of how these texts mute and blur any confident articulation of cultural positioning'.[26] Despite the self-conscious postmodernist phraseology, the project is misconceived and seriously flawed.

Donnell studies very few poems, all selected precisely because they are *not* assertively nationalistic. The argument about *A Small Place* reflects some confusion about what constitutes nationalism. It is the entire work, not discrete lexical elements isolated from their contexts, that constitutes Kincaid's nationalist argument, and honest nationalism has always involved intelligent recognition of countervailing forces within the nation.

For its own part, Katherine Frank's pseudo-feminist work, based on five novels altogether by Nwapa, Emecheta, Aidoo and Mariama Bâ, belongs to the 'Africa expert' school of colonialist criticism. Ritually reciting 'the historically established and culturally sanctioned sexism of African society' (a formula for disgorging racial stereotypes instead of offering new arguments or undertaking new investigations), the author vaguely speculates over African women's need for liberation from African men, concludes on Lloyd Brown's infallible authority that this need does indeed exist, and promptly proclaims an apocalyptic gender war in Africa.[27] Interestingly, such gender war scenarios do not envisage a universal alliance of women against a universal patriarchy but a joint-project by Western men and women against Third World men. Soyinka's argument that neocolonialist critics project *'their* history [and] *their* social neuroses' onto their subject finds demonstration in Katherine Frank's representation of her personal fantasies as African women's desire for the 'solution of a world without men', 'a liberating ideal of potentiality, of a rich, active, and fulfilling future . . . a future without men', achieved through a fight to the death:

> there is no possibility of a compromise, or even truce with the enemy. Instead, women must spurn patriarchy in all its guises and create a safe, sane, supportive world of women: a world of mothers and daughters, sisters and friends. This, of course, amounts to feminist separatism, though only obliquely in Aidoo's *Our Sister Killjoy* do we find the logical outcome of this ideology: lesbianism.[28]

Unless one assumes that the inhabitants of Katherine Frank's lesbian utopia are all born through immaculate conception which does not engender males, or perhaps cloned in laboratories which destroy male foetuses, or that her lesbian paradise practises gender eugenics, one must view this argument as a species of sympathetic magic.

Anne McClintock's recent work on such gender discourse has traced it to the economic foundations of colonialism, specifically the labour-and-profit calculations of European settlers-farmers in polygynous colonial cultures:

> Colonial documents readily reveal that the assault on polygyny was an assault on African habits of labor that withheld from the resentful farmers the work of black men and women ... [This was] a direct and deadly threat to the profits of the settlers. As Governor Pine complained: 'How can an Englishman with one pair of hands compete with a native with five to twenty slave wives'?[29]

In 'Mother Africa on a Pedestal: the Male Heritage in African Literature and Criticism', Mineke Schipper recklessly asserts that 'in Africa, illiteracy is four times more prevalent among women than among men and in the school the proportion of girls falls as the level of education rises'.[30] No source is given for the fantastic statistics, as it is traditional in this field of scholarship that assertions about Africa or Africans do not need to be proved, hence similar racial gossips are the staple of small talk at academic conferences. Unknown to many gender theorists, many of the statistics they recite like mantras are mere variations upon Margaret Mead's *Coming of Age in Samoa* hoax. They have their origins in undergraduate long essays, get disseminated when lazy supervisors plunder the essays for their own 'learned' publications, and attain the status of established truth through constant unreflecting repetition.

Florence Stratton's *Contemporary African Literature and the Politics of Gender* combines Mineke Schipper's and Katherine Frank's flaws with fresh failures. Stratton advertises her 1994 work as a pioneer effort in deploying gender 'as a social and analytic category' and bringing to light African women writers who 'have been rendered invisible in literary criticism'.[31] Consulting a widely accessible journal like *Research in African Literatures*, which periodically publishes lists of undergraduate dissertations from the Department of English, University of Nigeria Nsukka, since the 1970s, would have revealed to her how far she lags behind the lecturers and students of that institution on this issue. Not surprisingly, her concept of African women writers does not go beyond Grace Ogot, Flora Nwapa, Buchi Emecheta and Mariama Bâ, all of whom are better known in African schools than Florence Stratton.

Stratton's gravest failing lies in her penchant for ignoring complexity, treating strictly local phenomena as universally African, uncritically relying on dubious authorities, and generally approaching her task with more passion than insight. All these flaws are evident in the representative passage below:

> Amadiume tells of a northern Nigerian state 'which outlawed rented accommodation for single women, considering them all to be prostitutes against whom punitive action should be taken.' And Carolyne Dennis tells of how, in its 'War Against Indiscipline', the Nigerian Federal Military Government in 1984–5 'singled out as being the cause of "indiscipline"' three categories of women: 'petty traders, single women, and working women with children' – categories which 'would appear between them to encompass most Nigerian women.'[32]

There is more fantasy here than interpretation of evidence. The citation of Amadiume omits the crucial detail that the state in question was enforcing its own peculiar interpretation of Islamic law rather than 'Nigerian' or 'African' custom. Most other Islamic and all the Christian state governments had no such legislation; neither did the Federal Government. The account of the Nigerian military government's 'War Against Indiscipline' attributed to Carolyne Dennis is simply ridiculous. Though the military establishment's own cesspool morality eventually perverted the programme into a war against the Nigerian populace, the programme as initially conceived was precisely what the slogan proclaimed. To claim that women were its primary targets or major victims betrays a reckless disregard for truth, the kind of fantastic travellers' tale on which many 'Africa expert' reputations have been built. With greater critical insight, the musician and social critic Fela Anikulapo Kuti captured the tragedy of the betrayed revolution in his lyric, 'Beast of No Nation':

> Make you hear this one
> War Against Indiscipline
> Na Nigerian government, dem dey talk
> 'My people are useless
> My people are senseless
> My people are indisciplined.'
> Na Nigerian government, dem dey talk be dat:
> ....

I never hear that before, this government talk:

....

Which kind talk be dat?
Na craze talk be dat
Na animal talk be dat.[33]

More confusion is betrayed over African writers' generic use of masculine (pro)nouns for humanity – a reflection of the gender biases of the European cultures in whose languages Third World people have to write. Many African cultures, such as Chinua Achebe's Igbo and Wole Soyinka's Yoruba, have gender-neutral (pro)nouns for such generic references. Barbara Christian has also pointed out that 'some Native American languages ... use female pronouns when speaking about non-gender specific activity'.[34] However, university-educated Anglophone African writers have generally followed the British custom, which is currently the norm also among the general British populace, government and academia. By contrast, Yoruba and Igbo writers with low mastery of English tend to employ the less elegant 'man or woman', 'he or she', 'his or her(s)', in an effort to recapture the gender-neutral forms provided by their indigenous languages. For illustration, Amos Tutuola's first novel, *The Palm-Wine Drinkard* (1952), contains such telling examples as: 'everybody would be returning to his or her destination or to where he or she came from' (p. 17), and 'they would catch him or her and begin to cut the flesh of his or her body into pieces' (p. 59).[35]

Finally, in her critique of specific texts, Stratton complains about the marginalization of women characters through naming. 'Achebe does not even bother to name Okonkwo's wives [in *Things Fall Apart*] until the narrative is well under way',[36] Stratton writes, raising an issue that would be familiar to readers of James Olney's *Tell Me Africa* published in 1973.[37] Achebe's use of names mirrors Igbo culture's investment of personal names with so much mystique that their use is privileged, and parents are honoured by being addressed as 'Father' or 'Mother' of some child. Chapter 2 narrates that 'a snake was never called by its name at night, because it would hear' (p. 7). Chapter 5 reveals that people never answered to their names when called 'from outside' even if they recognized the voice of the caller, 'for fear it might be an evil spirit calling' (p. 29). Stratton missed these clues because, like many anthropological critics, she started off determined to shoehorn the literary facts into her borrowed theoretical mould.

Given Stratton's stated objection to the ethnocentrism of European gender theory, her continued application of its methodology and assumptions betrays the pitfalls of a derivative or tributary academic practice. Unfortunately, her confusion falls within a long-established tradition. Some two decades earlier, Maryse Condé had set the pattern with an essay which manages to combine pseudo-feminism with pseudo-nationalism in its discussion of Flora Nwapa, Ama Ata Aidoo and Grace Ogot. Condé rebukes Ogot for being 'blinded by her respect for the European codes of behaviour' but in the same breath advises her 'to join some Women's Lib. Movement to see how European females question the code of values and behaviour imposed upon them, and to replace her Bible by Germaine Greer's book'.[38] Condé obviously could not see her idolatrous reverence for Germaine Greer as a form of self-enslavement to 'European codes of behaviour'.

Against the saccharine platitudes and utopian imagery of a lesbian 'world of mothers and daughters, sisters and friends', history offers the sordid reality of the South African black nanny whose husband had been killed or jailed, her children (including her daughters) exiled to a remote, blighted *bantustan* to die of starvation and lack of mother-care while she slaved for the European lady and her mixed-gender family and friends. Chinua Achebe has given a real-life account of his own mother's psychological and physical torment at the hands of a typical female colonial missionary, Edith Ashley Warner, Principal of a girls' college in colonial Eastern Nigeria.[39] Alice Walker's *The Color Purple* (1983), Toni Morrison's *The Bluest Eye* (1970), Grace Ogot's *The Graduate* (1980), and Jamaica Kincaid's *A Small Place* (1988), all of which postcolonial gender theorists are desperately trying to incorporate as their canonical texts, offer memorable paradigms of the predicament of Third World women in subjection to Western women.

Alice Walker's work demonstrates the unbridgeable gap between socially responsible feminism and the self-aggrandizing practice of gender theorizing. Walker is painfully conscious that imperialism is gender-blind, that every murder of a man means some woman's loss of some male relation, and that destruction of 'women and children' is evil irrespective of their race. Herself a mother, she does not hesitate to invoke her motherhood or general parent–offspring bonds, contrary to the faddish fringe who erroneously believe that their own lifestyles are actually humanity's proper destiny. Her famous letter of 13 March 1996, to American President Bill Clinton, protesting the massive destruction of Cuban lives and property through America's obsessive hostility to Fidel Castro's regime, is character- istic. Cuban children are 'as dear as any on earth, as dear as [the Clintons' daughter] Chelsea, or my daughter, Rebecca'. About the bill signed by Bill Clinton (Walker intends no pun here) tightening the embargo against Cuba, Walker pronounces:

> The bill you have signed is wrong...the embargo is wrong... Given [Cubans'] long struggle for freedom, particularly from Spain and the United States, they cannot help taking understand- able pride in who they are...Is [anti-Cuban, hawkish Senator] Jesse Helms, who speaks of Cuban Liberty, as he urges our coun- try to harm Cuba's citizens, the same Jesse Helms who caused my grandparents, my parents and my own generation profound suf- fering as we struggled against our enslavement under racist laws in the South?...One cannot justify starving [Cuban children] to death because their leader is a person of whom some people, themselves imperfect, human, disapprove.[40]

In Walker's *The Color Purple*, the African-American woman Sofia's show of mental integrity and high self-esteem convinces the Euro- American mayor and his wife Millie that Sofia's true destiny is to be white lady's nanny. For rejecting this honour, Sofia is beaten to a pulp by the mayor's police while Millie watches with sadistic satis- faction:

> They crack her skull, they crack her ribs. They tear her nose loose on one side. They blind her in one eye. She swole from head to foot. Her tongue the size of my arm, it stick out tween her teef like a piece of rubber. She can't talk. And she just about the color of a eggplant. (p. 77)

Morrison's *The Bluest Eye* unerringly pinpoints the ideological function of postcolonial gender theory within neocolonialism's hegemonic strategy of subverting all those institutions which have proved pivotal to social cohesion and anti-colonialist resistance. It reveals why marriage, family, reciprocal parent–offspring obliga- tions and other social values are relentlessly assailed, calumniated, stripped of dignity and misrepresented as structures of patriarchal conspiracy against women. Morrison's black heroine Pauline is employed by a white woman to whom 'female solidarity' means

isolating black women from the psychologically supporting structures of marriage, family and black society itself in order to exploit
them with unhindered ruthlessness. The employer confiscates Pauline's accumulated salary in order to coerce her into breaking up her
marriage and then enslave her. In Pauline's words:

> I really begged that woman for my money ... She wouldn't let up
> none, neither, ... and then she told me I shouldn't let a man take
> advantage over me. That I should have more respect, and it was
> my husband's duty to pay the bills, and if he wouldn't, I should
> leave and get alimony ... A seen she didn't understand all I needed
> from her was my eleven dollars to pay the gas man so I could
> cook ... 'You leave him, and then come back to work, and we'll let
> bygones be bygones.' 'Can I have my money today?' I said. 'No'
> she said. 'Only when you leave him. I'm only thinking of you and
> your future ... '[41]

In *The Graduate*, the female European secretary Mrs Jane Brown
proves implacably hostile to the Kenyan junior secretary Anabell
Chepkwony who, though more skilled, has been shunted aside in
favour of Mrs Brown. Anabell Chepkwony has no illusions of sister-
hood with Mrs Jane Brown, and no doubts about her patriotic
duties. Many Western postcolonial gender theorists conveniently
ignore this kind of situation, for they know that their scenario of a
gender war 'with no possibility of compromise, or even truce with
the enemy' is designed to unfold in Third World societies while
Western men and women close ranks. Anabell Chepkwony is not
deceived, however, and casts her lot with a fellow Kenyan despite
the risks involved. The model of action which she invokes is her
people's folk wisdom, not an alien theory of gender relationships
(pp. 65–6).

More examples abound in Jamaica Kincaid's *A Small Place*, from
the European woman who was 'notorious for liking Antiguans only
if they are servants' (p. 47) to the notorious female Irish-British
teacher who denied education to black children by rejecting girls
born outside marriage, and delighted in comparing black Antiguan
girls with 'monkeys just out of trees' (p. 29).

The market value of sex and gender has inevitably led to the spon-
sorship of anthologies of Third World women's writing by astute
publishers, with the attendant risk of corrupting artistic creativity
and subverting the liberation agonistic at its source. *The Heinemann*

Book of African Women's Writing, edited by Charlotte H. Bruner, represents this trend. Bruner claims in the Preface that she and Heinemann searched out 'new writers, or hitherto unpublished ones' who were 'recording the *new* Africa...since independence, since "modernisation," since westernisation, since the feminist movement'.[42] Yet almost all the women featured here achieved success as writers, scholars, administrators, or cabinet ministers long before Bruner 'discovered' them. As many were born in the 1920s and 1930s, they hardly represented Bruner's 'new [African] generation' in 1993. The possibility of Third World women being conscripted into collusion with neocolonialist interests by the lure of publication in the West is highlighted by Bruner's ominous admission that 'several [women] wrote short stories for our consideration. One novelist decided to try out the short-story format for the first time. In rare cases, a chapter of an autobiography served as a story unit as it stood.'[43]

THE SCOURGE OF POSTMODERNIST MIMICRY

Besides infiltration by hostile ideological priorities, postcolonial discourse is intellectually hobbled by its derivation from Western postmodernist theories of culture and knowledge. This is seen in the uncritical acceptance of philosophies of reading and criticism whose primary purpose is the obfuscation rather than explication of literary works, with prime examples being Roland Barthes' 'The Death of the Author' and Michel Foucault's 'What is an Author?'

Both Barthes and Foucault claim to be accounting for the process by which meaning is created in a literary work, the agency of which they transfer from the author to the reader. But what they have effectively done is lay the foundation for a tradition of misreading which substitutes the critics' resourcefulness and ideological agenda for the author's intelligence and intentions. As Terence Hawkes summarizes this approach, texts do not contain an essential meaning revealed by the author but 'function as resources which we use to generate meaning for our own purposes'.[44] However, the accuracy or otherwise of Foucault's account of the development of the concept of authorship in Europe over centuries of cultural change or Barthes' description of the relationship between author, text and reader are irrelevant to the task of elucidating meaning from any particular text. The two theorists' occasional literary criticism amply bears this out. Whether a writer's private letters, random jottings,

marginal notes made in books, and other similar materials are classi-
fiable alongside his/her books as 'works' 'authored' by him/her is
more properly treated as a question of nomenclature rather than of
meaning.

'What is an Author?' is usually accepted by the unwary and the
gullible as a definitive proof of the irrelevance of authorial intentions
in the construction of meaning. It is nothing of the sort, and this
error must be rejected outright. All Foucault has done is declare his
preference for neutralizing authors other than himself in order to
indulge in endless wordplay generating a 'proliferation of meaning'.
'Proliferation of meaning' is particularly precious to him, as if there
were some humanity-liberating virtue in Babel:

> The author allows a limitation of the cancerous proliferation of
> significations within a world where one is thrifty not only with
> one's resources and riches, but also with one's discourses and
> their significations. The author is the principle of thrift in the
> proliferation of meaning... [The author] is a certain functional
> principle by which, in our [European] culture, one limits, one
> excludes, and chooses; in short, by which one impedes the free
> circulation, the free manipulation, the free composition, decom-
> position, and recomposition of fiction... The author is therefore
> the ideological figure by which one marks the manner in which
> we fear the proliferation of meaning.[45]

For its own part, Barthes' argument betrays a misconception of
the operation of fictional works in general, misunderstanding of
some of the particular literary works he cites, and persistent confusion between final effects and the techniques by which such effects
are produced. The effacement of the speaker in Balzac's *Sarrasine*,
for example, is precisely the effect that author Balzac aimed to produce, not a spontaneous emanation from a free play of signifiers, as
Barthes implies. Barthes' invocation of the 'constitutively ambiguous
nature' of classical Greek tragedy is quite unfortunate, for, once
again, what he takes to be intrinsic in words is actually a product of
the tragic dramatist's successful and conscious exploitation of extant
conventions of drama and theatre. Aristotle's theory of tragedy in
the *Poetics* explicitly identifies such structures of irony/ambiguity
and peripeteia or reversal as precisely what judges and audiences
were interested in, while literary theorists from the Renaissance to

the present day have properly linked them to the Greek view of the cosmos and humankind's place in it.

Foucault and Barthes obviously assume that the reader should construct a single meaning from their essays, as expressions of their intentions rather than merely sites in which frolicking signifiers await resourceful readers to draw them out into 'a proliferation of meaning'. To deny such an assumption would raise the question of why they bothered to write in the first place; to admit it raises the question of why other authors' works should be treated differently. This self-contradiction is not resolved by Linda Hutcheon's argument that in 'Foucault's challenging of the possibility of knowledge ever allowing any final, authoritative truth', Foucault, like Derrida, 'knew that he must include his own discourse in the radical doubting, for it is ineradicably dependent upon the very assumptions it seeks to uncover'.[46] In Barthes' famous conclusion to 'The Death of the Author' – 'the birth of the reader must be at the cost of the death of the Author' – 'reader' is only a convenient public mask for the self-anointing theorist. Putting the matter mildly, Dominic Strinati has pointed out that:

> The postmodern popular culture produced by certain occupational groups within the cultural industries is clearly not just concerned with a celebratory populism or a know-nothing relativism. The quotes and references that are part of this process are meant to appeal to those 'clever' enough to spot the source of the quote or reference. Rather than dismantling the hierarchy of aesthetic and cultural taste, postmodernism erects a new one, placing itself at the top.[47]

Human discourse is governed by what Jean-François Lyotard calls a 'rule of consensus between the sender and addressee of a statement with truth-value'.[48] H.P. Grice refers to that unstated 'rule of consensus' as a 'co-operative principle' which 'binds speakers to express themselves in such a way as not to impede interpretation – and hearers to assume that whatever is addressed to them is designed to make sense, so that they make an effort to find an interpretation even when the language does offer difficulties'.[49] Denial of the co-operative principle through abrogation of the authorial intelligence has become a strategy for the disempowerment of decolonization literature and the deflection of its agonistic purpose – on the authority of theorists whose own language is deemed by their disciples to be precise, stable and non-negotiable! Barbara Christian puts the matter more starkly: the postmodernist-derived postcolonial mode of critique is no less than a neocolonialist Trojan Horse:

> [It] has begun to occur to me that the literature being produced *is* precisely one of the reasons why this new philosophical-literary-critical theory of relativity is so prominent. In other words, the literature of [colonized peoples] as overtly 'political' literature was being preempted by a new Western concept which proclaimed that reality does not exist, that everything is relative, and that every text is silent about something – which indeed it must necessarily be.[50]

Containment is further continued through the self-negating practice of contesting European hegemony through European cognition schemes, codified in binary conceptual categories like 'Self /Other', 'Metropolis/Periphery', 'Centre/Margin', 'Major/ Minor'. In valorizing the first item in each pair, this terminology perpetuates the Négritude errors (1940s to 1960s) of countering anti-black myths by reformulating the same myths as positive ontological categories. For ex-colonized peoples, the centre is themselves and their cosmos, a point emphatically made in decolonization literature. Thus, Albert Wendt in 1992 maintains that Samoa is 'the centre of the Pacific' and New Zealand 'the periphery', while Witi Ihimaera asserts: 'wherever I go now, I think of the world I'm in as being Maori, not European'.[51] Themes of cultural conflict and alienation would be inconceivable if the colonized world were merely conceived as the periphery of the colonizer's.

One can, however, understand the paradoxical attraction that the Europe-centred binary scheme holds for some cultural theorists from the ethnic minorities who constitute the Third World underbellies of Western countries. 'Universality' has a fascination for hegemonists and weak people alike, though for different reasons: the former from a desire to subordinate the rest of humanity to their own value systems through homogenization, and the latter from a need to construct a counter-weight coalition which either invests their powerlessness with some grand significance or offers a platform for bargaining with the dominant order. Gayatri Spivak's confession in this regard is illuminating:

> I would like to comment first on the idea that we are not assimilated by the first world ... I think of myself as basically a United States

academic...In fact, I say over and over again when I am lecturing, that I put aside your definition of me as a marginal...I put aside your construction of me as speaking for the third world...I have put in a great deal of time precisely assimilating, and so listen to me not as some sort of self-agonizing Caliban, but as one of you, you know...I am not the Other, capital O. I am part of the Same, with a difference.[52]

A related tendency is at work in the North American phenomenon of 'Minority Discourse', defined by Abdul R. JanMohamed and David Lloyd as 'a theoretical articulation of the political and cultural structures that connect different minority cultures in their subjugation and opposition to the dominant culture'.[53] JanMohamed and Lloyd are confusing relativities with absolutes. It is unrealistic to expect Western European women and East Europeans to forge a common front with non-European peoples against the dominant culture to which the former belong and the latter aspire. The repetitious use of 'we/they', 'Europe/non-Europe' and 'white/black' dichotomies in Joseph Conrad's *Heart of Darkness* expresses Eastern Europe's quest for the West's recognition as 'Europeans' by opposing an undifferentiated Europe to non-Europe. Despite the internationalist propaganda of the East Bloc during the Cold War, it is actually among successful imperial nations like Great Britain, France and Italy that racial tolerance is a goal that governments actively try to promote.

Even the concept of an anti-Western Third World coalition collides with the reality of racism, ethnicity and imperial ambitions among non-European peoples. Indonesia's annexation of East Timor in 1975, with the attendant atrocities by which colonial occupation has been perpetuated (about a third of the indigenous population exterminated in 22 years of occupation), provides a stark reminder that neither the imperialist nor the genocidal impulse is exclusively European. Within particular Third World states, ethnic imperialism or colonialism every bit as virulent as the European variety affects daily life in ways that, to the subjugated, are more easily identifiable than the more devious Western conspiracies. Against the dynamic policies of the government of the United Kingdom to open up institutions like the armed forces, the police and the judiciary to ethnic minorities stand the ethnic-cleansing policies by which most tribe-based African governments transform these institutions into bastions of tribal power. It is with a sense of wonder that people from former British colonies but resident in the United Kingdom, for example, realize that Her Majesty's government accords them civil rights and other securities they could not expect in their home countries outside their ethnic homelands. During the Nigerian elections of 1983, to take another instance, a state governor openly lamented the end of British colonial rule despite British contributions to the chaos.

The Kenyan writer Grace Ogot captures these contradictions in her novels. In *The Promised Land* (1966, 1990) the protagonist Ochola, from Kenya's Luo ethnic group, journeys to the 'promised land' of Tanganyika (mainland Tanzania) and amasses considerable wealth through hard work, only to fall victim to a vicious local sorcerer who bluntly tells him in a dream-vision: 'You Luo people ... I hate all of you' (*PL* p. 128) and proceeds to inflict unimaginably cruel diseases upon him and his family. But the narrator also traces the sorcerer's enmity to local resentment of decades-long Luo dominance as conquerors. Ogot's *The Graduate* offers an even more sophisticated treatment of ethnicity. The Kenyan Minister for Public Affairs Mrs Juanina Karungaru's mission to mobilize Kenyan students in the United States of America for the task of national reconstruction runs headlong into the intractable issues of ethnic animosities, the ugly memories surviving from the anti-British war of independence, and the sheer irresponsibility of a myopic government that cannot even see the country's own graduates as a resource pool for national reconstruction. A student, Ngure, whose Mau Mau father had executed the minister's father, a traitor, during the war of independence, now fears reprisals from the minister's now-powerful family (p. 35), and yet secretly thrills to the knowledge that, among the Kenyans present, he and the charismatic minister share special ethnic bonds as Gikuyu (p. 34).

Furthermore, though the field of postcolonial studies is focused on Euro-Christian imperialism and colonialism, the spread of Islam into Africa (and Europe) by Arabs of the Arabian peninsula constitutes a colonization enterprise whose beginnings predate that of Europe and whose effects have proved equally enduring. It is a failure of postcolonial theory, and further proof of its Eurocentrism, that it ignores this major dimension of history. Yet a few writers, such as Yambo Ouologuem in *Bound to Violence* (1971), Cheikh Hamidou Kane in *Ambiguous Adventure* (1972) and Ayi Kwei Armah in *Two Thousand Seasons* (first published 1973) have treated this Arab-Islamic counterpart to Euro-Christian colonialism. Kane actually portrays Arab-Islamic culture as indigenous African in his search for a framework of values to combat the West whereas Ouologuem and Armah place it in the same category as its Western counterpart. Only a few postcolonial theorists, such as Soyinka in Chapter 3 of *Myth, Literature and the African World*, have commented at some length on this current in African postcolonial literature.

It is important, therefore, to recognize that literary/artistic opposition to neocolonialism represents a special kind of liberation agonistic conducted by an ideologically conscious, politically motivated elite who properly assume the task of awakening the general population to the forms and agency of their predicament, and leading them to contest European hegemony. Colonial conquest occurred in discrete territorial spaces, and this is reflected in patterns of perception and resistance. The decolonization novel is thus primarily an ideological construct projecting the author's perception of history and cultural life rather than an empirically accurate documentation of the historio-cultural realities of a society. What the theorist or critic studies is not absolute, unmediated social reality but particular writers' interpretation of aspects of reality, a fact which underscores the centrality of the authorial consciousness. Failure to recognize this accounts for the futility of much postcolonial literary and cultural theory.

Decolonization writers' conception of the novel within the larger field of liberation agonistics places a particular onus on criticism to make the writing accessible to ordinary readers of fiction beyond academia's narrow confines. Yet the development of postcolonial discourse as a tributary of postmodernist discourse renders it peculiarly incapable of performing this function. Despite frenzied theorizing, or perhaps because of it, much less is known globally in the 1990s about the literature than was the case in the 1960s and 1970s, for the theorizing has been oriented towards securing a niche in the dominant culture by demonstrating extensive assimilation of its esoteric practices, rather than explicating the literature. The decolonization novel is neither a 'human condition', nor 'sexual neurosis', nor 'gender war' genre, though elements of these may be woven into its exploration of contemporary social experience or interpretation of history. It is a genre rooted in the history of (neo)colonial negation and motivated by a nationalistic commitment to a liberation agonistic, a tradition willed into being by individuals and groups as an extension of political struggles against colonialist negation.

As even a glance at the histories of the decolonization literary traditions reveals, the critical factor that drove the emergence of the novel, once literacy had been achieved, was nationalism. Emerging in Africa and the West Indies in the first decades of the twentieth century, this factor gave rise to the Négritude movement of the 1940s, but attained critical mass only in mid-century. Among the Polynesian societies of Samoa and New Zealand Maoris, this point was reached in the 1960s and 1970s and quickly assumed a pan-Pacific magnitude. By Witi Ihimaera's account:

> It was the age of...'No Maoris, No Tour.'... Of trying to mould a new future. Of making the linkages with our own culture, with Pakeha New Zealand, with the South Pacific, and with Third World concerns... We say that continued alienation of Maori land and the Maori people from their culture meant that the Maori was becoming landless in his own country.
>
> This was the time which therefore saw Nga Tamatoa petitioning Parliament for the establishment of courses in Maori language and culture in all schools... It was the time of sit-ins in Parliament grounds and annual protests at Waitangi Day celebrations to draw attention to Maori grievances.[54]

Albert Wendt has stressed the indigenous initiative behind this cultural reawakening: it was 'inspired and fostered and led by our own people... across the political barriers [and] artificial frontiers drawn by the colonial powers'. Two of the highlights of this awakening were the 1972 and 1976 South Pacific Festival of Arts held in Fiji and New Zealand, respectively.[55] Related cultural programmes in Africa, Polynesia and the West Indies included the establishment of all sorts of magazines to stimulate literary interest and provide outlets for such interests.[56] These origins give the literatures a uniqueness, specificity and social mission that set them apart from the literatures of Europe and its diaspora as well as such non-European nations as China and Japan.

METAHISTORIES AND METAFICTIONS

Of special importance in the quest for genuine decolonization was a recognized need for a cosmographic revision: the reinterpretation of the worlds of colonized peoples to reflect their authentic histories and cosmic perceptions. European historiography and the current concept of postcoloniality date the histories of non-European peoples from the day a European adventurer stumbled into their world, leading to such absurdities as the claims that America was 'discovered' by Christopher Columbus, Australia by Captain James Cook, and the 2600-miles long River Niger by the Scottish explorer Mungo Park who was led to it by 'natives'. Many critics are wont to argue that concern with the revision of this historiography is out of step with contemporary reality and academic trends. Yet until a universal denunciation from formerly colonized peoples dissuaded them, Western powers had been pushing the United Nations Organization to commemorate the year 1992 as the five hundredth anniversary of the 'discovery' of America by Christopher Columbus.

The role of the European novel (including its imperial outpost sub-set) in the propagation of a Europe-centred view of the world and rationalizing the depredations committed by colonialism must be viewed within this historiographic tradition. In his admirable work on Joyce Cary, M.J.C. Echeruo compares the 'European foreign novel' (which I have called the imperial-outpost novel) with 'a letter home from abroad', whose author exploits a long-established and culturally validated mythology of the foreign scene to entertain the reader. Even phenomena which have European equivalents are ascribed to some imaginary philosophical or moral predisposition of non-European races, and interpreted through Freudian and Jungian theories of 'primitive' cultures.[57] Of the European 'novel of Africa', Echeruo argues that the mind it studied:

> was really the European mind; the imagination it finally under-
> stood (or delineated) was inevitably the European imagination.
> But the occasion was conveniently Africa and the various myths
> of Africa provided the terms of argument and demonstration. If
> there is anything 'true' of such novels, it is not essentially (or
> 'properly') in its depiction of character and personality, but in the
> accuracy of its reflection of the imaginative temper of the author's
> culture.[58]

Albert Wendt has made similar observations on European fiction about South Pacific societies:

> Much of this literature ranges from the hilariously romantic
> through the pseudo-scholarly to the infuriatingly racist; from the

noble-savage literary school through Margaret Mead and all her comings-of-age, Somerset Maugham's puritan missionaries, drunks and saintly whores, and James Michener's rascals and golden people, to the stereotyped childlike pagan who needs to be steered to the Light.

The Oceania found in this literature is largely *papalagi* fictions, more revealing of *papalagi* fantasies and hang-ups, dreams and nightmares, prejudices and ways of viewing our crippled cosmos, than of our actual islands.[59]

Decolonization novelists have therefore always seen mythoclasm and creation of counter-myths, metahistories and metafictions as integral to the task of rehabilitation.[60] There is a remarkable agreement between Albert Wendt's 1982 observation that Third World peoples must endeavour to transcend 'the tragic mimicry' and 'grotesque colonial caricatures' into which colonialism has transformed them, and Aimé Césaire's claim that through Négritude the black man 'whose grotesqueness or exoticism' European literature 'sets out to emphasise is made a hero', and a world created 'where only the junk-shop's exotic inhumanity rose before'.[61] The tasks which engage decolonization writers in the 1990s are not only the same as those of the pioneers but have acquired a special urgency as a result of the resurgence of Europe's sense of a divine mandate or 'manifest destiny' to reorder the universe. Albert Wendt unequivocally reiterates this point in 1992:

> Most of my books are an analysis of colonialism and its effects on the colonised ... The New Zealand section [of *Ola*] is a look at colonialism in New Zealand. It was intended to disturb ... Some Pakeha have taken exception to it, and accused me of racism. They ought to look at where they're coming from.[62]

Without any roots in this literary tradition, prevailing Postcolonial Discourse has failed to nurture a virile culture of criticism for this literature. Whereas theory and criticism have always fed into each other in European traditions, a survey of the postcolonial literary scene reveals an immense disparity between the vast flood of re-cycled theory reformulating the commonplaces of traditional literary criticism as earth-shaking discoveries, and the meagre amount of sustained work of textual explication. The chasm separating the theorists from the creative writers and from the larger populace whose 'liberation' and 'empowerment' are being theorized about is manifest in the anarchic, anti-democratic and gratuitously mystifying language inherited from Postmodernist discourse, a form of jabberwocky but bereft of Lewis Caroll's original inspiration, design and sparkling humour.

A measure of the irrelevance of such scholarly self-indulgence is provided by the unanimous decision (18 December 1996) of the school board of Oakland, California, to adopt 'African-American Vernacular English' (for which the term 'Ebonics' was coined in the 1970s, a neologism created from 'ebony', for black, and 'phonics') as the medium of instruction for African-Americans in its schools 'to facilitate their acquisition and mastery of English language skills'.[63] One may agree or disagree with this startling perception of African-American Vernacular as a language other than English, but it is on record that the Board was able to convince the Rev. Jesse Jackson.[64] Yet of the 18 essays in *The Nature and Context of Minority Discourse*, the founding text of the 'Minority Discourse' campaign in North America, only a few are linguistically accessible to normal educated people. Most are not just incomprehensible but stylistically repellent. Unfortunately, such language is typical of much postcolonial discourse.

Postcolonial discourse (with its 'Minority Discourse' variant) is thus caught in a terminal identity crisis rooted in the politics of its Western origins. To European theorists and their Third World followers, it represents the application of European theoretical perspectives and models of cultural relationships to the analysis of a global reality of which the Third World is a subsidiary. To Third World decolonization theorists, however, it is an integral part of a discourse of resistance whose concern is the development of a theoretical practice and modes of critique for approaching ex-colonial peoples' literature of anti-colonialist resistance. The European approach is antagonistic to this aspiration, for the attempt to homogenize the colonial experience as a postmodernist existential condition in which colonizer and colonized are uniformly implicated is analogous to a homogenization of fishing as a partnership between the fisherman and the fish.

To break out of this schizophrenic bind, it is important to develop a discourse that re-affiliates theory and practice with the political activism of the decolonization literature. Ketu H. Katrak has identified major questions that should preoccupy such a discourse:

What theoretical models will be appropriate for this task? How can theory be an integral part of the struggle of these writers as presented in their novels, poems, dramas, essays, letters, and testimonies? How can we make our theory and interpretation of postcolonial texts challenge the hegemony of the Western canon? How can we, within a dominant Eurocentric discourse, make our study of postcolonial texts itself a mode of resistance? And... what theoretical models will be most constructive for the development of this literature?[65]

The issues raised by Ketu Katrak are engaged in the present study.

2

The Politics of Form: Ideology, Form and Technique

Decolonization agonistics begins with a search for adequate form to embody the novelist's vision of history and the universe. In Africa, Polynesia and the West Indies, the existence of a rich indigenous tradition of literature, albeit an oral tradition, means that novelists' first and formative aesthetic experience comes from the indigenous culture. Many novelists have therefore generally begun by looking inwards to their own myths, epics, legends, folktales, songs, riddles and proverbs, and other literary performances.

The importance of orality in the first generation of novels certainly eluded the first generation of readers and critics, whose responses defined European approaches to the novel for half a century. European readers who had no difficulty accepting their culture's oral ballads as literature generally found it difficult to accept oral cultures' products. This difficulty has usually been explained in terms of inextricable etymological links between literature and writing, though as Wellek and Warren have shown, this connection found in English does not exist in such major languages as Russian and German.[1] The major obstacle was the anthropological perception of non-European oral literatures not as individual creations but as immutable products of a 'group mind', serving the utilitarian functions of inculcating moral values, preserving communal beliefs and histories, and curtailing social change. So enduring is this error that Barthes confidently writes that in oral cultures 'the responsibility for a narrative is never assumed by a person but by a mediator, shaman or relator whose "performance" – the mastery of the narrative code – may possibly be admired but never his "genius"'.[2]

Barthes is wrong. And so are the generations of anthropologists from whom he borrowed his opinion. Oral literatures are art forms which place great emphasis on aesthetics, individual genius and the individual artist's career. Every performer is expected to imaginatively enrich his/her work within the bounds recognized by generic and formal conventions, performance contexts of situation and canons of moral propriety. His/her reputation and career depend on satisfying an audience that is not passive but highly critical and participatory. Robert Te Kotahi Mahuta's work on Maori performance, for example, has revealed that the audience audibly critique the performers' techniques and wisdom.[3] 'Among the Ibo the art of conversation is regarded very highly', Achebe narrates in *Things Fall Apart*, 'and proverbs are the palm-oil with which words are eaten' (p. 5).

In the absence of writing, oral literatures also constitute frameworks within which, as Soyinka has argued, 'traditional society poses its social questions or formulates its moralities'.[4] In the novel *Pouliuli*, Albert Wendt portrays the protagonist Faleasa searching Samoan myths for 'the essence of pre-papalagi Malaeluan beliefs about the cosmos and man's place in it' (p. 94). Obiechina has thus rightly described proverbs as 'kernels' of wisdom which 'derive their effectiveness and force from the collective imagination which apprehends the underlying connection between a literal fact and its allusive amplification and which vivifies an experience by placing it beside another which bears the stamp of approval'.[5] Such use of proverbs is more easily understood in the context of the philosophical needs of an oral culture, for whom proverbs function as mnemonic devices for packaging and transmitting experience in convenient, memorable doses.

It is important in this connection to correct a common misunderstanding of the concept of 'tradition' (with its adjectival form, 'traditional'). In colonialist cultural discourse, this usually means a non-European society's indigenous culture, hence synonymous with 'antiquated' and 'primitive', as distinct from the European, taken to be 'modern' and 'civilized'. Properly speaking, 'tradition' is, as the *Merriam-Webster's Collegiate Dictionary* (10th edition) defines it, simply 'an inherited, established, or customary pattern of thought, action or behaviour', such as 'a religious practice or social custom'. The true antonym to 'traditional', therefore, is not 'modern' or 'Western' but 'alien', and European culture is merely its own tradition, without any connotation of modernity or universality. Use of indigenous literature is thus part of the central preoccupation with ending the people's alienation from their world, their present from their past, through the reclamation and authentication of their entire cosmos. In the search for adequate form and idiom, indigenous narrative modes and aesthetic codes are hybridized with those of the imported written genre, exploiting the elasticity of the hybrid form for a more effective exploration of the complexities of contemporary social reality.

THE NOVEL AND THE PSYCHODYNAMICS OF ORALITY

For oral cultures, words exist only as sound. This has manifold implications for any writer who exploits oral literatures to give narrative shape to experience. Walter J. Ong's *Orality and Literacy: the Technologising of the Word* effectively links the formal properties of oral discourse with the noesis or 'psychodynamics' of orality. Ong further shows that to meet the needs of the performer who depends entirely on memory for composition and reproduction of the discourse, and the audience who depend solely on the ear to seize the fleeting word in its brief existence, oral discourse tends to be aggregative rather than analytic, redundant or copious, agonistically toned, empathic and situational rather than abstract, and to adopt additive rather than subordinative syntax.[6] Writing produces different effects, for, as Jack Goody has shown, it can embody thought and discourse in visible, permanent and cumulative form capable of endless scrutiny and revision. It is therefore instrumental to the development of great intellectual abstraction and 'decontextualization of knowledge', for any desired segment of human discourse can be isolated for concentrated, abstract scrutiny.[7]

From misunderstanding the nature and extent of novelists' exploitation of indigenous forms, criticism of the first generation of decolonization novels rarely went beyond identifying and describing specific occurrences of oral forms, thus reinforcing the general misperception of their presence as mere anthropological details. Ideally, criticism should endeavour to uncover the principles and aesthetic conventions (if any) underlying such writing, distinguishing between conscious experiment, inadequate mastery of formal demands, and cultural interference, for there is no value in criticism that indicts a novelist for not achieving effects that s/he has chosen to avoid. Robert Plant Armstrong's work on the novels of Amos Tutuola (who had only a basic competence in the use of English) shows greater sensitivity in relating Tutuola's style to interference from his indigenous language and oral literature.[8]

It is therefore possible to construct a hypothetical model for comparative evaluation and analysis of novels conceived within the decolonization tradition, particularly those from older societies with a pre-European history and a living indigenous language, as the intimate, oral culture develops towards global culture. In the African and Polynesian traditions, this results in a broadly common pattern of thematic and structural development along a roughly triangular path according to certain principles of composition. A preoccupation with cultural affirmation in a relatively uncomplicated oral setting at the left base angle gradually broadens thematic emphasis to grapple with more complex contradictions at the apex. The linear or chronological plot characteristic of novels in the left base angle gives way to a more convoluted structure, and the teller narrator moves closer to the position of a reflector narrator as the fictive tradition itself reveals the increasing influence of the Euromodernist tradition. A greater clarification of artistic vision here frequently leads, however, to a search for ideological solutions to what is now recognized as neocolonialism's asphyxiating hold on the societies that have been granted nominal independence. Thus begins an ideologically driven structural decomplication as the novel moves down the right gradient towards what may be designated as the novel of radical traditionalism. The return to traditional values is nevertheless accompanied with a greater harnessing of chirographic amenities. Principles of composition operating within this model may be summarized thus:

(1) Novels in which affirmation is most central are most pervaded by the features of oral discourse, particularly when such affirmation involves an imaginative reconstruction of an autonomous, pre-colonial universe. Conversely, concern with satire or criticism of post-independence society generally results in greater exploitation of techniques developed within the written tradition. Such techniques are best suited to the exploration of the chaos, ambiguities, uncertainties and contradictions of modern society.

(2) Language strategies are directly related to the latent noematical or psychodynamic characteristics of the dominant cultures along an orality–literacy, rural–urban continuum, and the apparent intellectual appeal of the language is largely a function of its ability or otherwise to assimilate English conceptual categories.

(3) Finally, the degree of a novelist's identification with the portrayed culture is reflected in the degree of proximity between the narrative prose and the dialogue. A novelist/narrator who identifies with the fictional culture endeavours as much as possible to bridge the language gap and, through this, harmonize the cultural consciousness, whereas a hostile narrator widens the gap as much as possible.

Literary criticism informed by these principles will benefit from the ease of isolating and scrutinizing any desired feature in a narrative. For example, character analysis can avoid the false flatness-versus-roundness scheme introduced by E.M. Forster (which serious European critics never apply to the evaluation of European texts and poorly informed critics always apply to Third World texts) and concentrate more rewardingly on relevant contextual issues. In comparative criticism, whether of an individual writer's corpus, works from one culture, or works from several cultures, it becomes possible to compare novels on the basis of discrete, objective criteria based on narrative features that are actually present in the novels rather than those subjectively perceived to be absent. A novel conceived in the tradition of the oral performance of a primary oral culture must necessarily differ in terms of plot structure, language and methods of character delineation from a novel conceived within the chirographic tradition, and there is no point in criticism which approaches the former in terms of the absence of features that properly belong to the latter.

Robert Fraser has pointed out this pattern or development in the works of Ayi Kwei Armah:

the usual direction of change [in the modern novel] is towards greater complexity and a more opaque texture. Armah presents us with a marked exception to this rule. His work has in no sense become harder. He is not one of those artists – James Joyce might serve as an example – whose work becomes more hermetic or convoluted as it develops. Rather the opposite: Armah's prose style has become increasingly transparent.[9]

At every point, this democratic transparency of language among creative writers constitutes a repudiation of the secret-cult obscurantism cultivated by many theorists of postcoloniality.

A writer may begin at any point along the triangle, with the work broadly following the principles dominant at that point, as is the case with Albert Wendt, Ayi Kwei Armah and Ben Okri, as well as many West Indians. Okri's early works, such as *The Landscapes Within*, set a pattern of experimenting with European forms transplanted to an African setting, but *The Famished Road* belongs firmly in the radical-traditionalist location. For his own part, Achebe has never favoured the structural disjointedness of the Euromodernist tradition. The nearest Achebe comes to Euromodernism is in *Anthills of the Savannah*, but even here he contents himself with the use of several narrators who constitute the joint-protagonists of the novel, recording their experiences as part of the larger experience of the fictional society of Kangan. In this sense, the novel is polyvocal. Polyvocalism in decolonization novels is not the same as the postmodernists' indeterminacy, instability of signifiers, or proliferation of conflicting meanings. On the contrary, it is a concert of voices revealing the various layers of a complex experience. Even in conflict, the relationship of the various narrators' voices is one of complementarity, and their ultimate function is the projection of a rich, unified vision of multidimensional reality.

Virtually all major African novelists who have published more novels after reaching the apex (or, as in Armah and Soyinka, who started there) have subsequently taken the path of decomplication. Wole Soyinka's first novel, *The Interpreters* (1965), for example, is located right at the apex with its five joint-protagonists and extremely convoluted plot which features several flashbacks and flashforwards but also flashbacks within flashbacks. Whereas many Western critics hailed this Euromodernist convolution as a sign of the technical coming-of-age of the African novel, many African critics denounced it as a product of an alienated consciousness. By contrast, Soyinka's next novel, *Season of Anomy*, is developed through a fairly linear plot and chronology. Whereas *The Interpreters* has no story line, *Season of Anomy* explores Nigeria's post-independence experience through an extended allegory. Both novels, however, are deeply rooted in the metaphysics and cosmogony of Soyinka's Yoruba culture, whose narratives provide the analogues against which the Nigerian reality is measured.

The writer whose works most typically conform to the pyramidal pattern is Ngugi wa Thiong'o, starting with *The River Between* and *Weep Not, Child* and then rising to *A Grain of Wheat* and *Petals of Blood* before moving down to *Devil on the Cross* and *Matigari*. The decomplication begins with *Petals of Blood*, and the last two novels are vatic narratives in which the narrator is also a prophet in the role of the traditional African artist. *A Grain of Wheat* and *Petals of Blood* are also polyvocal narratives which reveal experience through several joint-protagonists. As in *Anthills of the Savannah*, the various experiences are unified through a background voice that embodies the communal consciousness. In *A Grain of Wheat* and *Petals of Blood*, this voice occasionally incorporates the reader into the events through second person pronouns, as in the following passage from *A Grain of Wheat*: 'as you'll remember, we had only just been allowed to hold political meetings ... Also the many wounds which our people had suffered were too fresh for the eye to look at' (*GOW* p. 75).

The device facilitates full exploitation of the possibilities of both first-person and omniscient third-person perspectives by creating ample room for the authorial ventriloquist to intervene with ideological polemics, historical exposition and moral denunciation without alerting the reader to the surprisingly global consciousness of the ostensibly peasant narrator.

Petals of Blood inaugurates Ngugi's decomplication of his writing. Appropriately, it is also his last novel to be written originally in a European language.[10] Both *Devil on the Cross* and *Matigari* (1982) are shaped by this new consciousness, the former being the revelation of vatic narrator and self-proclaimed 'Prophet of Justice' while the latter is conceived as a performed oral narrative. The oral conception of *Matigari* is assertively acknowledged in the dedication, in the 'Note on the English Edition' and in yet another note 'To the Reader/ Listener'. The dedication commends the novel 'to all those who love a good story; and to all those who research and write on African oratures; and to all those committed to the development of literatures in the languages of all the African peoples'.

Ayi Kwei Armah's case is clearly a democratization process driven by an ideological desire to make his writing speak for the voiceless, confused millions of Africa. Armah's first novel, *The Beautyful Ones Are Not Yet Born* (1968), is a work of deep disillusionment whose structure has been strongly influenced by the Euromodernist tradition, as are *Fragments* and *Why Are We So Blest?* The last two novels, *Two Thousand Seasons* and *The Healers*, are racial sagas revealed, like Ngugi's *Devil on the Cross*, through a vatic narrator in the decomplication process that prompted Robert Fraser's comment noted earlier.

As in Ngugi, this development is not as abrupt as it might seem, for the novelists distinguish between individuals or institutions and the larger society whose redemption is the goal of decolonization literature. *The Beautyful Ones Are Not Yet Born* reveals strong indigenous roots in its network of anecdotes, parables and other short oral forms, and its sixth chapter unfolds a long sequence of anguished reminiscence in mythopoeic language which differs from the rest of the novel and belongs more with *Two Thousand Seasons*. In *Fragments*, passages revealed through the ancestral consciousness of Naana have an unmistakable oral-aural elegiac quality which anticipates the elegiac opening section of *Two Thousand Seasons*. Even while marking the peak of Armah's development as a prose stylist in the Euromodernist tradition, the third novel, *Why Are We So Blest?*, also exhibits a palpable tension between Euromodernist form and African nationalism. It is profoundly anti-Western in spirit, and involves a reverse application of Europe's racial Manichean principles in exploring the historical relationship between the white race and Africa. The novelist's fictional *alter ego* and *raisonneur*, Solo, unequivocally repudiates the Western myth of the artist as a hyper-sensitive being isolated in philistine society, in favour of the social responsibilities of the traditional African artist (p. 231).

It is in *Two Thousand Seasons*, however, that Armah's pan-Africanism and Ngugi's Marxism finally converge in narrative forms which conceive the narrator as prophet and conscience of the race. The artist-narrator's self is completely integrated in the community's identity, and both are represented through the first person plural pronoun and separated from the oppressors, 'they'. Armah's communalism must not be confused with Marxism, which Armah unequivocally rejects as 'the whitest of all white philosophies' (*WAWSB* p. 163). In this as in his general perception of the history of colonial relationships, Armah reveals a more acute insight into those relationships than African Marxists have shown, for as Robert Young has pointed out:

> Marxism's universalizing narrative of the unfolding of a rational system of world history is simply a negative form of the history of European imperialism: it was Hegel, after all, who declared that 'Africa has no history', and it was Marx who, though critical of British imperialism, concluded that the British colonization of India was ultimately for the best because it brought India into the evolutionary narrative of Western history, thus creating the conditions for future class struggle there.[11]

The communal orientation of this literary tradition accounts for Armah's simultaneous exploitation and subversion of the epic form. Against the epic's celebration of aristocratic heroes and their exploits *Two Thousand Seasons*, again like Ngugi's novels, celebrates the heroism of the ordinary people while trenchantly denouncing the leadership whose treachery dooms African peoples to European domination. Like the biblical prophets, the vatic narrator admonishes Africa to abandon Europe-fostered atomistic individualism and revive the indigenous African virtues of reciprocity and 'connectedness' which Armah designates as 'The Way'. As in Ngugi's *Devil on the Cross*, 'connectedness' is not just an ethical but also an aesthetic principle which shapes the narrative. Thus, in *Devil on the Cross* Ngugi's narrator pulls himself up to establish the proper links (*DOC* p. 10) while Armah's fabulist rebukes himself for letting his proud tongue fly 'too fast for the listener' (*Healers* p. 2).

Among the Polynesians, the novels of Patricia Grace, Witi Ihimaera and Albert Wendt all manifest increasing anger against what they perceive as the worsening racism in New Zealand under European settler domination. Ihimaera and Grace start with lyrical recreations of traditional Maori culture, but Ihimaera's evaluation of this early work suggests a programmatic conception of his artistic mission. 'It was as if we'd all been given sleeping pills, tranquillisers', he writes. 'Even the literature we were writing lacked strength and direction ... and, with very few exceptions, the work lacks anger and political thought.'[12] Behind this was a long-term vision, however, for Richard Corballis quotes him as declaring:

> My concern is for the roots of our culture, the culture that we carry within ourselves and which makes us truly Maori ... rather than about the Maori in urban areas where – so I've been informed – all the action is. But only when I have completed writing about the rural Maori to my satisfaction will I uncurl my toes and write about how hard the city pavements are to our feet.[13]

Exploration of the 'hard pavements' of the city is undertaken by Ihimaera in *The Matriarch* (1986) and by Grace in *Cousins* (1992). *The Matriarch* does not actually explore Maoris' experience in the city except insofar as 'the city' may be taken to represent the bastion of Pakeha power and ideology. In terms of technical development of the novel form, the movement from *Tangi* (1973) and *Whanau* (1974) is remarkable. Though *Tangi* is by no means a linear narrative (several levels of time and action are actually telescoped within the hero Tama's narrative), *Whanau* is structurally more complex, with a chronologically fragmented plot and multiple narrative centres or spots of concurrent activity. Its themes mark the beginning of Ihimaera's analysis of Maori–Pakeha relationships through explicit materialist-historical perspectives that causally link Pakeha racial and economic aggression to Maoris' inability to compete with the Pakeha. Expropriation of Maori lands, racially oppressive legislation and Maori exclusion from the political-economic mainstream are located in a historical pattern that has persisted over a century of Pakeha attempts to remake the land in their own image. The action lasts a mere 16½ hours (from four o'clock on Sunday morning to half past eleven in the night) but within this time span Ihimaera manages to evoke a sense of eternity.

With *The Matriarch*, Ihimaera undertakes the historiographic task of reinterpreting the Maori–Pakeha encounter from predominantly Maori viewpoints, blending a medley of forms – epic, history, parliamentary records (the *Hansard*), mythology, newspaper reports, diary, and conventional narrative, among others. Mark Williams' 'Witi Ihimaera and the Politics of Epic' has demonstrated the length to which Ihimaera has gone to subvert European historiography, arguing that 'Ihimaera misrepresents history in order to make his partisan case more convincing'.[14] But C.K. Stead's review of the novel for the *London Review of Books* reveals great umbrage. Complaining, rather naively, that 'the Ihimaera of sensitive, lyrical, rather plangent evocations' has been replaced by 'the novelist as *warrior*, the novel as *taiaha* or *mere*, the reader as ally or enemy', C.K. Stead reviles Ihimaera's revision of history as 'intellectually puerile and imaginatively futile'.[15] The text itself occasionally reads like a primary epic and occasionally like a secondary epic, as the need arises. The primary epic is certainly the dominant tradition in the apostrophe to the eponymous heroine's great uncle, the Honourable Wi Pere Halbert, to whom the narrator apologizes for introducing him rather late in the saga:

> I apologise, my ancestor. Blame it on the narrative process, which would only have been confused if you had made too early an entrance. Better still, consider that I have at least given you the stage to yourself. Quickly now, without any authorial prompting from myself, tell it all in your own words. But one stage direction, just one – while you are telling it, think of yourself

as *the Maori with his own hands around his neck.* (p. 301. Ihimaera's emphasis.)

Racial themes and political commentary have always had a strong presence in Grace's work. However, the movement from *Mutuwhenua* and *Potiki* to *Cousins* (1992) shows mounting impatience with the Pakeha's concept of biculturalism. The central theme of *Potiki* is Maori determination in the present to resist further dispossession by the Pakeha as had happened in the 150 years of Maori–Pakeha encounter. Through a theme of conflict between the Tamihana family, whose territory lies on a beautiful stretch of seaboard, and a consortium of estate developers who want to take over this property, the novel links the consortium's predatory scheme to the larger process of legislated disempowerment and dispossession during this encounter. The novel is also characterized by polyvocal narration conducted through several joint protagonists, as in Achebe's *Anthills of the Savannah* and Ngugi's *A Grain of Wheat* and *Petals of Blood* and Soyinka's *The Interpreters* (1965).

Cousins explores Maoris' contemporary problems through the experiences of three cousins: Mata, Makareta and Missy who symbolize different dimensions of the Maori predicament, and offer different perspectives on the problems of Maori–Pakeha relationship. Missy, product of a Maori woman's marriage to a deserter from the British navy who 'only wanted a slave for him and a prospect of [getting Maori] land' (*Cousins* p. 45), represents a variation on the plot developed in *Mutuwhenua* about the Maori caught at the Pakeha–Maori cosmic interface, and her story is one of eventual return. Her experience further stresses one of Grace's major themes of struggle: nobody would give you a turn, you have to fight for your rights. Makareta's own story explores the meaning of biculturalism for the Maori. Even when she rejects the marriage arranged by the family to consolidate family lands and inter-family relationship, she devotes her learning and experience to the Maori cause. Missy is the one who fills the role rejected by Makareta, and to do so she has to sacrifice her own dreams of a glamorous life as a pop singer in Pakeha society. Through their meshed lives, Grace projects the totality of the Maoris' quest for their rightful place in contemporary New Zealand, in a narrative form that is radical-traditionalist.

Among the Polynesians, Albert Wendt is an exception to the practice of beginning with a pastoral reconstruction of the indigenous order. His first novel, *Sons for the Return Home*, is a work of critical realism which recognizes both the flaws of Samoan culture and the reality of the European presence in Samoan life. But there is a relative lack of structural complexity from this novel through the next, *Pouliuli*, to the third, the chronological *Leaves of the Banyan Tree*. From *Ola* (1991) and *Black Rainbow* (1992), increased complexity becomes a marked feature of Wendt's globalized vision, greater concern with the position of women in patriarchal cultures, and deepening disenchantment with the Pakeha of New Zealand. Set in the twenty-first century and inspired by lithographs painted by Ralph Hotere to protest successive French governments' poisoning of the South Pacific environment with nuclear explosions, *Black Rainbow* also marks Wendt's departure from 'writing well-structured novels', preferring now 'to throw all the bits and pieces together and see where the novel goes'.[16] Structurally, it reveals the same Euromodernist tendency as Soyinka's *The Interpreters*, marked by a chronologically staggered plot and a rejection of conventional closure to the plot. Going further than Soyinka's, however, Wendt's novel offers a set of alternative resolutions in the last chapter ('Endings/Beginnings') whose last sentence declares that 'Readers are free to improvise whatever other endings/beginnings they prefer.'

Nevertheless, though *Black Rainbow* is very much a futuristic novel of the twentieth-century technological revolution, its central theme is the West's use of its technological superiority to pursue its scheme of global domination. Lack of closure to the plot is not a statement about any inconclusiveness to the experience, or ambiguity about its form, as some readers may be inclined to interpret it, but of the fact that none of the alternative endings will significantly alter the fundamental situation. Further underscoring the antinomy between form and political message is Wendt's mocking of the post-structuralist and postmodernist schools by employing the word 'deconstruct' in the negative sense of killing.

INTERSTICES IN ETERNITY: TIME, SPACE AND NUMBER

The Racial Debate

Consciousness of time (that is, perception, representation, and attitudes to time) is one of the cultural behaviours that, in European racial theory, is taken to distinguish the white from the non-white races. Europeans supposedly possess an advanced consciousness of time whereas non-Europeans lack it. The American critic Charles Larson has published two books of anthropological literary criticism linking consciousness of time to the racial binaries of rational, analytical white and irrational, emotional black. On Spengler's authority, Larson blandly asserts that 'interest in time is peculiar to the Western civilization'.[17] In *The Novel in the Third World*, the second chapter 'History without Time' is devoted to proving that same thesis of non-Europeans living 'outside of time', in mythical time or 'anti-history' that is 'removed from any specific time warp'. A discussion of Vincent Eri's *The Crocodile* leads to an address to white readers: 'The conflict here is against the Australians instead of the Europeans, but this is still black against white, the emotional versus the analytical.'[18] When one reads the entry 'African time' defined as 'unpunctuality' in the *Collins English Dictionary* (1991), it is difficult to miss the assumption underlying the racial slur.

Alternatively, Jack Goody and several others have shown that perceptions of time are functions of the state of literacy and technology rather than racial ontology. Goody points out that 'with regards to concepts of time, we find differences in technology, to procedures for the measurement of time', hence 'the concept of chronology is linear rather than circular [because] it needs numbered series starting with a fixed base, which means that some form of graphic record is a prerequisite'.[19] Anthony Giddens has argued in a similar vein that:

> the development of writing underlies the first emergence of the linear time consciousness which later in the West became the basis of historicity as a feature of social life...Its very linearity as a material form perhaps encourages the consciousness of the elapsing of time as a sequential process, leading from one point away to another point in a progressive manner.[20]

Pre-literate European cultures actually apprehended and measured time like other oral cultures, and Ian Watt has shown that even European Renaissance writers (a prime example being Shakespeare) showed 'a-historical attitudes...associated with a striking lack of interest in the minute-by-minute and day-to-day temporal setting'.[21] Finally, Lewis Mumford writes that 'in terms of the human organism itself...time is measured not by the calendar but by the events that occupy it. The shepherd measures from the time the ewes lambed; the farmer measures back to the days of sowing or forward to the harvest.'[22]

Modes of measuring elapsed time must be distinguished from actual perception of time as well as from relativistic theories of time and space which, though their validity has been amply demonstrated by science, lie outside human history and everyday spatio-temporal experience on earth. Experiments with time and space by a postmodernist writer like Jeanette Winterson must be understood in their proper context. Winterson's *Sexing the Cherry* (1989) comes easily to mind here, with its epigraphs questioning the reality of time and matter, and its plot constructed to enact this questioning. Winterson's first epigraph asserts that perception of time as present, past and future 'does not exist' among the Hopi Indians even though their language is as sophisticated as English. This is an error, for absence of tense markers that English has evolved in its own entirely different cultural context does not mean absence of the time dimensions denoted by those markers. Similarly, that matter is made up of 'empty space and points of light', as her second epigraph observes, does not annul the lethal materiality of a knife, a bullet, or a nuclear bomb; neither does it obviate the need to feed.

For all human purposes connected with life on earth, representation of time in most cultures follows the pattern attributed by Thorleif Boman to Western cultures:

> Western minds represent time as a straight line upon which we stand with our gaze directed forward; before us we have the future and behind us the past. On this line we can unequivocally define all tenses by means of a point. The present is the point on which we are standing, the future is found at some point in front of us, and in between lies the exact future; behind us lies the perfect, still farther back the imperfect, and farther back yet the pluperfect. At first one does not think about whether this straight line is finite or infinite, for all our attention is concentrated upon the present and upon the times that are grouped about it.[23]

Boman's model is no more exclusively Western than the Atlantic Ocean. However, cultural theorists of the Larson school are wont to introduce quixotic criteria in describing cultural behaviour in order to maintain their ontological myth. In *The Emergence of African Fiction*, Larson points out what he considers to be typically African usage as exemplified by the Nigerian, Amos Tutuola; in the course of this, Larson reveals his own supposedly civilized European practice:[24]

[Tutuola's] numbers tend to be whole units instead of fractions. Time is usually referred to in complete hours (such as eight o'clock p.m.) rather than by minutes or portions of hours, as if Tutuola is not quite used to having to pinpoint exact periods of time. (p. 102)

Now here is Larson's habitual denotation of time, number and space:

The distance from the school where I taught in Eastern Nigeria and the Onitsha market was thirteen miles, yet I was rarely able to cover this distance ... on my motor scooter in less than an hour. (p. 105)

No dispassionate reader will miss the total identity between Tutuola's habitual usage and Charles Larson's. From his own self-revelation, Larson is clearly 'not quite used to having to pinpoint exact periods of time' or fractionalizing the units of space measurement (hence his 'thirteen miles' and 'an hour'!).

Many readers are likely to be confused by statements by such writers as Witi Ihimaera and Wole Soyinka about time in their cultures. Ihimaera, for instance, has asserted that 'For Maori people the past is not something behind us. It is before us, a long unbroken line of ancestors whose guidance must be accepted and to whom we are accountable.'[25] Similarly, Soyinka has declared that Yoruba thought operates a cyclic conception of time, creating a paradox by which 'the unborn' are older than the living just as the latter precede the ancestors, and 'the world of the unborn is older than the world of the ancestor'.[26] Such models of time/reality merely express the importance of the historical past for understanding the present, and there is nothing here to suggest that time literally unfolds in endless cycles. Soyinka's model also accommodates the belief, found among many cultures, in reincarnation and the literal existence of both the ancestors and the unborn in their own worlds. Patricia Grace clarifies this issue in *Potiki* in the major narrator Roimata's awakening to the relevance of past to future:

It was a new discovery to find that these stories were, after all, about our own lives, were not distant, that there was no past or future, that all time is a now-time, centred in the being. It was a new realisation that the centred being in this now-time simply reaches out in any direction towards the outer circles, these outer circles being named 'past' and 'future' only for our convenience. (p. 39)

The Spatio-Temporal Deixis

Decolonization novelists are aware that ordinary Europeans' beliefs about the perception of time in non-European cultures are more influenced by wide-circulation works like Larson's and the *Collins English Dictionary* than specialized books like Jack Goody's. They have therefore had to devise means of representing, within their plots, oral cultures' apprehension of dimensions of time (past, present and future) and the *parts* of time (days, nights, months, years, and their various subdivisions and aggregates) in the absence of writing and the mechanical clock. E.N. Obiechina's study of the representation of time in 'urban' and 'rural' West African novels has revealed that in the latter 'the fixed nature of the seasons, the rhythms of agricultural work and the distribution of festivals give important temporal signposts'. So do regular daily events, habitual actions and the diurnal movements of the heavenly bodies, while historical time is measured by events which have left their marks on the corporate destiny or experience.[27]

However, the proper opposition is not urban/rural but writing/ orality, for it is these which determine the modes or technologies for measuring time. Rural Britons do not normally measure time by the sun or cockcrow but by the clock because theirs is not an oral culture. Consequently, while novelists endeavour to structure unfolding events within definite temporal grids, cultural verisimilitude demands specifying time/space through appropriate cultural psychodynamics by denoting time as the duration of a communally known event or phenomenon, and space as the time spanning two events/phenomena.

In Merle Collins' *Angel* the distance of Joy's mother's hill-top house from the university campus is given through time as 'a full day's journey from campus' (p. 160). The *ilo* (stadium) of Umuachala in Achebe's *Arrow of God* is so large that the only way to convey a measure of its dimensions (a measure of distance) is the time taken by the fastest runners to cover its perimeter: 'It was sometimes called Ilo Agbasioso because its length cowed even the best runners' (p. 195). 'During the planting season', it is related in *Things Fall Apart*, 'Okonkwo and his family worked daily on his farm from cock-crow until the chickens went to roost' (p. 10). In *Arrow of God* Akukalia's party 'set out for Okperi about the time when most people finished their morning meal' (*AOG* p. 20). In Wendt's *Banyan Tree*, Toasa concludes a tale when 'the sun had clambered past noon and chased the shadows from the two men' (p. 69). Tauilopepe's labourers stop working 'when the sun squatted on the shoulders of the Western ridge' (p. 75). And Taifau comes to take up a job with Tauilopepe just as Tauilopepe's aiga 'were sitting down to their Monday morning meal' (p. 97).

Erna Brodber's *Myal* provides a glimpse into the beginning of the use of a remarkable event to date historical time. In this race-conscious district in Jamaica, 'a white woman and a black woman walking together quietly and comfortably like equals was news. It would be an incident which people used to mark events' (p. 24). Often, however, it is cataclysms like wars, earthquakes and outbreaks of disease (such as the European influenza epidemic that followed the end of World War I, in Wendt's *Banyan Tree*), or supposedly 'portentous' phenomena like eclipses of the sun that are used for historical dating.

In urban settings as well as European-dominated locations in rural culture (such as the seats of colonial governments), European clock and calendar are very prominent. Their increasing use in Part III of *Things Fall Apart* (which shows the overthrow of the indigenous order by the British) over indigenous collectivized systems becomes a strong indicator of the cultural interfacing that is developing. 'A few *months*' (not 'moons') in Mr Brown's school equipped a person for a clerical job or employment as a court messenger (p. 128), and some of Mr Brown's pupils 'were *thirty* years old or more' (not twenty and ten years, as Umuofia's indigenous decimal system would have it in the traditional setting: for example, p. 91).

Urban settings, as the seat of government, industry and commerce, involve clock-based time references, especially if the agent in an incident works in any of these establishments. An apt illustration comes in Armah's *The Beautyful Ones Are Not Yet Born*, set in Takoradi in Ghana. The hero works in the Traffic Control Office of Ghana Railways. Punctuality where train movements are scheduled by the clock and detailed recording of train time/space movements is mandatory. Horological references are intimately woven into the plot. To Armah's highly observant hero, a Space Allocations clerk's early arrival indicates that some chicanery is being planned (pp. 104–5). So organically is time structured into the plot that it serves to reveal the central thematic statement about the failure of independence: the years have been passing while the nation stagnates. This theme is sharply focused through personal stories of characters whom time has also passed by. Even the change in government is signalled, to sensitive characters, by a change in the national radio's programmes schedule, as is also the case in Merle Collins' *Angel*.

When Armah turns to myth and legend to explore African history in *The Healers*, his time scheme changes accordingly. The spiritual corruption (and undermining) of the Asante cosmos is first suggested through the symbolism of the 'ritual games of remembrance' held 'every chosen year' (pp. 3–7). In George Lamming's *In the Castle of My Skin*, the annual floods become a time marker for the young hero, G., though in the negative sense of coinciding with and ruining his birthday celebrations. A slightly more extended use of nature and annual rituals is found in Ngugi's *The River Between* in Ngugi's exploration of the conflicts between Gikuyu nationalism and British imperialism, and another between rivals for leadership. The former conflict occurs over the annual ritual of circumcision, which Ngugi pointedly juxtaposes with the Christian converts' annual cycles of Christmas and baptism. The analogous relationship between these is further emphasized by exploiting the connotations of the Christian phrase of being 'born again'. Among the traditionalists, 'preparations for initiations went on, while Joshua and his followers prepared for the birth of a saviour' (*RB* p. 32). The juxtaposition has a major bearing on present cultural debates, for whereas Europeans locate their anniversary celebrations along a progressive time scale, they have formulated various theories of eternal returns which locate similar celebrations among non-European cultures outside time and history.

Time in Thematic Structure

For many cultural theorists, a major problem arises from a failure to distinguish between generalized temporal deixis in narrative, which requires no more than an indication of time lapse or a pinpointing of a specific moment in time, and the function of time as structural element or thematic dimension. The former is usually self-evident, though European critics frequently quarrel with the indigenous mode of notation, while the latter is more subtle and demands closer attention to narrative structure than many postcolonial theorists are disposed to give.

In Ihimaera's *Tangi* and *Whanau*, the bicultural realities of Maori life are partly marked by time references, most conspicuous as Tama moves from the capital city, Wellington, to his family home in Gisborne in what is recognizable as Ihimaera's subversion of the European motif of a hero's journey from European civilization to self-knowledge in a non-European hell, underworld, or pre-creation. Tama's journey takes him into the future–past continuum defined by Ihimaera, without any of the social Darwinism of the European motif which would transform the Maori world into hell. It is among his people in Gisborne that Tama achieves the necessary intellectual and emotional growth, and his progress is charted through time references, with clock references gradually giving way to nature rhythms the farther away from Wellington and closer to home. Moreover, clock references occur predominantly in association with train and airplane schedules – modern mass-transit systems whose operations are strictly regulated by the clock:

> Time ... suddenly so important. A phone call from home, just a few hours ago and here I am bringing the last moments of a boy with his father to a close ... E pa, if I could I would force these ticking hands back from the top of the clock, back to the faraway side of the hour. But I cannot. The clock still ticks.
> – You got the time, Tama?
> – Almost five to four, Mr Ralston.
> – Good. You don't have to check into the airport until ten past. Plenty of time.
> – Time to catch the plane. (*Tangi* p. 61)

In *Whanau*, Rongo Mahana laments the passage of the period when a family 'would fix a time for the planting, calculating it in the old way by the shape of the moon and the position of the stars in the night' (*Whanau* p. 50). Within the plot, however, time functions within a panoramic revelation of several interrelated blocks of activity in a single day which proves critical for the community. The action is structured through the daily motion of the sun, but time segments, particular moments, and events of specific duration are located by the clock, for the novel is set at the Maori–Pakeha cosmic overlap. Each of the 25 chapters deals with a block of action set in a definite clock-measured time grid, one-hour intervals between the chapters in the first half of the novel and shorter intervals as the crisis draws closer. Before the crisis (the temporary loss of the Kau-matua, Nanny Paora) erupts, a sense of impending crisis is created partly through constant references to the clock, and events are given an irreversible temporal progression despite the fact that until the search begins there has been no story line in the novel. When the search for Nanny Paora and Pene ends towards midnight in Rongopai, the ancestral meeting house, the two systems are merged.

Conception of the conflict as an archetype of Maori life and Maori–Pakeha relations results in a deliberate withholding or blur-ring of time markers in Patricia Grace's *Potiki*, for the desired effect here is one of historical continuity. The three parts of the novel sym-bolize pre-European Maori society, the conquest by the Pakeha, and a projected future of Maori self-assertion, but Grace's structure of the narrative belies the fact that long time spans separate these historical phases. Although the first incident of Part 2 (the meeting between the Tamihanas and Mr Dolman who represents the West-ern consortium) is a major crisis which erupts after a long period of peace, yet it is introduced in a low-key narrative: 'There was in the meeting house a wood quiet' (p. 87). The aftermath of the historic confrontation between the Tamihana and their potential dispos-sessors is similarly revealed: 'The hills are quiet and the machines have been taken away' (p. 159).

The time scheme becomes much more complex but also more subtle at the symbolic level in Wendt's *Pouliuli* and *Banyan Tree*, the level at which Wendt explores socio-historical transition and the rites of passage of individuals and the community. In *Pouliuli* this involves a sophisticated time–space–number construct organized on the number 7 and its multiples 14, 21 and 42, which also refer to years in the lives of the central characters Faleasa and Lemigao. *Pouliuli* is thus full of incidents which mark temporal progression in the different phases and forms of coming of age for Malaeluans (Samoans), a theme which also delivers a side swipe at Margaret Mead and her *Coming of Age in Samoa*. World War I and the year it broke out fall within this pattern. At the personal levels, Faleasa and Lemigao 'saw their first papalagi' in 1921 (p. 41). That same year, they also attained the age of 21, for Faleasa was already 14 years old in 1914 when he betrayed the old man (p. 112), and he and Lemigao were born 'a week apart' (p. 19). Three weeks or 21 days before Christmas 1921, they visited Apia the national capital for the first time (p. 46). And they saw their first Americans in 1942 (p. 55). Each of these landmark occurrences also introduces many 'first' experiences which both individually and cumulatively constitute a loss of innocence and a coming of age.

In Achebe's *Things Fall Apart* and *Arrow of God*, the sense of time is very intimately woven into all aspects of the narrative. The first sentence of the third paragraph of *Things Fall Apart* provides a fitting illustration of temporal deixis as mere pointing: 'That was many years ago, twenty years or more...' This is directly linked to the temporal focusing of the narrative event through the narrator's consciousness, rather than the culture's apprehension of time. The narrative performance is conceived as occurring in the present, which is the time of reading for every reader. From this present, time stretches backwards and forwards. Time pointers such as 'ago', 'yesterday' and 'tomorrow' are accordingly employed instead of 'before'/'earlier', 'the previous day', or 'the following day' (the usual forms in formal reported speech). Grammatically, the clue to this is the predominance of the simple past tense over the past anterior in these novels.

Within the plot, cultural apprehension of time is embedded in the use of collectivized activities. In Chapter 2 of *Things Fall Apart*, Okonkwo is given custody of a boy, Ikemefuna, offered by the neighbouring clan of Mbaino in appeasement for the murder of a daughter of Umuofia at Mbaino market. Ikemefuna arrives during the season 'between harvest and planting', and begins to adjust to his lot 'only a few days before the Week of Peace' which is soon violated by Okonkwo (*TFA* pp. 20–1). Other passages show the development of a father–son relationship between Okonkwo and the sacrificial boy, in the light of which Okonkwo's participation in Ikemefuna's sacrificial killing after three years exposes the psychologically crippling flaw of unreasoning inflexibility arising from his own slothful father's irresponsible response to time.

Arrow of God is plotted through a rigorous lunar calendar which opens in the planting season and ends in the harvest, with every major event in-between being meticulously integrated within this frame. At the centre of this plot are Time/History and the New Yam festival through which Umuaro commemorates its own origination. During this annual festival, every man offers a yam to the god Ulu, an act of piety which also serves as an annual census besides providing the 13 yams with which the priest marks the calendar, eating one yam every new moon. The dislocation of this Time/History frame by the colonial District Commissioner mirrors the European intervention that disrupted colonized people's histories. In contrast to this is the normal process of change and self-contemporization, by which Umuaro sheds historically obsolete, superfluous, or dysfunctional customs and institutions, as dramatized in the fates of minor gods:

> Some of them would be very old, nearing the time when their power would be transferred to new carvings and they would be cast aside...At last year's festival only three of these ancients were left. Perhaps this year one or two more would disappear, following the men who made them in their own image. (p. 202)

The interlocking of Time/History with number in the festivals is important. Achebe uses number in *Arrow of God* to reveal another dimension of the human mind's ordering of chaos. The opening scene reveals the Chief Priest, the clan's representative intellectual, in the sacerdotal role which fuses time and number: for three nightfalls he has been watching the sky for the new moon (p. 1). Several conflicts are related to reckoning, counting, measuring, equating and calculating. Ezeulu is ever using numbers in his probes into reality, from measuring the number of white men who led the party that exterminated Abame against the amount of damage caused by the party (p. 131) to attempts to quantify the power of his office (pp. 3–4). When he refuses to announce the date of the New Yam feast, his assistants use numbering to suggest his alienation from Umuaro's world: they assumed he had 'lost count' because of his detention at Okperi (p. 203). Finally, Umuaro people process his calamity through a measuring proverb which asserts that the community is greater than even the greatest of men (p. 230).

MYTHS OF THE NATION: FROM REALISM TO RADICAL-TRADITIONALISM

Myths, legends and ritual archetypes are important strategies of resistance and self-affirmation in postcolonial novels, where they serve both as content and as organizing principle or prefiguration technique in the plot. Their thematic functions range from asserting a culture's development of a civilization to staking claims upon territory and providing models for human conduct. As John J. White has suggested, 'the role of mythological motifs [and ritual archetypes] is analogical, describing the modern world in the light of a readily available set of models'.[28]

For many novelists, a favoured myth is the origination myth which symbolizes man's conquest of chaos,[29] or the cosmogonic myth that provides blueprints for normative institutions. Wole Soyinka's *Myth, Literature, and the African World* opens with an assertion of the centrality of Yoruba cosmogonic myths in the people's 'quest for the explication of being'.[30] Soyinka's novels, rarely recognized in conventional criticism as works of cultural affirmation, demonstrate his nationalist argument that indigenous African myths provide the fundamental principles for organizing society's institutions and ethical principles, and it is against such principles that the performance of post-independence society is measured. Though Soyinka complements the African myth with Graeco-Asiatic myth, he has also pointed out the sharp contrast between the strict principles of accountability enjoined by Yoruba mythology and the unchecked outrages that characterize Greek gods.[31]

The Yoruba myth tells of a primal act *ab initio* that was both a deicide and an archetype of revolutionary self-assertion: the fragmentation of the original godhead by a human slave, with the consequent emergence of a multiple godhead and the separation of gods and humans across different sides of the elemental abyss or realm of chaos. When the gods' quest for reunion with mankind was frustrated by the abyss, Ogun hacked a path through it in an exemplary act of community-oriented heroism, and survived his own dismemberment through a supreme exercise of will.

So central is this myth to Soyinka's artistic nationalism that a reader without some acquaintance with it can hardly plumb the depths of Soyinka's major works, whose thematic and stylistic complexity comes from its metaphysics. His major protagonists are either modelled on Ogun or created as composites of the major gods of the Yoruba pantheon; plots tend to re-enact the myth at an allegorical level, with the 'Road' (which belongs to Ogun) as a central structural principle and thematic symbol; themes tend to be variations on the threats of 'Chaos' to mankind's potential for self-fulfilment, and the paradoxical complementarity which comes from the latency of creation and destruction within chaos. As Ogun is also the god of science and technology in Soyinka's reworking of the Yoruba myth, the Road, Ogun's Road, represents the entire potentiality of the human race to utilize its science and technology for genuine progress or self-destruction.

Thus, it is no exaggeration to say that a single cluster of related themes, explored by Soyinka at varying degrees of elaboration, runs through plays like *A Dance of the Forests* (1963), *The Road* (1965) and *Death and the King's Horseman* (1975); poems like 'Abiku', 'Death in the Dawn', 'In Memory of Segun Awolowo', 'Idanre' and 'Ogun Abibiman', and the two novels *The Interpreters* and *Season of Anomy*. All these works explore social phenomena in terms of rites of passage, with differentiating details coming from the particular sociohistorical experiences explored in each work. The prayer 'May you never walk/When the road waits, famished', in 'Death in the Dawn' recurs in an identical context (death in a car crash on Ogun's road) in Part II of 'Idanre': 'Fated lives ride on the wheels of death when,/ The road waits, famished.' In *The Road* the character Samson, a lorry driver's assistant who is steeped in Ogun's lore, prays: 'May we never walk when the road waits, famished' (p. 66). Yet a reader unfamiliar with the Yoruba myth or its reworking by Soyinka is unlikely to read back to it from the novel, for, with the exception of the fairly long poetic peroration which opens Chapter 16 of *The Interpreters*, Soyinka hardly mentions it.

Readers familiar with Ben Okri's *The Famished Road* (1991) will recognize Okri's indebtedness to Soyinka's work for the inspiration, title and central metaphor of 'the road', though the 'abiku' (the 'ogbanje' of Achebe's and Emecheta's novels) motif is found throughout West Africa.[32] The short opening paragraph of *The Famished Road*, which simultaneously builds on the opening formula of the narratives of an oral culture (particularly creation myths and aetiological tales) and the opening sentence of Saint John's Gospel ('In the beginning was the Word'), points to the Soyinkan inspiration: 'In the beginning there was a river. The river became a road and the road branched out to the whole world. And because the road was once a river it was always hungry' (*FR* p. 3). Professor, the central character of *The Road*, who is searching for the meaning of 'the word' in the mythology of 'the road' pronounces:

> When the road is dry it runs into the river. But the river? When the river is parched what choice but this? Still it is a pleasant trickle – reddening somewhat – between barren thighs of an ever patient rock. The rock is a woman you understand, so is the road. They know how to lie and wait. (Part II, p. 58)[33]

Even Okri's protagonist, the 'abiku' Lazarus (shortened to Azaro), is traceable to Soyinka's *The Interpreters* rather than the dead man resurrected by Jesus Christ (John 11: 1–44). The biblical Lazarus is not an 'abiku', and the focus of the story is not Lazarus himself but the power of the Christ over death. Conversely, in *The Interpreters* Soyinka's Lazarus is conceived to function as the Yoruba spirit Esumare – the Rainbow, bridge, rope, link – who will restore the links between spirit essence and human materiality, past and present, the dead/unborn and the living (see Chapter 16 of *The Interpreters*). It is this role that Azaro fills in *The Famished Road* with his cycling between the human and the spirit world.

For both Soyinka and Okri, the 'abiku' or 'ogbanje' myth offers a ready model of recurrence in social phenomena (the Igbo word 'ogbanje' actually translates as 'repeater' or 'one who repeatedly comes and goes'), in terms of which the alternation of promise and betrayal, hope and failure, in post-independence African states could be critiqued. Generically, however, Okri's work is direct heir to the tradition of realism–fantasy fusion inaugurated in West African europhone writing by Amos Tutuola with *The Palm-Wine Drinkard* in 1952. Okri's university education has endowed him, however, with not just a far greater competence in English but also an extensive immersion in the currents of world literatures, and a cosmopolitan consciousness that enables the exploitation of these literatures as intertexts within his own work. Theorists and critics who seek to root it in the Latin American so-called magical realism are in error. Folk narratives have always overridden the barriers between various domains of existence, blending realism with fantasy in the adventures of human or spirit protagonists who traverse the human and the spirit world. As the Yoruba myth of Ogun shows, such narratives are constantly being contemporized to encompass new developments in science and technology.

Major problems with Okri's extension of Tutuola's form and elaboration of Soyinka's tropes include its repetitiousness, the superfluity of the Lazarus evocation and the comparatively marginal status of Okri's Lazarus in relation to the major crises in the novel, unlike Soyinka's 'abiku' who incarnates the rebellious spirit of 'repetition' or cyclicism that society must contend with in its search for self-fulfilment. It is this departure which constitutes Okri's innovation, however, for Azaro symbolizes the betrayed hopes and promises. Azaro and the other 'abiku' are victim-rebels, their rebellion lying in their insistent quest for earth-life. Azaro is 'a spirit-child rebelling against the spirits, wanting to live the earth's life and contradictions' (p. 487). As representations of 'nations, civilisations, ideas, half-discoveries, revolutions, loves, art forms, experiments, and historical events' that have been denied full self-actualization: 'They are all part-time dwellers in their own secret moonlight. They all yearn to make of themselves a beautiful sacrifice, a difficult sacrifice, to bring transformation, and to die shedding light within this life, setting the matter ready for their true beginnings to cry into being...' (p. 487).

Other novelists usually introduce their myths as literary references and allusions in a manner which makes their identity fairly obvious to the reader. The opening paragraph of Achebe's *Things Fall Apart* introduces, in Umuofia's origination myth, an illustration of the use of such narratives to generate thematic statements about the development of a civilization and to structure the conflict. Okonkwo's defeat of the renowned champion Amalinze the Cat in a wrestling match is transformed into a paradigm of consecration of territory through combat with and triumph over a monster: Umuofia's ancestral hero successfully engaged such a monster for seven days and nights (p. 3). From this cryptic invocation of Umuofia's myth of origins, wrestling constitutes a *leitmotif* for exploring the interwoven conflicts between the hero and his community, between Umuofia as cosmos and the British invader as chaos, and internally between Okonkwo's more human impulses and his neurotic response to his father's failure.

Another form of cosmicization myth transforms the story of Achebe's *Arrow of God* into a people's struggle to secure the cosmos they have consecrated out of chaos. Umuaro was founded in the mythical past expressed in surprisingly accurate palaeontological imagery as 'when lizards were still few and far between' or 'when lizards were still in ones and twos'. Actually, that time is not so remote, and this mythopoeia should be understood in terms of the history-making consciousness striking the limits of memory in an oral culture. Six independent villages threatened with extinction by marauding Abam armies form a federation, make for themselves a guardian deity, Ulu, give themselves a name, Umuaro, and thereby acquire a new and distinctive identity (*AOG* pp. 14–15). This act of self-creation has been instituted into an annual ritual, complete with a validating myth, during which chaos is combated again through communal atonement for evils committed in the year just ending.

An indication of the direct relationship between writers' choice of myths and their people's colonial experience is provided by the difference between the practices of writers like Achebe, Soyinka and Armah who come from societies that did not fight a decolonization

war, and those like Ngugi, Grace and Ihimaera whose people had to
wage prolonged wars of liberation against colonial regimes and set-
tlers. Writers in the latter category generally employ cosmogonic
myths to reinforce their people's claims to their territory.

Ngugi's *The River Between* states that the creator Murungu made
the primogenitive pair Gikuyu and Mumbi and 'gave the country to
them and their children and the children of the children, *tene wa
tene*, world without end' (*RB* p. 18). *Weep Not, Child* has a fuller version with the same conclusion, with Murungu making a covenant
with the pair:

> This land I hand over to you, O Man and Woman
> It's yours to rule and till in serenity sacrificing
> Only to me, your God, under my sacred tree ...
>   (*WNC* pp. 23–4)

To render the myth meaningful within colonial history, Ngugi exfo-
liates it into historical processes. The usurpation of Kenyans' patri-
mony, first by the British, and then by indigenous ruling classes in
post-independence Kenya, leads to themes of liberation struggle, to
explore which Ngugi draws upon another Gikuyu myth about a
prophecy made by an ancient seer, Mugo wa Kibiro (*RB* p. 19; *GOW*
p. 11). Mugo prophesied both the British conquest and the emergence of a messiah. He also provided a blueprint for the liberation
struggle: the saviour should not precipitate the reclamation struggle
until he has learnt the invaders' behaviour and acquired their 'wisdom and secrets' (*RB* p. 20). This blueprint finds implementation as
it unfolds from myth into successive historical epochs across Ngugi's
six novels, from the would-be messiah's acquisition of literacy and
formal education in *The River Between* to armed rebellion using
effective firearms in *Weep Not, Child* and *A Grain of Wheat*, socialist trade/student unionism in *Petals of Blood*, *Devil on the Cross* and
Matigari. The progressive increase in the number of 'heroes' from
the third novel marks the reformulation of Ngugi's nationalism in
revolutionary Marxist terms, seen further in *Petals of Blood* in the
transfer of the agency for cosmicization from a divine being to a
human hero, Ndemi, who conquered all antihuman forces to found
the first human settlement, Ilmorog, established agriculture and
crafts, and transformed pre-creation chaos into a human habitation
(pp. 120–1). Continued neocolonialist aggression projected through
local pimps, academic collaborators and the International Monetary

Fund sets the stage for a recourse to armed struggle in Ngugi's last three novels.

The crucial issue of loss of inheritance pervades all the Maori novels, and in Patricia Grace's *Potiki* and Witi Ihimaera's *Tangi, Whanau* and *The Matriarch* cosmogonic myth asserts their prior claim to New Zealand and serves as a rallying cry to Maori nationalism. In Wendt's *Black Rainbow* in which the Pakeha have not only disinherited the Maori but also reduced them to the status of the Proles in Orwell's *Nineteen Eighty-Four*, this myth forms the basis of their resistance. 'We were the first, our ancestors, no matter what lies the Tribunal says', maintains Manu, one of the disinherited youth. 'So our maps are at the bottom of the bloody heap. They're still there though the bloody otherworlders have tried to fucking well erase them' (*Black Rainbow* p. 134).

All these novels draw upon the myth of the Polynesian folk hero Maui-tikitiki-a-Taranga, who fished out the North Island of New Zealand (or Aotearoa, 'Land of the Long White Cloud', as the Maori know it) and brought numerous promethean benefits to the people. Grace deploys this myth in *Potiki* as a background to the struggles of the Tamihana against a powerful Western consortium of estate developers. She has explained that her use of Maori mythology in this novel is much more deliberate than in her preceding fiction, and 'the events in *Potiki* have been legitimised by real events that I have been involved with, associated with, or felt deeply about'.[34] Employment of the myth is designed to arouse Maori nationalist resistance. For his own archetype, Ihimaera goes back to the creation of the world and separation of the primogenitive pair, Rangitane and Papatuanuku (Sky Father and Earth Mother, respectively), with the consequent emergence of their offspring into the world of light:

> My mother was the Earth.
> My father was the Sky.
> They were Rangitane and Papatuanuku, the first parents, who clasped each other so tightly that there was no day. Their children were born into darkness. They lived among the shadows of their mother's breasts and thighs and groped in blindness among the long black strands of her hair.
>   Until the time of separation and the dawning of the first day.
> (*Tangi* p. 26)

The myth is symbolically enacted on the human plane through the death of Rongo Mahana and Tama's subsequent journey in *Tangi*, and through the loss-and-search motif in *Whanau*. Different aspects of the myth serve to complicate structure and contribute thematic details beyond narrative assertions. Thus, the separation myth sets up the paradoxical theme of fragmentation leading to individuation; the legend of the Seven Canoes which brought the ancestral heroes to Aotearoa proclaims that the original wilderness was cosmicized by Maoris and therefore belongs to them; and Maui's snaring of the sun to lengthen the daytime further attests to the people's attempts to master their universe. However, *The Matriarch* foregrounds Maori mythology as a variety of history, following Ihimaera's intention of rewriting the history of New Zealand.

The Matriarch treats myth and history as a continuum which began with the creation of Te Po, the Night, from Te Kore, the Void. Ihimaera's grand design becomes manifest right from the Prologue which opens with two paragraphs of allusion to contemporary Italy before plunging into a detailed recounting of the cosmogonic myth. As the heroine Artemis Riripeti Mahana (later Artemis Riripeti Pere), the Matriarch of the title, instructs the hero-narrator Tamatea, the myth also becomes a kind of genealogical lore which ends, significantly, with 'Then came the Pakeha' (p. 6). The Matriarch advances a theory of autochthonous origins for the Maori. 'We are the tangata whenua, the people of the land...Ancients descended from the Time of the Gods', she declares, quickly telescoping time from the mythical beginnings to the arrival of subsequent waves of Maoris around 700 AD and the legendary Seven Canoes from Hawaiki (*Matriarch* p. 4). From this follows the kind of nationalist charge with which readers of Ngugi's and Grace's novels are familiar, to love and care for the heritage, to know every part of the territory. This relationship to the land and territory, she tells Tama, is necessary to fight against any prospective dispossessors (*Matriarch* p. 95).

Another distinctive feature of use of myth and legend by writers whose people went through the horrors of colonial wars is their location of the people's experience within the paradigm of the biblical Israelites' experience of exile in Egypt and subsequent exodus. Egyptian exile and subsequent redemption from the house of bondage have become common motifs in decolonization literature, such as George Lamming's *In the Castle of My Skin* and V.S. Reid's *New Day*. In its exploration of Jamaica's near-century epic struggle (1865 to 1944) against colonialism, *New Day* actually encompasses the historical span of Ngugi's novels, from the Patriarch to exile, warrior leaders, the arrival of the New Testament messiah, and the evolution of the messianic function according to socio-economic developments. Paul Bogle and his Stoney Guts men's rebellion against a heartless colonial regime follows the Mosaic tradition. But armed struggle gradually gives way to a more constitutional process, and it is the Christ-like lawyer Garth who leads the people out of colonial servitude. Armed struggle in the present is thus given cosmic dimensions and justified through being presented as historically inevitable response to a pattern of oppression which has existed since the dawn of history.

It is at a nationalist political rally in Ngugi's *Weep Not, Child* that Kiarie, one of the consciousness raisers, proclaims the resistance manifesto: 'Today, we, with one voice, we must rise and shout: "The time has come. Let my people go. Let my people go! We want back our land! Now!" ' (*WNC* p. 58). The major protagonists of *New Day*, Ngugi's Mau Mau novels and Ihimaera's *The Matriarch* all consciously define their positions through biblical reference. In *The Matriarch*, direct accounts of the anti-colonialist war evoke biblical Old Testament mythopoeia and historiography. For instance, Chapter 6 deals with the circumstances of the divine call of the resistance hero Te Kooti, in the mythopoeic language of the biblical accounts of wars and prophecies, while Chapter 7 evokes a logbook kept in the scholarly language of a historian. Te Kooti Rikirangi Te Turuki is Moses and the warrior kings of the Old Testament rolled into one, for 'Jehovah chose him at birth to lead His Children of Israel, the Maori nation, out of the land of the Pakeha, out of slavery to Egypt' (*Matriarch* p. 133).

A significant exception to the dominant patterns of employing myth in decolonization novels is the work of Ayi Kwei Armah. For Armah, ritual archetypes are very important, but he distrusts all myths and other narratives which have the potential to ratify existing class structures, hence his tendency to subvert heroic narratives even while exploiting them. Seeking to create a new myth of the African race, he harnesses existing myths to the task of transforming Africa's racial experience into a rite of passage. Armah would obviously accept Christopher Caudwell's analysis of epics as a degeneration from free people's metaphysical inquiry into the universe, to a superstitious worship of deified men by a powerless, enslaved mass. Such tales, argues Caudwell, have 'a childishness and servility' which distinguishes them from 'the creations of an undivided society'. They show 'the adaptation to the role of an exploited class', are 'tainted with the idiocy of exploitation', and are 'full of luck and gold and magic meals and lucky sons – the fortunes this class so conspicuously lacks'.[35] A related point is made by J.G. Frazer, who in *The Golden Bough* maintains that classless society develops class structures when, influenced by a priesthood, people relinquish to gods the powers they had formerly claimed for themselves, and demean themselves in the same scale as they magnify the gods.[36]

Consequently, though the entire saga of *Two Thousand Seasons* is presented as a fulfilment of the vatic revelations of the mythical seer Anoa, it is the entire race that is the hero of the epic migration from the desert to the fertile lands near the sea. A similar approach is adopted in charting the collapse of the Ashanti empire in *The Healers* through a series of apocalyptic wonders (pp. 245–51). The structural principle behind these novels is the ritual archetype derived from Akan metaphysics, consecrating the harmony between the living, the dead and the unborn.[37] The perversion of these rituals into a Cargo cult is the subject of Armah's critique of post-independence African society in virtually all his novels, but most notably in *Fragments* and *Why Are We So Blest?* (see Chapter 5 of the present book).

Use of mythology in the terms discussed here is quite different from the creation of 'myths of the past' which mainstream criticism often attributes to decolonization literature. The novelists are creating myths of the present which is continuous from the past. As (ex)colonial societies have developed away from oral cultures, and the certainties of the 'village as harmonious world' have disintegrated with the emergence of nation states competing on a global stage with other nation states and alliances of states, decolonization writers are experimenting with new agonistic idioms for interpreting the new forms of colonialism that have emerged in the post-Cold War era. There will be bold experiments with literary form and idiom, bolder harnessing of the amenities of writing and of techniques developed in competing media like television, the cinema and computer entertainment. But the major concern will remain unchanged from the 1950s: resistance to colonialism and neocolonialism. The direction of development will, therefore, be more towards the kind of radical traditionalism manifested, for example, in Albert Wendt's *Black Rainbow*, Witi Ihimaera's *The Matriarch*, Chinua Achebe's *Anthills of the Savannah*, Patricia Grace's *Cousins* and Merle Collins' *Angel*. The radical-traditionalist form, fondly mislabelled as 'magical realism' in homogenizing critical traditions, represents the ideal form for nationalistic assertion. It is not a reaction against realism, with which it will always co-exist, but a more versatile medium for accommodating and combining a variety of experiences without the constraints of formal realism. Realism is not an exclusively European form, and critics who number the 'subversion of Western realism and historicism' among modes of Third World anti-colonialist resistance are actually engaged in a quest for non-Western literary exotica with which to titillate themselves. Radical-traditionalism, however, enables the foregrounding of indigenous cosmic perceptions within a narrative mode that has its reference frames within the indigenous cosmos.

3

The Agonistic of Tongues

Meaning in language is not natural but conventional. Linguists say that the coding of meanings is arbitrary, by which they mean that any sounds or letters could be used to represent any concept. But what concepts come to be represented is not an arbitrary or accidental matter. Over long periods in the history of a society, a vocabulary and phrasings develop to suit the needs of the society – those 'needs' being the interests of the dominant, privileged groups...Language thus becomes a part of social practice, a tool for preserving the prevailing order.[1]

THE SPEECH PACT

Language and Order

It was Jean-François Lyotard who wrote in *The Postmodern Condition* that 'to speak is to fight...and speech acts fall within the domain of a general agonistics'.[2] The rules of language, Lyotard points out, 'do not carry within themselves their own legitimation, but are the object of a contract, explicit or not'.[3] Before Lyotard, Benjamin Lee Whorf, in a hypothesis later modified by Edward Sapir, maintained that we dissect nature, organize it into concepts, and ascribe significance as we do 'along lines laid down by our native languages', because we are parties to an agreement *'whose terms are absolutely obligatory'* (Whorf's emphasis) codified in the patterns of language within the speech community, with the grammar of each language guiding the individual's mental activity, analysis of his impressions and synthesis of 'his mental stock in trade'.[4]

The Sapir–Whorf hypothesis has often been attacked as deterministic, in contrast to the postmodernist version of post-Saussurean linguistics, with its obsession with indeterminacy. Outside the ivory tower of politicized postmodernism and post-structuralism, however, language use bears out the Sapir–Whorf hypothesis and its more recent developments, seen for example in the work of Roger

Fowler. Language, Fowler maintains, 'creates a grid of meaning which encourages a slanted perspective on what is being presented', the grid being the speaker's 'theory or ideology . . . his analysis of the communicated content according to the system of relevant beliefs he has been socialized into holding and into coding in his habitual language use'.[5] Decolonization novelists are concerned with language in use in human social and historical experience, particularly in the context of European expansion into non-European territories and the power relationships that have resulted from that expansion. They are concerned with use of language in all walks of life, from the street, the football stadium and the bar room to the classroom, from the shopping mall, the boardroom and the workplace to business premises and political establishments, from global power politics to the activities of the United Nations Organization.

From their historical approach to language use, decolonization novelists recognize that there has been little fundamental change since the fifteenth century either in the relationship between Europe and the Third World or in the language which encodes, transmits, rationalizes and reinforces this relationship. They recognize that in the geopolitical contests of the present day, characterized by the triumph of perception over substance, victory begins with the seizing of the language initiative, and in this Europe has enjoyed a centuries-long advantage of naming and labelling other peoples.

European public reactions to reports of crime, for example, are usually conditioned by the racial identities of the criminal and the victim. The electronic and print media's deliberate practice of racially specifying the accused or victim (a 'Western youth', 'Western teenager', 'Western tourist', 'West Indian immigrant', 'African/Asian accused') capitalizes on cultural and racial stereotypes to manipulate public perceptions. 'Western' connotes 'innocence'; 'African', 'Asian', or 'Arab' connotes guilt. No argument or proof is required. The pattern underlies not just politically inspired academic disciplines but also relationships in workplaces and larger questions of social justice and government policies, and persists despite the unquestionable increase in racial tolerance among Europeans. There is no contradiction in this. Race relations in most Western countries are healthier than ethnic relations in many African, Asian and Latin American countries. Racial tolerance has not significantly affected European assumptions of cultural superiority, however. For a very large minority, indeed, 'tolerance' is merely an attitude rather than a conviction – a limited acceptance even while holding fast to their entrenched racial prejudices.

In geopolitics, there is a long list of tags and labels for pasting onto Third World leaders – 'extremists', 'moderates', or 'fanatics' are just a few – on the basis of those leaders' advancement of or resistance to Western economic and strategic priorities. In effect, these labels perform not only the function of prejudgement but also that of pre-ratification of whatever actions are taken on the basis of the pre-judgement. More than any other period of history, the late twentieth century is exceptional for the saturation of all discourse with verbal tags, labels, clichés, shibboleths and other prefabricated verbal formulas designed to oust independent thinking and manipulate public perceptions.

Consequently, decolonization writers' concern with language is driven by the need to contest the history and the labels, rather than quibble with the subtle philosophic distinctions between *'différence* with an "e" ' and *'différance* with an "a" ' – distinctions built upon a pun that exists only in French and a few related European languages. Postcolonial theorists influenced by Ashcroft and partners have failed to address this specific concern of the literary language, largely because the ragbag concept of postcoloniality can only deal with the lowest common denominators of the 'postcolonial literatures', but also because the concept is designed to concentrate on the ephemera of style rather than the deeper motivations of language use. Conversely, a decolonization theory of language must uncover these deeper aspects because they constitute the genuine sites for nationalist agonistics. For this reason, it is important to revise the primary paradigm for colonizer–colonized contest in language, namely, the Prospero–Caliban paradigm.

Re-reading the Prospero–Caliban Paradigm

Ever since O. Mannoni's *Prospero and Caliban: the Psychology of Colonisation* drew an analogy between Shakespeare's *The Tempest* and colonial relationships,[6] critics have used the 'Prospero–Caliban relationship' as a paradigm for the colonial victim's indictment of imperialism in the latter's own tongue. Yet the real nature of this relationship has been only hazily understood, and for half a century cultural theorists have assumed, as George Lamming memorably but erroneously puts it, that Caliban was indebted to Prospero for 'speech and concept as a way, a method, a necessary avenue towards areas of the self which could not be reached in any other way'.[7] A proper reading of Act 1, scene 2, of Shakespeare's play quickly overthrows this interpretation.

Being fully conscious of their material universe, Caliban and his mother Sycorax had explored and named its features and started intellectual probes into the non-material forces governing it, long before Prospero's irruption into their lives. Naming, Dwight Bolinger has observed, plays a crucial role in 'solidifying and objectifying experience' by 'enabling us to create entities practically out of nothing'.[8] Sycorax, imprisoned for witchcraft by the sorcerer Prospero, had developed an advanced concept of deity, with a pantheon headed by Setebos and a set of magical rites through which she related with these supernatural beings. Caliban has been able to show Prospero 'the fresh springs, brine-pits, barren places and fertile' because he has studied, understood and named their properties. Moreover, his political vocabulary ('I am all the subjects that you have, / Which first was mine own king') entails political concepts of self-determination which no usurper would teach the person s/he has dispossessed. It should be obvious, therefore, that what Caliban owed to Prospero was no more than competence in the colonizer's language. The exchange between him and Prospero leaves no doubt about this:

PROSPERO. Abhorred slave...
   [I] took pains to make thee speak, taught thee each hour
   One thing or other. When thou didst not, savage,
   Know thine own meaning, but wouldst gabble like
   A thing most brutish, I endow'd thy purposes
   With words that made them known...

CALIBAN. You taught me language, and my profit on't
   Is, I know how to curse. The red plague rid you
   For learning me your language!

Prospero's contemptuous dismissal of Caliban's language as a 'gabble like/a thing most brutish' has a familiar twentieth-century ring. One of its most widely known incarnations comes in Joseph Conrad's description of African languages in *Heart of Darkness*: 'they shouted periodically together strings of amazing words that resembled no sounds of human language, and the deep murmurs of the crowd, interrupted suddenly, were like the responses of some satanic litany'.[9] By denying human status to the language, Prospero and Conrad also deny the humanity of the speakers – one of the rationalizations of the exterminations that accompanied colonial conquests. David Spurr has pointed out that

> for Western thought, one of the fundamental measures of a culture is the quality of its language. Language comes to be judged according to its richness and complexity, its refinement from mere cry and gesture, its capacity to make distinctions, its multiplicity of names, its range from particularity to abstraction, and its organisation of time and space.[10]

Furthermore, Spurr notes the ancient Greeks' practice of representing those who did not speak Greek, 'the language of civilized humanity', as 'barbarians', hence Aristotle's thesis that 'barbarians' were comparable to slaves and must therefore be ruled by Greeks.[11] Conrad's attitude to language, therefore, forms an integral part of his racial identity politics, the quest to end his and Poland's/Eastern Europe's 'othering' by the West by linguistically constructing what may be called 'alternative others' – the 'barbarians' placed by their language outside the sphere of 'civilized' humanity.

A measure of Conrad's success is the facile argument frequently offered by his defenders, that he 'explains Africa to Europe', not minding that his own native name of Józef Teodor Konrad Korzeniowski was so 'barbarous' to genuine Britons' ears that he had to anglicize it to Joseph Conrad.

Caliban's account of his initial encounter with Prospero is familiar from the five-hundred-years-old history of the colonial encounter that began with Christopher Columbus' arrival in the 'New World'. In a typical scenario, the sick adventurer is treated hospitably, fed and nursed back to health, and shown around the land; then he unfurls a tiny flag and in performative language proclaims possession over his hosts and their territory on behalf of his monarch and country. For good measure, he shoots a few of the hosts dead to demonstrate his power. A character in Merle Collins' *Angel* sums up the Columbus attitude: 'Who dere already could go to hell! Is who comin dat matter!' (*Angel* p. 169). Another pointedly links this 'backward history' to the mind-enslaving strategies of (neo)colonialism: 'The backward history tell us, for example, that Europeans discover the Caribbean an act as if the Arawaks an them was nobody' (*Angel* pp. 172–3).

To European historians, however, the explorer's performative language that proclaims ownership effectively becomes an act of creation, and the murders accompanying the invasion are sanctified through language that speaks of discovery of territory, taming of the jungle and planting of civilization. This is the force of Jamaica Kincaid's argument in *A Small Place* (1988) about the language of European historiography and the dilemma of decolonization writers compelled to write in the colonizer's language:

> Isn't it odd that the only language I have in which to speak of this crime [of European dispossession of her people] is the language of the criminal who committed the crime? And what can that really mean? For the language of the criminal can contain only the goodness of the criminal's deed. The language of the criminal can explain and express the deed only from the criminal's point of view. It cannot contain the horror of the deed, the injustice of the deed, the agony, the humiliation inflicted on me.[12]

Redefining Language Nationalism

Decolonization agonistics in language involves a debunking of the Prospero–Conrad myth that the colonizer's tongue was 'language' while the victim's was no more than a 'brutish gabble'. But it also goes beyond merely asserting the humanity of the colonized through reclamation of language, important as this is; it involves use of language to reverse the erasures performed through the language of European historiography, and reinserting into history and human memory the brutal realities that have systematically been edited out over the centuries.

It is very important, however, to clarify what is meant by language nationalism and other related phrases which have become the staple of postcolonial language theory. As has been noted, major repercussions of the ragbag concept of postcoloniality include the failure to distinguish between mere personal style and ideology-driven reconfiguration of language, and emphasis on innocuous common features which can be traced across a wide range of decolonization and imperial-outpost novels but have no significance in decolonization agonistics. Conquerors gunning their language into conquered peoples in North America, Australia, New Zealand and Latin America, the Trinidadian V.S. Naipaul and the Nigerian Buchi Emecheta labouring to write like true Britons, and the Nigerian

Amos Tutuola doing his best to overcome his educational limitations and write in English, all become heroic crusaders against British imperialism.

A precondition for language nationalism in decolonization literature, however, is that it must be conscious, and must involve a recognition of the role of language in colonialist subjugation and an active will to challenge this role. This is an entirely different matter from grappling with the grammar, syntax and idioms of one's own mother tongue in order to fashion a personal voice. For the British Diaspora, language nationalism could only mean asserting the English language, their mother tongue, against the languages of the conquered peoples which they regarded as 'brutish gabble'. It could not be otherwise, as this was the language that encoded the world views that rationalized their very presence and activities in these territories. Adaptation of the language to its new environment did not at any time purge it of these world views. Confronted with the colonizer's language as a potent tool for validating past and current social practice, decolonization literature assumes the role of contesting the interpretation of the past and the present, and disrupting through counter-propaganda any tendency towards language stabilization that would have the same effect as eternalizing Western dominance.

Over the years, language nationalism has become so common in decolonization literature that postcolonial language theories generally ignore the fact that, until a relatively few daring pioneers engaged the anglophone world's attention with their startling use of English, the prevailing practice was to write in one's 'best English'. For historical reasons connected with colonial education, such 'best English' was culturally and ideologically British even when the setting and themes were not. Colonialism's assault on colonized people owed much of its psychological success to its infiltration of its own subversive codes into the latter's linguistic processing of reality. Colonial regimes frequently outlawed indigenous languages in schools, a recurrent theme in Patricia Grace's *Cousins*, where Maori school children live in absolute terror of being overheard speaking Maori at school (e.g., pp. 160 and 179). Indeed, many of the writers who were to spearhead the Maori cultural renaissance in New Zealand, including Witi Ihimaera, had to learn the language in schools following the Pakeha government's reversal of its language policies (*Cousins* pp. 210–15). An exception to this common pattern was the white minority regime that ruled South Africa between 1948 and 1994, which adopted a policy of indigenous-language education as a means of isolating the various oppressed ethnic groups from one another and from the outside world.

Even in territories where the ban on indigenous languages was limited to schools, as in Nigeria, language nationalism was missing from the first crop of English-language writing. The so-called Onitsha Market writers who produced chapbooks in that Nigerian commercial centre between the 1940s and the 1960s were typical. For purposes of illustration, however, it is better to refer to writers who are internationally known, namely, the Nigerian Cyprian Ekwensi, who has turned out to be the highest achievement of the Onitsha Market tradition, and the Trinidadian V.S. Naipaul, who exemplifies the most thoroughgoing triumph of colonialist usurpation of consciousness through language.

Neither Naipaul nor Ekwensi manifests any language nationalism, although the former is a fairly competent prose stylist and the latter merely average. Naipaul's conscious *assimilado* ambitions and self-contempt are incompatible with nationalism, and language use in his fiction never goes beyond a conscious artist's efforts to embody thought in effective language. For author and characters alike, reality lies in the metropolis and mastery of the metropolitan standard becomes a kind of vicarious assimilation. The characters fail and the novelist mocks them and their ambitions. In *The Mystic Masseur* (1957), for instance, the emphasis in portraying characters' language is on deviance and mimicry rather than subversion of the metropolitan standard which actually constitutes Naipaul's frame of reference. Shifts between the narrator's language, the 'Victorian weightiness' of Ganesh's 'correct English' (p. 76), Ganesh's everyday dialect and Leela's everyday dialect and curious snob English, as well as other distinctive speech habits, are frequently pointed out, but Naipaul's treatment of such speech events confirms his continued association of Creole with the grotesque. In *A House for Mr Biswas*, the authorial narrator incessantly points out whether an utterance was originally made in 'broken English', Hindi, or standard English, and relationships among characters are linguistically signalled. Mr Biswas's insistence on speaking English in the Tulsi household where Hindi is the norm signals his rebellion against Tulsi values.

Moreover, while Naipaul renders Hindi in standard English he gives Creole and 'broken English' to uneducated non-Hindu characters. Racial variations which serve other West Indian writers to portray multicultural realities become for him only a means of entrenching racial stereotypes. In his Africa tales, like the short-story collection *In a Free State* (1971) and the novel *A Bend in the River* (1979), the attempt is to mimic as closely as possible the European imperial-outpost narrative. In terms of possession of language, the African characters are only marginally advanced beyond those of Conrad's *Heart of Darkness*, which is Naipaul's model.

For his own part, Ekwensi is an unconscious *assimilado* in most of his novels even while staking out a role as a cultural nationalist at every stage of his career. Thus, he is able to declare in a 1964 essay that the role of African literature was the 'reinstatement of the dignity and pride which the black man lost through slavery in the New World and colonialism in the Old',[13] in the same breath as he rejects the prominence of race in African-American writing up to the early 1950s (in Ekwensi's erroneous dating) and Black South African literature of the 1960s – long before the Civil Rights marches of the 1960s in America and the 1976 slaughter of hundreds of African school children by the racist white government's police in South Africa.

Such contradictions can be traced back to Ekwensi's beginnings as an impressionable schoolboy (much more impressionable than some of his peers) raised on a literary diet of imperial outpost literature, and an adult who began writing under the auspices of the British Council in Nigeria. It was the Council which sponsored one of the very first anthologies of African writing, *African New Writing* (1947), to which Ekwensi contributed 5 of the 14 short stories. It is illuminating to compare Ekwensi's treatment of the subject matter of his early short story 'The Cup Was Full' with Wole Soyinka's treatment of the same subject in the play *Death and the King's Horseman* (1975). Both deal with the British colonial administration's arrogant intervention in the funeral of a Yoruba king to prevent the king's chief minister's suicide required by custom. But whereas Ekwensi focuses on the suicide requirement and portrays the incident as a conflict between atavistic custom and forces of modernization, Soyinka explores the threat posed to the people's universe by this arrogant, self-righteous intervention. The difference is not merely that of the Yoruba Soyinka's more intimate understanding of his people's customs than the outsider Ekwensi, or that of Soyinka writing nearly thirty decades after Ekwensi, for much of Ekwensi's writing up to the mid-1970s reveals the same split consciousness that shaped his earliest writing.

Evidence of this pervades such works as *The Passport of Mallam Ilia* (1960), *An African Night's Entertainment* (1962), *Burning Grass* (1962), *Lokotown and Other Stories* (1966), *Juju Rock* (1966) and *Samankwe and the Highway Robbers* (1979). Ekwensi retains the colonizer's white-versus-black colour symbolism. Fatimeh the heroine of *Burning Grass* attains heroine status only because she has European features, and is contrasted with the anti-heroine, Kantuma, the evil dark temptress 'dressed in Oriental fashion' and 'beautiful in a dark way' (p. 110). In 'Glittering City', one of the stories in *Lokotown*, the heroine has 'the fair skin that went with most beautiful Nigerian girls'. By contrast, Ekwensi's villains are hulking, grimacing figures, 'dark-faced', 'very black', or 'dark visaged'. Some of them are 'black magicians' doing evil with their 'black magic'. In *Juju Rock*, a European-traveller-in-Africa story narrated by a school boy, one such African walks straight out of a Henry Rider Haggard novel-of-Africa:

> At that very moment one of the most formidable men I have ever seen rushed past me. In one short glimpse of him I saw his huge hairy black chest. His hands were enormous and hairy too. His arms hung down to his knees like a gorilla's. He ran with a kind of lurching hop...
>
> I was still gazing after this horrible man when another, and a very different-looking man, came out of the house. He was a tall Englishman in clean white shirt and trousers, and his hair was golden like sunshine. (p. 16)

The colonialist language and imagery of godlike Englishman and ape-like African is an embarrassment which Ekwensi tried to edit out in a 1971 revision; but no editing short of total rewriting can purge such language from a story that was wholly conceived within the European imperial-outpost tradition.

In a special category are writers like Buchi Emecheta who believes that her long stay in Britain has given her a mastery of metropolitan English and its 'nuances', and that this makes her literary language superior to the 'stilted' language of 'writing coming from Nigeria, from Africa'. 'I know this because my son does the criticism,' she proudly informs Adeola James during a 1990 interview. 'After reading the first page' of such African writing, she boasts, 'you tell yourself you are plodding. But when you are reading the same thing written by an English person or somebody who lives here [that is, Buchi Emecheta] you find you are enjoying yourself because the language is so academic, so perfect.' Her ultimate boast is that her paperback publisher, Collins, 'has now stopped putting my books in the African section'.[14] Unfortunately, not even the magisterial authority of her son-critic can rescue her language from its Sociology-book dreariness. Even Katherine Frank, who excitedly cites her as the epitome of the militant African feminist writer, nevertheless dismisses her most ambitious novel, *Destination Biafra*, as 'aesthetically simplistic, empty,...boring', and languishing 'in a shadowy region between manifesto and fiction'.[15] Emecheta, who is an Igbo, also revealed to Adeola James that she did not go to her village until after her education, and cannot write the Igbo language,[16] though her implausible women-in-African-culture plots frequently abound in stock incidents ostentatiously labelled as 'typically Igbo', 'typically African', or 'African through and through'. Her confession and the evidence of her novels expose the futility of postcolonial cultural theory that reads subversion of metropolitan norms into the language of all postcolonial novels even when the authors are completely indifferent to the politics of norms or, as in Emecheta's case, have those norms as their ideals. Language nationalism is a political programme consciously undertaken, and implemented with a clear vision of objectives and effects.

THE LANGUAGE-OF-LITERATURE DEBATES

From decolonization writers' recognition of the role of language in mind-enslavement and therefore its potential role in liberation agonistics, the emergence of decolonization literature was accompanied in many (ex)colonial states by vigorous debates about the proper language in which the literature should be created. At the 1962 conference on the language of African literature, Obiajunwa Wali argued that 'until [europhone African] writers and their Western midwives accept that any true African literature must be written in African languages, they would be merely pursuing a dead end, which can only lead to sterility, uncreativity and frustration'.[17] The Indian writer B. Rajan has similarly been quoted as declaring that 'the Indian who writes in English is *ex hypothesi* unIndian...His sensibility is mixed and impure.'[18] Translating resolution into action, the Kenyan writer Ngugi wa Thiong'o has abandoned English, but only after some twenty-two years of writing in that language. In a prefatory 'Statement' to his 1986 book *Decolonising the Mind: the Politics of Language in African Literature*, he proclaims his new manifesto: 'This book... is my farewell to English as a vehicle for any of my writings. From now on it is Gĩkũyũ and Kiswahili all the way. However, I hope that through the age old medium of translation I shall be able to continue dialogue with all.'[19]

With this break, Ngugi has also escalated his attacks on Africans who opted for English during the 1962 conference, and takes particular issue with Achebe's admission that despite 'a guilty feeling' over abandoning 'his mother tongue for someone else's', he intended to go on writing in English.[20] Yet Ngugi's abandonment of English is largely a symbolic gesture by a writer secure in the knowledge that his international reputation, consolidated over two decades of writing in English, provides him with an international audience eager to read his views, and capable translators to satisfy that audience. It is quite in order to confront Ngugi with the challenge thrown to Obiajunwa Wali by Soyinka during the 1960s debate: 'What has [he] done to translate my plays and others into Igbo or whatever language he professes to speak?'[21]

More recently, the critic Adewale Maja-Pearce has ridiculed the entire idea of cultural nationalism in europhone writing. Maja-Pearce has no coherent language theory of his own, however, and futilely labours to construct one from loopholes he thinks he has espied in African writers' arguments, leading to such banal assertions as that 'the problem is not with English *per se*... but with those for whom English is not a first language, but who nevertheless insist on writing novels in a language they effectively consider an alien import'.[22] A critic who cannot understand why a writer in a society fragmented among over two hundred distinct languages would choose to address his/her compatriots in the only language common to all of them, or why a decolonization writer would reach for an international audience through a world language, is certainly ill-equipped to investigate the implementation of language programmes in the literature.

Many other decolonization writers share Achebe's uneasy relationship with the colonizer's language. Albert Wendt has Ola, the eponymous heroine of his 1991 novel, complain that 'From the moment we're born we are fed on words/language; we're controlled by words; we're classified/described/identified, etc., by words; we're enslaved by language as prescribed by those who control our societies' (*Ola* p. 39). Confronted with the same issue, Witi Ihimaera has proclaimed: 'My own belief is that Maori writing at its truest can only be that literature which is written in Maori, where the spiritual, emotional and political dynamics control the content. For us, Maori is a sacred language as opposed to English, which is profane.'[23] They have continued writing in English, however, from a recognition that in the battle for minds and in the mobilization of opinion against imperialism, decolonization literature must address a global audience. Many also share Achebe's goal of 'pushing back' the limits of 'conventional English' to accommodate the world views of the indigenous culture.[24]

Through language agonistics, the self is reconstructed and redefined in its autonomous being rather than non-being to reclaim its world which constitutes a universe in its own right. Lewis Nkosi has written that 'black consciousness really begins with the shock of discovery that one is not only black but is also non-white'.[25] Self-redefinition through language goes far beyond the superficial inscription of 'difference' which has become one of the hallowed buzzwords of postcolonial cultural theory, as if acknowledgement of cultural difference were a new development in human history. 'Difference' has always been emphasized in colonialist discourse and representation, but through negation in terms of the 'non-white' and 'non-European'. Decolonization agonistics rejects such negation and substitutes the cultural self as the positive and absolute: as African or Asian or Polynesian; as Nigerian, Jamaican, Indian or Maori. Reality erased in colonialist historiography is thus reinstated, and this reconstituted self becomes the point of reference. Language becomes the interface through which the two worlds meet, interact and overlap, but the novelist endeavours to reproduce the overlaps and intersections without compromising the uniqueness of the indigenous culture. Novelists' exploration of the forms and progression of the encounter at this interface frequently constitute modes of denoting society's historical progression.

Dismantling the euphemisms through which colonialist historiography masks the brutal realities of conquest frequently results in language calculated to shock with its explicit naming of colonialist acts of violence, as in parts of V.S. Reid's *New Day*, Armah's *Why Are We So Blest?*, Ngugi's *Weep Not, Child* and *A Grain of Wheat*, and Ihimaera's *The Matriarch*. This is a remarkable departure from the understated 'Abame is no more' with which the extermination of that clan is reported in Achebe's *Things Fall Apart*, and the novels have attracted much denunciation on this account. Adewale Maja-Pearce denounces Armah's attitude as 'self-castrating racism'[26] (Armah shows the castration of one of the joint-protagonists by officials of the French colonial regime). Derek Wright excoriates it as 'a racist fiction about racist fictions', on the grounds that 'instead of establishing counter-truths the novel is itself heavily implicated in the proliferation of some stale, white-originated myths of sex and race'.[27] W.J. Howard complains that Ngugi has made the British colonial official Howlands into a monster and satyr in the tradition of Hollywood melodrama[28] for showing the man's sadistic cruelty, which includes castration of Gikuyu men, in the torture chamber known as the 'House of Pain'. And C.K. Stead's denunciation of Ihimaera's *The Matriarch* has already been noted in Chapter 2.[29]

Ihimaera's language is particularly noteworthy. Against European historians' presentation of the encounter between Maoris and the British explorer Captain James Cook, Witi Ihimaera in *The Matriarch* points out that in just 'two days and fourteen hours' of their stay Captain Cook and his men murdered six Maoris and kidnapped three (*The Matriarch* p. 37). The denunciation is direct and bitter, frequently propelled home through second-person pronouns and direct mode of address which will not countenance any post-structuralist verbal legerdemain with the 'instability' of 'the text', 'inconclusive ironic mediation', 'relative insignificance of authorial control', or other similar postmodernist evasions about slippery texts that 'can never be pinned down'.[30] Ihimaera knows that to the native audience of the imperial-outpost histories and literatures, the text is an unproblematic, definitive embodiment of the wisdom and/or testimony of an authoritative witness.

At all times and places, writer and reader alike subscribe to the convention that the writing represents the writer's thoughts or utterance, which is the only rational justification for the scholarly practice of citing supporting 'authorities' and the entire academic industry of writing about other writers. Consequently, Pakeha historians' selective memories and accounts are decisively countered: 'Yes, Pakeha, you remember Matawhero. Let me remind you of the murders at Ngapata' (*Matriarch* p. 177). Ihimaera's own account of the murder of Maoris and the Pakeha colonial government's nomination of the murderer to serve on the jury during the inquest ends with: 'The killing of innocents, Pakeha. The blood is on your hands' (*Matriarch* p. 174). An earlier reference to the Matawhero affair is remarkable for the precision of the nouns, verbs and modifiers used to reinterpret it through Maori perspectives. The 'Matawhero Massacre' is in reality:

Te Kooti Rikirangi's *retaliation* against a whole history of Pakeha abuse of Maori people, custom and land . . . [and] is surely no more horrifying than the atrocities committed on the Maori people in the name of civilisation. Of course, the difference is that *white* people were killed at Matawhero. The blood of a white man, woman or child, spilt by natives, is called an atrocity. The blood of a [Maori] man, woman or child, spilt by a white man, is called an act of self defence. (*Matriarch* p. 71)

The precision of the language in such counter-discourse constitutes an act of renaming which serves to reveal incidents in specific moral lights. It is significant that in all these cases the colonized people are fighting a decolonization war, usually represented in European history as acts of terrorism by savages unable to appreciate the value of the civilization the colonizer is bringing to them at great personal sacrifice.

Language agonistics also involves confronting the political implications and artistic demands of writing in English. For a non-British person to write in English, the risks of unwitting self-subversion by cultural values and world views encoded in the language are always present, as the example of Cyprian Ekwensi shows. In Samuel Selvon's *A Brighter Sun*, the revelation of the dangers is conscious on the part of the novelist, as distinct from the cases of Ekwensi and Naipaul who are themselves victims of their own mishandling of the language. When Selvon's growing protagonist, Tiger, abuses an unhelpful fellow-Indian doctor as 'a nasty coolie man', a European term of racial contempt for Indians, he manifests that lack of dignity and self-esteem, that tendency to see himself through the colonizer's eyes, which Achebe has pointed out as one of the worst psychological ravages of colonialism's denigration of its subjects. Several other characters in the novel manifest even more severe symptoms of low self-esteem. As the Creole woman Rita laments to the Indian woman Urmilla, 'why we creole can't live like Indian, quiet and nice?' Urmilla inwardly laments that 'it was the same thing all over. Only white people. If they could only be like white people' (*BS* p. 31). More examples abound in George Lamming's *In the Castle of My Skin*, where the language of the local overseer employed by the English feudal landlord, Mr Creighton, reveals a consciousness that has been thoroughly contaminated by the master's contempt for local people.

LANGUAGE APPROPRIATION AND EXPERIMENTATION

The need to break out of this language trap results in much experimentation. English has to be transformed into a new kind of world language disburdened of its original racial bias. The first act in this regard has consequently been a historic act of reverse appropriation. Novelists as geographically separated as George Lamming of Barbados and Raja Rao of India have argued that the English language belongs as much to them as to any native English person, even though Rao admits the enormous problems of trying to 'convey in a language that is not one's own the spirit that is one's own ... [and to] convey the various shades and omissions of a certain thought-movement that looks maltreated in an alien language'.[31] To appropriate a language is to make it a vehicle for one's own point of view, an embodiment of that world whose reality it is desired to convey, the consciousness or sensibility that mediates the narrative to the reader. Many novelists have accordingly proceeded to break English down and reconfigure it into a pentecostal instrument by impregnating it with the psychodynamic characteristics of their own cultures, which are thus restored to primacy in the centre of their universe.

A proper appreciation of these experiments demands rejecting the 'death of the author' fallacy. Decolonization writers recognize that the so-called 'disappearance' of the author from twentieth-century fiction is never more than a stylistic convention. Even in those texts where the author does not engage the reader in imaginary banter, whether these be European, Third World, or other ideological texts, s/he still mediates between the reader and the imaginary world of the text through his/her language strategies. Theorists and writers who pride themselves on having dismissed the 'Author-God'[32] to concentrate on the writing are simply misapplying the metaphor, for it has never been the habit of God to roam the streets advertising his presence or his works. What M.A.K. Halliday has described as 'the communication role that [the author] adopts, of informing, questioning, greeting, persuading, and the like', is performed by using language as a strategy for 'intrusion into the speech event'.[33]

In the europhone postcolonial text, authorial intrusion actually begins with his/her exploitation of the convention of reading to offer speech events generated in the indigenous language as if they were originally in the English language. It is partly for this reason that those who consciously treat language as an issue choose to represent the standard form of the indigenous language as a form of standard

English. In an August 1991 interview with Jane McRae, Patricia Grace makes this point about the book she was working on:

> I am writing in English. But I don't want to write the dialogue in what could be called Maori English. So I have chosen to write the dialogue in 'standard' spoken English because the characters are speaking 'standard' spoken Maori.[34]

In all of Grace's full-length novels as well as the novels of Achebe, Ihimaera and Wendt, such indigenous oral art forms as oratory which should normally exhibit the greatest features of oral psychodynamics are consistently represented in some form of standard spoken English for this very reason.

This strategy gives special importance to narrative point of view in decolonization writing which is concerned with fidelity to cultural psychodynamics. Point of view determines the kind of world that the text can bring into life through language, the narrator's relationship with this world, and the strategies for authorial intrusion into the text, hence any liberties that might be taken with the grammar, syntax and other aspects of the language. Extant criticism, such as Keith Watherhouse's critique of the language of Achebe's *No Longer at Ease*, has also shown that these factors greatly affect readers' responses to the language. Of Achebe's language, Waterhouse sneers:

> It is usual, almost traditional, to pay tribute to the simplicity of style of novels such as this... as if short words were something new in fiction. I suppose the fact of the matter is that simplicity is all we ask for in the African novel... not the new luxuries of characterization, motivation, depth psychology and all the rest of it.[35]

Contrary to Waterhouse, the fact of the matter is that he has read the novel with too much presumption about how novels should be written. Though *No Longer at Ease* deals mainly with the predicament and ultimate failure of a university-educated protagonist, the society is still predominantly oral and even the city dwellers are peasants who are just developing into an urban proletariat. Deictic features like first-person pronouns in the narrative prose suggest the presence of a peasant consciousness which circumscribes the range of vocabulary that could be employed outside the central character's academic circles.

This leads us to one crucial feature that prevailing postcolonial theories of language have ignored, namely, that language politics in decolonization literature set up a measurable relationship between fidelity to cultural psychodynamics and the verbal repertoire of a text. This relationship may be demonstrated with three first-generation decolonization novels: *New Day* (1949) by the West Indian V.S. Reid, *Things Fall Apart* (1958) by the Nigerian Chinua Achebe, and *Leaves of the Banyan Tree* (1979) by the Samoan Albert Wendt. Attempts to assimilate oral narrative techniques within the written form set up an oral resonance in each novel. Yet the oral resonance in each novel is primarily a function of the dominant psychodynamics of the cultural setting. Achebe's and Wendt's cultures possess a first language other than English while Reid's Jamaican culture has a variety of English as its first language. Whereas Achebe's and Reid's narrators are peasants whose consciousness is oral, Reid's has also acquired some literacy in English, and Wendt's narrator is university-educated. In contrast, *New Day* is the only one directly conceived as a live oral performance before a fictive 'listening audience' rather than 'reader'.

These permutations determine the verbal repertoire from which each novelist draws: for example, the range of alien vocabulary and concepts that can be assimilated into the cultural psychodynamics. Reid's narrator's language is the English speech of his Jamaican experience, plus any specialized English words which he has acquired through association with educated people. Wendt's university-educated narrator can employ educated diction in his normal thinking and speech, that is, the narrative prose and instances of Free Indirect Discourse. When s/he is a participant in the action, his/her idioms and verbal repertoire are restricted only by the themes and the kind of audience to whom the discourse is addressed. Conversely, any words or idioms with a discernible specialized or foreign tinge would be out of character in Achebe's novel, particularly in the pre-European first two parts. Achebe is not entirely successful or consistent in implementing the strategy, but it is the principle governing his language use.

Many English-language abstractions and specialized terminology would, of course, equally be implausible in a British novel if they lie outside the social experience of a British character to whom they are attributed. Beyond the conventional demands of plausibility, however, looms the question of congruence between the characters' cultural consciousness and that of the narrator who is conceived as a participant in the culture rather than an Olympian elite looking down upon it. The issue here is not whether oral cultures are capable or incapable of conceptual abstractions or scientific thinking but whether language is in character with the totality of cultural experience it is designed to express – and, therefore, with the verbal repertoire which would have grown up to express the culture's material and non-material universe. Oral cultures do distil alcohol from grains, as in the rural novels of Flora Nwapa and in Ngugi's *Petals of Blood*, but they do not discuss it in the language of commercial alcohol production or that of the organic chemistry laboratory. In Flora Nwapa's novels, they 'cook' it. Language here operates on the analogy of food preparation within the homestead. Cooking is frequent in Achebe's ethnic novels. Logs glow in the huts, but there is no 'combustion'. The writer who fully participates in his/her culture endeavours to harmonize the narrator's language with that of the fictional characters, for, as Ann Banfield has noted, 'narrative statements describing a character's actions, especially when in a vocabulary the character would not use in dialogue, presumably adopt a point of view outside the character's own'.[36]

In *Petals of Blood*, Ngugi makes this a point of his cultural assertion when, witnessing the fermentation and distillation process involved in rural Ilmorog people's production of the alcoholic Theng'eta liquor from maize, the school boy Karega exclaims: 'But this is chemistry!' The language is in character because Karega belongs also to the world of 'college' and its organic chemistry classes, but out of character for Nyakinyua and her group. Karega's exclamation articulates Ngugi's affirmation of the indigenous intellectual and technological potential which colonialism programmatically subverted and the post-independence elite have betrayed. Similarly, words like 'capitalism', 'Mercedez Benz', 'jet', 'yacht' and 'psychological engineering', which all occur in Achebe's *Anthills of the Savannah* have no place in *Things Fall Apart* and *Arrow of God*. They are in character for the university-educated writer-narrator and social critic, Ikem; but their presence in this poor, low-technology, predominantly peasant society portrays a schizophrenic national elite enslaved to Western lifestyles and material products.

Observing these permutations, Peter Crisp linked Wendt and African writers as 'artistic kinsmen [who know] first-hand the art of holding an audience with the voice' in such novels as *Pouliuli* (1977) and *Leaves of the Banyan Tree*.[37] His insight was, however, promptly challenged by Roger Robinson who, interpreting Wendt's imagery literally and out of its context in order to locate Wendt within the Western tradition, argues that: 'There are no sunny limitless plains in Samoa; the diseased beast is a European, not a Pacific archetype … "honour and integrity and courage", and "the excitement of original ideas" convey abstract ideas and have no special oral quality in structure, sound or reference.'[38] There are, of course, no 'sunny limitless plains' anywhere in Europe or the Americas, and the 'diseased beast' is not European but Middle Eastern in origin, though Wendt's protagonist actually employs 'beast' to denote a morally degenerate person just as Achebe's Igbo peasants denounce Obi Okonkwo as an irresponsible 'beast of the bush' in *No Longer at Ease*.

Leaves of the Banyan Tree unfolds in Samoan, and the narrator constantly points out when utterances are made in English as well as the speaker's competence in either language. The power struggle between the city-based businessman Malo and the feudal farmer Tauilopepe is virtually decided in an oratorical contest in which Malo pits his adulterated-Samoan city language (*LBT* p. 35) against Tauilopepe's virtuoso performance. Tauilopepe approaches the contest knowing that his performance is under the 'expert, critical scrutiny of Sapepe', for whom 'style and technique were the justification for almost everything' (*LBT* pp. 36–7). With this background, a Samoan who spoke anything but standard Samoan would be a deviant. Yet Wendt also restricts the vocabulary of such Samoans to non-specialized words and expressions. The expression 'style and technique', for example, is the educated narrator's language unveiling Tauilopepe's thoughts through Free Indirect Discourse.

A distinction should therefore be made between novels, such as those of Achebe, Ihimaera, Grace, Wendt and Collins, in which language is itself of thematic importance in the decolonization agonistic, and the vast majority in which it is not. Novels of the latter category are not necessarily less nationalistic, but for them language is primarily instrumental and only incidentally ideological in function. This point is very important, for its implication is that only the first kind of language use has any place in a genuine postcolonial language theory. Any language theory that embraces the second kind of usage will apply equally to any instance of language use by non-native speakers, for example, Germans using English or French people using Greek.

The truth of this is demonstrated by Ashcroft and partners' futile and self-contradictory attempt to develop a theory of 'postcolonial' language use based on the practice of Amos Tutuola whose sole concern in using English at the onset of his career was to express himself intelligibly in the alien language. Tutuola's language, they argue, 'may be seen as paradigmatic of all cross-cultural writing, since the development of a creative language is not a striving for competence in the dominant tongue, but a striving towards appropriation, in which the cultural distinctiveness can be simultaneously overridden-overwritten'.[39] That Ashcroft and partners have to abandon their own definition of postcolonial literature in order to wander in this cul-de-sac is symptomatic of the confusion in which mainstream postcolonial cultural studies is mired.

To say that language nationalism is not operative in a particular novel or novels does not say anything about their aesthetic merits. Indeed, writers like Tutuola (though not Ekwensi or Naipaul, for reasons already discussed at some length) are in good company here, for the same may rightly be said about the novels of Soyinka despite Soyinka's peerless control of the language. Stylistically, Soyinka's *The Interpreters* is a product of the Euromodernist tradition acting on a poet-dramatist's sensibility while *Season of Anomy* is refreshingly free of the Euromodernist burden. To the numerous charges of obscurantism that have followed *The Interpreters*, Soyinka has explained: 'I have to concede I tend towards what's called the elliptic style of writing...But I deny absolutely any attempt to mystify or to create obscurities...Generally, I certainly never set out to be obscure. But complex subjects sometimes elicit from the writer complex treatments.'[40] Many readers will hear in this some echo of T.S. Eliot's comment on Euromodernist poetry:

> We can only say that it appears likely that poets in our civilization, as it exists at present, must be *difficult*. Our civilization comprehends great variety and complexity, and this variety and complexity, playing upon a refined sensibility, must produce various and complex results. The poet must become more and more comprehensive, more allusive, more indirect, in order to force, to dislocate if necessary, language into his meaning.[41]

Niyi Osundare has pointed out that 'because of the way words and ideas seem to throng Soyinka's consciousness, he sometimes piles up a series of sentence fragments [the type referred to as graphological sentences]', and run-on sentences or 'psychological sentences, not guided by the grammar book's rubric on punctuation ...but directed by the pulses of the mind and the rhythm of consciousness'.[42] Nevertheless, despite the presence of some 42 Yoruba words and phrases which are explained in a glossary, there is no attempt to simulate the rhythms of Yoruba speech or thought except when Yoruba proverbs are quoted by a character – and in such instances Soyinka reproduces the entire proverb in Yoruba.

Going beyond mere appropriation, language nationalism at its best expression involves some form of experimentation to insert the indigenous world as a living presence in the alien-language text. It is no experiment when a writer occasionally drops indigenous words or other sociological particularities into an English-language passage, whether the practice is motivated by a nationalistic impulse or compelled by the absence of functional equivalents in British English. Such indigenous expressions effectively infiltrate a culture's uniqueness into the text and subvert complacent reading, but unless they also evoke the realm of consciousness, ideas and values they do not perform a psychodynamic function, for mere disruption of complacency can be achieved with any specialized register or vocabulary in the midst of conventional language. Experimentation involves a deliberate construction of sentences to simulate the latent consciousness that processes information or reality. Almost invariably, this involves some reconfiguration of the syntax of the alien language to subvert metropolitan conceits about norms of appropriateness. This is why experimentation is possible only with utterances conceived in the indigenous language. For writers who undertake this experimentation, the choice of strategy is directly related to the linguistic and cultural landscape created in each locale by colonialism.

Reconfiguration of syntax must not be confused with the quaint exercise undertaken by Chantal Zabus in Chapter 4 of her book *The African Palimpsest: Indigenization of Language in the West African Europhone Novel* (1991). Writing on languages in which she has no competence, Zabus is unable to personally translate her West African speech samples into English or analyse their syntax, and relies on others to a degree that more prudent researchers would recoil from. Her reliance on Austin Shelton's notoriously inaccurate translations of Igbo proverbs is particularly ruinous, as most of the time what she is really discussing is an imaginary language of his or her own manufacture.[43]

Following the practice of European collectors of folklore, Zabus prefers what she takes to be verbatim translations of West African speech into English, resulting in absurdly disjointed syntax strings that are reminiscent of the work of nineteenth-century European writers who caricatured black people as overgrown infants babbling in exotic half-language. Her Igbo-to-English translations generally ignore the phenomenon of polysemy, frequently render inflexional affixes/morphemes as independent words, and pervert structures of modification, particularly cases of post-modification, by ignoring the logical relationship between modifier and modified. She also fails to appreciate that, like European languages, African languages have idiomatic and figurative expressions whose meaning cannot be arrived at by verbatim translation. What is particularly surprising is that she engages in these parodies of translation without bothering to search out the original Igbo proverbs, for it is these originals rather than novelists' or anthropological collectors' translations that are Igbo cultural facts/artefacts. This omission is as indefensible as the entire idea of verbatim translation, for indigenous speakers of a language speak the standard formal or colloquial idioms, without any reference to, or mediation by, some other language.

Until Postcolonial Discourse came into vogue to revise the palimpsest of history, many Western critics responded with hostility to decolonization writers' linguistic experiments. Thus, one finds Norman Simms querying the 'validity' of Patricia Grace's and Witi Ihimaera's experiments. 'If, in reality, the Maori writer of today thinks and speaks partly in English and partly in his own language', Simms asks in 1978 apropos of Patricia Grace's writing, 'should the literary language, even when "echoing" real thoughts and real conversations, reproduce the mixed language?' Contrasting this 'macaronic' approach with his own ideal of an 'integrated approach ... in which there is no sense of disturbing English syntax beyond its normal bounds and the experience of [Maoriness] is made to flow through the narrative shape of a European story',[44] Simms maintains that:

> The validity of a Maori literature in English depends on its ability at once to be integrated into (while enhancing) already existing categories of literary endeavour – the regional, dialect and ethnic novel, for example; and also to open new possibilities of artistic expression by transferring to English generic and conceptualising categories either no longer present, never existent, or vaguely present in the English tradition.[45]

Decolonization novelists have no interest in locating themselves or their work within the imperial 'great tradition' whose language has been a major instrument in their subjugation, or pouring their people's experience into the 'narrative shape of a European story' which can only divert resistance into harmless channels of elitist, self-massaging aestheticism. Compelled by history to write in the colonizer's language, they seek to transform it from a hegemonic instrument into an agency of self-empowerment and identity reintegration.

The Experiments

For the mid-century West Indian novelist, the problem was largely that of developing an effective creative language from the numerous varieties of 'Creole English' (hereafter 'Creole') that have evolved in the various islands, and devising a functional orthography for a written style that achieves psychodynamic and sociological fidelity without the encumbrances of any extreme localisms. Barbara Lalla has pointed out, for instance, that:

> Jamaica differs from much of the English-speaking Caribbean in the survival of a conservative (basilectal) Creole. This is not only incomprehensible to uninitiated Standard English speakers but also difficult for speakers of decreolized varieties in other Caribbean territories. Jamaican literature is linguistically distinct from other literature in English to the extent that it includes selected features of this Creole.[46]

Peter A. Roberts in *West Indians & their Languages* has identified the multiplicity of historical factors that 'militated against stability and relatively homogeneous language development', such as a high mortality rate, replenishment of the labour force through importation rather than natural increase, displacement of one colonial ruler by another, revolts by the colonized population and various waves of migration, including post-Emancipation influxes from Asia.[47]

A second level of difficulty for writers arises from characters' tendency to run words into one another, creating for the writer the problem of determining which unit of utterance to treat as a discrete morphological element and which to treat as a syntax string even while grappling with the dialectal variations. An incident in Merle Collins' *Angel* portrays this phenomenon from the vantage point of users. Trying to explain away her inability to speak the dialect that is dominant among the students, the heroine Angel claims that she comes from Aruba rather than Grenada, and invents an 'Aruban' sentence on the spot:

> Maria was impressed. 'Say something again.'
> 'Mammie say I must talk English all the time now so as I could learn quick,' said Angel...
> 'I feel if was me I woulda talk a lotta Aruban.'
> 'Ah don know. Ah tink...'
> 'We always telling you not to say "Ah don know". It soun real country. Why you caan say, "Me en know"?'
> Angel asked Doodsie [her mother] to teach her Aruban. Doodsie brushed her aside, impatiently.
> 'In Aruba we used to talk English same as here and a little bit o Pappiamentu.'
> 'Ah don even know Patwa. Allyou does only talk Patwa for us not to understand.'
>
> (*Angel* p. 91)

Constructions like 'woulda', 'lotta', 'caan' and 'allyou' clearly combine aspects of morphology with those of syntax, which the novelist recognizes but which the speaking character is not concerned with. The fact that, in real life, speakers also adapt their language to the context or audience means that the reader of a West Indian decolonization novel must be prepared for apparent discrepancies within the same novel and even from the same character.

Driving this experimentation is the nationalistic desire to free the language from the traditional stigma which associated it with the grotesque and the primitive, or, as Merle Collins observes, considers it 'a sign of inferior intelligence'.[48] For this reason, every attempt to create a substantial portion of a novel in Creole is a form of experimentation. Though Creole (as pidgin) had been used earlier by European writers, such writers' practice was part of the colonialist construction of the Prospero–Conrad myth, and the decolonization writer has to devise his/her own language strategies. Jean D'Costa has summarized the range of favoured strategies. The novelist:

> can simply make use of words and idioms with a distinctive West Indian meaning and flavour in what is otherwise more or less standard English. Or secondly, he can decide, say, to use dialect simply for the conversation of certain characters while using standard English for narrative prose and perhaps for the dialogue

of other characters. Or, a third possibility, he can decide to... reflect in his writing the wide spectrum of dialectal usage – from very broad vernacular to educated local usage – which is a feature of the verbal behaviour of many West Indians.[49]

West Indian writers have faced the language problem with considerable courage and success. By lacing their own narrative prose with the flavour of oral speech, exploring serious themes and positively portraying peasant protagonists, the novelists have remarkably succeeded in freeing Creole from the stigma attached to it. There is a world of difference between V.S. Naipaul's hollow caricatures and the living beings of the other writers, seen most emphatically in the difference between Mohun Biswas's search for a house in *A House for Mr Biswas* and Tiger's quest in Samuel Selvon's *A Brighter Sun*, and readers tend to respond to characters' language through cues provided in the characters' portrayal. Most writers also attempt to strike a balance between extreme local forms and more broad-based forms, except when extreme forms are required for special effects in sociological verisimilitude.

V.S. Reid's *New Day* was the first West Indian full-length novel to be narrated entirely in Creole, and Reid faced before any other West Indian novelist the problem of lack of models for his linguistic enterprise. He approaches the challenge by adopting an amalgam of standard English and median Jamaican Creole, as spoken by an octogenarian peasant narrator, Johnny Campbell, whose consciousness is deeply steeped in the oral tradition. In Frederic G. Cassidy's model of 'Jamaica Talk', Jamaican English exists along a continuum with the educated model at one end, 'the inherited talk of peasant and labourer' at the other, and subtle gradations in between. 'Moving towards the middle from the educated end', Cassidy writes, one encounters an increasing inclusion of 'Jamaicanisms', mainly 'Jamaican rhythm and intonation', words that have their meaning only within the immediate environment, and 'turns of phrase that have grown up in this island'.[50] The narrator's language effortlessly oscillates along this continuum as the occasion demands, and demonstrates the viability of Creole as a vehicle for national celebration as well as profound social commentary. A passage eulogizing the Jamaican bullhorn shows this language at its best:

Bullhorn O, how often ha' you led into battle your Jamaican men? When first we heard your voice in the hurry-hurry hills... was it

no' of war you talked of ? Did no' the English redcoats and traitor
Juan de Bolas sweat in terror as you spoke o' death in the bush?
Then again in 1690, did they no' hear your voice in Clarendon
parish when African slave-princes would sever their bonds? . . .
    Wartime, hunting-time, hear the shells talk! . . . *human you are,*
Bullhorn?

(pp. 119–21. Narrator's emphasis.)

Of the settler farmers, Johnny comments: 'I am a-think that buckra
are great people; for ride, they ride horses all the time . . . live, they
live in Great Houses' (p. 24). The opposition between the purported
greatness of the buckra, their economically unproductive lifestyles
and their ownership of 'the Great Houses' effectively portrays a
parasitic class that lives off the labour of their victims.

Critics have reacted in various ways to this amalgam. To R.B. Le
Page, the language 'had a very literary flavour . . . and failed to carry
conviction'.[51] R.J. Owens, Louis James and W.I. Carr have all been
quoted by Mervyn Morris as arguing: that the language is neither
'art speech' nor 'vernacular' (Owens); that though 'more concentrated
than the vernacular', it lacks 'the variation, the acerbity, the vigour
that exists in the spoken word' (James); and that its rhythms are
monotonous (Carr and James).[52] Such criticism ignores the fact that,
despite being designed as an oral performance, *New Day* is a novel
to be read by the eye rather than listened to. The language
is particularly effective in capturing the latent consciousness of
the narrator and other characters, offering a channel for authorial
injection of comments and observations, marking the tempo of 'historical' events that are narrated as well as mood-shifts in the story-
telling act itself.

For his own part, Selvon in *A Brighter Sun* uses language to convey the multi-ethnic richness of West Indian life as well as the
relationship between language and power. Selvon is one of those
writers whose narrator's language belongs to a different standard
from that of the local characters. Yet there is no sense of cultural or
intellectual superiority over the society or the fictional characters, for
by restricting his vocabulary and simplifying his syntax Selvon
creates an impression of equating standard English with standard
Creole. Language marks out first-generation Hindi-speaking characters, the younger generation, African West Indians, literate characters and the hero Tiger at different stages of his growing consciousness.
For instance, the English language of Hindi-speaking characters like

Lamlal, Sookdeo and Tiger's father is characterized by grammatical, syntactic and lexical features which suggest that thought is conceived in another language and then translated into English speech. Their English is strictly for imparting a message, with no rhetorical embellishment or stylistic flourish, as in Ramlal's direction to Tiger to organize his married sexual life on the model of what his parents do:

> Well, is dat self. You doam same thing. You gettam house which side Barataria, gettam land, cow – well, you go live dat side. Haveam plenty boy chile – girl chile no good, only bring trouble on yuh head. You live dat side, plantam garden, live good. (p. 7)

By contrast, Sookdeo's English speech reveals the confident volubility of one who, being literate in English, can afford to strive after heightened stylistic effects. Thus he proudly imparts his philosophy of farming to Tiger: 'Listen, boy, Ah cud see yuh still young. Yuh have plenty tings to learn. In de first place, yuh have to love de tings yuh plant' (p. 77). He can even afford to indulge in English-language punning (p. 77).

When Selvon portrays African West Indians, their language reflects the narrator's assertion that 'the Negroes were never farmers, and most of them did odd jobs in the village or the city' (p. 10). Being spoken as a mother tongue, the language exhibits a relatively more complex grammar and syntax than that of rural Hindi-speaking characters, as well as a stronger persistence of a French substrate retained from an earlier period of French dominance on the island. Selvon's African characters, including lifelong rural dwellers, are more likely than Indians to incorporate French patois into their speech. Joe Martin's language is thus fairly sprinkled with 'oui', while an elderly milk vendor is fond of 'eh bien'; among Indians only city dwellers like Boysie reveal this habit, as when Boysie challenges a woman: 'And is why you lookin' me so, *macoumere*?' (p. 86). Important sidelight is thrown on this issue by Peter A. Roberts' demonstration that 'crystallisation of the language' in Trinidad and Guyana occurred in the early nineteenth century, following the arrival of thousands of French speakers fleeing from revolutions in France and Haiti but before post-Emancipation labour shortage led to 'massive influx of East Indians'. Trinidad remained 'linguistically and culturally more French than English' until its economic and strategic importance re-excited American and British interest.[53]

More than any of the other peasant heroes, Selvon's Tiger realizes that language and writing hold an important key to the mastery of the world which the Second World War and an American team of road builders are changing. His initial attempts involve a comic error – he acquires a dictionary, proceeds to build up a diction of polysyllabic words, and then, intuitively searching for the essence behind the words-as-names-or-labels, substitutes phrasal definitions of objects for the names themselves. This new language is a private code to which his wife Urmilla, on whom he tries it out, does not possess the key, with predictable failure in communication. Tiger's project is ironical but not as wrong-headed as it appears, for it reveals an intuited need to assert control over a concept by giving it a linguistic embodiment, as noted by Sapir,[54] even as his abrogation of names handicaps his quest. Selvon accordingly treats the error as an aspect of his growth-process.

Like Selvon, Mais employs a modified form of standard English for the narrator's prose and that of the eponymous hero in *Brother Man*. Within the narrative, however, he constantly employs code-switching to attain his mission of being 'a hundred percent Jamaican writing about a hundred percent Jamaicans'.[55] Liturgical and obeah language frequently intersect with language of the slum or yard, the law court, the formal essay, the city street, or the language of the 'Chorus of People in the Lane' to portray the plight and anxieties of a people living on the margins of society as colonial Jamaica approaches self-rule. For Mais, fidelity to the Jamaican world demands transcribing the language of the Chorus with little modification, as in:

- Mis' Brod's clubfootbwoy get run over...
- You hear wha' Bra Ambo say? Say we is gwine get nodder breeze-blow dis year yet...
- Cho Missis, no mind Bra' Ambo, after him no eena Big Massa council...
- Coal-price gone up since todder day
- Ee-ee Ma him do an' get run over...
- Oonu lissen hear wha' Bra Ambo say... (p. 7)

On the matter of developing a suitable orthography, the West Indian experiment has had mixed results, and should be understood as an ongoing process. The novelists are, it must be admitted, not trying to develop a single region-wide Creole standard but working from living examples of their own communities. Nevertheless, there are wide variations between writers from the same community, such as the Jamaicans Roger Mais and V.S. Reid, and sometimes even in the same novel. A comparison of the works of earlier novelists and those from the 1980s shows little convergence. The difference between Selvon's 'nutting' and Mais's 'nutt'n' (for 'nothing') may be attributed to dialectal differences between Trinidadian and Jamaican Creole; but within the work of each of them grammatical forms also reveal some inconsistency. 'Dem' and 'them', 'you' and 'yuh', 'I' and 'ah', are all used to serve the same grammatical function, sometimes as subject, sometimes as indirect object, and, in the case of 'you' and 'yuh', as possessive pronoun. Abbreviation of standard spelling, phonetic adjustment, hyphenation and fusion of words may also be used to give an appearance of Creole to a standard word, exploiting the amenity of writing and therefore the fact that the text is to be read rather than heard or listened to, giving such forms as Reid's ''cept' for 'except', and 'y'know' for 'you know', or Mais's 'todder' for 'the other', 'tek-up' for 'take up', and 'so-much' for 'so much'.

Lack of consistency does not mean lack of success, however. The novelists' concern is not with writing *per se* but with its agonistic function in reclaiming the universe on behalf of the people. In this nationalistic task, they have been eminently successful. Subsequent generations of novelists have built upon this. In Merle Collins' *Angel*, even university-educated characters speak Creole by habit, just like the peasants. The same situation obtains in Merle Hodge's *Crick Crack, Monkey*. In these novels, it is standard English that sometimes sounds out of place. As an undergraduate in a Jamaican university, Angel considers 'funny' the metropolitan English of her friend who has lived in England most of her life since the age of two (*Angel* p. 136) while in *Crick Crack, Monkey* an attempt by Auntie Beatrice, of mixed African and European blood, to distinguish herself by ponderous standard English merely provokes ridicule from a shopkeeper and his amused clients: 'I wonder whe' this one come-out, boy? Mus' be land yesterday!' (*CCM* p. 89).

Collins and Hodge confidently employ phonetic spelling without any taint of quaintness. In dealing with expressions of French origin, they refuse to follow Selvon's practice of retaining something of the original French spelling, choosing instead to transform them into local words. In *Angel*, Selvon's 'macoumere' becomes 'Makomè', 'eh bien' becomes 'é ben' while 'oui' becomes 'wi', and V.S. Reid's 'buckra' becomes 'bukra' ('backra' in Erna Brodber's *Myal*). Others include 'gadé' for 'regardez' (second person French verb, 'look at'), 'mwen' for 'moi' ('me'), 'palé Patwa' for 'Parlez Patois' ('speak patois'), 'diab o' for 'diable' ('devil'), and 'vyé nèg' for 'vielle/vieux nègre' ('old Negro'). Merle Hodge similarly adopts her own orthography.

Nothing is accidental in these practices. Every choice testifies to a conscious striving to root the language in the indigenous soil. Such practice has forcefully validated George Lamming's boast that the West Indian novel 'has restored the West Indian peasant to his true and original status of personality' by transforming him from a mere 'cheap source of labour' into 'a living existence'.[56]

For Africans and Polynesians, rendering in English a discourse conceived in the novelist's or narrator's own mother tongue demands similar skills in effecting transcultural transfers, particularly when dealing with realities (for example, object names, institutions, abstract ideas) that have no equivalent in English or, in Raja Rao's words, when trying to 'convey the various shades and omissions of a certain thought-movement that looks maltreated in an alien language'. In particular, the novelists have to confront the irony that indigenous language elements stand out as 'alien' in the English-language text. Going beyond orthographic representation, problems here include the technical and psychological tasks of integrating indigenous material into the English-language medium without alienating those foreign readers who are willing to make some effort to understand a different culture. There is also the inevitable confrontation of the Prospero–Conrad mentality of cultural monists who see their own local cultures as universal models, as represented by the anonymous reviewer of Witi Ihimaera's *Tangi*:

> Most of the time there is too heavy a reliance on the reciting of strings of exotic names...the rehearsing of strange beliefs, and the charting of, to us, uncustomary religious customs involving Earth Mothers and Sky Fathers and many another Frazerian trapping. Even a Maori novel needs to be bulked out with other than dollops of native lingo, endlessly repeated.[57]

In many first-generation decolonization novels from Africa and Polynesia, novelists approach this task by relaxing the syntax of English just enough to accept direct translations of phrases and idioms from the local language, or creating syntactic structures that simulate the psychodynamic characteristics of the indigenous language but are not true translations. The new English utterance is close to acceptable forms of colloquial or informal usage. In *Things Fall Apart* a town-crier's message is related as 'every man of Umuofia was asked to gather at the market place tomorrow morning' (*TFA* p. 7) while Akuebue in *Arrow of God* tells Ezeulu: 'I asked her did she want her husband to go to the market for a when his wives kept fowls' (*AOG* p. 7). In the first of these sentences, convergence between the narrator's and the town-crier's points of view results in the unusual deixis of 'tomorrow' rather than 'the following day' which one would expect in formal reported speech.

Here again, language use is inseparable from a conscious national-ist agonistic. The writers confront problems arising specifically from their society's experience of European colonization rather than any 'modern condition' that transcends time and place. In consonance with this, they place a high premium on transcultural accessibility. The various strategies for achieving this are examined in the next section.

Transcultural Accessibility

Infiltration of the English-language text with lexical elements from the indigenous language has its concomitant in the use of various strategies to make the indigenous terms accessible to a multinational or multicultural audience. Decolonization writers want to reach other ex-colonized peoples whose nationalistic efforts could con-ceivably complement one another in the struggle against neocolo-nialism, as well as those sections of Western populations who share the vision of the world as a heritage of all humanity rather than a booty for the powerful nations or ideological blocs.

The question of providing or withholding translation equivalents poses a special dilemma. Patricia Grace has pointed out that just as 'using some Maori vocabulary can be seen to be political, [not] pro-viding a glossary can be seen to be political'.[58] Contrary to prevailing postcolonial cultural theory, however, it is not translation but its absence that poses a risk of marking the indigenous term as exotic, for without some form of transcultural re-rendering the reader is offered no means of coming to terms with the usage as part of the reading experience. On the one hand, besides the risk of alienating such a reader is an equally potent risk of incomprehensibility if a particular indigenous term is crucial to the meaning of the passage in which it occurs. On the other hand, provision of a tourist-guide kind of translation tends to shift effort from reading to learning a foreign vocabulary. In either case, though the desired disruption of complacency and cultural assumptions is still achieved, this comes at the cost of incurring the reader's active resentment and thus defeating one major goal of the language agonistic. The real choice that faces the decolonization writer, therefore, is that of deciding what kind of purchase to offer the reader, and the strategies for delivering it.

Early in his writing career, Chinua Achebe experimented with direct translation, or what Chantal Zabus designates as 'cushioning': 'tagging an English calque onto the indigenous word' so that the English term 'shadows [or] provides a fainter representation or adumbration' of the indigenous word and prevents the use of culturally misleading expressions.[59] In *Things Fall Apart*, Umuofia's powerful medicine 'was called *agadi nwayi*, or old woman'; 'the elders, or *ndichie* met to hear a report of Okonkwo's mission' (both p. 9); Okonkwo's 'own hut, or *obi*, stood immediately behind...' (p. 10). In *No Longer at Ease*, an Igbo-language doggerel with which Protestant school children mock Roman Catholics is followed by a telling narratorial gloss: 'which translated into English is as follows...' (*NLAE* p. 50). Though pedagogically effective, in keeping with Achebe's concept of 'the novelist as teacher', this device carries the ideological risk of emphatically tagging the indigenous expression with lexical deviancy.

More subtle and aesthetically more satisfying are the various devices which establish semantic equivalence between indigenous and foreign lexical items. In *Arrow of God*, a reader understands the Igbo word *obi* as equivalent to the English 'huts' in the structure: 'His *obi* was built differently from other men's huts' (*AOG* p. 1). The clue to meaning lies in the relationship of the two items to the main verb of the sentence.

Sometimes, the indigenous lexical element and its English-language equivalent are related through apposition or through explanatory post-modification. The device can be traced back to *Things Fall Apart*, where it is sometimes developed into a narrative description. Thus, Ekwefi 'remembered the night, long ago, when she had seen *Ogbu-agali-odu*, one of those evil essences loosed upon the world by potent "medicines" the tribe made in the distant past against its enemies but had now forgotten how to control' (*TFA* p. 73). In *Arrow of God* Ezeulu is saddened by the knowledge that the cosmic dislocation caused by the New Yam crisis 'would afflict Umuaro like an

ogulu-aro disease which counts a year and returns to its victim'
(p. 219). The adjectival clause here explains *ogulu-aro*. Much of the
time, though, there is simple apposition, like Beatrice's 'World inside
a world inside a world, without end. *Uwa-t'uwa* in our language', or
'Nwanyibuife – a female is also something', both from *Anthills of the
Savannah* (*AS* pp. 85 and 87, respectively).

A similar device is employed in Soyinka's *The Interpreters*, though
this is not immediately apparent owing to the poetic compactness of
Soyinka's implicit metaphors. Thus, of the encounter between Egbo
and his guardian, Soyinka writes: 'But his guardian was awaiting
him, his flabby paunch overflowing downwards, huge rolls of soft
amala over a leather rim' (p. 15). Here the reader does not need to
know exactly what the Yoruba word 'amala' designates, but can
infer its function as a substance which a flabby paunch may re-
semble. Though Soyinka also provides a glossary, as many African
and West Indian novelists do, it is the semantic replication within
the immediate context rather than the glossary that offers the transcultural access needed by the reader – and does so in a more aesthetically pleasing manner that does not disrupt reading as a glossary
would do.

An item in one language may also be repeated later in the other
language in the unfolding narrative. Thus, in *Arrow of God* an Igbo
phrase occurs first as *ora obodo* and is later repeated as 'folks of the
village' (p. 64). In a variation on this device, Witi Ihimaera sometimes introduces an item in a series of successive phrases or sentences before the translation comes as a climax. Chapter 26 of *Tangi*,
for instance, begins by portraying Mere as something of a cry baby
before Ihimaera slips in the Maori term of 'tangiwheto': 'My Mere,
my sister, you're still a tangiwheto' (p. 122). It is also through a similar device that Grace explains the meaning of the Maori 'Kaua
e harawene mona' as 'Don't be jealous of him' (*Cousins* p. 109).
Ihimaera frequently exploits Tama's bilingualism by which the hero
switches from one language to the other in his grief, as well as the
dirge convention of repetition. Thus, Tama apostrophizes his dead
father:

> E pa, I remember
>   Mum has called me
>   – Tama! Tama Mahana! Come home! Come home!
>   Kua mate to papa . . . To papa . . . Kua mate
>   Your father is dead. (*Tangi* p. 22; also *Whanau* p. 169)

With their painful memories of Pakeha attempts to legislate Maori out of existence, Grace and Ihimaera rarely concede to English more eminence than they are compelled to do by historical circumstances or the demands of the narrative. They rarely employ an English lexical element when a Maori original is available, and rarely indulge in translation that is not absolutely necessary to intelligibility. In these novels, a Maori can hardly be isolated in a Maori setting unless s/he cannot communicate in the language, though, as in Collins' *Angel*, parents sometimes ensure confidentiality to their discussions through language the children do not share. Grace's *Cousins* is full of instances of Maori children being punished at school for speaking Maori, hence the elderly woman Kui defiantly addresses her young ones in Maori within the school compound. 'This old woman speaks her very own language wherever she is, wherever she goes', Kui maintains (p. 179).

Grace's novels are notable for the high frequency of untranslated Maori expressions. This practice is her contribution to the reinvigoration of what she describes in *Potiki* as 'a language that was in danger of being lost' (p. 60) as well as a contribution to the debate about biculturalism in New Zealand. In *Potiki* the value of the Maori ideal of mutual support is reaffirmed through a Maori proverb, '*He aha te mea nui i te ao? He tangata, he tangata, he tangata*'[60] within a paragraph devoted entirely to showing how Te Ope people, having successfully recovered their land from Pakeha dispossessors through united effort, would now help the Tamihanas cope with a similar adversity (p. 61).

In Achebe's novels, contextualization is often facilitated through seriation, syntax and grammar. Once the proper semantic field has been established, untranslated items are introduced within a series of lexical elements of equivalent rank, as in Unoka's introduction of the musical instruments *ekwe, udu, ogene* and, in English, 'flute' (*TFA* p. 5). In the same novel, Okonkwo is rebuked for committing *nso-ani* (p. 22); and then in English for committing 'a great evil'. Any attentive reader will recognize that 'great evil' and *nso-ani* have semantic equivalence as direct object of the transitive verb, 'committed'.

Quasi-Translations

From the knowledge that striving for psychodynamic fidelity in language often results in translation of lexical elements from indigenous languages into English, readers and critics have tended to treat all instances of syntax reconfiguration as direct translations from the indigenous language. Many such instances, however, are really quasi-translations, novelists' own creations based on recognizable generic features of traditional models. Commentators who have hailed Achebe's masterly direct translations of sentences from Igbo into English in his ethnic novels would be surprised to learn that much of the time what Achebe offers are really such quasi-translations. Considerable light is thrown upon this strategy by J.H. Nketia's comment on the stylistic value of proverbs. 'The proverb is a model of compressed or forceful language', Nketia observes. 'In addition to drawing on it for words of wisdom', the writer familiarizes himself with its 'verbal techniques – its selection of words, its use of comparison as a method of statement, and so on' in order to create his own proverb or avoid hackneyed expressions.[61]

This point may be illustrated with two of Achebe's numerous proverbs: 'The world is like a Mask dancing. If you want to see it well you do not stand in one place' (*AOG* p. 46), and 'A man of sense does not go on hunting little bush rodents when his age mates are after big game' (*AOG* p. 169). The Igbo original of the first proverb is 'anoro ofu ebe ekili mmuo' while the second is 'Ndi munafa gbalu ngwele agbabago osa' (literally: 'Those with whom I shot lizards are now shooting squirrels'). Properly speaking, no translation is involved in either case, though the sense of each has been effectively conveyed. Achebe's nationalistic and pedagogic purpose has come up against the language problem pointed out by Vladimir Ivir, namely, that

> languages are differently equipped to express different real-world relations and certainly do not express all aspects of meaning with equal power ... [Some] linguistic units of the source text will have no formal correspondents, while the formal correspondents of others will inevitably carry somewhat different meanings.[62]

Furthermore, with its ability to encapsulate subject, modality, tense, action and the conclusion or outcome of action within a single verb, Igbo language can achieve a degree of precision and conciseness which is impossible in English.

In each case, Achebe constructs an utterance that renders the sense but not the words of the original, modelling it on the partite structure, generic syntax and epigrammatic crispness of proverbs.

The contrast between the five-word Igbo original of the Mask proverb and the twenty-one-word, two-sentence English rendering arises partly from the greater precision and conciseness of Igbo over English, partly from the pedagogical need to infuse the sense of the original into the English version, and partly from the aesthetic need to evoke the orality of the original through rhythmic balancing. With the second proverb, Achebe takes care to evoke the moral thrust of the original, which distinguishes between behaviour or achievement acceptable in very young children and that expected of adults. Yet so effective is Achebe's art that Adewale Maja-Pearce, who sneers endlessly at Achebe's themes and language experiments, adopts Achebe's English version of the Mask proverb as the epigraph, source of the title and shaping philosophy of his work *A Mask Dancing: Nigerian Novelists of the Eighties*, but misidentifies it as 'Igbo proverb' rather than credit it to Achebe.

In an article, 'English and the African Writer', Achebe has explained that the ideological motivation of language use in his ethnic novels was to create language that was culturally 'in character' rather than 'idiomatic English'.[63] In this connection, E.N. Obiechina's 'translation' of the Mask proverb into Igbo, as 'Uwa di ka nmo egwu. Onye cholu ifu ya ofuma a d'akwu (adi akwu) n'ofu ebe,'[64] must be understood as a 'translation' of what Achebe has given in *Arrow of God* but not the Igbo original. This is also true of the translation made for Austin Shelton, though in a different dialect of Igbo,[65] with the important difference that Obiechina is aware of the existence of the original in a way that Shelton is not.

From the expansiveness into which Achebe is forced by the combined demands of psychodynamic fidelity and pedagogical impulse, it is clear that there is a fundamental flaw in the criticism which lauds the language of Achebe's ethnic novels for its lucidity, dignity and economy. The language of these novels could not be economical because the psychodynamic features of oral culture such as copiousness and redundancy, through which the pedagogical narrator achieves clarity, are incompatible with linguistic economy, although syntactic and lexical balancing endows them with a rhythmic dignity. Susan Rubin Suleiman has indeed observed that 'a novel written in the realistic mode and seeking to persuade its readers of the validity or the falsehood of a particular doctrine' is necessarily characterized by linguistic redundancy, 'for it is by means of redundancy that plural meanings and ambiguities are eliminated and a single "correct" reading imposed'.[66] The narrative prose of *Things Fall Apart* is often reminiscent of that of Amos Tutuola's language in *The Palm-Wine Drinkard* reworked by a university-educated conscious artist, particularly in their use of redundant constructions. In a typical passage, Tutuola's hero narrates:

> God was so good, we began to snuff the sweet smelling and we were very satisfied with it and we did not feel hungry again. (*PWD* p. 51)

Similarly, Achebe's narrator describes Unoka as 'ill-fated' and cursed with 'a bad chi or personal god', pursued by misfortune 'to his death, for he had no grave':

> He died of the swelling which was an abomination to the earth goddess...The sickness was an abomination to the earth, and so the victim could not be buried in her bowels. (*TFA* p. 13)

Yet this difference has fundamental implications for language theory in Postcolonial discourse. Achebe's practice has an ideological purpose beyond mere language appropriation for narrative purposes, whereas Tutuola's is limited to appropriation. Writers like Achebe are engaged in 'extending the frontiers of English so as to accommodate [indigenous] thought-patterns', and doing this 'through their mastery of English and not out of innocence'.[67] Without this ideological impulse, even the most daring innovations in language are matters of style rather than language nationalism.

LANGUAGE AND HISTORICAL DYNAMICS

Language does not merely portray the world in these novels, it also shows it in motion. At the most obvious level, movement from rural to urban setting enlarges the world of the novel, with corresponding enlargement of vocabulary and range of imagery, as noted earlier. It is also a movement from the 'harmony' and certainties of the ethnic world to the heterogeneity and uncertainties of a global world in which the decolonization text competes with other texts to define and influence reality. The developmental pattern is best illustrated with Achebe, who not only began his writing by portraying a pre-European world but also made language a central issue in his first novels. The inward gaze of the early novels imposes a constraint on language, limiting it to local phenomena and experience. Beyond its exploitation of Yeats's 'Second Coming', imagery in *Things Fall Apart* is scrupulously restricted to local phenomena until the third part, where the entrenchment of colonialist political, religious and educational institutions occurs. Part III locates the novel in the world of books by bringing books into the novel, from religious texts to the District Commissioner's proposed *The Pacification of the Primitive Tribes of the Lower Niger*.

With the District Commissioner's book in the final chapter, the narration of Umuofia's encounter with Europe is wrested from the Umuofia raconteur, a historical development reflected in the novel through the shift in narrative point of view from the peasant narrator's to the District Commissioner's. There is an immediate conflict between the language of Umuofia's self-perception as a great people and the language of this adversary who sees Umuofia as just another 'primitive tribe of the lower Niger' to whom the white man toils to 'bring civilisation' (*TFA* p. 149). This becomes apparent in the opposition between the raconteur's and the District Commissioner's respective uses of the concept of 'pacification'. For Umuofia, it means restoring wholeness by purging out the abominations committed by converts to the alien religion, but for the District Commissioner it is a euphemism for destruction and conquest. In rapid order, the conflict is extended from the cultural-political arena to the historiographical. Thus begins the intertextuality by which Achebe's novels join the world of books and simultaneously become an arena where the world's books interact in dialogue and conflict. An extract from a chapter, 'The Call', of the District Commissioner's book is inserted as an intertext in *Arrow of God*, where its cultural jingoism and imperial arrogance clash with the novel's nationalism and connect the British presence in Igbo land with the larger historical phenomenon of World War II which is itself a product of competing imperial enterprises. This intertextuality will be discussed in the next section.

Just as language in *Things Fall Apart* additionally charts the gradual integration of different parts of Igbo land separated by distinctive dialects in pre-European times, language in *Arrow of God* shows the gradual integration of Igbo land into a nation state that will itself become a part of a larger world. When the District Commissioner Captain Winterbottom's messengers arrive to take Ezeulu to Okperi, they baffle Umuaro elders with what sounds in local ears like a masterful rendering of the whiteman's language:

'Sometine na dat two porson we cross for road,' said the corporal.

'Sometine na dem,' said his companion. 'But we no go return back just like dat. All this waka wey we waka come here no fit go for nating'. (*AOG* pp. 153–4)

What one observes here is threefold: first, the emergence of new social hierarchies, in which literacy and the book-culture will dominate orality and traditional ways; next, beginnings of the ethnic culture's incorporation within a national and then a supra-national state; and finally, the beginnings of the Igbo variety of what will eventually become, first, Nigerian, then West African, pidgin. This becomes much clearer barely a page later, when pidgin becomes the interface between two Africans who do not share one mother tongue, namely, the Igbo who is the District Commissioner's steward, and the non-Igbo who is the Assistant District Commissioner's steward (p. 155). In *Anthills of the Savannah*, so pervasive is the transformation in culture, consciousness and social facts that, in the cultural melting-pot of Kangan, pidgin is one of the many varieties of English used to encompass the different levels of criss-crossing social relationships.

Narratives of social histories and individual experiences in *Anthills of the Savannah* will unfold predominantly in the language of this new world. As 'teller-narrators' in the earlier novels are supplanted by 'reflector-narrators'[68] playing the 'dual voice' role of 'intertwining of objective and subjective statement, of narratorial account and free indirect speech',[69] the short simple sentences in paratactic syntax and basic vocabulary of the ethnic novels yield to long complex sentences in hypotactic syntax, unrestricted range of vocabulary and imagery, and a plethora of such multi-barrelled formations as 'second-class, hand-me-down capitalism', 'root-and-branch psychological engineering', 'trudging-jigger-toed oppressed', 'always-taken-in-vain reality' and 'Mercedes-Benz-driving, private-jet-flying, luxury-yatch-cruising oppressor'.[70] In such passages, Achebe achieves the linguistic economy which his admirers erroneously attribute to *Things Fall Apart*.

Language in *Anthills of the Savannah* also consolidates the movement begun in *Arrow of God* towards naming in place of the periphrastic strategies of *Things Fall Apart*. For the first time, Achebe begins to employ English-language puns and neologisms to charge his language with social criticism. Compounding, through fusion or hyphenation, is, of course, also used by other novelists. 'Clubfootbwoy' in Roger Mais's *Brother Man* is just one example out of many in that novel, and Niyi Osundare has commented on Soyinka's predilection to neologisms and compounding.[71] For Achebe, however, this marks a definite phase in the continuum from *Things Fall Apart*.

Ashcroft and partners have argued that 'successful neologisms in the english text emphasize the fact that words do not embody the cultural essence, for where the creation of new lexical forms in english may be generated by the linguistic structures of the mother-tongue, their success lies in their function within the text rather than their linguistic provenance'.[72] This argument misses the point, and its illustration is inappropriate. The compound chosen by them ('purity-heart', from the Bengali poet Sri Chinmoy's *From the Source to the Source*) cannot express a Bengali essence because it is not of Bengali origin. 'Semantic categories', Fowler reminds us, 'are not simply properties of language, but products of the society in which the language is moulded'.[73] Aspects of a culture's essence can therefore be conveyed only by indigenous concepts, such as 'ndichie' from Achebe's Igbo culture, 'Matai' from Wendt's Samoan culture, and 'Maoritanga' from Maori culture. 'Ndichie', for instance, designates an institution that is equivalent to the Roman 'senate' (both roughly translate as 'elders' or 'council of elders'), hence its presence, even as a word, debunks the colonizer's myth of bringing order to a people with no sense of civil organization.

The problem here, as in much of *The Empire Writes Back*, is that the authors confound imperial-outpost writing with decolonization writing. Indeed, the entire second chapter ('Re-placing language: textual strategies in post-colonial writing') is merely a broad survey of style in anglophone writing outside the British Isles rather than a discussion of language nationalism in postcolonial literatures, hence their preoccupation with the imperial-outpost 'monoglossic texts of the USA, english-speaking Canada, Australia, and New Zealand'. Expatriation and domestication of a mother tongue by native speakers who have occupied foreign lands in the name of the motherland has nothing to do with colonizer–colonized contradictions, for these writers are themselves the colonizers.

In a europhone postcolonial text, conscious neologisms (which can only be in the alien language) can function thematically primarily as bearers of attitude and commentary rather than of cultural essence, though they may also be used to achieve stylistic economy. Such neologisms must be distinguished from unconscious misuse of words by characters and various morpho-syntactic contractions and/or inversions resulting from writers' orthographic experiments to recapture the culture-specific and noetic characteristics of dialect speech. As bearers of attitudes, they often have a satirical thrust.

In Wendt's *Black Rainbow*, for instance, neologisms like 'dehistory-ing' and 'reordinarination' are satirical comments on the Stalinist programme of the New World Order government in New Zealand. In Achebe's *Anthills of the Savannah*, such a purpose is served by two striking neologisms, the portmanteau words: 'Mandingauls' (p. 38) and 'Harmoney' (p. 120). 'Madingauls', a fusion of Mandingo (a Sen-egalese ethnic group) and Gauls, the ancient name of the French people, is a comment on the French colonial policy of assimilation and the ambivalent politics of Senegal's first president Léopold Sédar Senghor whose excessive adoration for French culture contradicts his Négritude philosophy. 'Harmoney' (a fusion of 'harmoney' and 'money' in 'Harmoney Hotel') indicts the soul-crushing enthrone-ment of the Carlylean 'cash nexus' as the governor of human relationships in the neocolonialist state of Kangan. Deliberate, them-atically functional puns include the play on 're-form', 'reform' and 'transform'. On the one hand, in Soyinka's *The Interpreters*, a con-struction like 'cloudburst' (*Interpreters* p. 5) is an instance of a nom-inalization used to achieve verbal economy while lending intensity to the phenomenon described. On the other hand, 'hurricanoes', a punning fusion of 'hurricane' and 'canoes', denotes the irrational rage of a religious bigot who is familiar with the terrors of sea storms, implacably cursing his son for marrying a Christian: 'Five years ago he had stood at the door of the Marriage Registry and implored the wrath of hurricanoes on the treachery of his blood' (*Interpreters* p. 98).

IMAGERY AND INTERTEXTUALITY

The significance of intertextuality in the development of decoloniza-tion agonistics has already been mentioned. Intertextuality trans-forms the novel into an extended metaphor for a polyphonic world with which it exists in whorls of relationships, for it participates in this world as an argument within a larger argument at the same time as it constitutes a space within which the world is integrated through imagery, literary allusions and echoes.

To understand intertextuality as a device both for figuration within the novel and for transforming the novel into an extended metaphor, it is important to address the metaphor–metonymy opposition that postcolonial cultural theory has inherited from controversies in Western structuralism and post-structuralism. Homi Bhabha's 1984 essay on representation in the colonial text set the pattern with its argument against critical mimeticism – treating the literary text as 'the image of the represented' or 'pre-constituted' reality – and the consequent appropriation of a (post)colonial text (actually V.S. Naipaul's *A House for Mr Biswas*) 'within the canon of the Great Tradition' by treating its tropes as metaphor rather than as 'metonymy and repetition'.[74] Here, Bhabha is merely indulging in the postmodernist practice of misinterpreting traditional critical concepts in order to formulate ostensibly new theories based on the old meaning they should have started with. The introduction of 'repetition' into the argument is merely gratuitous, and his re-reading of Naipaul's novel is entirely traditional. His argument does not derive its cogency from his metaphor/metonymy distinction but simply from his reading against Western 'strategies of naturalization and cultural assimilation'[75] as many traditional critics before him have done.

All theories of mimesis ultimately derive from Aristotle's theory of modes of imitation or representation in his *Poetics*. The sheer range of human activities to which Aristotle applies this term – from various forms of drama and poetry to music, dance, sculpture and painting in all their varieties – shows that he never conceived mimesis as point-to-point correspondence between life and art. Further confirmation of this comes from his discussion of 'possibilities', 'probabilities', 'probable impossibilities and improbable possibilities'; and his recognition that things may be represented as they are, better, or worse than they are, in a realistic or non-realistic mode. Aristotle was not, however, developing a theory of language or writing, and theorists who pretend that his theory of mimesis applied to these phenomena are themselves the originators of error, for as Gérard Genette has pointed out:

> no narrative can 'show' or 'imitate' the story it tells. All it can do is tell it in a manner which is detailed, precise, 'alive,' and in that way give more or less the *illusion of mimesis* – which is the only narrative mimesis, for this single and sufficient reason: that narration, oral and written, is a fact of language, and language signifies without imitation.[76]

Of metaphor, students of literary criticism above beginners' classes know that metaphoric representation rarely implies total identification of one thing with another. Metaphor operates on a principle of selection or filtration, by which specific features or values of entities are abstracted and equated, with metonymy and synecdoche constituting the actual vectors of those values. Thus, the Thane of Ross's metaphorical description of Macbeth as 'Bellona's bridegroom' in Shakespeare's *Macbeth* abstracts from Macbeth and Bellona's bridegroom the prized quality of 'courage' or 'martial prowess', on the basis of which the two entities are equated, while filtering out all the nuptial connotations of 'bridegroom'.

Umberto Eco has therefore argued in 'The Semantics of Metaphor' that 'each metaphor can be traced back to a subjacent chain of metonymic connections which constitute the framework of the code and upon which is based the constitution of any semantic field'.[77] Jacques Lacan in 'The Insistence of the Letter in the Unconscious' suggests that 'any conjunction of two signifiers would be equally sufficient to constitute a metaphor', for the creative spark of the metaphor 'springs from two signifiers one of which has taken the place of the other in the signifying chain, the hidden signifier then remaining present through its (metonymic) relation to the rest of the chain'.[78] Better guidance is provided in more transparent language in A.E. Darbyshire's definition of imagery as the harmonization 'of disparate elements, or bits of lexical information from different and not obviously related sets' through cross-transference of lexical information between analogues, to create 'an experience in which the universe or a portion of it is not analyzed but integrated'. Darbyshire's 'analogue' would obviously function as metonymy or synecdoche, for he defines it as 'a word or expression of a different lexical set, and therefore different lexical information from some other word or expression'.[79]

Integration of the universe or a portion of it is not annulment of difference but illumination of affinities and conflicts. The development of the decolonization novel away from its preoccupation with the village-as-world to engagement with competing nation states, ideologies and books comes with a corresponding unleashing of language and, in particular, explosion of imagery. Definition of local phenomena through foreign references becomes quite common. In Achebe's *Anthills of the Savannah*, Beatrice's reference to 'Russian dolls' comes as naturally as the reference to 'the bird nza' in *Arrow of God*. But it is the role of books which is the most important aspect of this explosion of language and imagery, for, unlike other cultural products, books are ideas and arguments. The decolonization novel itself develops its argument with reference to the real world and to representations of this world in other books.

Many postcolonial theorists influenced by post-Saussurean theories of language have misinterpreted the development of plural voices or polyphonic narratives within the decolonization novel, often basing their error on a misreading of Catherine Belsey's statement that:

> the notion of a text which tells a (or the) truth, as perceived by an individual subject (the author), whose insights are the source of the text's single and authoritative meaning, is not only untenable but literally unthinkable, because the framework which supported it, a framework of assumptions and discourses, ways of thinking and talking, no longer stands.[80]

Belsey is not arguing that truths no longer exist, or that language lacks the power to express definite meanings, but that truth can no longer be defined by complacent reference to such traditional authorities as revealed religion, age-old custom, or mere 'common-sense'.

Within the decolonization novel, language and intertextuality serve a paradoxical function. On the one hand, the clash of voices in argument recreates the contests of the real world, complete with alliances and antagonisms. On the other hand, as exploratory strategies consciously deployed by the novelist, all these voices together constitute the author's unified field of vision, his/her theory or interpretation of reality. The novel consequently speaks with a single voice about multiple voices and clashing realities. Examination of Ben Okri's use of myth in *The Famished Road* (see 'Myths of the Nation' in Chapter 1) has demonstrated how Okri embeds Soyinka's themes and images as intertexts in *The Famished Road* to project his own vision of reality, but more extended illustration may be made with Ngugi's *Petals of Blood* in which intertextuality is more effectively exploited for thematic structure.

Petals of Blood is structured through an integration of indigenous myth and legend with the gyral dialectic of Yeats's 'Second Coming', and further elaborated with ideological-thematic motifs from Walt Whitman, the Bible, William Blake and Amilcar Cabral, and historical lessons from the anti-imperialist revolutions in such countries as China, Laos, Guinea and Mozambique. The title itself comes from Derek Walcott's poem 'The Swamp',[81] and G.D. Killam has

demonstrated in a short but incisive article how even this title provides Ngugi with access to a throve of additional useful thematic
references to Blake's 'The Tyger' as well as Hemingway's 'Big
Two-Hearted River'. Killam convincingly establishes Ngugi's fruitful
harnessing of Walcott's vision of life as a movement 'toward ultimate chaos' with the blackman being 'a special kind of victim in the
process'.[82] The effect of such variety is not any 'proliferation of
meaning' or construction of a Tower of Babel but a sharper focaliza-
tion and concentration of the novel's central themes. Ngugi himself
has explained that the novel uses the metaphor of how a 'very huge
tree prevents little flowers from reaching out into the light' to
explore how 'the social system of capitalism acts to stifle life'.[83]

For many novelists who began by focusing predominantly on the
indigenous world, such as Chinua Achebe, this has meant a major
paradigm shift. It is a remarkable leap from Achebe's ethnic novels
to *No Longer at Ease*, which takes its title from T.S. Eliot's poem 'Journey of the Magi'. Exploration of themes and delineation of character
are developed through a multi-layered structure of allusions to many
other books and literary characters. Achebe's anti-hero, Obi Okonkwo, specifically alludes to T.S. Eliot's 'The Love Song of J. Alfred
Prufrock' and Graham Greene's *The Heart of the Matter*; but the
reader can also identify subtle allusions to Evelyn Waugh's *A Hand-
ful of Dust*, W.H. Auden's 'Musée des Beaux Arts', Joseph Conrad's
Heart of Darkness, and A.E. Housman's 'Easter Hymn'. The criss-
crossing intertextuality extends the novel's thematic range beyond
what a straight narrative could reach. *Anthills of the Savannah* continues this integration of the universe through reference to other
books, including Achebe's own *Things Fall Apart*, and through pervasive figurative language that evokes the wider world.

Albert Wendt similarly moves beyond *Sons for the Return Home*,
and the four novels following it are firmly positioned in a global
culture of books and other mimetic arts. All Wendt's plots are partly
developed by reworking Polynesian myths or their Samoan vari-
ants, and one can detect intertexts from W.B. Yeats, T.S. Eliot and
Albert Camus. *Pouliuli* additionally evokes themes from Shakespeare's *King Lear* as a readily available set of analogies for the protagonist Faleasa's abdication of political and moral responsibility.
Faleasa himself is later fused with another apocalyptic figure, a mysterious old man driven to eschatological despair by the horrors of
the Second World War which are symbolically represented in the
metaphors of all light being 'sucked up by the ground' while 'the air

without the word drives us into silence' (pp. 104 and 113). As the old man descends the church steps (*Pouliuli* pp. 98–9, 113, 142, 144), he simultaneously evokes Yeats's 'vast image out of Spiritus Mundi', the beast of the apocalypse emerging after 'twenty centuries of stony sleep' (the twentieth century), Shakespeare's King Lear raging on the heath, and Edvard Munch's famous lithograph 'The Cry' (1894), better known as 'The Silent Scream'. The old man in *Pouliuli* 'maintained this posture [of Lear and "The Silent Scream"] in absolute stillness until Osovae had counted up to twenty. Then he began to advance down the steps of the church' (pp. 98–9). He enters *Banyan Leaves* as the apocalyptic Galupo and *Black Rainbow* as the Other-Worlder regime of Joseph Starr Linn which runs post-twentieth century New Zealand on behalf of a world dictatorship, the Council of Capitalist Presidents.

Galupo himself has been extensively influenced by the books he has read (Chapter 14 of Book 3), whose presence as intertexts elaborate the themes of Wendt's novel for any reader acquainted with the worlds of those texts. The list includes the Bible, Milton's *Paradise Lost*, Camus's *Myth of Sisyphus* and *The Plague*, Frazer's *The Golden Bough*, Dostoevsky's *Idiot* and *Crime and Punishment*, the unexpurgated edition of Lawrence's *Lady Chatterley's Lover*, Dreiser's *American Tragedy*, Norman Mailer's *The Naked and the Dead*, V.S. Naipaul's *A House for Mr Biswas*, and Luis Borges's *Ficciones* (*LBT* p. 366). Together, these serve to explore the bewildering complexities and element of the absurd in the historical development of an ex-colonial culture. But with the exception of V.S. Naipaul all these books are European. *Ola* and *Black Rainbow* reveal increasing interest in the worlds of European/American, African–American, Caribbean, New Zealand and Polynesian books, including Wendt's own. Some New Zealand writers are even cast as characters in the plot under names formed from anagrams of their real names.

Black Rainbow is in a sense so much a novel about other novels that the central conflict is imagined to be re-enacting an analogue to the plot of Borges's novel. Several characters besides the protagonist (the Questor) and some of his antagonists are endowed with awareness of their roles as fictional characters in Wendt's reinterpretation of other fictions, and the protagonist even compares his trial with 'trials in other novels (and films)' by Fyodor Dostoyevsky, Franz Kafka, Albert Camus, Jean Paul Sartre, Bernard Malamud and Albert Wendt himself (*Black Rainbow* p. 247). Yet *Ola* and *Black Rainbow* are first and foremost concerned with the (neo)colonialist dynamics of

Pakeha–Polynesian relationships. By paying particular attention to Polynesian writing and mythology, Wendt emphasizes the uniqueness of the Polynesian world even as he integrates it into global history and the geopolitics of the New World Order.

Explicit figuration, such as undertaken by writers like Achebe and Wendt, is only one of the two approaches to metaphorization of social evolution in a (neo)colonialist context. A more oblique approach, preferred by some writers, is exemplified in Wole Soyinka's work. Many readers miss the web of allusions and echoes in Soyinka's novels as a result of their being embedded in a matrix of cultural assumptions of which those readers are unaware, especially as Soyinka's clues are extremely subtle. Thus, Chapter 16 of *The Interpreters* opens with a 401-word epic invocation, comprised overwhelmingly of prepositional phrases and clauses, giving a synopsis of the Yoruba creation myth and the 'drama of the gods' derived from it, beginning with:

> And of those floods of the beginning, ... of the first messenger, the thimble of earth, a fowl and an ear of corn, seeking the spot where a scratch would become a peopled island; of the first apostate rolling the boulder down the back of the unsuspecting deity – and shattering him in fragments, which were picked up and pieced together with devotion; shell of the tortoise around divine breath; of the endless chain for the summons of the god . . .

The opening phrase/image links the text to archetypal floods in numerous myths of beginnings and endings, and a reader familiar with the epic tradition, Milton's *Paradise Lost* in particular, will quickly recognize the literary convention to which this invocation belongs. But familiarity with the Yoruba myth is a precondition for understanding the elliptic allusions, while knowledge of Soyinka's cultural theory in *Myth, Literature and the African World* is required to link the referents to their Graeco-Asiatic analogues. Further integration with the world begins with the narrative sentences that follow the invocation: Sagoe's wistful statement that all that is required is a link, a 'bridge, or the ladder between heaven and earth. A rope or a chain' (*Interpreters* p. 227), which call up similar tropes in other mythologies. Assisted by much back-scanning and the metaphoric cluster formed by words like 'bridge', 'ladder', 'rope', 'chain' and 'link', the reader eventually infers that the myth in the peroration is indeed the subject that Sagoe has painted on his canvas, and that both are concerned with the quest for individual and communal (re)integration. What Sagoe has been searching for is someone to model the god Esumare, the rainbow, the link between humanity and gods in the painting.

In *Season of Anomy*, the two layers of myth (Yoruba and Graeco-Asiatic) are linked in an allegorical plot which explores post-independence political chaos in Nigeria by fusing the myth of Orpheus and Eurydice with the Yoruba creation myth. Names of personages in the Graeco-Asiatic tradition are rendered in Soyinka-invented quasi-Yoruba forms. Hence the protagonist is Ofeyi, a character modelled on the Yoruba god Ogun but also corresponding to the Greek Orpheus (Orphée in French, and Ofee to Iriyise), the heroine is Iriyise (Eurydice, also Iris, the Rainbow) and the gaoler is Karaun (Charon). Ofeyi's search for Iriyise occurs across a Nigerian wasteland that terminates in Hell. At the same time, the five-phase movement of the plot is controlled through an indigenized, politicized variation on conventional seasonal imagery – 'Seminal', 'Buds', 'Tentacles', 'Harvest' and 'Spores' – which charts the development of resistance to the treacherous alliance between the Nigerian government and Western capitalism. In contrast, the language in which Soyinka presents the ceremonial commissioning of the Cocoa Fountain built by the Cocoa Corporation's chairman (pp. 32–49) reveals the alienated consciousness of the leadership through the imagery of 'the glory of Italian marble', resplendent costume reminiscent of 'a nineteenth-century Venetian court', and 'a Florentine moment in the heart of the festering continent' (p. 44).

Soyinka's prose offers one of the best examples of how language in decolonization fiction is charged with ethnographic information to foreground cultural 'uniqueness' even as relevant 'bits of lexical information' are used to integrate the culture into the universe and history. Like 'globalization', 'integration' must be understood as a construction of relationships of analogy and opposition rather than a homogenization. Beginning with, but going beyond, a refutation of the Prospero–Conrad myth, language serves as the instrument as well as the stage for political and ideological action. It serves to install the indigenous world as a living presence within the alien-language text, by standing as a structure of order constructed from 'disparate elements and bits of lexical information', containing and interacting with other worlds similarly constructed.

4

Cultural Affirmation and Resistance

SOCIETY IN MOTION

Cultural affirmation in the first generation of decolonization novels is often viewed as time-bound by mainstream criticism, and it is quite common to hear the literature of the 1950s and 1960s contrasted with 'contemporary' writing. In recent years, a revisionist school of criticism typified by Adewale Maja-Pearce has questioned the validity of the literature itself. Though Maja-Pearce restricts his comments to African writers, the comments suggest a very shallow acquaintance with this literature as a historical phenomenon which has manifested itself among all formerly colonized peoples. Particularly astonishing is his confession that he has dispensed with all principles of literary criticism and analysis and 'simply read the novels and responded to them as directly as possible' on the authority of D.H. Lawrence's profound observation that 'literary criticism can be no more than a reasoned account of the feeling produced upon the critic by the book he is criticizing'.[1] Unfortunately, neither the authority of D.H. Lawrence nor that of any other mentor can miraculously confer knowledge or insight where either is lacking, and gut feelings are no substitute.

Challenging Achebe's assertion that colonialism robbed African people of their dignity, Maja-Pearce argues that this:

> begs the related question: dignity in relation to whom? The answer – to the European – suggests that the definition of dignity which Achebe has in mind is relative, and was to be measured in terms of the other, that is, the European ... How, then, did one begin to negotiate one's dignity in the face of what was, after all, a matter of historical fact?[2]

The absence of a coherent vision of the subject is glaring, despite the desperate wordplay with relativity, otherness and negotiability. The psychological carnage inflicted on the colonized by the colonizer is real, its effects long-lasting, not just in the people's relationship with Europe but also in the colonized people's own concept of self-worth. There is no relativism in this, as the study of language in Chapter 3 has partly shown. To dismiss the humiliation as 'a matter of historical fact', with all that this implies of the futility of resistance, bespeaks the kind of confusion that is itself one of the strongest proofs of the necessity for decolonization literature.

Self-assertion or rehabilitation in the first generation of decolonization literature was not a matter of offering point-to-point correspondence between indigenous and European cultural institutions, or staging blind claims of superiority to Europe. It is not a question of spicing up narrative with details of customs that might transform novels into some kind of tourist brochure for armchair tourists. Rehabilitation involves a serious attempt to relate past to present by portraying the indigenous world as an ordered universe that generated its own dynamics until its historic encounter with the colonizer. It is therefore primarily concerned with states of being and of becoming, the dynamic presence of the past in the present within which the future may be glimpsed. On this basis, all decolonization novels are novels of self-assertion, whether the emphasis is on cultural affirmation or on criticism of post-independence society.

The prevailing concept of cultural affirmation in first generation decolonization novels has usually been based on the models of African novels in which conflict between indigenous societies and European invaders culminates in the overthrow of those societies. Such overthrows have frequently been interpreted in isolation from the society's continuity in the new dispensation that emerges. When one turns to novels from Polynesia and the West Indies, the inappropriateness of such interpretations emerges even more strongly, for these novels tend to portray societies that already include a strong European presence. Lacking a pre-European history, present West Indian societies obviously do not provide fertile ground for such themes, though cultural affirmation and conflict are important. What unites the novels examined in this chapter is their common concern with reintegration of identity through establishing a concord between the historical past and the historical present.

One of the more notable aspects of decolonization novelists' approach to, or execution of, this task is the centrality of the Irishman W.B. Yeats's reworking of the biblical apocalypse theme in his poem 'The Second Coming', and the Anglo-American T.S. Eliot's reworking of the nativity story in his 'Journey of the Magi'. Both are also important in explorations of post-independence collapse (see Chapter 5), but Yeats's model is more central in explorations of the overthrow of indigenous civilizations because of its inbuilt dynamics, useful for portraying the end of an era as a phenomenon in itself and as a threshold of a new beginning.

The society of the novels is forever in motion, and novelists examine the past for patterns that may guide the task of reintegration within the present. In African and Polynesian novels, this frequently involves some reconstruction of that past in terms which transform cosmic disintegration into a new genesis. Thus, every collapse also involves a survival of a core of values around which a new order coalesces, and on the basis of which the society copes with new realities.

The Making of a Nation

In African and Polynesian novels, reconstruction of those institutions through which precolonial society had ordered its universe is a historical necessity, for a conflict of cultures is hardly possible unless the contesting cultures are each conceived as an autonomous universe. The novels set up the pre-European world as a paradigm of order, and conflict with European invaders is explored in idioms of defending a hard-won cosmos against the forces of chaos. However, in weaving the operations of political, judicial, spiritual and commercial institutions into their plots, novelists are not so much concerned with idealization as with showing the essential humanness of the culture. Culture, Wendt has argued, is 'like a tree ... forever growing new branches, foliage and roots', and even in pre-*papalagi* days Samoan culture was neither perfect nor unchanging:

> There is no state of cultural purity ... from which there is a decline: usage determines authenticity. There was no Fall, no sun-tanned Noble Savages existed in South Sea paradises, no Golden Age ... Our quest should not be for a revival of our past cultures, but for the creation of new cultures, which are free of the taint of colonialism and based firmly on our own past.[3]

Nevertheless, the need to debunk European claims of moral superiority entails some implicit comparisons of indigenous institutions and their counterparts in the aggressor's own culture. For instance, the reconciliatory principle of Igbo justice (as in Chapter 10 of *Things Fall Apart*) is contrasted with the European adversary system which also operates in many of Europe's ex-colonies. The reconciliatory principle seeks to end conflict by addressing the underlying cause, with the larger objective of restoring harmony. Conversely, the adversary system's objective is not justice but victory, and the outcome of a litigation depends partly on the relative skills of professional legal teams to manipulate the law on behalf of their clients, partly on the whims of judge and jury, and partly on the financial resources of the litigants, with the result that many cases linger for decades. In *Things Fall Apart*, the colonial regime's hanging of a man for manslaughter, contrary to the purificatory and expiatory exile that was the clan's judgement, raises an issue which has a direct bearing on present-day debates about the role of capital punishment in various cultures.

Wendt and Achebe also challenge Western claims of originating democratic principles and institutions. Indigenous democracy, they suggest, was one of the casualties of European conquest. Achebe himself has expressed this point forcefully in reply to interviewer Bill Moyers' suggestion that 'it was a great gamble that Nigeria and other new nations in Africa took when, leaving colonialism, they embraced democracy'. To this Achebe replied:

> That is not true at all. The colonial regime itself was...a most extreme form of totalitarianism. The colonial governor was not responsible to anybody in the territory. He was responsible to a minister in Paris or in London... [The Western claim of introducing democracy] is, of course, totally spurious. There's no way you can inculcate democracy through dictatorship. The colonial system in itself was the very antithesis of democracy.[4]

For Samoa, New Zealand rule and military aggression necessarily meant an imposition of its political structures over indigenous ones, but there are also more subtle forms of subversion. In *Leaves of the Banyan Tree*, economic dominance is a major but subtle factor. Conversion from subsistence farming to cash-crop production serving Western market interests inexorably erodes the moral authority of indigenous institutions which are infiltrated by the cut-throat ethics of that market – witnessed in the vicious contest between Tauilopepe and Malo for individual ownership of land that would normally be communally owned. The delicate balance of power between the Matai and the ordinary people is the first casualty of this economic subversion of the political and moral order. In this sense, the significant thing about the first Matai council in the novel, which determines the contest between Malo and Tauilopepe, is not its flaws but its effectiveness, and it is noteworthy that major decisions are still taken in such councils until the end of the novel.

Things Fall Apart is framed by such consultations, an open meeting of all men of arms-bearing age in the market place to devise a response to an external threat, and this democratic system is contrasted with the dictatorship of the colonial regime. The first instance occurs in the pre-European period, and the narrator's revelation that 'the elders, or ndichie met to hear a report of Okonkwo's mission' (*TFA* p. 9) moves the argument from the general forum where able-bodied men vote on a military issue, to the executive deliberation by the *ndichie* (literally, 'senators'). There is considerable irony in Chapter 24 of *Things Fall Apart* when the colonial dictatorship sends its police force to disperse a peaceful democratic assembly. In Selvon's *A Brighter Sun*, the deal between the British colonial government and the American government, giving American military forces a free run of the island, involves no Trinidadian consultation or representation. And Armah's *The Healers* shows a kingdom as effectively organized and administered as any in Europe being subjected to imperial aggression for which colonialist historians have had to invent fanciful rationalizations.

Colonial regimes' establishment on the ruins of indigenous democratic structures serves as a comment on the charade of belated 'democratic reforms' which they stage just before they withdraw. For many ex-colonial states in Africa and the Caribbean, such 'reforms' have masked a programme for building instability and mechanisms for neocolonization into the political culture and institutions. Often, administrative divisions and electoral constituencies have been gerrymandered to ensure dominance by the ethnic group favoured by the departing colonial ruler.

There is no suggestion that the indigenous institutions are perfect, but then perfection is not the issue in the debate between imperialism and its subjects, and the extremely violent history of Europe between the eleventh and the mid-twentieth century is not itself a model of perfection. Emphasis in the novels falls on the interaction between internal flaws and external aggression in the collapse of the culture. The opening of Armah's *Healers* portrays a society whose viability has already been considerably undermined by its own internal fissures, but it is the British expeditionary force and its local collaborators who are literally portrayed as agents of darkness. Wendt's novels do not disguise the corruption which had begun to corrode the moral authority of the aiga administration and Matai institution even in pre-European times, just as Achebe's *Things Fall Apart* highlight the cruelty of a culture that, driven by considerations of cosmic survival, fears and throws away twins. But when Achebe's *Arrow of God* portrays the British District Commissioner in Igboland as psychologically deformed by the experience of losing his wife to another man while fighting to expand the British empire during the Second World (European) War, the subtext is that Europeans embroiled in their own centuries-long wars have no claim to a higher rationality than the people on whom they were imposing themselves. The two World Wars are similarly incorporated into Wendt's plots in *Leaves of the Banyan Tree*, *Pouliuli* and *Ola*, Patricia Grace's *Cousins*, and Samuel Selvon's *A Brighter Sun*. *Pouliuli* actually interprets the second War as the final turning point in human history towards an era of darkness, and it is as such that it gives rise to the Orwellian society of *Black Rainbow*.

Novels like *Ola*, *Cousins* and *Black Rainbow*, all of which were published between 1991 and 1992 expose the weakness of the brand of postcolonial theory that consigns cultural nationalism to the 1950s and 1960s, denies the complicity of European women in the historical atrocities that accompanied colonial conquests, and casts the European diaspora as victims of 'European imperialism'. In all these Polynesian novels, as in African disillusionment novels, the nationalist cause remains paramount, as the novelists' indictment of the apostasy of the ruling elite and the general citizenry derives its moral authority from a specific vision of the nation. Indeed, virtually all novels published since the 1980s by Grace, Ihimaera and Wendt articulate anti-colonialist attitudes that are far more uncompromising than the Polynesian novels of the 1970s.

Overthrows and Rebirths

In their treatment of the colonial encounter, many novelists have come to terms with it and therefore contain cultural overthrow within the larger history of society's evolution. Novels like Armah's *Two Thousand Seasons* and *The Healers* are important exceptions. Armah insists on a total separation between Africa and the white world as a precondition for Africa's unfettered development. Branded as racist or xenophobic by literary critics in the 1980s, Armah's vision is neither of these, and has received much validation from the new forms of imperialism that have emerged in the post-Cold War era. At its idealistic best, it is also the kind of vision that conceived the United States of America and the European Union.

In *Things Fall Apart*, the subsuming of cultural affirmation within the dynamics of historical evolution begins with the tri-partite plot structure, representing pre-European culture with its flaws and strengths, the European invasion and the fragmentation which resulted from the interaction of internal flaws and external aggression. The contrast between the initial and the final situations is revealed in the opening scenes of Parts I and III: on the one hand, a validation theme derived from the myth of the clan's origins, on the other hand, individual dispensability and communal continuity within inevitable change as expressed in the proverb about the lizard's regeneration of a lost tail. The lizard imagery alerts the reader to the doom awaiting Okonkwo who is implacably opposed to change, and the philosophy implicit in that imagery also accounts for Ezeulu's tragedy in *Arrow of God*. In both novels, the heroes' activities constitute major obstacles on the road to regenerative change, and they have to give way.

Okonkwo lives by a warped code of exaggerated masculinity dictated by his own neurotic personality, a perversion of cultural ideals in the past and a dangerous anachronism in the present. Contrary to this warped perception, Umuofia's success ethic is predicated upon a complementarity of masculine and feminine values (the so-called male and female principles), seen also in: the elaborate ritual balancing of the three cosmic planes of female Earth, male Sky and the spiritual domain; patrilineal, warlike Umuofia's dependence on a female deity (Ani or Earth, the earth goddess) as its principal deity and this deity's emanation (Agadi Nwayi or Old Woman) as source of its military prowess; the assignment of priestesses to male deities and priests to female deities; the designation of the powerful male oracle, served by the priestess Chielo, by the name Agbala which is also a designation for women and effeminate men; and the practice of burying a married women among her own rather than her husband's kindred. In the tale of the quarrel between Earth and Sky, harmony is restored only when Earth's emissary softens Sky's heart with a song (p. 38). Such songs represent the 'poetry' of life which Achebe symbolically associates with the female principle, and Okonkwo's repudiation of this principle marks him out as a doomed man from the beginning of the novel.

This delicate male–female balancing in *Things Fall Apart* has frequently been distorted by many gender critics, who invariably and erroneously assume that mere knowledge of Western gender theories has equipped them to discuss non-European cultures to which they are aliens. The importance of the priestess Chielo, particularly in her brief encounter with Okonkwo (Chapter 11), is often dismissed with the preposterous argument that she has power *only when playing the role of priestess*, even though no major European religion has successfully developed an equivalent office. Carole Boyce Davies vaguely states that this episode 'is one of those situations over which Okonkwo has no control...His machete, the symbol of male aggression, is of no use at all in this context', after which she concludes that women are 'peripheral to the larger exploration of man's experience'.[5] It is difficult to see how male aggression comes into the scene of a man taking up arms to defend his wife and daughter against even the gods themselves, but Carole Boyce Davies apparently cannot resist the lure of the prefabricated phrases of the foreign gender theory which she has made her Bible.

Florence Stratton cites the passage to buttress her own flawed argument which reduces Chielo to a derivation from 'Conrad's "savage and superb" African woman' in *Heart of Darkness* and the 'femme fatales' of Rider Haggard's *King Solomon's Mines* and *She*. Even Chielo's memorable rebuke to Okonkwo to beware of exchanging words with a god (p. 72) is to Stratton only another proof of the novelist's and culture's oppression of women,[6] whereas a critic unburdened with preconceptions would have seen the supreme irony of this rebuke to the masculinity-obsessed Okonkwo from a woman embodying the authority of a male deity whose name connotes 'woman'. Stratton also conveniently sees a phallus in Chielo's entering her god's shrine on her belly through a hole in the wall (p. 77; also Chapter 3, p. 12), as if Umuofia people developed their customs in accordance with a blueprint from Freud. Yet this hole serves as passage for all who come to consult the oracle, and, in *Arrow of God*, it is narrated that even the great Masks which were ancestral spirits emerged from 'ant holes' (Chapter 17, p. 195). Such obstinate misreading suggests an assumption that the novelist and the culture are as dependent on foreign models for their art as she herself is for her critical theory.

As a patriarchal culture, Umuofia certainly suffers from gender contradictions, which Achebe presents as a form of self-violation that, next to the European invader's superior firepower, contributes to its collapse. In its preoccupation with survival, the clan has violated its male–female complementarity principle by alienating those members who are not achievers (metaphorically female in male-defined terms), such as unsuccessful men, women who have given birth to twin or female children only, and the caste of ritual slaves. The arrival of Christianity offers such people a means of transcending their alienation. The conversion of Nwoye, the son despised by Okonkwo, follows and illustrates the pattern. Nwoye was captivated not by the doctrine of the Trinity, which appeared insane to him, but by the 'poetry' of the alien religion (p. 104).

Yet Achebe also portrays Umuofia's collapse as a rite of passage, an end that is also a beginning, by exploiting the gyral dialectic of Yeats's 'Second Coming', with Umuofia as the civilization that has reached the point of maximum expansion. An explanation for the specific situation is provided by Obierika's adaptation of Yeats's phrase to explain the clan's loss of its will and cohesion (pp. 124–5), the parable of the bird Nza's challenge to his *chi*, and the hunt imagery of the hunter's dog that unaccountably attacks its owner (p. 118). This archetype of the disintegrating centre is employed in an all-encompassing way that transforms it into a symbol of self-violation in a broad range of decolonization novels. The historical theme is not that colonialism forced change upon a static culture, for in *Things Fall Apart* even a sacrosanct ritual observance like the Week of Peace dedicated to the Earth has also undergone modification, while in Soyinka's and the Maori novels the primal disintegration is also an act of creation. Colonialism transformed a normal process into an apocalypse, hence the appearance of the first colonizer in *Things Fall Apart* evokes the Beast of the apocalypse, a spectre with abnormal skin colour 'riding an iron horse' and identified by the oracle as a harbinger of a pestilential visitation by others of his kind (pp. 97–8).

In action constructed on the model of classical Greek tragedy, the attempt to thwart the prophecy by killing the apparition ensures its grim fulfilment; the clan is exterminated by the white man and colonialism begins its pestilential spread. When a local convert desecrates an ancestral spirit in Umuofia, it is the Mother of Spirits' lament here (p. 132), rather than Okonkwo's suicide later, that marks the passing away of the old dispensation, and the occasion of Okonkwo's death merely confirms this by the District Commissioner's wresting of the narrative from the unnamed raconteur who has hitherto told the story of Umuofia. Umuofia elders' preparation to offer 'sacrifices to cleanse the desecrated earth' (p. 147) underscores the survival of the ritual core around which a new order will coalesce.

In *Arrow of God*, the birth of the Umuaro clan is again a statement about the creation of political order in pre-European Africa, and how colonial aggression undermined this order. This novel explores a deliberate process of nation-building in terms that make it a political allegory of Africa's fatal encounter with Europe. Every act in Umuaro's origination is an act of will, as six militarily weak villages threatened with annihilation by a vicious enemy accept symbolic death in order to achieve rebirth as a strong single community. The new community project their aspirations into their self-made founding deity, and, furthering this historic act of self-definition, give a name to themselves. This death-and-rebirth is what they have instituted into an annual ceremony of self-reconsecration enacted during the harvest festival of the New Yam.

Emphasis in *Arrow of God* is not on war, however, but on intellectual mastery of the universe, and the major internal conflict is between a majority that places its faith in physical pre-eminence and the chief priest who seeks intellectual mastery of history. Violent rivalries generated by the circumstances of their federation deprive Umuaro of the benefits of the priest's great intellect in their struggles against British colonialism, while disposing the priest to pursue a dangerous experiment to clarify the ambiguities of his office. Beneath the surface is a struggle between spiritual and secular interests in the evolution of a polity. Ezeulu's antagonists' repeated accusation that he wants to unite the offices of priest and king has some justification which is, however, undercut by the fact that the priestly office was specifically created to counter a military-political threat and perform civil services like the conduct of an annual census. British intervention imposes an external resolution on the conflict.

Umuaro's fate thus becomes paradigmatic of that of every other colonized people. However, the solution is also consistent with the conception of the overall conflict in spiritual/intellectual terms, as the British colonial government's abandonment of its contentious programme of imposing its lackeys as chiefs over formerly self-governing polities now sets the scene for the spiritual dimension of the struggle to be determined. This further clarifies the nature of the theme Achebe has been developing, for this conflict actually pits the European sky god against his Umuaro counterpart, the sky god Idemili, rather than the man-made earth deity Ulu. This explains why all critical events of cosmic proportions are marked with the myth and rituals of Idemili whose emanation is the royal python: from the consecration of Ulu to Umuaro's various struggles and, finally, the collapse of the universe that had been consecrated 'when lizards were in ones and twos'.

For a novelist like Ayi Kwei Armah who has learnt from history to be suspicious of colonizer cultures, progress can only mean a reversal of those relationships that have historically subordinated Africa to Europeans and Arabs, the two being identified as branches of the white race in Armah's history. Armah's novels have therefore moved from the pessimism of *The Beautyful Ones Are Not Yet Born* to the idealism of *The Healers* and *Two Thousand Seasons*. This ideological shift is paralleled by the emphatically diasporic perspectives of the last two novels which encompass the black race's historical experience all over the earth. Always conscious of the immense potential of continental Africa, with a population that matches that of the West, Armah sees Africa's subjugation by the white world as consequence of apostatic self-fragmentation.

The Healers explores the overthrow of the Ashanti kingdom in what is now the West African country of Ghana by imperial Britain between 1873 and 1874. Armah attributes the collapse to a moral rot bred by the emergence of kingship, which Armah views as a violation of Africa's communalist and democratic spirit, and hence the emergence of this institution is treated as a symbolic descent into hell, and Armah subordinates the historical events to the movements of myth. Through seven parts of six chapters each, the story unfolds through the clear, uncomplicated outlines of historical narrative to work out the consequences of the people's betrayal of their own 'rituals of remembrance': 'festivals made for keeping a people together' to ensure their survival 'in spite of unbearable pain' (p. 4). The festival games now celebrate individual excellence, producing 'a single winner riding over a multitude of losers' (p. 7). Kingship as the apotheosis of parasitic individualism finds its most devastating demonstration during the final British onslaught, when the crafty courtier Ababio schemes to gain kingly power by betraying the kingdom to the British.

As antetypes of the venal leadership that will pimp for neocolonialism in the post-independence era, characters like Ababio in this novel and Koranche and Kamuzu in *Two Thousand Seasons* are apocalyptic beasts in the primary sense of Yeats's 'Second Coming' and the dialectical sense of Eliot's 'Journey of the Magi'. But other eschatological omens are pressed into service to transform the historical event into a conflict between life and death, creation and destruction, harmony and dissolution, cosmos and chaos (e.g., pp. 245–51). Ababio's treacherous overture to Densu, introduced with the solemn observation that 'the king is old', occurs in physical and emotional surroundings that presage a kind of death: a room weakly illuminated by a single lamp whose 'fretful flame' seemed to spring from oil adulterated with water (p. 28).

In the dénouement, the reader finally discovers the reason for Armah's subordination of history to myth, as the dance of death which opens the novel is now morphed into 'The New Dance' in the racial cradle of the last chapter. Armah's diasporic perspectives of history are clearest here, as is his idealism, for the light of dawn becomes for Ebibirman and the diaspora a light of knowledge, dispelling the darkness of ignorance on which the novel opens and the darkness of death which is the colonial army and its local collaborators. As all dance to the music of West Indians producing joyful music from the enemy's 'instruments of the music of death' (*Healers* pp. 308–9), the initial fretful flame is transmogrified into a Pentecostal symbol: a plurality of people speaking a motley of tongues but who understand one another and enjoy perfect harmony from a rediscovery of their common origins and destiny. The transformation of a potential Babel into a racial symphony against the designs of the alien enemy is the supreme irony which reveals Armah's vision. Ebibirman dies and is reborn through rediscovering its origins.

Ends, Beginnings and Biculturalism

The end that is also the beginning as well as a progression into the future features in Maori affirmation novels sometimes in terms of the reclamation of a prodigal as in Ihimaera's *Tangi* and Grace's *Mutuwhenua* and sometimes as a discovery of a new strength to cope with the present through renewed awareness of the past, as in Ihimaera's *Whanau* and Grace's *Potiki*. Linda the heroine of *Mutuwhenua* and Tama the hero of *Tangi* seek personal fulfilment out of a culture they consider stultifying, but the novelists use their discontent to explore the broader social problems of colonial relationships. The novelists are working from a realization that a member of a submerged culture cannot attain any genuine self-fulfilment that is denied to the culture itself, hence the central character's life becomes a growth towards an affirmation of Maori culture.

Through the subject matter of cross-racial marriage, Patricia Grace's metaphor for Maori–Pakeha biculturalism, *Mutuwhenua* explores an issue which, though of particular application to New Zealand, has a wider relevance to ongoing global debates about multi-culturalism. The marriage metaphor points to the novelist's view that New Zealand biculturalism must be based on cultural equality, hence the need for the Maori to relate to the Pakeha from a position of strength. The heroine Linda is tenderly conceived as a naïve Maori girl who will eventually overcome her enthralment to the Pakeha world and embrace her people's own. Patricia Grace has recently commented that, though some Maori and Pakeha can communicate effectively, sometimes the Pakeha expect the Maori to make all the sacrifice to bridge the gap between them.[7] In the novel, the Maori world symbolically exacts the required concessions from the Pakeha society.

Yearning to escape into the Pakeha world she considers more ful-filling, Linda transforms the event of entering a new school into a rite of passage by which she will be born into a new identity by shedding her Maori name Ngaio and her bicultural name Ripeka to assume the Pakeha name of Linda (*Mutuwhenua* p. 24). Unknown to her, Linda already contains both worlds in herself through her second name Ripeka, Maori for Rebecca, hence her attempts at a crossover is a form of self-mutilation. Maori novelists frequently use name symbolism to denote their people's dual-cultural reality, in-cluding the attendant dilemma. Often, elderly people call a char-acter by a Maorified version of a Pakeha name while the younger generation use the Pakeha original, as in Anaru/Andrew Whatu in Ihimaera's *Whanau*; or for an elder person to bear the Maorified ver-sion while an offspring bears the Pakeha original, as in Hemi and his son James in Grace's *Potiki*. But Linda's action additionally illumi-nates the psychological mutilation inflicted by economic and polit-ical disempowerment, the source of Maori youth's discontent with their culture and consequent hankering after Pakeha lifestyles. In this vicious cycle, self-devaluation such as Linda's merely results in further negation by the Pakeha. The implication is that Maoris can fight for equal opportunities only from a strong position as Maoris.

Consequently, Linda's proposed cross-racial marriage to the Pakeha Graeme does not receive her family's blessing until Nanny Ripeka is satisfied that she has emotional and intellectual commitment to Maori values (pp. 96, 101, 112). Nevertheless, the marriage plunges Linda into a psychological nightmare in which bizarre sensations of violent motion symbolize her loss of anchorage, as soon as she and Graeme arrive in the Pakeha city (pp. 115–27). Though her experience is eventually traced to the location of their house on an ancient Maori burial ground, thematically it is a dissolution of the absurd identity she has assumed. Rebirth or salvation comes only through the agency of her mother, in the form of an owl that leads her to the seashore, making her rebirth a deeper immersion in Maoritanga and her marriage to Graeme a more positive construction of biculturalism. Their first child is named after Linda's grandfather (who dies just as the child is born) and given to Linda's mother to wean.

Linda's success is also Patricia Grace's tribute to the enlightened sector of the Pakeha population, represented by Graeme, who share this vision of biculturalism as Maori–Pakeha equality. Albert Wendt's *Ola* suggests that such understanding is frequently absent in cross-racial relationships, and several strands of the plot explore the crises of marriages that are terminated by Pakeha husbands as soon as they discover that the wife with whom they have lived for years has Maori blood. *Mutuwhenua* is an anti-racist, not an anti-Pakeha novel, and the ideal of racial harmony is affirmed in the tree symbolism of the opening pages. Of the three trees represented, the *ti kouka* (cabbage tree, *Cordyline australis*), which was planted in Linda's father's childhood, and the *ngaio* (*Myoporum laetum*), which was planted at Linda's birth and gave its name to Linda, are indigenous trees with Maori names and cultural significance. Conversely, the Macrocarpa (*Cypressus macrocarpa*) was imported from California by the Pakeha to form a windbreak around their homes in the early days of their settlement, and its inhospitable 'tangle of dead twigs' now represents unreconstructed Eurocentrism in their view of biculturalism or integration.[8] Linda's addition of a *ti kouka* for her son therefore constitutes a statement of Maori continuity within a Maori–Pakeha society.

Like *Mutuwhenua, Tangi* is remarkable for its muted politics which leaves its social commentary to be inferred from the protagonist's remembrances and the Maori world recreated at the funeral ceremony. This protagonist, Tama, left his Maori village of Waituhi in pursuit of 'the bright lights of Wellington' four years before the story opens (p. 159), and, until compelled by his father's death, defies all family pleas to return home. This makes his resolve to return permanently to Waituhi a political statement, a physical journey that is also a psychological reconciliation with his Maori heritage and a growth into his social responsibilities as a Maori in Pakeha-dominated

New Zealand. The keynote of an end that is also a beginning is struck in the opening scene, with Tama at the Gisborne railway station at the start of his homeward journey. There is a counterpointing of an image of a little boy who is embarrassed after kissing his mother with the image of Tama who has now accepted his adult responsibility. Any temptation to read this ritual motif as a Freudian death wish or longing for the womb is decisively squelched by invoking the myth of Maui's strangulation while entering the womb of Hine-nui-te-Po (Hine of the Long Night) through her vagina (p. 104), with Tama's arrival being marked by Hine's transformation into Hine-the-Dawn-Maiden (pp. 201–2). This is the same myth employed to make a similar statement in Wendt's *Sons for the Return Home*.

Corballis and Garrett have rightly interpreted Tama's experience as that of 'one representative Maori family making its way in a world more and more dominated by the materialistic values of the Pakeha'.[9] It should be stressed, though, that the conflict in this and other Maori decolonization novels is not between Pakeha 'materialistic values' and Maori spirituality. Maoris want their full share of opportunities and the material resources of their country. As Mark Williams has argued, 'they are concerned with money and appearances' and the products of modern technology. But all these have been integrated into existing value systems 'which do not coincide with those of the ruling culture' but serve to reinforce family unity.[10]

Ihimaera uses Tama's school experience for some sociological commentary. The taunts of 'Maori boy!' at school, the budding cross-racial friendship that is abruptly terminated by Pakeha parents (p. 77), the loneliness of being the only Maori in a class (p. 78), and the general contrast between Maori school children's poverty and the obvious affluence of their Pakeha mates are among the pressures to which a Maori child is subjected. These have their parallels in Grace's *Cousins*. Such pressures generate their own vicious cycle, such as the high dropout rate of Maori schoolchildren which further impedes their development of skills necessary for improved competitiveness. Alternatively, Tama's recollection of life with his family highlights the general hardship but also the strength of Maoritanga, the totality of Maori cultural values, which has sustained the race through centuries of oppression. The tangi or funeral ceremony itself celebrates this rich but threatened heritage, and Tama's participation in it becomes a rediscovery, a reconciliation and a growth. The young boy of Chapter 1 now emerges as a man in his community.

Enclosing the experience within the myth of Rangitane and Papatuanuku, the Maori first parents whose painful ordeal of separation
was also a release into the world of light for their children, symbolizes
the latency of life in death. Ihimaera objectifies this meaning in the
restoration of Napier town from the rubbles of a 1931 earthquake,
which Tama takes as a symbol of his own life (p. 108). Thus *Tangi*, a
novel about death and the meaning of death for a people whose
world is threatened with dissolution in a conqueror's world, also
becomes an affirmation of life and the love or aroha which expresses
itself in 'to manawa, e taku manawa' or 'your heart is my heart'.
Writing it was, in Ihimaera's own words, 'my way of responding to
the charge, "you must work for the Maori people" ', an 'endeavour
to convey an emotional landscape for the Maori people . . . across the
wastelands where we now live'.[11] Pointing out that 'until the 1960s
the major writers of imaginative fiction on Maori people were
Pakeha',[12] Ihimaera had to make this 'novel by a Maori', by 'the first
Maori novelist', a thoroughgoing Maori creation.

Sociological and economic details that are merely implied in *Tangi*
are brought to the fore in *Whanau*, at the heart of which lies the concept of 'family' and its sustaining ethos of 'aroha'. The title of the
novel literally means 'family', not just the nuclear or the extended
family but also the Maori nation who seized destiny in their own
hands when they broke through the imprisoning embrace of Rangitane and Papatuanuku to thrust themselves into the world of light.
Ihimaera identifies the threat to the Maori family institution as the
most potent threat to Maori survival, and traces this threat to two
sources: racially motivated uneven development, and government
attempts to legislate the family structure out of existence (p. 69),
ostensibly to speed up biculturalism, which to the Pakeha means
'integration of the Maori into the European way of life' through
'more movement of Maori from the lower classes into the middle
class bracket' (p. 35). The wealth of the Pakeha city exerts a siren lure
on Maori youth, many of whom become broken by racial discrim-
ination and thwarted ambitions, and this further undermines the
family institution.

Ihimaera uses the experiences of several Maori families to evalu-
ate and comment on this process. The family of Pita and Mariama
Mahana illustrates the vicissitudes of increasing economic pressures,
declining farm productivity and escalating expectations of the youth
(pp. 20 and 81); but it also demonstrates the couple's unflagging
courage, industry and dignity derived from the Mahanas' faith in

the whanau spirit: 'the eldest look after the young ones, but when they are old, it is the young who must look after them' (p. 22). In the middle-class Walker family, Hepa Walker's attempts to consolidate his toe-hold in Pakeha society put his children under enormous pressure to distinguish themselves, and also alienate him from the Maori community (pp. 34–7, 91–2). He has surrounded himself with the material trappings of Pakeha middle-class life, 'but they had given only a semblance of middle-class standards. Actually attaining the attitudes that went with them was much harder' (p. 36). Conversely, the economically less successful Jacksons lead a dignified life and hold the guardianship of the Kaumatua, Nanny Paora, whose destined successor is the family's precocious youngest son, Pene.

Ihimaera's exploration of the family follows the pattern found in many other decolonization novels from societies where the family is also an economic institution which prevents society's polarization into antagonistic classes. Wealthy family members (or, frequently, the family pooling its resources together) provide many of the amenities provided by governments in the affluent West under various welfare and social security programmes. In Achebe's *No Longer at Ease*, for example, the clan sponsors academically gifted members on university studies overseas, and in Albert Wendt's novels the aiga serves analogous functions. In *Whanau*, the family provides solace and emotional healing for youth defeated by the Pakeha world, such as Andrew/Anaru Whatu whose budding romance with a Pakeha girl faces stiff opposition from her parents (pp. 54–5). It also makes life meaningful for the bigger losers who have no foothold in either world, such as the 'no-hoper' Sam Walker who has crumbled under his father Hepa's pressure, Mattie Jones burdened with an illegitimate child and a deceptive lover, and Jack Ropiho who lacks the personal discipline to succeed anywhere. This makes the family institution the last bastion of organized resistance to neocolonialism.

Umelo Ojinmah has undoubtedly misread the functions of characters like Hepa Walker, Pene Jackson and Andrew Whatu in Ihimaera's critique of Pakeha social theories and attitudes. Such characters do not 'fit into both worlds without being strangers in either' as Ojinmah argues, and Hepa Walker's negative role goes beyond viewing racial integration solely in terms of 'enhancing [his own] prestige'.[13] Ihimaera casts Pene in the symbolic role of successor to the Kaumatua, Andrew Whatu as a victim of racism, and Hepa Walker as a creation of Pakeha tokenism. In his love of the Pakeha girl, Josephine, Andrew is thwarted by the 'strange world ... outside the village. A

European world', (p. 66); 'he is caught in between, a Maori forcing himself against the values of a Pakeha world' (p. 67). Hepa Walker has succumbed to the reality-distorting economic theory which portrays Maori lack of upward mobility and Maori poverty as cause and effect rather than as a single phenomenon produced by racial marginalization. Having risen to the position of Lieutenant in the Maori Battalion during World War II and earned social eminence in postwar Maori society, he has been adopted by the Pakeha for his propaganda value and as a salve for their guilty conscience:

> [The Pakeha] had tolerated him, he was quite a fine chap really, and anyway they needed a Maori to sit with them at their opening ceremonies... and to appear with them in the social pages of the local newspaper. Yes indeed, one had to remember to include a Maori on any guest list, for the Maoris were important to the community weren't they? And wouldn't they be proud to see how well they were becoming integrated?
>
> And so Hepa had found himself being groomed to fulfil a particular social role. (*Whanau* p. 35)

Ihimaera certainly believes in the values of modern education and a socially effective Maori middle class. But he also suggests that such ideals stand little chance under present social institutions with their built-in mechanisms to undermine the cultural strength from which the Maori could compete. Maoris must therefore revitalize their own cultural values, and draw strength from them. Appropriately, from Chapter 13 the search for solutions takes the action into the symbolic past/future, signalled by the Kaumatua's walk to Rongopai, and later a race between ageing Charlie Whatu and his son Andrew/Anaru, a symbolic race between old/past and new/present. Andrew wins, but yields honour to his father.

The crisis is provoked when pakehafied Rosie's plot to secretly send Nanny Paora to a Pakeha-run old people's home prompts Pene to flee with the Kaumatua to Rongopai, the ancestral meeting house. The search for the runaways temporarily revives the whanau spirit (p. 171), but the discovery of the pair also reiterates the imperatives of the bicultural, biracial present, for young Pene's attempt to warm the old man merely gives him the old man's cold instead (p. 163). An even stronger statement for biculturalism is inscribed in the interior mural decorations which blend the Maori and the Pakeha worlds (p. 124).

In *Potiki*, Patricia Grace extensively develops the theme of economic aggression in the conflict between the Tamihana family who inhabit a beautiful seaside village, and a Pakeha consortium of estate developers who covet this desirable property. Without repudiating the ideal of racial harmony, the novel uncompromisingly asserts Maoris' unique identity and their rights to restitution for the dispossession they have suffered. This is manifested most strongly during their negotiations with Mr Dolman, the consortium's representative (pp. 88–95), as well as in the related experience of Te Ope people (pp. 71–84). Against the consortium's genocidal campaigns – including arson, terrorist bombing and various attempts to flood them out – the Tamihanas tenaciously hold onto their land. Threat of extinction revives the family spirit and strengthens resistance, with crucial support coming from the Te Ope community who have survived similar aggression. Patricia Grace emphatically develops the conflict as paradigmatic of Maori–Pakeha relationships since the Pakeha invasion, and deploys the Polynesian myth of Maui to organize the resistance. This is the meaning Roimata derives from the 'stories' of the different members of the family, the central significance of her assertion that 'all time is a now-time, centred in the being', which reaches out in other directions 'named "past" and "future" only for our convenience' (p. 39).

This pattern is subtly incorporated in the novel's structure: a Prologue and three main parts. The Prologue strikes the central theme of creation as a continuous process to which each succeeding generation must contribute its creative energies. A master carver commissioned to carve a communal meeting house and include in it all their famous ancestors, symbolizing the link between humanity, the earth and the heavens from the ancestral past to the future, had left one pillar to be completed by a future carver, a symbolization of the need for a leader of a new politics of self-reinvigoration. Entrusting this responsibility first on Hemi and then on Hemi's son James eloquently ratifies the continuity of 'creation' as well as the central motif of interdependence: between past, present and future, the old and the young. The economic hardship which sends Hemi home (Chapter 10) is a bit of historical realism and an artistic strategy for equipping the Tamihanas for the ordeal.

At the immediate level, the title *Potiki* refers to Tokowaru-i-te-Marama, the Maui-like 'potiki' or 'youngest', but it also refers to James, for in the line of craftsmen-creators he is currently the youngest, the 'potiki'. Evidence in the novel suggests that the concept of 'potiki' refers both to the youngest member of a nuclear family and to an heir in a line of succession. In the Prologue the master carver-creator has no son of his own, hence his apprentice becomes his 'potiki', and this is the chain of continuity along which Hemi takes his place, to be followed eventually by his son James. In the novel's political idiom, 'potiki' also refers to a generation that is succeeding another – in this case, the vigorous new Maori generation emerging from the ruins of the past to lead Maori resistance to their 'broken-ness, a broken race ... decrepit, deranged, deformed' (p. 102). The alternative to resistance, the novel suggests, is annihilation.

MODERNIZATION AND THE PERILS OF WESTERNIZATION

It is customary in Western discourse to define as 'westernization' any social transformation that entails some economic and technolo-gical advance, the assumption being that the West's advantages in these areas make them uniquely Western, though the West never regards its own progress as 'orientalization' despite owing the foundation of its civilization to the Orient. To most decolonization writers, however, progress and modernization are integral aspects of their societies' historical dynamics which colonialism arrested and mutilated. Textile and metal-working industries in Africa, for in-stance, were undermined to create markets for home factories. Local liquors and salt production were outlawed outright in many colonial territories.

In the novels of Flora Nwapa and Ngugi wa Thiong'o, alcohol production is presented both in terms of hospitality rituals as well as dimensions of technological and economic resistance. In the novels of Ngugi, Grace, Ihimaera and Wendt, the desire for comforts of-fered by technology is presented as part of cultural progression rather than westernization. By contrast, 'westernization' is employed in the sense of development of antisocial, neurotic tendencies or predatory competitiveness, as in Armah's *The Healers*, Ngugi's *Mati-gari* and Wendt's *Leaves of the Banyan Tree*. A notable exception is V.S. Naipaul whose self-perception as assimilated native denies the validity of indigenous civilizations. Nevertheless, even Naipaul con-ceives his writing as a contribution to West Indians' need for cultural self-clarification, hence a form of decolonization agonistic. 'Living in a borrowed culture', he once wrote, 'the West Indian ... needs writers to tell him who he is and where he stands.'[14]

In *A House for Mr Biswas*, Naipaul portrays the collapse of the Hindu world of the Tulsi family as a form of cultural conflict and overthrow analogous to the situation in Achebe's *Things Fall Apart*. Michael Neill has observed that *Biswas* reveals 'one facet of the colonial experience' which is peculiarly West Indian: 'the anxiety of displacement, with the attendant sense of missing the real world'.[15] Biswas's struggle to escape from Trinidad Hindu culture is in fact a fictionalized rendering of Naipaul's own flight to Europe, and Andrew Gurr has identified a eurotropic pattern of movement which constantly takes this absurd antihero ever 'westwards' to a centre of European culture.[16] There is little support for Ngugi's Marxist description of Biswas as a 'peasant' hero.[17] Biswas is a barely articulate rebel, and his impulse to revolt is repeatedly matched by an instinct for imitation of the Tulsis whom he claims to despise. His quest for westernization, symbolized in the desire for a house for his nuclear family outside Tulsi communalism, constantly collides with the absurdist tenor of Naipaul's narrative, with its cynical vacillation between endorsement of Biswas's rebellion and ridicule of his ambition, between rejecting the Tulsi order and questioning the claims of the European world. A hostile universe mocks Biswas's best efforts and unrelentingly reclaims into void each house he builds, reclaiming the one in Greenvale through a deluge and the one near Shorthills by fire, until he adopts absurdist role-playing and clowning as an antidote to his anguished sense of littleness, impotence and inconsequence. Gordon Rohlehr errs in blaming this role-playing on what he calls the Tulsis' mind-enslaving strategies.[18] It is Biswas's self-therapy.

Given the absurdity and grotesquery, Mr Biswas's ultimate success is ambiguous, an exchange of the 'alien white fortress' of Hanuman House (p. 80) for an unsafe and uncomfortable 'squat sentry box' (pp. 8–9) which turns out to be the worst of available bargains. Even this reversal is contained within a larger ironic process, for the eurotropic search for pools of light/whiteness merely takes him from the sepulchral gloom and darkness of houses he has lived in throughout his past life to this 'sentry box' that is rendered uninhabitable by excessive sunlight during the day (p. 572) – effectively sentencing him to nocturnal life. 'Irretrievably mortgaged', the house becomes a potentially tragic legacy to his children, which Naipaul highlights through comparison with the heroine's calamity in Guy de Maupassant's short story 'The Necklace' (pp. 564–5), and this is reinforced by the funereal imagery of 'his own half-lot of land, his

own portion of the earth' (pp. 8 and 14). This deletes the few positive aspects of the acquisition, such as the new relationship that
develops between Biswas and his wife Shama, and the revelation
that in death he has left a void which lends him posthumous significance after living most of his life 'unnecessary and unaccommod-
ated' (p. 14).

In treating Hanuman House or Tulsidom itself, Naipaul obviously
cannot appreciate the implications of portraying it as doomed from
its origins, or of denying it any authentic framework of values by
which the members' performance should be evaluated. As in his
treatment of Biswas's quest, Naipaul is not really exploring the Tulsis'
predicament as a historical phenomenon but merely using it to demonstrate his thesis that the West Indies is trapped in an eternal futility. The characters are mere puppets programmed to go through
certain motions before the curtain falls, a fact which makes *A House
for Mr Biswas* a naturalistic novel in the European tradition rather
than a genuine decolonization novel. What unfolds in the novel is
not the destruction of a society in a colonial conflict but the rigor
mortis of an organism from which the historically naïve novelist has
withheld the vitality for survival.

Everything about the Tulsis, from the house to its inhabitants, is
accordingly conceived as a parody of the real, and in Naipaul's
terms the real is Europe. The fortress aspect of the house suggests
retreat and vulnerability rather than strength, and within it centri-
petal forces are also building up. Even its name, Hanuman House,
its proclamation of its own identity, is voided through the pun
which literally renders it as 'monkey house', thus stripping it of the
more positive association of the Hindu Monkey-god, Hanuman.
Whereas writers with greater understanding of historical cause and
effect would see adaptability or the perils of transition in the Tulsis'
cultural syncretism (for example, their observance of some Christian
as well as Hindu rituals, and their combination of Western and
Hindu medicine), Naipaul mocks this as mindless and effete compromise, just as he derides their attempt to exploit the resources of
their Shorthills estate as a parody of the more virile exploits of European colonizers. Mrs Tulsis' proprietary tour of her estate accordingly
runs headlong into the Christopher Columbus Road, the ultimate
origins of the Tulsis' predicament. In a novel where history is constantly repeating itself, the Tulsis' Greenvale 'enterprise' re-enacts
the history of the old slave estates while the Shorthills adventure
re-enacts the occupation of decayed slave plantations by liberated

slaves. In the end, Tulsidom collapses into its own void, following the departure of Mrs Tulsis' male heirs either to England or to European-style nuclear families, and an intensification of an anarchic American presence during the Second World War. In the celebrated verse of T.S. Eliot's 'The Hollow Men', this end occurs 'not with a bang but a whimper'.

Naipaul's failure in *A House for Mr Biswas* stands out even more starkly in comparison with Selvon's *A Brighter Sun*, which is also set in Trinidad during the Second World War among a predominantly Hindu community and has the quest for a house as one of its central symbols. Selvon uses the story of Tiger, a 16-years-old Trinidad Indian, to explore the urbanization of a representative Trinidadian rural community, Barataria, during the Second World War. Unrelated to the people's needs, this urbanization responds solely to American needs for military facilities and supporting infrastructure, and quickly initiates the catastrophic development whose culmination is exemplified by the slums explored in *Brother Man*. With the arrival of American military personnel and the hoisting of the American flag over Trinidad in 1941 (p. 17), the deleterious effects of their culture on the moral fabric of the local society begin, and the permanence of these effects is made palpable in the ominously named Churchill-Roosevelt Highway (p. 197).

Tiger's abrupt uprooting from Chaguanas and transplanting in Barataria, following his marriage, subtly re-enacts his ancestors' original severance from India and sets the stage for exploring his search for anchorage in the emerging order. Unlike Naipaul, who laments the emergence of a multiracial West Indies as a degradation of the Aryan culture of Trinidad Indians, Selvon explores it as the formation of a new community which can ameliorate the ravages of westernization. Seeing every assault by the alien force as a personal challenge, Tiger embarks on a self-education mission to conquer the stifling 'unknowingness' which had initially enfolded him (p. 11). He dreams of power that comes from knowledge so that he can anticipate events and preserve, for his future reference and the benefit of posterity, an enduring record of the process of change (pp. 126–8). Tiger's growth therefore involves his 'awakening to the requirements of a multiracial society under neo-colonial domination and of the limitations necessarily caused by his background'.[19]

Racial, communal and personal lessons converge in a series of events that compel Tiger to critically reassess all racial and gender orthodoxies in which he has been brought up. On the one hand, his pregnant wife's illness following a cruel beating from him, and his search for a doctor, brings him into critical contact with a fellow Indian, a Negro and then a white doctor, in that order (pp. 178–87). The experience reveals to him the existence of both good and evil across racial divides, as only the white doctor responds sympathetically to his appeal. Next, his suffering and the stillbirth of the child who turns out to be a boy compel his outgrowing his wrong-headed belief that beating his wife and having 'a boy chile' are necessary adjuncts to manhood. On the other hand, Tiger's journey to Port of Spain exposes him to the inescapable realities of racism in colonial relationships, as he witnesses the unbearable arrogance of white people and the responsive cringing of non-whites.

Though Tiger is only modestly successful, even this qualified success is positively viewed by Selvon. The last two chapters show him sinking new roots – signified by his building a house, that symbolic bulwark against disintegrative forces and testament to his attainment of self-definition, manhood and roots. A house is 'something standing up for years after it was built', as Joe Martin aptly puts it (p. 208). The contrast between this solid house and the ramshackle 'sentry house' with which Naipaul mocks his antihero's efforts in *A House for Mr Biswas* says a lot about the two writers. Tiger's victory is reaffirmed in his rejection of Boysie's invitation to exile: a man with 'a wife and child and house' does not betray such bonds or his social duties to flee into irresponsible self-worship (p. 213).

With the termination of the war corresponding with the completion of Tiger's house, Tiger's personal story is merged again with the destiny of the community which the reign of American chaos has transformed from a slumbering rural outpost to an urban settlement with few urban amenities but with its moral fabric shredded and its gardens destroyed to accommodate roads and army camps. Nevertheless, Selvon's idealism snatches some optimism from this rubble, for first-hand experience of American imperialism has forged in the people a sense of common Trinidadian destiny which identifies imperial America and her military bullies as the 'Other' (e.g., p. 200).

Selvon's nationalistic ideology gives *A Brighter Sun* an optimistic ending confirmed in its clinching image: 'overhead a cloud fled the sun, moving in a swift breeze' (p. 213). In *Brother Man*, Roger Mais completes the social portrait with a close-up view of the traumatic effects of westernization on a rural population of Kingston, Jamaica's capital, during its urbanization in the last phase of colonial rule. Mais's portrait of life in Kingston slums focuses on the psychology of poverty and powerlessness in a transplanted colonial society doomed to a crepuscular existence by the government's inability to provide a welfare safety net and the absence of traditional family structures to fill the vacuum left by the government. Poverty, disease and lack of hope breed an acute insecurity which finds outlet in crime and other forms of negative rebellion. Despite an absence of explicit political commentary, the opening Chorus's portrayal of a society plagued with sudden death on the roads, natural disasters, inflation, drug peddling, currency counterfeiting and domestic violence encourages reading these as products of what the narrator refers to as the people's 'hunger and haltness and lameness and rightness and negation' (pp. 7–9). Between Girlie and Papacita, even the sexual act becomes both a fulfilment of emotional yearnings and an outlet to sadomasochistic impulses (pp. 27–9) of powerless people who can hurt only themselves and those close to them. Similarly, Cordy bewailing her lot, pining for her husband imprisoned for drug trafficking, and terrified of loneliness (pp. 17, 124) manifests the psychic terrors of life lived under the shadow of death.

Focusing his themes on the psychology of poverty and powerlessness enables Mais to offer a glimpse into the crippled polity that is emerging. Such powerlessness and loss of hope breed a messianic longing, for which the people expect fulfilment from the eponymous hero John Power (Bra' Man or Brother Man), the Christ-like Rastafarian. But though endowed with the gift of healing, Bra' Man does not see himself as a messiah and his other-worldly message of 'peace and love' runs counter to the people's desperate need for an amelioration of their material lot. His rejection and 'crucifixion' may therefore be read as a spontaneous discharge of long-repressed frustrations by a people brutalized by their own impotence, enacting on the public stage the drama of pain which Girlie enacts privately in murdering her lover Papacita. Juxtaposing the two scapegoat incidents illuminates each in terms of the other, and Girlie speaks for the crucifying crowd with her lament, just before plunging a clasp-knife in Papacita's unprotected back: 'Life is cruel, cruel, Papa-Joe, better to be dead' (p. 187).

A more comprehensive examination of the political and economic processes involved in the march of westernization is undertaken in Wendt's epic *Leaves of the Banyan Tree*, which deals with the social and moral dislocations attendant upon the emergence of a western-oriented market economy in an agrarian community. Wendt's nationalism does not involve staging an opposition between capitalism and any other socio-economic system, or between Western 'decadence' and Samoan 'innocence', a romantic myth he scorns. At the same time, he recognizes the spuriousness of economic theories which pretend that capitalist economies are governed by a 'free play of market forces', in brazen denial of the role of governments. He therefore emphasizes the hostage status of local producers in their relationship with Western market interests. Sapepe, which is Samoa thinly disguised as well as a typical weak Third World country, is compelled to produce cash crops for the Western market and purchase goods from that same market, all at prices dictated by the West. Such master–slave relationships subject Third World societies to all the moral dislocations associated with the growth of capitalism in the West but without the compensatory benefits, making the emergence of the so-called Third World 'economic man' an unmitigated disaster. Wendt is disturbed by the destruction of those human bonds which were the foundations of the faa Samoa, the Samoan way of life. 'I know that "humanism" is under attack by Rogernomics and some postmodernists', he told Michael Neill during a 1992 interview, 'but I'm afraid free-market forces are not my thing. There's no "level playing field". The game is stacked against the poor and the benighted!'[20]

Leaves of the Banyan Tree opens on an image of Tauilopepe Mauga 'mentally adding up the profits he hoped to make from the copra he was going to sell at Malo's store the next day', while the rest of his family say the evening prayer. The reader soon learns of the bitter rivalry between the middle-man Malo and the farmer Tauilopepe, a rivalry which will later engulf and fragment the community. But dislocation has already begun in Tauilopepe's own family, pitting his enthralment to Western Mammon against his mother's enthralment to Western 'Christianity', and his fanaticism against the lack of conviction shown by his surrogate father and his eldest son Pepesa, who together ineffectually represent the last bastion of the faa Samoa. Tauilopepe's victory is all the more significant because he is so vehemently anti-nationalist that he quits the Legislative Council set up by the New Zealand colonial administration in its version of the charade of last-minute 'democratic reforms' (p. 276).

Employing the same title of 'God, Money, and Success' for Book 1 of the novel in which Tauilopepe achieves his personal triumph and for Tauilopepe's inaugural sermon as a deacon effectively dramatizes the triumph of the new culture of Mammon worship which equates prosperity with righteousness and divine approval. In terms of human relationships, the emerging society bears more than a passing resemblance to Victorian England which equated poverty or uncompetitiveness with criminality. Like the Utilitarian business-man Mr Gradgrind of Charles Dickens's *Hard Times*, who organized his relationships on the principle that 'the good Samaritan was a bad economist', Tauilopepe strives to root Samoan generosity out of Pepe, brutally overriding the boy's protestation that 'everyone in Sapepe does [that]'. 'You're not just everyone,' Tauilopepe insists. 'You work for something. You keep it. That's the new way. That's the way to get ahead' (*LBT* p. 152). His decision that Pepe must acquire 'a good papalagi education' to learn 'what life is all about' (p. 153) under-lines the link between his new morality and the papalagi way of life.

Nevertheless, Wendt does not portray Tauilopepe as totally evil, and there is no longing for a reversal of the transformation which has come through his agency. Galupo, his enigmatic vanquisher, is every bit as ruthless. Wendt's teasing suggestion that Galupo is a product of Tauilopepe's rape of Malo's wife, Moa, makes his victory a form of poetic justice and his career a metaphor for the continua-tion of his 'father's' policies. The triumph of these two agents of apocalypse suggests the novelist's acceptance that progress comes at some cost; yet it also distinguishes between progress for which sacri-fice of some customary practices is acceptable, and westernization with its cult of individual aggrandisement at communal expense. Tauilopepe's and Galupo's careers are accordingly contrasted with the revolt of Pepe and his friend Tagata ('mankind') which, though directed against Tauilopepe's obsessive drive for material success, lacks a clearly articulated goal and is in some ways disturbingly reminiscent of Western absurdist revolt. Rather than use his novella 'Flying Fox in a Freedom Tree' (Book 2 of *Banyan Tree*) to offer *his own* vision of society, Pepe produces a parody-Western whereas Galupo strides in from the same tradition (Book 3) as the menacing 'stranger', the good cowboy come to gun down the bad sheriff. With Galupo as a conscious exponent of the existentialism which is merely intuitive in Pepe, the Galupo section may rightly be seen as mount-ing a satiric critique of the Pepe section.

Wendt's use of the gyre from Yeats's 'The Second Coming' for his model of historical change, elaborated with indigenous Samoan myths and Albert Camus's reworking of the Greek myth of Sisy-phus, further emphasizes the dialectics of progress, acknowledging the absurd in civilization without reducing existence itself to Western-type Absurdism. Pepe's trial for various crimes in Book 2 (the section

'Trial of the Native Son', pp. 194–202) strongly echoes the trial of Meursault, the absurdist antihero of Camus's *L'Etranger*, and, less strongly, that of Bigger Thomas in Richard Wright's *Native Son*, without Pepe becoming either of these protagonists. The extended unravelling of the plot thus begins in Chapters 8 and 9 ('The Cost') of Book 3, where preparations for Samoan independence are counterpointed with Tauilopepe's erection of his church to immortalize himself, and climaxes in the aptly titled Chapter 10 ('The Second Coming') in which Tauilopepe with prophetic irony cues in the apocalypse: 'The old must make way for the new' (p. 310). The old church is promptly reduced to 'only the concrete floor and the twenty steps which now led up to a sky of memories, like a tomb which had been plundered by efficient thieves' (p. 310), a Yeatsian 'Spiritus Mundi' from which emerges the 'rough beast' going to Sapepe to be born again after 'twenty centuries of stony sleep'. But Galupo's hold on 'the power and the glory' is temporary (p. 413).

Galupo also represents a far more articulate manifestation of the Western drive for world domination. Despising conventional morality, the ruthless 'sheriff' figure admires the 'otherness' of the West, and accordingly designates the West as the 'Other-World' and 'Other-Worlders'[21] (first introduced in Chapter 14, 'The Mythology of Night-Wave', of Book 3). In Wendt's *Black Rainbow*, an Orwellian novel set in twenty-first century New Zealand, the triumph of Other-Worlders is complete. However, the movement towards this begins in Wendt's first novel, *Sons for the Return Home*, in which the world of order (as distinct from anarchy) is represented as a series of pebbles in circular orbit around a central pebble, holding anarchy and its attendant horrors at bay. One etymology of Samoa, interestingly, is 'Sa-moa', the sacred centre. In *Pouliuli*, this circle takes its final form of 20 circumferential pebbles around 1 central pebble, used by a mysterious old man to 'exorcise the horror being born out of the world's collective memory' (p. 113).

Pouliuli, Wendt's second novel, explores the disintegration of this centre in terms of a universal collapse of responsibility and rationality, manifested locally in Samoan politics and globally in the First World War. Young Faleasa Osovae, who in later life as an all-powerful political power broker will pollute Samoan political culture with his amorality, violently prevents the mysterious old man (another 'beast of the apocalypse', see Chapter 3 of this book) from completing his thirteenth pebble circle (p. 112) despite the father–son relationship that has grown up between them. Two novels later, in *Ola*, Wendt identifies the 'horror' with yet another European war (the Second World War) and the Holocaust (*Ola* p. 31).

Black Rainbow is a dystopian novel of the New World Order in which a triumphant power bloc identifiable as the West has established a Stalinist global regime and is currently executing a programme of reality-control through a process of 'Dehistorying' – total erasure of memory followed by substitution of false remembrance (pp. 32–3). Officially, Deshistorying is designed to reprogram people into robot-like conformity, a variation on the 'zombification' programme in Erna Brodber's *Myal*. Resistance incurs the penalty of 'reordinarination', the alteration of personal 'preferences' (p. 83). In the immediate context of New Zealand power relationships, these programmes have as their objectives the eradication of Maori nationalism and sense of unique identity as a prelude to their absorption into Pakeha culture. Acceptance of cultural conversion is made a precondition for escaping the grinding, dehumanizing poverty of the majority of Maori people in the novel.

Questor, the central character, is thus not necessarily an individual but a type, a representative prominent Maori equipped with an intellectual alertness and nationalist consciousness to lead a Maori resistance. This protean personage is variously named Patimaori Jones, Supremo Jones, and Eric Mailer Foster. The object of his quest is none other than a recovery of authentic Maori/Polynesian consciousness, though Wendt casts it as a game of 'hunter-and-hunted' designed by the Tribunal, in which the Questor has to earn the enviable status of Free Citizen by searching out his family while eluding his hunters. The central issue in the novel, therefore, is Maori nationalist resistance to what Wendt perceives as a new form of Pakeha racism and oppression in which even academics and other intellectual classes are deeply implicated. But the struggle is not racial, as the 'Tangata Maori' or True Maori have joined hands with the Tangata Moni, the True Ones, 'descendants of ancient Maori rebels and urbanized Polynesians from the islands, and rebel Pakeha' to defend *human* values against the new global Stalinism.

Wendt's critique therefore operates along two tracks which frequently intersect, sometimes converge, but also remain distinguishable. As in many decolonization novels, oppression is most acutely felt as a dominant political group's denial of economic opportunities to a disempowered population; but with the linkage between political and economic dominance, the fact that political power is monopolized by the West (the Pakeha in New Zealand) strikes racial chords that are inevitable. Of the three Tangata Moni who aid the Questor, one, Aeto, is born of a Tangata Maori-Niuean-Samoan-Pakeha-Irish father and a Maori-Tokelauan-Cook Island-German mother. Aeto's early experience of adoption by an elderly Pakeha couple who steal pigeons from a public park, despite their immense wealth, becomes a parable of all-consuming greed that dehumanizes and finally destroys life itself. Like the Proles of Orwell's *Nineteen Eighty-Four*, whose position they occupy in the novel, these under-dog classes have retained their humanity, their personal and racial memories, preferring material deprivation to the literal mindless-ness which purchases the status of Free Citizen. They accordingly constitute sparks of hope in the bleak vision projected by the novel.

COLONIAL WARS AND DECOLONIZATION FICTIONS

Western accounts of colonial conflicts have generally been presented in terms of the 'pacification' of childlike savages by noble-minded European generals. Though physical resistance by the victims of colonialist aggression is acknowledged, the dual need of emphasiz-ing the genius of the imperial army's commander and the altruistic pretensions of the colonial enterprise frequently results in distorted, derisory portrayal of resistance as the instinctive gestures of be-nighted peoples. In the rare case of determined military resistance being acknowledged in colonialist writing, the nationalist fighters are portrayed as terrorists while the ferocious terrorism of colonial regimes is represented as maintenance of order. Many decoloniza-tion writers have therefore felt the need to counter such misrepre-sentations. Chinua Achebe, for example, has expressed some concern over the tendency among 'people who read novels like history books' to interpret the temporally telescoped duration of Igbo resist-ance to Christian missionary advance in *Things Fall Apart* as a measure of the real historical process. In reality, Achebe points out, the mis-sionaries' progression was merely 'seven miles in thirty-five years, that is, one mile every five years'.[22] Erna Brodber in *Myal*, V.S. Reid in *New Day*, Ngugi wa Thiong'o in *The River Between*, *Weep Not, Child* and *A Grain of Wheat*, and Witi Ihimaera in *The Matriarch* have all confronted the issue of (mis)representation of anti-colonialist resist-ance in colonialist texts.

Erna Brodber's concern embraces the history of resistance, the his-toriography that denies such resistance, and the mind-enslaving strategies that the colonizer uses to paralyse the will to revolt. Like Armah's *Why Are We So Blest?* Brodber's *Myal* deals with the colonizer's transformation of colonized peoples into zombies by sucking out all their vitality. This is the phenomenon Brodber calls 'spirit thievery', the plundering of someone else's soul and intellect for the purpose of dehumanizing and enslaving the person with the soulcontent. Brodber's heroine Ella O'Grady will eventually discover the 'principles of spirit thievery': first, 'let [the victims] feel that there is nowhere for them to grow to. Stunt them ... Let them see their brightest ones as the dumbest ever. Alienate them' (p. 98).

Travelling to Baltimore, Maryland, as companion/maid to the rich European lady Mrs Burns, the mixed-race ('black' in American terms) Jamaican heroine Ella is drawn into an affair, then a marriage, with Selwyn Langley, the unpromising son of middle-class American parents. Ella's story of her Jamaican society provides the stimulation and raw material needed by Selwyn's dormant mind to develop some creative vision. Selwyn repackages Ella's story as tourist theatre under the title of 'Caribbean Nights and Days', a gaudy paste-up of racial clichés featuring the Hollywood staple of rape-minded, cartoon-black characters and would-be ravishers chasing a blonde maiden (pp. 83–4) in what is ultimately a thinly disguised Caliban–Miranda motif. Ella's complaint sums up the plunder: 'He took everything I had away. Made what he wanted of it and gave me back nothing' (p. 84).

Brodber's novel suggests that absence of resistance to oppression and dispossession is a reliable sign that the victims' self-esteem has been destroyed through denigration and spirit thievery or zombification. Ella's experience with Selwyn Langley, which Brodber presents at a mystical level, is therefore illustrated allegorically with the story of an abortive rebellion of farm animals – written by Selwyn. In this remarkably Naipaul-like view of decolonization, the collapse of the animals' week-long rebellion argues a thesis that bondage is their true destiny (*Myal* pp. 96–104). Standardizing such texts in colonial schools has been among colonizers' most effective strategies for getting the colonial subject to collude in their own subjugation, hence the nationalist and history-wise Ella refuses to teach the pernicious story to her class of seven-year-old children, and insists on reinterpreting it to expose and subvert its spirit-thieving thesis. The character Mr. Dan links spirit thievery and the colonialist literature to the strategies of colonialism:

My people have been separated from themselves...by several means, one of them being the printed word and the ideas it carries...[Now] we have people who can and are willing to correct images from the inside, destroy what should be destroyed, replace it with what it should be replaced and put us back together, give us back ourselves with which to chart our course to go where we want to go. (*Myal* pp. 109–10)

Brodber's exploration of this phenomenon constitutes an effective answer to O. Mannoni's postulate about a so-called dependency complex which disposes enslaved people to relish their enslavement as a form of security. In Mannoni's confused reading of *The Tempest*, 'Caliban does not complain of being exploited; he complains rather of being betrayed' by the ruthless dispossessor and enslaver on whose protection he has purportedly come to depend.[23] Ella's contempt for such enslaving propaganda is a necessary first step in countering the brainwashing. Many decolonization novelists recognize mind-contamination as a potent tool of enslavement, but Erna Brodber is one of the few to represent it as a clearly formulated doctrine of zombification by 'separation and insertion' (p. 108), and the concept of 'spirit thievery' is an important contribution to the study of the strategies of imperialism. The 'separation and insertion' process is a particularly imaginative adaptation of the biblical story in which a man from whom a demon has been expelled is soon repossessed by the same demon and a reinforcement of 'seven other spirits more evil than itself' (Luke 11: 14–26; Matthew 12: 43–5). In Brodber's adaptation, however, it is the positive features that are fraudulently separated from the victim and replaced with the debased and destructive.

In V.S. Reid's *New Day*, Ngugi wa Thiong'o's trilogy and Ihimaera's *The Matriarch*, self-redemption involves actual military struggles which explode the colonialist myth denying the colonized people's active challenge to colonialism. Reid in his Author's Note describes the novel as 'a tale that will offer as true an impression as fiction can of the way by which Jamaica and its people came to today'. The novel celebrates Jamaica's long struggle against brutal and remorseless colonial exploitation, from the Morant Bay rebellion of 1865 to the eve of self-rule in 1944. A combination of the sheer barbarity of colonial exploitation with a succession of natural calamities provokes the colonized into challenging the entrenched position of their dispossessors. Though the rebellion is bloodily crushed, the spirit of resistance is never suppressed, as Davie's escape in Part II (1865–82) to Morant Cay/Salt Savannah Cay with his young brother Johnny and Lucille Dubois keeps the flame of rebellion alive. The symbolic progression from night to day is structurally reiterated by enclosing the struggle between 'The Evening' of the first prologue and 'The Morning' of the epilogue, so that the unfolding historical nightmare corresponds to the long night of dissolution and self-regeneration. Here, Reid paints a picture which is standard in all decolonization wars.

In a pattern that would ultimately become widespread in decolonization literature, the resistance is cast in biblical language and imagery. The Campbell lineage from the 'patriarch' Pa John to the messianic Garth is transparently conceived as a parallel to the biblical messianic line from Abraham to Jesus Christ. Though Davie's pioneering ardour, in the bid to transform the place of refuge into a 'Zion', degrades his Zion into an emotional desert, the point is nevertheless made that the people are entirely capable of ordering their own lives. James Creary Campbell, who succeeds Davie, is portrayed as a visionary and competent administrator who, as soon as practicable, introduces a cash economy while his own successor, Garth, introduces trade unionism and collective bargaining even as he leads a political agitation for self-determination.

The celebratory spirit of Reid's novel leaves little room for extended critical analysis of socio-historical forces, but Reid charges his imagery with some of the task of commenting on the development of the struggle. Within the controlling exodus trope, images of movement serve to reveal and critique every phase of the unfolding process. In Part I, the conflict between the conservatism of the Bible-enslaved older generation of the patriarchal Pa John Campbell and the radical spirit represented by Davie is reflected in the imagery which associates Pa John with slow, ponderous walking and Davie with frenzied movement. Part II, being a pause, reveals no significant image of movement despite Davie's monomaniacal drive for prosperity. And Part III is defined by the vigorous images of the racing horse and the locomotive engine. Pa John's faith in a divine scheme for the universe cannot comprehend Aaron Dacre's haste expressed in racing horse imagery (p. 33), and it is as a pilgrim that he leads his family out of Salt Savannah to escape Governor Eyre's savage fury (Chapter 32) and later leads the remnant to sacrificial death (Chapters 33 and 34). From hindsight, the reader can later interpret the failure of the 1865 rebellion in terms of the racing horse being guided by inexperienced hands (p. 33). Conversely, in Zion 'the engine stands quiet in the yard without ever moving' and the fires 'are banked' (p. 253). Finally, in the era of constitutional struggles, Johnny Campbell must ensure that the fires are not banked and yet the locomotive is not driven at reckless speed (pp. 253–4). This principle of conducting the liberation struggle through ways and means that are appropriate to the historical moment is later elaborated further in Ngugi wa Thiong'o's trilogy.

Ngugi deals with Kenyan resistance across the entire colonial period, from the era of creeping colonization for which European Christian missionaries served as the advance guard, to the prosecution of the Mau Mau nationalist war which broke out in 1952. One of Ngugi's major triumphs in these novels is his ability to locate these events simultaneously in Kenyan cosmogony and history, in a manner similar to Maori cultural nationalistic writing. The whole of Kenyan history from the onset of colonialist aggression to the decolonization wars is related to the prophecy of the mythical Gikuyu seer Mugo wa Kibiro while the experience of the biblical Jews forms a second level of elaboration. *The River Between*, written before though published after *Weep Not, Child*, shows the role of the colonial church in implementing 'spirit thievery' to paralyse the will for self-assertion.

As in *Things Fall Apart* and *Arrow of God*, Gikuyu nationalism in *The River Between* has to contend with the activities of both the foreign enemy and the Gikuyu converts to the foreign religion. Even more insidious is the effect of colonial education on the consciousness of Waiyaki, the would-be messiah. Waiyaki becomes enmeshed in the paradoxical consequence of Mugo's injunction that the messiah should expel the usurper with the latter's own weapons, which at this stage of Kenyan self-assertion is literacy and formal education. In sending him to 'the Mission place', his father Chege faces the same dilemma as Ezeulu's under similar circumstances in *Arrow of God*, and Waiyaki's quandary is a replication of that of Ezeulu's son, Oduche. Their problem, Gerald Moore has explained, is that 'the white man's alleged "wisdom" is not some detachable commodity' but 'part and parcel of a certain view of the world, a certain scale of values, which tend subtly to adhere to that wisdom, like burrs on a golden fleece'.[24] Waiyaki's mission begins as part of the Gikuyu counter to Christian missionaries' religious imperialism, but the missionaries' 'spirit thievery' beclouds his judgement and alienates him from 'those things that mattered to the tribe' (*RB* p. 39). A compounding of this alienation with the clan's polarization between the

nationalists of Kameno and converts of Makuyu, and bitter antagon-
ism from ambitious Kabonyi, blunts the edge of nationalist resistance,
as Waiyaki concludes that his most pressing task is reconciliation of
these factions.

Ngugi's exploration of the problems in *The River Between* is not
entirely successful, largely as a result of his attempt to reconcile
European-Christian and Gikuyu religious values – a fact he conveniently ignores in his Marxist attacks on non-Marxist African writers.
As Andrew Gurr has revealed, Ngugi conceived the novel as an
exploration of a 'rejected black messiah' theme, under the title of
'The Black Messiah', but later altered the title to avoid representing
Waiyaki as a tragic hero in the classical Greek mould.[25] Ngugi has
himself explained that he 'was trying to remove the central Christian doctrine from the dress of Western culture [to see] how this
might be grafted on to the central beliefs' of Gikuyu people.[26] In
pursuing this syncretism, he fails to distinguish between the Christ-
like messiah of the New Testament and the Moses-type messiah or
tribal warrior-hero of the Old Testament, which the prophecy fore-
tells and Gikuyu traditionalists expect. It is for this confusion, reminiscent of that of Brother Man in Roger Mais's novel, that Waiyaki is
rejected, not for any 'romantic individualism' as suggested by Gerald Moore,[27] for it is a hallmark of Ngugi's novels that the hero is
invariably paired with a heroine. In awakening the people to the
value of formal education, however, Waiyaki is in fact successful.

In *Weep Not, Child*, the Mau Mau guerrillas have no doubt about
their messianic mission, and the liberation struggle is portrayed in
Fanonian terms as an apocalyptic process. The eschatological theme
is first established through the epigraph taken from Walt Whitman's
poem 'On the Beach at Night'. The consolation proffered in the
poem is not realized here, however. At the level of the personal
story of Njoroge, the boy hero, *Weep Not, Child* is a conventional *bil-
dungsroman* tracing Njoroge's growth from ignorance to knowledge
of his people's historical predicament and his role in their struggle.
This is reflected in the novel's organization into two roughly equal
halves – 'The Waning Light' and 'Darkness Falls' – linked by an
Interlude. From the precarious security of the twilight first part, subsequent events in the Interlude expose the frangibility of this world
as Njoroge and the Kenyan nation descend into the abyss of
the Emergency declared by the colonial government. The apocalypse syndrome of 'war, disease, pestilence, insecurity, betrayals,
family disintegration' terrifies Njoroge into wondering whether 'the

Second Coming' would 'see the destruction of all life in this world' (p. 91).

Picking up again the issue of education, Ngugi takes it beyond formal, schoolroom book learning and makes it an instrument of the people's own self-empowerment. Njoroge's egocentric perception of education as a ladder to a personal 'bright future' in a universe regulated by a benevolent divinity (pp. 3 and 4) is swiftly punctured through a series of incidents that suck him into the maelstrom of history. Unlike Njoroge, the Mau Mau recognize that security can come only through the agency of the people themselves, for the messiah prophesied by Mugo wa Kibiro is not an external agency but the people's own fighting will.

This linkage between education and liberation is so crucial that all important characters who cannot consciously integrate the two are dead by the end of the novel. In the novel's pervasive darkness-and-light symbolism, Njoroge's school represents a world of light whereas the world of his father Ngotho and the older generation is enveloped in darkness. Friendship between him and Mwihaki, daughter of Ngotho's enemy Jacobo, makes them 'oblivious of the bigger darkness over the whole land' (p. 96), for Ngugi is also exploiting the conventional symbolism of the child being the seed of the future. Njoroge's fall out of the school world into the colonial regime's torture chamber called the 'House of Pain' is a descent into hell (pp. 114–17). For the adult generation, there is neither hope nor consolation; their darkness is terminal. Ngotho himself is literally castrated by the settler Mr Howlands, a mutilation that is both real and symbolic of attempts to emasculate the people's will (pp. 118–20). However, an offspring of each of the three major adult protagonists survives: Ngotho's Njoroge, Jacobo's Mwihaki and Howlands's Stephen.

By the time Ngugi comes to write *A Grain of Wheat*, the last novel in the decolonization trilogy, his concept of heroism has evolved under Marxist influence beyond individual lone heroes to a mass heroism of the peasantry. Yet *A Grain of Wheat* also elaborates one theme introduced in *Weep Not, Child*: the ravages inflicted on individual and collective psyches by the horrors of the state of Emergency. The character Githua, though eventually exposed as an impostor, sums up these ravages in the simple statement: 'The Emergency destroyed us' (*GOW* p. 5). Ngugi's re-creation of the violence of these times is not gratuitous. As a historical fact it is part of Ngugi's discursive counter to the British version of Kenya's independence struggle. It also serves Ngugi's cultural affirmation purpose: a celebration of the Gikuyu people's sacrifice and heroism against a ferocious, militarily superior enemy. Finally, the background of pain and grim resistance establishes a reference frame for evaluating the performance of the Kenyan state born out of the struggle. Ngugi's prefatory note effectively dedicates the novel to the heroic 'peasants who fought the British yet who now see all they fought for being put on one side'.

Several disturbing premonitions of this betrayal are revealed in a magnanimous spirit which argues the need to forge a new social harmony unshackled by traumatic and vengeful memories rooted in the Emergency. The novel demands a re-assessment of events and people's roles (actual or merely suspected) within the total historical context, a revision of its canon of martyrs, heroes and villains, as a precondition for harmony in the emerging nation. 'Read your own heart, and know yourself ' (p. 54), Wangari admonishes her son Gikonyo, a traitor who is nevertheless being consumed with implacable, self-righteous vindictiveness against his wife Mumbi for her supposed adultery.

The plot structure is most appropriate for this theme. The story line barely spans five days that culminate in independence (Uhuru) on 12 December 1963. But a series of flashbacks, characters' reminiscences, interior monologues and direct exposition fills in details reaching back to the dawn of this century. Four days to the formal flag-hoisting ceremonies marking the 'birth' of the Kenyan nation, local Mau Mau leaders in Thabai district launch a massive manhunt for the hitherto unknown betrayer of their leader Kihika. Through this whodunit plot is unravelled an intricate web of poor judgements in a community tumescent with secret guilts, where villains are not just white characters like Dr Lynd, Mrs Thompson, and especially Mr Thompson who as District Officer had presided over concentration camps in which many Kenyans had died, but also major Kenyan characters like Karanja, who had collaborated with the enemy, Gikonyo, who had betrayed the Mau Mau oath, Mugo the supposed hero who turns out to be the betrayer of Kihika, and even the Mau Mau leaders themselves. This plot is no less than a probe into the emerging nation's own heart. The anti-climactic 'disturbing sense of an inevitable doom' (p. 188) which mars the independence celebrations is an ugly prognosis, summed up in the bewildered elder Warui's anguished lament of the unexpected isolation of the leadership from the populace: 'it was like warm water in the mouth of a thirsty man. It was not what I had waited for, these many years' (p. 208).

Of all germs of betrayal discernible in the trilogy, the most threatening is Gikonyo's transformation from creative, charitable craftsman (p. 68) to predatory middle-class business man who joins Asian merchants in the practice of hoarding commodities so as to reap huge profits from the artificial scarcity thus created (pp. 51–3) – a foretaste of the emerging Western-style economic system. Gikonyo's activities are all the more reprehensible because he is not just another Kenyan. His name is almost certainly a variation on 'Gikuyu' of which, according to Jomo Kenyatta, 'a strict phonetic spelling would be Gekoyo'.[28] Hence he and his wife Mumbi symbolize the Kenyan nation as Gikuyu and Mumbi, the first parents. His activities therefore prefigure the self-betrayals that will blight the independence era in *Petals of Blood*, *Devil on the Cross* and *Matigari*.

Different readers will interpret the resolution of the plot of *A Grain of Wheat* as either optimistic or ambiguous. Gikonyo and Mumbi are reconciled, and Gikonyo prepares for Mumbi a 'wedding gift' of 'a stool carved from Muiri wood' in the form of 'a woman big – big with child' (p. 213). On the balance, however, it is essentially optimistic, for, transcending the immediate present and near future, Ngugi's vision encompasses the whole historical future in which the house of Gikuyu and Mumbi will be reconstituted. This is why the woman in Gikonyo's carving is not neutrally described as 'pregnant' but emphatically portrayed as 'big with child'. In Ngugi, a child is latent with the ultimate fulfilment of the historical future, as the examination of *Weep Not, Child* has amply demonstrated. An unborn child is not an unknown or indeterminate product of a pregnancy but the future and its promises.

Witi Ihimaera's *The Matriarch* goes much further than Reid's and Ngugi's novels in its reinterpretation of colonial conflicts. Towards the end of the novel Ihimaera's narrator, Tamatea Mahana, offers what amounts to the novel's *raison d'être*: 'All truth is fiction really, for the teller tells it as he sees it, and it might be different from some other teller. That is why histories often vary, depending on whether you are the conqueror or not' (*Matriarch* p. 403). For Ihimaera and many Maori nationalist writers, New Zealand history written by Europeans has not only been blatantly self-justifying but, even more insidiously, has also employed 'spirit thievery' to condition many Maoris into accepting their dehumanization. Consequently, whereas most historical novels in this tradition generally use history as a background, or occasionally introduce actual historical events into the plot, *The Matriarch* has Maori history as its subject matter and adopts Maori perspectives in recording major landmarks in the encounter with the Pakeha. Yet the novel is also an epic in every sense, lending cosmic significance to Maori history by deeply rooting it in Maori cosmogonic myths and legends as well as biblical traditions of exile and redemption. The grand setting of the novel spans time from pre-creation to the 1980s.

The Matriarch is a logical development from Ihimaera's resolve, cited by Richard Corballis: 'only when I have completed writing about the rural Maori to my satisfaction will I uncurl my toes and write about how hard the city pavements are to our feet'.[29] Ihimaera himself regards his earlier writing as lacking in 'anger and political thought'.[30] More recently, he has suggested that earlier Maori writing was further restrained by the political climate of an era when the principal outlet for Maori writers was the magazine *Te Ao Hou* published by the Pakeha-run Department of Maori Affairs. The first drafts of his early novels, he informed Mark Williams during an interview, reveal 'an undercurrent or tension in them which accepts the political reality of the Maori situation. I think what we sometimes forget ... is that [Maori] writers are locked into the prevailing philosophy of the times.'[31] By contrast, *The Matriarch* is a novel in which the writer shows the whites of his eyes in anger. In the Prologue, Artemis Riripeti Mahana (later Artemis Riripeti Pere), the Matriarch of the novel's title, teaches Maori creation myth to the narrator Tamatea Mahana, later revealed as the heir to 'the mantle of [her] mana' (pp. 219–20). A measure of Ihimaera's metahistorical project is glimpsed from the account of Captain James Cook's arrival in Aotearoa/New Zealand. Against Pakeha historiography which represents the landing as a 'glorious' event and 'the stuff of romance', Ihimaera maintains that 'the glorious birth of the nation has the taste of bitter almonds when one remembers that six Maoris died so that a flag could be raised and that the *Endeavour* had lain in Poverty Bay for only two days and fourteen hours' (pp. 36–7).

The early introduction of this revision is crucial to Ihimaera's strategy and themes. From challenging this historical falsehood of European accounts of 'discovery', Ihimaera lays the ground for other challenges. The Treaty of Waitangi by which the British crown claimed sovereignty over North Island of New Zealand (South Island was claimed by 'right' of 'discovery'!), the Maori liberation wars which British and Pakeha historians represent as 'The Maori

Wars', use of parliament and the judiciary to dispossess and marginalize the Maori, and emotional consequences of these injustices from the past to the present are all re-examined from Maori perspectives. Ihimaera's account of the rapacity of the Reverend Archdeacon Henry Williams who stole some 50 000 acres of Maori land is historically true. So is the account of the Reverend gentleman's self-defence, when accused of the robbery by an aggrieved Maori chief during the signing of the Treaty of Waitangi, that he needed the land for his eleven children (p. 72). Equally important is the rehabilitation of the reputations of nationalist heroes maligned as terrorists and cut-throats in Pakeha histories, a notable example being Te Kooti Rikirangi. The language strategies employed by Ihimaera for this task have already been examined in Chapter 3, and repetition is not necessary here.

It is only to be expected that *The Matriarch* would devote considerable space to the Treaty of Waitangi, signed on 6 February 1840 (*Matriarch* pp. 46 and 73). D.F. McKenzie has revealed that five versions of the Treaty had been sent abroad, of which three had 'minor differences', two bore a different date and a differently worded preamble, all 'differ critically from each other in the second article', and 'the extant Maori version, the actual treaty signed by the chiefs on 6 February, is not a translation of any of these five English versions, nor is any of the English ones a translation of the Maori'.[32] Yet, falling back upon racial stereotypes, McKenzie blatantly contradicts himself by asserting that the Treaty 'offers a prime example of European assumptions about the comprehension, status and binding power of written statements and written consent on the one hand against the flexible accommodations of oral consensus on the other'.[33] The issue of literacy *versus* orality is beside the point here, for the Maori chiefs who signed the Maori-language version of the Treaty were complete masters of their language and its nuances, and the Maori agreement they signed had the same meaning to them whether written or spoken. Indeed, it is the Maori who insist on a strict interpretation of the Treaty, hence Ihimaera's contention (*Matriarch* p. 73) that 'the Pakeha signed it knowing that it was worthless' (in the sense of never intending to honour it), whereas 'from te taha Maori, the view is different. The British Crown has consistently broken its contract (and all you Pakeha lawyers can argue until the cows come home that the Treaty wasn't a legal document but *we* believe it is)'.

Perception of the Treaty as a Pakeha fraud is echoed in Wendt's *Ola*, where the character Shona denounces it as 'Absolute bullshit.

The Treat's a bloody fraud!' (p. 74), while Patricia Grace's *Cousins* focuses on the Treaty's potential as 'a covenant that must reside as the base on which our society builds' if only the Pakeha would interpret it in good faith (pp. 216–17). Outside fiction, *The Encyclopaedia Britannica* (electronic edition, 1997) under the heading of 'New Zealand History: Annexation and Further Settlement' reveals that it was a decision upon at least partial annexation of New Zealand that led the government to commission the naval officer William Hobson, as lieutenant governor, to negotiate the treaty which enabled the New Zealand Association, 'combining skillful propaganda with outright trickery and brutality', to claim immense tracts of Maori land.

Ihimaera's charge that the Pakeha signed the Waitangi treaty 'knowing it was worthless' receives much validation from Adam Shoemaker's observation that the Waitangi Tribunal (set up under the Treaty of Waitangi Act) was initially conceived 'as an apparently superficial gesture towards Maori autonomy'. Shoemaker also cites Paul Havemann as arguing that 'judging by how the Tribunal was set up originally, [the Treaty] must have been conceived as a way merely to placate Maori and to provide some cathartic moments'.[34]

The Matriarch is a fighting novel, in the tradition that has become familiar from the Gikuyu novels of Ngugi and the Jamaican novelist V.S. Reid's *New Day*: each generation fights with the weapons appropriate to its era. Thus, the military resistance of the nineteenth century had gradually given way to resistance, led by the parliamentarian Wi Pere within the constitution, followed by the mass action which began in the second half of the twentieth century and in which the novelists are participating. As in the other decolonization fictions about colonial wars, revision of the history of the struggle serves both to reaffirm the values that sustained that struggle and to serve as a lesson to the present generation.

5

Casualties of Freedom

THE INTERNAL ROT AND THE EXTERNAL PLOT

Addressing the 1968 Uppsala conference on 'The Writer in Modern Africa', Wole Soyinka declared that 'the stage at which we find ourselves is the stage of disillusionment', a time for the writer to cease looking backwards 'to prospect in archaic fields for forgotten gems which would distract the present'.[1] With this, Soyinka summed up the new themes and mood that had quickly emerged in African decolonization literature so soon after the euphoria of independence in the preceding decade. Disillusionment was not peculiar to African writers and peoples, however. In the Caribbean, writers who had taken stock of their societies' performance following the end of direct rule by European colonizers were drawing similar conclusions. Among Polynesian writers, Albert Wendt began serious writing on a note of disillusionment,[2] like Nigeria's Wole Soyinka, but for the Maori novelists disillusionment did set in only after an initial period of hopes in the promise of biculturalism collided with the reality of Pakeha conceptions of biculturalism as assimilation of Maoris into Pakeha culture. Maori novels like Patricia Grace's *Mutuwhenua* and Witi Ihimaera's *Tangi*, which express some cautious optimism over biculturalism, have accordingly been followed by novels expressing disillusionment with Pakeha bad faith, such as Grace's *Potiki* (1986) and *Cousins* (1992) and Ihimaera's *The Matriarch* (1986). Interestingly, Wendt's novels of the 1990s, such as *Ola* (1991) and *Black Rainbow* (1992), have denounced New Zealand Pakeha racism in stronger terms than any of Grace's novels, so that it is safe to assert that there is a common Polynesian disenchantment with the Pakeha's performance.

Critiques of the societies cover a broad range of ills. In African, West Indian and Wendt's Samoan novels, society is perceived as having re-enslaved itself through self-violation and a frenzied pursuit of the material trappings of Western middle-class lifestyles, while governments are portrayed as having betrayed not only the nationalist ideals of the decolonization struggle but also the opportunities for self-reconstruction that independence has opened up. In their exploration of these failures, some novelists have begun with colonial society itself, probing the inchoate society on the eve of independence for clues to the post-independence miasma. The novelists recognize that the destruction of indigenous structures of order by colonialism leaves an ethical crisis when the colonial regime departs, as the normative structures or institutions of colonialism are incompatible with the needs of a sovereign people. Colonial institutions were created to facilitate the plunder rather than the development of colonial subjects. As Belgium's building of a nuclear power plant in Zaire after the Second World War shows, European colonial powers never seriously contemplated relinquishing power to the colonial subject at some future date until compelled to do so by a combination of the decolonization struggles of the mid-century, the exhaustion of the European powers themselves in the Second World War, and the rise of America and the Soviet Union as competing superpowers.

As they move into the independence era, many novelists have foregrounded the relationship between internal failures and global political-economic forces. A crucial issue until the late 1980s was the Cold War rivalry between the West and the Soviet Bloc frequently fought by proxy in the ex-colonial world. Treating their ex-colonies not as human beings nor independent states but as mere counters in their strategic manoeuvres, the West continued to interfere secretly or intervene openly in these states' affairs to overthrow governments that they considered ideologically unacceptable, murder leaders whose policies were considered hostile to Western interests, foment civil wars to destabilize some countries, or install puppet regimes. These states have thus had to contend with government by brigands, morons, lunatics, psychopaths and zombies in army uniform thrust upon them by America and her allies. The role of the West in Third World poverty and instability has been that of pirates who, having plundered and sunk a merchant ship, take up positions along the shore and shoot any survivors trying to swim to safety.

The career of Joseph Desiré Mobutu (alias Mobutu Sese Seko) in Zaire, the former 'Belgian' Congo now renamed Democratic Republic of Congo, is illustrative, but the Mobutu tragedy has been replayed on such other theatres as Nigeria, Uganda under Idi Amin, Angola and Mozambique whose farmlands have been sown with millions of landmines, and many parts of Asia and the Arab world. Now reviled in the Western press as one of history's most venal leaders of a postcolonial state, Mobutu was enthroned in Zaire by the Americans following the 1963 murder of Patrice Lumumba, the first post-Belgian prime minister of the country, whom the West considered a communist. Thrice in the following three decades, American and French governments employed ruthless military force to crush attempts by the Congolese people to overthrow the vainglorious and corrupt Western puppet.

This cynical policy was publicly acknowledged and defended by former American Assistant Secretary of State for Africa Mr Herman Cohen in a BBC Television interview in May 1997 – when, with the Soviet Union extinct, the West decided to discard Mobutu and enthrone the same man, Laurent Kabila, whose insurgency they had previously crushed. Mobutu's venality was therefore literally the venality of his masters. One finds here the full force of Robert Young's observation that 'European philosophy reduplicates Western foreign policy, where democracy at home is maintained through colonial or neocolonial oppression abroad'.[3] The spectacle of Kabila on television signing away immense chunks of Zairean mineral and forest resources to predatory American businessmen even before the exit of his used-up predecessor pointed to a replay of the Mobutu tragedy under Kabila, who was literally a hostage to his sponsors.

Given the West's total control of the production and dissemination of information, these destabilization programmes are easily hidden from the Western public, and the immense human tragedy attendant upon them has been attributed to some primordial savagery that supposedly lurks in the sub-conscious of black peoples. The West's removal of a leprous dictator it installed promptly triggers massive rewriting of history and dissemination of the new authorized version by the mass communications media, historians and academics, many of whom belong to the think-tanks that developed the policies in the first place. Accounts of the Congo/Zaire tragedy rarely mention the successive French presidents who regularly hunted with Mobutu, the Franco-American crushing of Congolese will, or the century-long unparalleled cannibalism practised on the Congolese by Belgium (with France and America biting off sizeable chunks too) which at the time of independence in 1963 left the huge country of over thirty million people with fewer than two dozen university graduates.

Decolonization novelists have accordingly initiated a counter-discourse which probes the undercurrents of history for forces that have contributed to the contemporary malaise of the ex-colonial states. While novelists like Chinua Achebe have adopted a broadly humanist approach, portraying post-independence failures in terms of the moral failures of the people and their leaders, and some like V.S. Naipaul have offered racial-ontological stereotypes, many others in Africa and the West Indies have interpreted post-independence failures as symptoms of a much deeper problem rooted in the colonial and neocolonial experiences of the societies. Debates between Europe and the Third World are also accompanied with debates among the novelists themselves about the origins, nature and processes of the ex-colonial states' predicament, and the solutions to which they are amenable. In the three sections below, the various responses are examined according to their broad affinities.

THE CROSS-ROADS OF HISTORY

Withdrawal of the occupying power leaves behind a mutilated society faced with the task of constructing a new self out of the ruins of precolonial culture in the face of new, countervailing forces unleashed by colonization. The crisis thus generated is one of the central themes of such novels as *No Longer at Ease*, *A Man of the People*, *Mimic Men*, *Mystic Masseur*, *Elvira* and *Sons for the Return Home*.

Achebe's *No Longer at Ease* (1960), set in the last years of direct British colonial rule, condenses the situation profoundly into its title, 'No Longer at Ease', derived from T.S. Eliot's 'Journey of the Magi', from which Achebe also takes his epigraph and controlling metaphor:

> We returned to our places, these Kingdoms
> But no longer at ease here, in the old dispensation,
> With an alien people clutching their gods
> I should be glad of another death.[4]

The 'alien people' met by Obi Okonkwo are, ironically, his own people. Obi Okonkwo, son of Nwoye (now called Isaac) of *Things Fall Apart*, returns after university studies in Britain to a Nigerian society in the lethal grips of that 'mere anarchy' loosed 'upon the world' in *Things Fall Apart*. In his own Igbo society, social values have become inverted and institutions fragmented. In Lagos, capital city of the emerging Nigerian state, ethnic loyalties and an amoral ethic of ravenous self-gratification have spawned a culture of corruption. Obi's nascent nationalism, with its vaguely formulated vision of a supra-ethnic Nigerian state, is inadequate to deal with the contradictions inherent in this situation, besides clashing with his Umuofia people's perception of themselves as a family competing with strangers in a territory which none of them identifies as 'home'. Achebe thus uncovers the crisis of building a modern nation state out of an agglomeration of ethnic states that have been indiscriminately amalgamated by colonialists to serve their own economic and strategic interests.

Umuofia epitomizes the numerous ethnic 'nations' in Obi's Nigeria. To each of these rival groupings, the new state is an ill-defined and alien territory presided over by an equally alien government. Spontaneous loyalty or patriotic attachment to such an entity is impossible. The narrator reveals that:

> The Umuofians...who leave their home town to find work in towns all over Nigeria regard themselves as sojourners...When they have saved up enough money they ask their relations at home to find them a wife, or they build a 'zinc' house on their family land. No matter where they are in Nigeria, they start a local branch of the Umuofia Progressive Union. (*NLAE* p. 4)

A little reflection reveals that this perception of the state is a direct consequence of the adversary relationship between the colonizer and the colonized. The colonial regime was 'other', an alien conqueror and immoral despoiler. Cheating or robbing the colonial regime was a repayment in kind for its own depredations. In *No Longer at Ease*, this relationship is linguistically embedded in the designation of the civil service as the 'whiteman's establishment' where the occupant of a 'European post' does the 'whiteman's work'. The state as mere territory rather than nation is thus conceptually polarized into 'home' and 'beyond'. 'Home' is the ethnic state, the human habitation, a moral universe regulated by clear concepts of right and wrong, while 'beyond' is the frontier, spirit land, the realm of chaos in which a quest hero/heroine pits his/her wits against rivals and monsters in a struggle for a boon which must be appropriated on behalf of the 'home'.[5] In effect, Umuofia perceptions of the new social formation are conditioned by attitudes to the colonial regime, Igbo traditions of representative government and models of human self-extension enshrined in myths, legends and folk tales.

This archetype is widespread in early African and Polynesian novels. In *Things Fall Apart*, Okonkwo whose fame has spread from Umuofia 'home' to Mbaino 'beyond' is mandated to lead Umuofia's delegation to Mbaino to demand reparations for the murder of an Umuofia woman. The Umuofia orator who addresses the assembly refers to Mbaino as 'those sons of wild beasts' (*TFA* p. 8). A similar attitude is expressed towards Okperi by Umuaro in *Arrow of God* (p. 20). Samoans in Wendt's *Sons for the Return Home* maintain that 'Samoa was the navel of the universe: the world ended within the visible horizons and reefs. Anything beyond that was [chaos]' (p. 179), and in *Banyan Tree* the cosmos is 'the familiar and secure world contained within the coral reef ' (p. 8). Seclusion, intimacy and security are strongly emphasized in Grace's *Potiki*. Here, the cosmos consists of small Maori communities like the Tamihana family and the Te Ope. In both *Tangi* and *Whanau*, the cosmos is Waituhi, where the Whanau a Kai 'live close together, clustered around the meeting house, the painted Rongopai, which is the heart of the village' (*Whanau* p. 7). Even in Ngugi's novels, whose subject is the history of the entire Kenyan nation, the 'world' in the first three novels is represented by the small Gikuyu communities bounded by the ridges, first introduced in *The River Between*. 'The ridges were isolated', Ngugi writes. 'The people there led a life of their own, undisturbed by what happened outside or beyond' (*RB* p. 3).

To Umuofia in *No Longer at Ease*, therefore, Obi's journey to England (which the community sponsored at immense personal sacrifice) to acquire university education is indistinguishable from his journey to Lagos to acquire a well-paid civil service job. The community, in other words, attempts to interpret and control the present through an existing paradigm. 'In our folk stories', one of the elders congratulates Obi, 'a man gets to the land of spirits when he has passed seven rivers, seven forests and seven hills. Without doubt you have visited the land of spirits.' Obi is now 'a little child returned from wrestling in the spirit world' (p. 51). This is only a short step to his installation in the gallery of the clan's legendary heroes (p. 54), and his equation with his famous grandfather 'who faced the white man single-handed and died in the fight' (p. 53). By extension of the paradigm, too, the clansman 'hero' working in the 'beyond' is viewed as the community's champion, charged with fetching its share of the nation's wealth (*NLAE* p. 33). The incompatibility between the colonizer's and the colonized subjects' interests, the justification for nationalist agitation for decolonization, now militates against the healthy development of the new state.

It is in these terms that Achebe explores the story of Obi Okonkwo, who sets out to eradicate bribery, immorality and other causes of social chaos but ends up succumbing to them.[6] Arthur Ravenscroft's description of Obi's story as 'a paradigm of a man caught between the irreconcilable values of different ways of life [African and Western]'[7] merely betrays that skewed sense of morality by which the West regards its own gargantuan levels of corruption as mere aberrations while treating the same phenomena in other cultures as racial characteristics. Unequivocally deflating the colonial regime's claims to moral superiority, an Umuofia man observes that '[white people] eat bribe...more than black men nowadays' (*NLAE* p. 33). Colonialism itself is literally a form of armed robbery on a national scale, and Jamaica Kincaid has put the case more bluntly but with self-critical irony in *A Small Place*:

> Have you ever wondered to yourself why it is that all people like me seem to have learned from you is how to imprison and murder each other, how to govern badly, and how to take the wealth of our country and place it in Swiss bank accounts? ...You came. You took things that were not yours, and you did not even, for appearances' sake, ask first...You murdered people. You imprisoned people. You robbed people. (pp. 34–5)

What E.N. Obiechina rightly identifies as polarization between rural and urban settings[8] is at the more fundamental level of historical development better explained in terms of contradictions between 'home' with clearly recognized norms and the pre-creation inchoateness of 'beyond'. In many African and Polynesian novels, the scheme is really not bi-polar but tri-polar, the home-versus-beyond polarity being complemented by the little enclave that ethnic migrants have tried to consecrate as home-away-from-home in the urban chaos, such as the Umuofia Progressive Union formed 'six years ago' in *No Longer at Ease*, and the Osa Descendants Union who in Soyinka's *The Interpreters* want their 'son' Egbo to leave his job in the Foreign Office and become their 'enlightened ruler' (*Interpreters* p. 10). Wendt's *Sons for the Return Home* unfolds through these three settings: Pakeha New Zealand as chaos, the Samoan world reincarnated in New Zealand by Samoans, and then the Samoan motherland which like Umuofia clings to its image of pristine purity. In

Cousins which advocates Maori exploitation of all the opportunities of modernization offered by the society, there are distinctions nevertheless between the Maori home, the Pakeha-dominated capital city, and the Maori home-in-the-city which Maoris create for themselves in their quest to achieve modernization without succumbing to westernization and/or Pakeha assimilation programmes. Thus, Makareta who rebels against her clan in *Cousins* nevertheless serves them with her modern education and bilingualism, from the knowledge that 'it's not sticking to the old ways that's important' but 'us being us, using all the new knowledge our way. Everything new belongs to us too' (p. 235). The pattern also exists, though less elaborately, in such novels as Merle Collins' *Angel* and Grace Ogot's *The Graduate*.

The home-beyond polarity persists through Achebe's *A Man of the People* (1966) and *Anthills of the Savannah* (1987) and actually receives some validation in the latter from the national government's irresponsibility. In the former, the moral chaos of 'beyond' is gradually overwhelming the 'home' order. The people who ecstatically welcome the federal minister M.A. Nanga in the opening scene of *A Man of the People* know that he is corrupt, but naïvely accept this as part of the political culture of 'beyond' which has nothing to do with 'home' (p. 2). By contrast, the local shopkeeper Josiah's cheating of a blind man provokes instant ostracism (pp. 84–6). A character aphoristically sums up the ethical principle behind this: 'Josiah has taken away enough for the owner to notice' (p. 86). Odili's father amplifies: 'the owner was the village and the village had a mind; it could say no to sacrilege. But in the affairs of the nation there was no owner, the laws of the village became powerless' (p. 148). In the increasingly numerous intersections and overlaps of village and nation, this distinction becomes increasingly blurred.

Uncanny similarities exist between Obi Okonkwo and the unnamed hero of Wendt's *Sons for the Return Home*, who is only three years old when his family emigrates to New Zealand on a twenty-year sojourn to garner their own portion of the fabulous wealth reported by preceding sojourners. Both have similar personal and family backgrounds (Obi's father is a catechist, the boy's a deacon, their mothers are fanatical though inconsistent Christians), suffer estrangement from their indigenous cultures and new societies, and get entangled in calamitous romance with socially 'unacceptable' women which ends in pregnancy and abortion. Finally, both are vehicles through which others try to live their own dreams. Of equal importance is the two novelists' use of the love affairs to demonstrate

that irrational dichotomies in human relationships are not constructed by white people alone. In Achebe's novel *Clara*, the Igbo
woman involved with Obi is unacceptable because she belongs to
the *osu* caste – a caste of ritual outsiders. For Wendt's Samoans, the
problem is reverse-racism: the hero's mother does not want a white
daughter-in-law and pressures her into aborting the baby.

Part I of *Sons* explores the background for this development. In
Part II, the private world created by the lovers collides with public
truths of race, and is irreparably fissured. Part III takes the story into
the future by returning the sojourners to their Samoan past and origins, a society whose claims of pristine purity contrast sharply with
its frantic pursuit of what Fanon aptly terms 'a kind of lactification'[9]
(Chapters 15 and 16). The house built by the hero's father with his
new wealth reveals a sick addiction to bourgeois papalagi culture,
an absurdly over-furnished, under-utilized, worshipped possession
within which the mother struts about preening her ill-fitting plum-
age and displaying all the ludicrous self-conceit of the Third World
parvenu. In the national capital, Apia, 'money and the quality of a
person's English were two of the town's peculiar ways of estimating
status... Good English was proof that one was educated, sophisticated, civilised, totally removed from an "uneducated villager from
the back" ' (p. 195).

Traditional criticism has treated protagonists like Obi Okonkwo
and Wendt's unnamed hero as epitomes of a 'child of two worlds'
crisis, enlightened individuals alienated from their societies by their
acquired Western values. This is mistaken, for the cultures encoun-
tered by the returnees are not the original cultures they had left
behind but new social formations spawned by the West as its own
parody. Whatever conflict does take place between the two is therefore better understood as one between two progenies of the West.
The 'gods' clutched by Obi Okonkwo's people and Wendt's Samoans – the sum total of their values – are not those of the original
culture but those of the new Western parody. As a member of a local
Christian family, Obi was estranged from Umuofia traditions even
before his departure, while Wendt's hero left Samoa when he was
too young to receive permanent imprints from Samoan culture.
Even the latter's birth through a Caesarean operation performed by
a European doctor in Samoa becomes, in retrospect, a pointer to his
entanglement with European culture.

Such heroes are not Prometheans ruined by philistine society
or any malevolent gods, but potential Prometheans who failed as a

result of flaws in their own character. Obi acquires Western self-centredness that resents his kinsmen's 'interference' in his affairs, but the clan still comes to his aid in times of trouble. And although Albert Wendt has revealed that his hero's disillusionment mirrors his own at a corresponding age yet, by defining the hero's abdication of his communal role and going into exile through the myth of Maui's dastardly attempt to gain immortality by entering Hine-nuite-Po's womb through her genitalia, Wendt critiques it as nihilistic (*Sons* p. 217).

Corruption assumes such endemic proportions in Armah's *The Beautyful Ones Are Not Yet Born* and *Fragments* and in Wole Soyinka's *The Interpreters*, that it is individuals rather than communities that can form islands of morality. Both novelists interpret moral and political decay in terms of apostasy, the perversion of indigenous values in their mindless pursuit of the ephemeral Western culture which Armah represents as 'the gleam' in the first novel. Though indigenous systems were not perfect, they nevertheless rested on moral foundations that are absent from the system spawned by colonialism. Armah's *Fragments* thus explores the perversion of the Akan cosmic model of past-present-future (or the ancestors-the living-and unborn) relationships into a Melanesian cargo cult, described by the hero Baako as 'the expectancy, the waiting for bounty dropping from the sky through the benign intercession of dead ancestors' (p. 228).

According to J.H. Nketia in *Funeral Dirges of the Akan People*, mourners seeking to portray the indispensability of the deceased ask him to keep in touch with survivors through exchange of gifts, this being a ritual codification of the normal exchanges, through 'someone who happened to be going in the desired direction', between friends or relations living far apart 'in the old Akan society, in which personal communication was neither easy nor quick'.[10] In the cultural chaos left by colonialism, this mentality stunts indigenous initiative and creativity while promoting vulgar consumerism and self-nullifying mimicry of the West.

As self-emasculating desire and the object of desire itself, 'the gleam' is incarnated in *The Beautyful Ones Are Not Yet Born* as the symbolically named Atlantic Caprice hotel owned by Europeans, and in *Fragments* as the Kalifonia Moonbeam Café (p. 23), representing in each the 'brothel of Europe' to which, in Fanon's theory of colonialism, the senile local elite reduce their newly independent state.[11] But neither Armah nor Soyinka exonerates the poor from culpability. 'The poor are rich in patience', Armah's hero sadly comments in

Fragments (p. 39), becoming totally demoralized and apathetic when called upon 'to resent the powerful' (p. 152). In the last three chapters of the *Beautyful Ones*, it is 'the poor' – the hero himself, the corrupt minister Koomson's own surly boatman and the harbour watchman – who, for various personal reasons, aid Koomson's escape. As a social critic, Armah is averse to deferring the villain's punishment, and Koomson's escape route is none other than the hero's latrine, but the hero's creeping after the fugitive underscores his own complicity in the politician's evil. Consequently, Armah objectifies the hero's contradictions in the image of the chichidodo, the bird which 'hates excrement with all its soul' but thrives on lavatory maggots (p. 45). One of his strongest comments on the phenomenon of corruption appears in the memorable last scene of the novel, when soldiers who have just overthrown the rotten civilian government rob travellers at check-points while the bemused hero watches and a chichidodo alights on the roof of the school lavatory.

In Soyinka's *The Interpreters* it is the elite who frustrate the emergence of the 'beautyful ones', but it is the masses' complicity that pushes Sekoni, an Ogun–Prometheus fusion, into a nervous breakdown. A qualified electrical engineer, Sekoni returns to Nigeria with patriotic visions of helping to transform the backward country into a modern nation through his skills. His revolt against misuse of these talents in administrative jobs within the civil service incurs a punitive assignment to Ijioha (p. 26) where, as Prometheus, he builds an electricity-generating plant for the people. But his vision is thwarted by an alliance of local and foreign interests who have made enormous profits from the people's deprivation. A similar rot pervades the academic community, whose intellectual and moral bankruptcy is embodied in the 'petrified forest' imagery applied to the gaudy furnishings and synthetic flora of Professor Oguazor's sitting room (*Interpreters* pp. 141–2).

Soyinka's 'masses' are not morally different from the elite, except insofar as they lack the power to indulge in their own greed and viciousness. Primitive tribal and religious chauvinism, hypocrisy, fickle-mindedness and a capacity for unimaginable cruelty are just some of their characteristics. The blood-thirsty mob which tries to lynch a petty thief (*Interpreters* pp. 114–18) will 'reform tomorrow and cheer the larger thief returning from his twentieth Economic Mission and pluck his train from the mud, dog-wise, in their teeth' (p. 114). The aptly counterpoised funeral processions, one for the rich Sir Derinola and the other for an anonymous peasant (pp. 111–13), show that through their greed, reverence for wealth and awed ob-sequiousness before the rich, the poor do indeed psychologically aid and abet the rich men's criminality.

THE PATH NOT TAKEN

Disillusionment has become so established in post-independence lit-erature that there is a danger of accepting it as the only discourse on the performance of the ex-colonial states. Yet a significant propor-tion of the literature of this period approaches the society's problems with an optimism which even the realities of neocolonialism have not shaken. Ready examples are the novels of female writers like Erna Brodber, Merle Collins, and, in particular, Grace Ogot. As Collins' novels are discussed in the next section, the present section concentrates on Ogot's *The Graduate*. These are all female writers, but, contrary to postcolonial gender theory, their novels derive their political strength not from a repudiation of male-dominated society or waging war against it, but from breaking down gender barriers. Novels by these three explore post-independence society in terms of new vistas that could be opened up by according women their proper position in the mainstream of political power. In a 1974 inter-view with the Voice of America's Lee Nichols, Ogot reveals that though she rarely tried to advance a thesis in her fiction an excep-tion is a short story 'Elizabeth', which explores the evil of treating women primarily as sex objects and is based on the experience of someone she knew.[12]

Unlike the major male African writers, Ogot does not see the leader-ship as venal, even though it is predominantly male. For her, just-ice for women does not mean replacing male tyranny with the female variety but providing a level playing field for both sexes, and her championship of marriage and family institutions in her novels and numerous short stories administer stinging rebuffs to gender theorists who seek to pervert her work to buttress their theories. Indeed, the most recent edition (published by Heinemann in 1990) of her first novel *The Promised Land* (1966) broadcasts her contempt for such theories in its dedication: 'for my beloved husband Bethwell Allan Ogot'. And, contrary to some gender theorists' gripes about Ogot's being addressed as Mrs Ogot by 'patriarchal' critics,[13] the novelist's insistent and positive address of her married heroines as 'Mrs' reaffirms the values of marriage and family in a manner that unequivocally shows her scorn for the denigration of marriage and the family institution in neoclonialist gender criticism.

The plot of *The Graduate* demonstrates the waste and self-negation to which the society is condemned by its failure to harness the intellectual and other resources of its women. While identifying ethnic divisions and lack of indigenous manpower as some of the problems of the new state, she pinpoints the marginalization of women not only as an injustice in itself but also as a waste of their potential contribution to the nation-building effort. It is only the death of the Minister for Public Affairs in a car crash that provides an opening for the Hon. Mrs Juanina Karungaru to join the all-male cabinet.

Mrs Karungaru is sent to the United States of America to recruit educated Kenyans into the civil service as part of the programme of mobilizing indigenous manpower for national reconstruction. There is a suggestion that the inspiration for this harnessing of the resources of Kenyan students in foreign universities is hers, for until now the government has ignored such students. The task is not as easy as it initially appears, for the government's insensitivity to the needs of such students has bred disenchantment with government and country among the students. Chapter 2 of *The Graduate* offers a detailed account of suffering, in which even the ambassador's appeal to the government merely exposes how thoroughly the new elite have been cloned from the colonial regime, eliciting negative responses in stock bureaucratic phrasing: 'The government regrets to inform you ...' (*Graduate* p. 20). Yet so convincing is Mrs Karungaru that Jakoyo Seda, who holds a Masters degree in Civil Engineering and Town Planning, sacrifices a lucrative lectureship offered by the University of California and accepts a job in his country's City Planners Department. 'The charismatic spell the Hon. Juanina Karungaru had cast upon her audience' afflicts them with a guilty conscience 'akin to that of the prodigal son in the Bible' (pp. 24–5).

Ogot's demonstration of the minister's charisma is not entirely convincing, coming as the climax of her private denunciation of the students as villains who could not appreciate Kenyans' sacrifices during the freedom struggle (p. 18). The ironic complications of this simple view are disturbing: the minister's family's collaboration with the colonial forces during the freedom struggle, her father's execution by a Mau Mau guerrilla whose wife was then murdered by the traitor's followers, and whose son Ngure is listening to the minister with fears that he may not be safe in Kenya where this offspring of traitors is a powerful minister (p. 35). In Ogot's patriotic vision, however, transcendence of that past is part of the demands of na-tion-building. Consequently, neither Ngure's fears nor his perverse pleasure in the shared Gikuyu identity which ethnically separates him and the minister while excluding his fellow students (p. 34) is examined further. However, a reader who does not share Ogot's idealistic vision sees in this fact a piquant reminder of the burden of the past on the present, and the reality that, while Africans in a for-eign country may be categorized by their passports as citizens of particular countries, back home in the 'independent' African states their identities are defined primarily in terms of ethnic groups rather than the nation in the distribution of amenities.

In the end, it is not just the minister's charisma but also a genuinely patriotic sentiment that sways Jakoyo to accept her offer, despite the scepticism, even the pessimism, of his friends (pp. 25–30). Neither the blood feud nor the ethnic animosities pose any problem to Jakoyo either upon his arrival at the airport or at any other time, suggesting that the novelist sees them as problems that could be solved through loyalty to the nation. A final source of anxiety is removed with his manifestly happy reunion with his wife and daughter in what is obviously Ogot's reaffirmation of the import-ance of the family in nation-building and individual happiness.

Jakoyo's only problem comes from a neocolonialist cabal of Irish staff who are determined to rob him of the job because they see him as a threat to their profitable entrenchment as expatriate experts. More immediately, they seek to retain the job for their compatriot, Ted O'Neill, whose contract the minister has decided not to extend because of his incompetence. Ogot's representation of neocolonialist conspiracy with an Irish gang rather than nationals of the former colonial ruler, Great Britain (which, surprisingly, is quite cooperative with the new government), introduces a new angle to the repre-sentation of neocolonial relationships. However, the fact of colonial history is that British imperialism in the Third World was frequent-ly an Anglo-Irish enterprise. Irish priests of the Roman Catholic Church were ferociously intolerant of all other faiths, and inculcated similar intolerance in their converts. Between 1961 and 1963, one such priest actually raged like a tropical storm through Eastern Nigeria, raiding homes and shrines for objects of indigenous reli-gious worship, some of which were publicly burnt while many were sent to Europe.

The conspiracy serves as a further comment on how the political culture of independent states facilitates neocolonialist entrenchment and subversion. The Irish staff's conspiracy owes its initial success to the minister's surprising naïvety in promoting Mrs Jane Brown as her own confidential secretary in preference to the very capable Kenyan junior secretary Anabell Chepkwony, on the recommendation of Ted O'Neill (p. 50) with whom Mrs Brown is conducting an adulterous relationship. The scenario poignantly illustrates the vulnerability of new states compelled by lack of indigenous expertise to retain in sensitive positions the very same foreign interests who profit from perpetuating the country's weakness. Driven by her white supremacist ideology and personal loyalty to her lover, Mrs Brown uses her position to spy on the minister, protect her lover's interests, and humiliate Anabell Chepkwony. Her own husband Trudy Brown has used his position as an educationist and 'expert adviser in the Ministry of Agriculture' to secure another strategic post in the Ministry of Education. From this post, he has helped another expatriate 'expert', Clive Calders, to fraudulently enrich his family by using Kenya as a base for selling throughout Africa a huge number of intellectually barren science books that his family publishing firm could not sell in Europe. Now Clive Calders returns the favour by using his own position to aid the conspiracy, and an even more sinister plot is hatched to give Jakoyo a university lectureship from which equally entrenched neocolonialist forces would ultimately eject him (pp. 57–64).

One is reminded here of the ex-colonial powers' policy of sending junk machinery as 'aid' to the pseudo-revolutionary Jimmy Ahmed in V.S. Naipaul's novel, *Guerrillas*. Sham independence is thus further subverted by depriving the country of its own human and material resources, or diverting those resources into useless ventures, and then saddling it with junk technology, junk experts and very real debts. Patriotism and advocacy of women's interests merge in the character and role of Anabell Chepkwony, who courageously and patriotically thwarts the conspiracy, protects the country's interests, and rescues Jakoyo himself from the fate of other would-be Promethean heroes of African fiction who are ruined by a combination of internal rot and external plot. Neither Ogot nor her heroine has any illusions about mutually supportive lesbian utopias. Jane Brown humiliates Anabell Chepkwony without any consideration of her womanhood because the latter is black, and Anabell herself sees Mrs Brown as just another racist whose conspiracy must be defeated. Anabell's inspiration and model of action come from indigenous lore, and her imagery is firmly indigenous:

She remembered quickly, that among her people, the Nandi, he who spots the man-eater-lion must report its whereabouts at once, so that the community could descend upon the killer to rid the society and their cattle of its menace. Even if it cost her her job it was her duty to expose this plot to fool the minister into pushing a fellow Kenyan into the cold, while the expatriate and his family kept warm and cosy within. (pp. 65–6)

Here, Ogot displays her superiority to a writer like Buchi Emecheta, who from the evidence of her novels has a much inferior understanding of African cultures but chooses to fill her fictionalized anthropological plots with stock incidents supposedly illustrating the predicament of women in African culture, as reported by a self-advertised insider. Yet, as has been seen (Chapter 4), Emecheta has not only confessed that she 'can't write stories in my own language ... Igbo' but also boasted that her 'Africanness is, in a way, being diluted' by her acquired Britishness to the point that her paperback publisher has stopped categorizing her novels as African.[14]

LEADERSHIP AND THE MERETRICIOUS PATH TO POWER

Analyses of the role of the leadership in many of these novels reveal varying degrees of the influence of those two philosophers of Third World decolonization: Frantz Fanon and Walter Rodney. Fanon identifies two types of post-independent leader: the feudal overlord and the modern head of government. 'Having been upheld by the occupying power', the feudal leaders feel threatened by radical new ideas that challenge the basis of their power, 'Thus their enemy is not at all the occupying power with which they get along on the whole very well, but these people with modern ideas who mean to dislocate the aboriginal society.'[15] With a consciousness moulded by colonialism, the post-independence elite:

organise the loot of whatever national resources exist [and] use today's national distress as a means of getting on through scheming and legal robbery, by import–export combines, limited liability companies gambling on the stock exchange, or unfair promotion ... As far as doctrine is concerned, they proclaim the pressing need of nationalising the robbery of the nation.[16]

Independence transforms the national leader from an embodiment of national aspirations into 'the general president of that company of profiteers ... which constitute the national bourgeoisie'. The bourgeoisie itself, 'afflicted with precocious senility', strives to perpetuate the inequalities of colonial society, and therefore taking on 'the role of manager for Western enterprise ... [sets] up its country as the brothel of Europe'.[17]

Going farther back than Fanon, Walter Rodney surveys the entire history of imperialism as an ideology and colonialism as the implementation of this ideology. The survey leads to three conclusions: first, that Europe's present wealth is founded upon the dispossession of (ex)colonized peoples; next, that to preserve this wealth, Europe employs all her resources, including overt and covert violence, to subvert the aspirations of the new states; and finally, that much of the Third World's chaos results either from a scramble for what the colonizers had not bothered to appropriate, or from direct instigation of sectional violence by Western governments and multinational corporations 'so as to keep the colonized from dealing with their principal contradictions with the European overlord'.[18] These forms of intervention noted by Rodney come in addition to the more direct forms involving overthrows of genuinely nationalist governments and replacing them with self-seeking traitors.

A major problem of leadership in the post-independence era, therefore, is what may be described as the meretricious path to power: the emergence of a leadership of political prostitutes, adventurers and opportunists who are bereft of nationalist consciousness or vision, and see themselves not as nation-builders but as heirs to the powers and privileges of the colonial regime. West Indian novelists like George Lamming (*In the Castle of My Skin*), Merle Collins (*Angel*) and V.S. Naipaul (*The Mystic Masseur*) all locate leadership failures partly in such circumstances, with the mid-century labour unrest in the Caribbean providing a ready pool of discontented workers who become malleable instruments in the hands of crafty, demagogic opportunists. In Wendt's *Pouliuli*, the morally and intellectually bankrupt Malaga Puta becomes Malaelua's parliamentary representative solely by virtue of his kinship with Faleasa Osovae, the ruthless king-maker of Malaelua (p. 124). 'His Excellency Joseph Koomson, Minister Plenipotentiary, Member of the Presidential Commission, Hero of Socialist Labour' in Armah's *The Beautyful Ones Are Not Yet Born* rose from mediocrity to national eminence as a thieving minister in an ostensibly socialist regime committed to eradicating the legacy of colonialism while actually perpetuating those same legacies. In Achebe's *A Man of the People*, Nanga rises overnight from the parliamentary back benches to ministerial eminence through crude opportunism (*AMOP* pp. 3–7), and Odili Samalu follows suit in execution of a puerile scheme to revenge himself on Chief Nanga, who has seduced his woman (pp. 68–73).

Despite the ideological differences between Achebe and Naipaul, *A Man of the People* and *The Suffrage of Elvira* share a common perception of the meretricious rise to power. Naipaul's narrator's comment that the 1946 elections 'had taken nearly everyone by surprise', but this time around 'people began to see the possibilities' of commercializing them (pp. 13, 46) resonates in *A Man of the People* in Odili's account of Nanga's rise to political eminence: 'It was easy in those days – before we knew its cash price' (p. 3). Politicians who buy their way to power feel no obligations to the electorate, and in *Elvira* Harbans not only reneges on his promises but also becomes transformed from humble candidate to arrogant legislator (pp. 196–9).

Whether the leadership gains power through chicanery or through Western intervention, the consequence is the 'precocious senility' identified by Fanon, and explored as the 'Man Child' phenomenon in Armah's novels. The lament of the hero's friend in *The Beautyful Ones Are Not Yet Born* finds echoes in many ex-colonial states:

> How long will Africa be cursed with its leaders? There were men dying from loss of hope, and others finding gaudy ways to enjoy powers they did not have. We were ready for big and beautiful dreams, but what we had was our own black men hugging new paunches scrambling to ask the white man to welcome them onto our backs. (pp. 80–1)

In *Why Are We So Blest?*, the central question is posed by a maimed veteran of the African revolution: 'Who gained? ... Who won?' (p. 24). 'The situation and the problems are real', Ngugi wa Thiong'o insists in a short note appended to his own *A Grain of Wheat*, 'sometimes too painfully real for the peasants who fought the British yet who now see all that they fought for being put on one side.' Armah graphically illuminates this debacle through analogy with the automotive internal combustion engine, especially through the pun on '*l'essence*, that which is essential; and *l'essence*, petrol' (p. 26). In a revolutionary war, the true militants 'are the essence.' But 'that also means they are the fuel for the revolution . . . Something pure, light, even spiritual, which consumes itself to push forward something heavier, more gross than itself ' (p. 27). The crippled veteran (counterpart of the crippled Mau Mau guerrilla in Ngugi's *Petals of Blood*) sums up the tragedy. 'All the best ones died. And many of those left are cripples.'

For Ngugi, the real beneficiaries of the freedom struggle are wartime collaborators like Hawkins Kimeria and Ezekiel Waweru 'those who ran to the shelter of schools and universities and administration' (*POB* p. 60), and modern reprobates like Nderi wa Riera, Chui and Mzigo in *Petals of Blood*, Mwaura in *Devil on the Cross*, and John Boy in *Matigari*. In the blighted villages, peasants scratch out a wretched livelihood from exhausted soil. The landless who cannot get wage employment are reduced to hawking goods, begging, or prostitution if they are women. Women like Wanja (*Petals of Blood*) and Jacinta Warringa (*Devil on the Cross*) and Güthera (*Matigari*) symbolize life blighted by the neocolonialist socio-economic system. The history unfolding in these and many other novels of disillusionment has become a grim fulfilment of the bitter *bon mot* of the disgraced collaborator, Karanja, in Ngugi's *A Grain of Wheat*: 'the coming of black rule would not, could not mean, the end of white power' (p. 35).

George Lamming's *In the Castle of My Skin* (1953) was published nearly a decade and a half before Fanon's *The Wretched of the Earth* was published in English translation (1967), and explores the independence struggle of a backwater Barbadian village. But so prophetic is its presentation of the career of the leader who emerges from this struggle that the novel may rightly be regarded as the prototype of the novel of post-independence disillusionment. A school teacher bearing the ominous name of Mr Slime is dismissed from his job (or compelled to resign) for scandalous involvement with the Head Teacher's wife. He quickly repairs his fortune by opening a Friendly Society and Penny Bank which his unsuspecting followers happily patronize. He promptly converts economic into political power by inspiring the workers and the general populace with his fraudulent vision of a golden Jerusalem in which they own the land and receive fair wages for their labour. But the overthrow of the English landlord, Mr Creighton, merely ushers in the vicious cycle of betrayed hopes and false starts whose re-enactment all over the ex-colonial world has thrown into question the value and logic of independence.

Lamming powerfully prefigures this vicious cycle that will be unleashed with Mr Slime's emergence as leader. From the opening scene, the artist-hero, the boy G., through whose sensibility the experience will be unfolded, comments on weather phenomena and other foreboding of a pattern of change without progress, climaxing in a cloud epiphany of betrayal in Chapter 6. In the epiphany tableau, one half of the sky is an Edenic scene while the other portrays elemental turbulence. Yet in the Edenic half a white man and a black man are engaged in a violent altercation:

> The figures were still, and they looked across at each other hard and steady as if they were involved in a common chaos which neither could understand but greatly desired to redeem...And as they looked the clouds curving over and about their heads made an arc of words that read: ARE YOU NOT A BROTHER? The shapes sharpened in outline, the white one getting heavier and darker. (p. 111)

Two developments are fused in the morphing of white into black within the epiphany tableau: the white man's adoption of a black mask and the black man's assimilation of the white's essence. Here one finds the proxy and the clone rolled into one, and the question of brotherhood asserts the sameness of white ex-ruler and black clone even as it articulates the bewilderment of the black populace confronted with this monstrosity. This prefiguration materializes in the collusion between the new leader Mr Slime, the Head Teacher who had forced him to quit teaching, and the white ex-landlord Mr Creighton, within the syndicate that dispossesses the peasants. The Old Man, also called Pa, properly traces the pattern back to Africa's collaboration with Europeans in the transatlantic slave trade (pp. 210–11). It is now that one appreciates the full force of the novel's epigraph, taken from Walt Whitman's poem 'This Compost': 'Something startles me where I thought I was safest.' This phenomenon of the leader as pimp and clone is aptly described by Kamau in Merle Collins' *Angel*: 'As long as we know dat even when we have black people in these parts, is really roast breadfruit we dealin wid. Is other people outside control dem. De profits not staying here. De blackness is only something de eye feel it see!' (*Angel* p. 157). One of the most memorable images of Leader's government is that of a bucket with a hole in the centre (p. 210).

White colonialism behind a black face, or the colonizer sneaking back through the backdoor, is illustrated clearly in Okri's mythical *The Famished Road* in the unexpected return of a murderous white man after five hundred years' supposed absence: 'His face and his nose and everything was exactly the same except that now he was a Yoruba man with fine marks on his face', and he follows the time-proven principle of neocolonalist infiltration, 'The only way to get out of Africa was to become an African' (*FR* p. 483). In Merle Collins' *Angel*, the people's misfortune begins with the emergence of a trait-orous self-seeker as leader of the independence struggle. Leader, as he is fondly known by his followers, is able to exploit the working people's grievances against their predatory employers, and weld those followers into a force for nationalist resistance. But intelligent, unemotional observers like Doodsie, the heroine's mother, are able to penetrate the mask and the rhetoric. 'Dat man like a lotta flash', she warns her brother Regal (p. 13). The discovery that Leader's boss (against whom he has been leading a struggle) is his bestman at his wedding (p. 17) points to the emergence of a puppet government. By the time independence is granted, he has emerged as a clone of the colonial ruler and plantation owners, a rampaging tyrant and despoiler of his own people, until his career is terminated in a *coup d'état*.

Angel is one of the few novels that work Big Power aggression into the plot and story line, the historical event being the 1983 murder of the populist Prime Minister Maurice Bishop and overthrow of his populist government by a military cabal sponsored by the American government. Collins' treatment of this historical event provides a chilling demonstration of how ex-colonial states' attempts at self-development and genuine independence are violently thwarted by Western government and business interests. To the American government, Maurice Bishop's attempt to free Grenada from the stranglehold of American multinational corporations, by construct-ing an international airport with Cuban help, was equivalent to 'communism'. The number of Grenadans slaughtered in that heroic crusade against communism has been suppressed in the interest of 'national security'. The operation itself retrospectively illuminates a brief earlier incident, in which Angel's younger brother Rupert plays Jimmy Cliff's famous anti-Vietnam War music, 'Vietnam', without understanding either the words or the message ('Vietnam' sounds like 'The Egg Nog' to him) – another instance of the Western powers forcing war and unimaginable devastation upon a people in the name of securing the world for 'free enterprise'.

A variation on this is the colonial dictatorship's installation of a handpicked mediocre leadership to be its successor and implement its neocolonialist objectives. V.S. Naipaul explores the careers of two such 'leaders' in *The Mystic Masseur* and *Guerrillas*. Set in a Caribbean territory on the eve of independence, *The Mystic Masseur* explores the meretricious ascent of Ganesh Ramsumair from obscurity to political leadership. Like Odili in *A Man of the People*, Ganesh drifts into politics to settle a personal score (pp. 151–60), but is then taken over by others who want to use him to settle their own personal scores (pp. 144–51). The relationship between him and the colonial regime is again paradigmatic of the incompatibility between nationalist and colonialist aspirations. Ganesh's initial mask of populist nationalism earns him the Colonial Office's hypocritical derision as 'an irresponsible agitator with no following' (p. 214). But no sooner does he discard his pseudo-patriotic mask by branding striking workers as communists than he is adopted by the colonial regime, knighted, appointed to the Legislative Council when his people reject him, and sponsored on foreign missions as his masters' mouthpiece. By that strange irony which sometimes patterns life on art, Naipaul's own career was later to climax in a similar decoration.

Ganesh's denunciation of the workers as communists reveals the animal cunning of his kind, for this is just the cry that guarantees a knee-jerk reaction of support from the American government. In *Guerrillas*, the playboy Jimmy Ahmed's exhibition of some leadership quality recommends him to the metropolitan establishment by whom he is promptly 'taken up', 'programmed', 'made famous' and sent back to his people as a Trojan horse of leadership to blunt the edge of indigenous nationalism. The moment his 'revolutionaries' seem to be taking the role seriously, the American government sends in the bombers and fighter planes. 'The Americans shoot everybody', Harry de Tunja reports, and 'are not going to let anybody here stop them lifting the bauxite' (p. 194). The eerie shadows cast by American helicopters over the land (p. 193) and the attack submarines lurking like death in the besieged country's waters (p. 201) come to life in Grenada in 1983, grim reminders that in the crushing tragedy of poverty and instability in many ex-colonial states it is the Big Powers who play the role of malicious deities.

VISIONS OF ALTERNATIVES

Despite the broad agreement among decolonization novelists in portraying the problems of the ex-colonial states, there is little agreement about the solution. Many novelists have been more concerned with diagnosing the ills of society than with prescribing cures, and given the complexity of the issues involved this is frequently the best that can be attempted through literature. Exposure of corruption goes hand in hand with indictment of villainy and demonstration of underlying historical processes, a linkage that is consistent with the novelists' decolonization agonistic. Others, such as Merle Collins, Armah (in his later novels), Ngugi and Soyinka go beyond exposure to offer a vision of an alternative social system.

Responses to post-independence failures therefore vary between the reformist and the tendentious. This contrast lies at the root of Ngugi's critique of Nigerian disillusionment literature of the 1960s. In 'Satire in Nigeria: Chinua Achebe, T.M. Aluko and Wole Soyinka', Ngugi assails the reformist artist for standing aloof to view society and highlight its weaknesses without attempting 'to seek out the source, the causes and the trends'.[19] The charge is amplified in his censure on *A Man of the People*. 'Achebe-cum-teacher', Ngugi complains, has either 'left too many questions unanswered', or 'left it to the pupils to find the answers', a 'failure' Ngugi attributes to the novelist's analysis of history from a moral rather than a Marxist ideological perspective:

> The novel seems to suggest the possibility of individual honesty, integrity and maybe greater efficiency [within the old system]. However, a given organisation of material interests dictates its own morality. Which do you change first in a society – its politico-economic base ... or the morality of individual men and women?[20]

There is some justification for Ngugi's criticism, for while *A Man of the People* offers a powerful exposure of the riotousness and corruption of independence politics in Nigeria and many other countries, the events are not integrated within the plot as the unfolding of a historical pattern. Achebe's interpretation of the crisis of independence is further blurred by his subsuming it within the rivalries between the academic elite and the non-academic elite within the ruling class. This in effect continues the debate between Obi Okonkwo and his friend Christopher in *No Longer at Ease* (pp. 20–1). Achebe obviously endorses the graduates' claims, as is inferable from the presentation of the economic crisis which follows the collapse of coffee prices in the Western-controlled international commodities market. The Minister of Finance Dr Makinde, 'a first-rate economist with a Ph.D. in public finance', presents to the Cabinet 'a complete plan for dealing with the situation' by 'cutting down the price paid to coffee planters'. But the Prime Minister rejects this plan from fear of antagonizing coffee farmers, whose votes he needs. The cabinet crisis culminates in the ignominious dismissal of Dr Makinde and his supporters, a full two-thirds of the Cabinet, 'all university people and highly educated professional men' (p. 4).

Achebe's pro-academics' bias is further seen in his characterization. The 'intellectuals' have impeccable private and professional credentials. His economists invariably come from the London School of Economics, as in *No Longer at Ease*, *A Man of the People* and *Anthills of the Savannah*. Ironically, the Finance Minister's 'complete plan', a typical International Monetary Fund formula, fails to address the crucial issue, which is not high producer price of coffee but economic hostage to Western interests. Reducing the farmers' payments will only spread the national misery without giving the country any control of its destiny, and this control cannot be achieved or even aspired to unless the leaders understand the forces behind the crisis. One may argue that the opinions expressed in the novel are the narrator Odili's rather than Achebe's. This would be untenable, however, for much as Achebe often makes Odili a satiric butt, overwhelming evidence in the novel suggests that he shares Odili's sentiments and moral positions on crucial issues, including this economic crisis. The recurrent invocation of the authority of the London School of Economics leaves no doubt that the novelist subscribes to its economic model.

Among those novelists who have interpreted the problem in terms of historical forces, individual ideological orientations also introduce wide variations in the novelists' visions of the road to New Jerusalem. Merle Collins' *Angel* clearly identifies American neo-colonialism as the historical roots of Grenada's problems, as it is America that violently thwarts the people's efforts to apply their own solutions to their problems. Though much of the story concerns the personal growth of the eponymous heroine, this growth is, like that of Lamming's G. in *In the Castle of My Skin* and Selvon's Tiger in *A Brighter Sun*, towards social, historical and political or ideological awareness, of which American imperialism comes as the climax. The ideals behind the decolonization struggle are clearly communalist, and the organization of the new society is envisaged as communalist too. Collins makes a point of demonstrating that imperialism or colonialism does not distinguish between the sexes, and whatever gender contradictions exist can be resolved through greater enlightenment. The national priority is solidarity. Hence in the brave but futile resistance to the American invasion it is a solid phalanx of men and women who constitute the citizens army.

In Armah, engagement with neocolonialism is arrived at after an initial period of moralist criticism in *The Beautyful Ones Are Not Yet Born*. By the time he comes to *Why Are We So Blest?*, he has identified neocolonialist economic oppression as the issue. Unlike Ngugi, however, he is not a socialist internationalist. His concern is with Africa and the (neo)colonialist domination of the black race by the white. Consequently, his solution to Africa's enduring humiliation and dispossession is separation of the two races so that Africa can take its destiny into its own hands. In *Why Are We So Blest?*, a revolutionary government in exile set up by a guerrilla army fighting for independence shows the disturbing germ of a racial hierarchy in its ranks, with positions of real power being occupied by mixed-race people while the menial posts are filled by real Africans. At its headquarters in the symbolically named capital city, Laccryville ('city of tears'), Solo, one of the protagonists, observes the black-white Foreign Minister Jorge Manuel socializing 'with suave travellers while down below the black one [his secretary Esteban Ngulo] licked the tasteless backs of stamps' (p. 51). *Why Are We So Blest?* thus constitutes the background to the racial separatism of *Two Thousand Seasons* and *The Healers*.

Against Armah's racial approach, Ngugi offers international socialism, from a perception of (neo)colonialism as colour-blind economic rather than racial oppression. In language reminiscent of Fanon, he has argued that (neo)colonialism has been perpetuated in post-independence Africa because apart from indigenization of personnel 'there has been little attempt at breaking with our inherited colonial past' through radical restructuring of economic and political institutions.[21] On the leadership, he argues that:

> the top few quickly identify their interests with the interests of the whole cultural linguistic group and cry wolf! The wolf here is another tribe or a supposed combination of tribes. Yet . . . there are no tribes in Africa [any more], only a linguistic cultural superstructure into which Western education aided by the colonial spiritual police (i.e. the missionaries) have made many inroads.[22]

Despite its accurate analysis of the elite's treachery and the insidious role of neocolonialism, Ngugi's dismissal of the ethnic factor has been repeatedly exposed as flawed by ethnic genocides that, though exploited and sometimes even sponsored by the West, nevertheless have developed independent momentum. Even the socialist model he fervently espouses with so much confidence has been thoroughly discredited by the inevitable collapse of the Soviet ideological bloc and its socialist economy between 1990 and 1992. The prescription also lacks political pragmatism, given the technological underdevelopment, the economic weakness and the examples of devastation wreaked by the West on ex-colonies that merely experimented with non-capitalist but not necessarily socialist economic systems.

These issues have always been at the heart of African Marxist critics' quarrel with Wole Soyinka. Like Ngugi, Soyinka has proclaimed his belief in 'the value of an egalitarian society ... egalitarianism in justice, in economic welfare, in the right of each individual to achieve maximum fulfilment ... [and] in retaining the means of production and the material benefits of production by the masses of the people'.[23] He maintains, however, that the ideological and organizational principles for achieving these goals already exist in traditional African social philosophy as exemplified by the World view of the Yoruba people of Nigeria. Social problems arise not from the economic system *per se* but from general apostasy and the Olympian mentality of the leadership. Soyinka's ideology thus shares some aspects of Armah's without Armah's racial focus, and some aspects of Ngugi's without the Marxist doctrine. 'Given equal opportunity', Soyinka argues without exaggeration, 'the black tin-god would degrade and dehumanise his victim as capably as [white] Vorster or Governor Wallace', and duplicate 'the intermittent European exercises in genocide'.[24] In his novel *Season of Anomy*, Soyinka unfolds a Fanonian programme for society's redemption through revolutionary violence.

By contrast, V.S. Naipaul has throughout his writing career interpreted the history of the ex-colonial states from a Western point of view. Views expressed in *The Middle Passage*, his early traveller's tale, were later fictionalized in a series of novels and short stories. The title of *The Middle Passage* consciously echoes the transatlantic journey of slaves from the West Coast of Africa to the Caribbean and the adjacent American coast, and the sub-title declares that the book represents Naipaul's 'impressions' of Trinidad, British Guiana, Surinam, Martinique and Jamaica. What Naipaul misleadingly calls 'impressions' are, however, no more than European-originated racial stereotypes. Naipaul's unreliability as witness or observer is betrayed in an illuminating passage where he preposterously declares in one of his mimic-European postures: 'It is hard to know exactly what a Guianese is thinking; *but if you made up your mind in advance you will find much corroboration.*'[25] Utterances like this explain why many serious Third World scholars have dismissed him as the model for the 'mimic man' of his fiction and cultural theory, the colonial mockery pursuing his own 'Christian-Hellenic tradition, which some might see as a paraphrase for whiteness'.[26] He has variously been denounced: as 'a despicable lackey of neocolonialism' by H.B. Synge; as 'a smart restorer of the comforting myths of the white race' by Chinua Achebe; as a man driven by inferiority complexes to write 'castrated satire' against his own people; and as a craven artist who 'assiduously flatters [British critics] by his stock-in-trade: self-contempt'.[27] Among recent critics, many share Fawzia Afzal-Khan's 1993 description of his work as 'a literature that is primarily self-hating', and the self-hate

> drives him incessantly to demarcate the difference between who he is today (an inhabitant of the world of 'light') and what his very distant past (with its link to India) was (a world of 'darkness'). What he is today...is an Anglicized West Indian with a remote Indian ancestry...As the westernized native par excellence, Naipaul succumbs to the syndrome of alienation so acutely described by Frantz Fanon...In so doing, Naipaul creates a literature of self-hatred that duplicates Orientalist strategies of containment in which myth is used neither to debunk itself nor to glorify the past, but as a symbol of petrified societies enshrouded in perpetual darkness.[28]

Naipaul ascribes the West Indies' postcolonial predicament to a single phenomenon: existential futility arising from lack of history or achievement. On this, Gerald Moore has commented:

> Here Naipaul is surely confusing a purely personal rejection with a historical fact...The salient impression upon the outsider who looks at West Indian achievement...over the past twenty years is precisely of intense creativity. But Naipaul also challenges the product [and his] charge is singularly unfair.[29]

If the West Indies strikes Naipaul as sheer futility, Africa incarnates the Hobbesian and Hegelian conceptions of raw nature, and his

Africa novels *In a Free State* (1973) and *A Bend in the River* (1979) are hardly more than nineteenth-century racial myths recast as fiction. Gerald Moore and Michael Neill have independently described Naipaul's early novels such as *The Mystic Masseur* and *The Suffrage of Elvira* as the work of a provincial writer,[30] but such provincialism actually characterizes all the novels. This is indirectly admitted even by ardent Naipaul admirers like Bruce King who has recently published a hagiography on his life and writing. King, who approaches Naipaul's writing with the unquestioning faith of a true believer, and eagerly repeats Naipaul's ill-informed comments on history and societies as if they were proven facts, has exonerated the blatant racial stereotyping found in the novels on the grounds of Naipaul's experience of bitter racial rivalry between Afro-Caribbeans and Indo-Caribbeans, and oppression of the latter by the former, between Naipaul's youth and the 1950s:

> the Indian socialists who won the elections were twice deposed, first by the British and later with American help. There have been bloody inter-racial riots and the country has been ruled by a tyrannical black nationalist government...Naipaul's view of decolonization has been influenced by such events and he has taken such knowledge with him on his travels where it has been confirmed by his observations about the situation of minorities in Africa and other parts of the third world.[31]

Bruce King fails to draw out the historical significance of the British and American neocolonialist overthrow of popularly elected governments and installation of puppet regimes. Like Naipaul, he confuses effects with causes and chooses the cheap escape from reality, and it is this which makes his attempt to explain Naipaul's vision of history as much of a failure as Naipaul's own vision. Naipaul's major problem is that, though a panoramic observer, he lacks a sense of history and causation. Perhaps this is not surprising from a novelist who by his own confession started writing from 'childish' and 'romantic' (his own words) delusions about the writer as a deified human.[32] In a 1958 article, 'London', he reveals that he was 'never disturbed by national or international issues'.[33] Thirteen years later, he expresses 'immense astonishment' at his own indifference to 'things like Mau Mau in Kenya in 1952', the Suez crisis of 1956, and America's decades-long atrocities in Vietnam.[34] None of his later novels suggests that he ever outgrew those 'childish' delusions and his indifference to history, or that he has learnt to understand history in terms of causation rather than racial stereotypes and the immutable, eternal patterns of myth. Karl Miller has indeed observed, *vis-à-vis* Naipaul's portrayal of Guyana, that:

> Since *The Middle Passage* and *The Mimic Men* were written, information has come to light which suggests that ten years [after Guiana's independence] the British and the American governments, and the CIA, were actually concerned to engineer a reversion to colonial rule.[35]

Guyana's tragedy has been re-enacted all over the Third World, but Naipaul portrays such neocolonialist subversion as proof that these societies are perennially doomed to existential futility by their inauthenticity, rather than as historical forces causally related to the problem. Michael Neill has observed that the decolonization theme in Naipaul's novels is a kind of riposte to Frantz Fanon's optimistic programme:

> Against Fanon's simple conviction that the colonial world can and must be made anew, Naipaul [in his *Overcrowded Barracoon*] poses a question about the foundations of power and legitimacy: 'How, without empire, do such societies govern themselves? What is the source of power? The ballot box, the mob, or the regiment?'[36]

In equating 'empire' with order, Naipaul easily falls into the trap of European historiographic fiction which denies the existence of indigenous foundations of order among many peoples before European conquest. This inevitably leads to his portrayal of decolonization struggles of all types as the nihilistic beginnings of a relapse into primordial savagery. Frantz Fanon wrote that 'decolonization is always a violent phenomenon' and 'a programme of complete disorder' whose historic goal is that 'the last shall be first and the first last'.[37] In *The Mimic Men*, *In A Free State* and *A Bend in the River*, the Fanonian vision is enacted as parody.

It is usual to follow the narrator Ranjit Kripalsingh's practice and describe *The Mimic Men* as an account of his own career as 'a leader of some sort, a politician' in the fictional Caribbean island state of Isabella. However, the major issue in the novel is not Ranjit Kripalsingh's political career – there is a more important politician in the story, the prime minister – but the powerlessness of ex-colonial states in the historical encounter with Europe. The pervasive imagery of shipwreck in the novel reinforces this theme. Like Adewale Maja-Pearce in *A Mask Dancing*, however, Naipaul also offers the powerlessness as argument against self-assertion, for Kripalsingh balances the state's predicament with the ruthless crushing of a workers' strike by employers and the consequent rise of religious fervour among the workers. The government's demand for a fair deal from the British exploiters of the country's bauxite deposits runs into a solid wall of hostility, bullying and blackmail from these foreign businesses (pp. 216–18). The workers' demand for better working conditions is ruthlessly crushed by their employers, who are foreigners.

To a writer with a sense of history, the connection between these phenomena should be obvious, but to Naipaul they are merely two parallel illustrations of the futility of action among a mimic people. Isabella gains a reprieve only when an action of the government of Jamaica breaks the foreign industrialists' stranglehold (p. 218), but this is entirely fortuitous, not part of a conscious coordination of policy by the two oppressed governments. Similarly, messianic hopes replace purposive action among the defeated workers, who quickly join the millennial cult led by the narrator's father Gurudeva, for whom religion provides escape from the psychologically devastating knowledge that he is a total failure as family head. Naipaul therefore presents the religious fervour and the political assertion in virtually identical terms. The former is 'an eccentric lower-class movement' (p. 123), 'a gesture of mass protest, a statement of despair, without a philosophy' (p. 133), while the latter is 'less a political awakening than a political anxiety' (pp. 189–90), offering mere political posturing and vague socialism garbed in 'borrowed phrases which were part of the escape from thought' (p. 199).

A.C. Derrick has rightly observed that Naipaul's exposure of what narrator Kripalsingh calls 'the malaise of our times' comprises 'mere verbal statement [without] enough concrete demonstration',[38] but this is itself part of Naipaul's even larger failure of recycling of 'borrowed phrases', borrowed thought and borrowed images under the delusion that he is seriously analysing or interpreting the world's history. For instance, the kind of industrial activity which Kripalsingh blithely dismisses as merely 'a process of filling imported tubes and tins with various imported substances' (pp. 215–16) is neither a peculiarly Third World phenomenon nor inherently unprofitable. A tiny island colony that has just gained flag independence amidst ferocious hostility from Western governments and trans-national capitalist corporations cannot do more. Besides, the lack of basic industrial infrastructure, which Naipaul presents as proof of Isabella's existential mimicry, is actually a legacy of underdevelopment by the colonial ruler.

It is, however, the Africa novels *In a Free State* and *A Bend in the River* that reveal most glaringly Naipaul's bemusement by history. The former is a collection of four short stories and a novella, 'In a Free State', all dealing with exile and spurious freedom, but it is the title story that is of interest in this study. 'In a Free State' is Naipaul's first reworking of Joseph Conrad's *Heart of Darkness*, the other being *A Bend in the River*, with which it shares a setting that is a composite of several East and Central African states which are clearly recognizable as Zaire/Congo, Uganda, Rwanda and Burundi. A European couple Bobby and Linda undertake a cross-country trip through the newly free African state. Bobby is one of the skeletal administrative staff of white expatriates who service the machinery of imperial rule on the eve of independence, and the cross-country journey is designed to bring him to an acknowledgement of Naipaul's thesis about African's lack of a viable future.

The opening paragraph rightly identifies the problems of independence politics: violent, ethnically oriented, frequently bereft of nationalist vision and constantly manipulated by cynical foreign powers. The language is appropriately mythopoeic, reminiscent of a creation myth, for Naipaul is presenting a scenario he wants his readers to accept as eternal:

> In this country in Africa there was a president and there was also a king. They belonged to different tribes. The enmity of the tribes was old, and with independence their anxieties about one another became acute. The king and the president intrigued with the local representatives of white governments. The white men who were appealed to liked the king personally. But the president was stronger; the new army was wholly his, of his tribe; and the white men decided that the president was to be supported. So that at last, this weekend, the president was able to send his army against the king's people. (*IFS* p. 103)

However, in imitation of his mentor, Conrad, Naipaul manipulates unfolding story events to demonstrate what he calls 'the pre-man side of Africa' (*IFS* p. 119), thus powerfully illustrating Bill Pearson's observation that racial stereotyping actually involves a writer's creating 'a puppet figure of his own, covering his own frustrated aspirations in a [racially coloured] skin, like a hermit crab'.[39] In this tale as in *The Mimic Men, A Bend in the River* and *Guerrillas*, Naipaul secretes not just his racial prejudices but also his own personal infirmities or deformities onto his generic 'African'. There is a complete breakdown of artistic objectivity and personal restraint as an atavistic impulse takes Naipaul back to his Caribbean youth of racial conflicts, which he vicariously re-enacts in the novels. As individuals and as a race, his Africans are almost invariably mentally defective, intellectually limited, physically repulsive, and oozing a characteristic stench. Any who is physically wholesome like Peter in 'In a Free State' is 'less like an African than a West Indian [such as V.S. Naipaul, perhaps?] or an American mulatto', or they have some non-African blood which humanizes them, like Hok in *The Mimic Men* and Jimmy Ahmed in *Guerrillas*. The unbridgeable chasm between Africans and human beings emerges clearly in the farcical scene where an Israeli military instructor drills African soldiers:

> The Israeli was doing one thing, the Africans another. The Israeli was using his body, exercising, demonstrating fitness. The Africans, their eyes half-closed, had fallen into a trance-like dance of the forest. Their knees hardly rose; their faces were blank with serious pleasure. ('IFS' p. 172)

In their embarrassing crudeness, vulgarity and puerility, these novels bespeak a drowsy imagination that, unable to soar, crawls through its own garbage heaps picking up bits and pieces of racial stereotype. Criticism that maintains that these portraits and opinions of Africa offered by Naipaul are those of the fictional characters rather than Naipaul's is no more than verbal hide and seek, for, as Bruce King unwittingly acknowledges, they are secretions of the mental and emotional baggage that Naipaul has dragged with him from his Trinidadian youth. It is impossible to imagine these racial stereotypes gaining scholarly acceptance if in place of 'African' one were to insert 'European', 'German', 'Asian', 'Jew', 'Chinese', 'Japanese', or any other racial/national group – as the noisy denunciations of Armah's much milder racial separatism amply demonstrate.

In *A Bend in the River*, the same atavistic racial memories are employed to account for the cycles of false starts at self-renewal in the newly independent state threatened by a pseudo-Fanonian guerrilla rebellion. The sprawling, incoherent plot is constructed out of strands of narrative each of which builds upon one aspect of the myth of Africa, and in the end both the author and his mouthpiece, the narrator Salim, prove dismally incapable of making any meaning out of the unfolding history. The vista of chaos is painted from within the fast-crumbling security of the retreating order of Salim, an Indian Moslem whose family has been settled for long on the East African coast and made their wealth from legitimate trade, crime and the selling of African slaves ('disguised as a cargo of rubber' after the end of the regular slave trade). People like Salim, Mahesh and Nazruddin constitute a predatory mid-level mercantile class who control the secondary levels of economic activity that are open to non-Europeans. They subvert the country's economic aspirations through syndicated operations in prostitution, currency forgery, commodities smuggling and the use of local fronts. Without any stake in the country's success, they are at present scurrying away from the rot to which they have contributed extensively, and scouting for safe havens for their abundant loot.

As in *The Mimic Men*, Naipaul identifies lack of indigenous manpower, finance and infrastructure as major constraints on development. This is brutally demonstrated in the Domain project. Conceived as a model metropolis and centre of excellence in intellectual research and development planning, the Domain quickly fossilizes as a glittering antiseptic city of glass, steel and concrete conjured out of the surrounding bush by European science and technology, and African money (*BR* pp. 94–110). Naipaul's real thesis, however, is that with the withdrawal of imperial order Africa is inexorably and literally reverting to jungle. A parody of Fanon's decolonization theory is introduced through the unseen Liberation Army with its blood-curdling rhetoric of apocalyptic dissolution, and its manifesto, 'The Ancestors Shriek', conceived by Naipaul in a rabid mockery of Third World revolutionary ideals (p. 219). In the terminal scene of the novel, the flight of white foreigners occurs against a background of absurdist and apocalyptic symbolism fused in the image of the steamer towing a barge occupied by the poorest passengers. Anarchy is let loose as numerous escape dugouts 'desperate only to be tied to the steamer' merely hamper its movement and get swamped in its wake. In the subsequent attack on the steamer, the barge is cut loose and set adrift, its occupants 'behind bars and wire-guards, as yet scarcely seemed to understand they were adrift'. The turning off of the steamer's lights following more attacks is supposed to prefigure the dissolution of the African world in primordial darkness and chaos (*BR* p. 287).

In Soyinka's *Season of Anomy* and Ngugi's *Petals of Blood*, *Devil on the Cross* and *Matigari*, the themes of neocolonialism and self-liberation receive much-needed intellectual analyses in place of the moral critiques of reformist novelists and the racial myth-making of V.S. Naipaul. *Season of Anomy* is a political allegory inspired by the Nigerian civil crises of January 1966 to January 1970, explored against the background of the country's origination as a British colonial creation and its entanglement in the neocolonialist web. The 'season of anomy' of the novel's title is, however, restricted to the pogroms which took place between June and October 1966, when northern Nigerians and the northern-controlled army slaughtered tens of thousands of southerners. Soyinka's allegorical plot fuses the Orpheus–Eurydice myth with the Yoruba drama of the gods to explore these historical issues in terms of constructing a new society from the debris of the old, or rescuing life from death. However, whereas the inspiration of the novel comes from the Nigerian pogroms, the relationship between the events depicted in the plot and those that actually occurred in Nigeria exists only at the symbolic level.

On the surface, the story is that of the artist-hero Ofeyi's cross-country journey in search of his mistress Iriyise. Ofeyi, the Co-ordinator of the Cocoa Corporation's sales promotion campaign, leads his team to shoot a commercial documentary film in the rural commune, Aiyéró, but becomes converted to its communalist ideals, which he sees as a model for the country: 'the waters of Aiyéró need to burst their banks. The grain must find new seminal grounds or it will atrophy and die' (p. 6). His subsequent revolutionary campaign of subversion against the Corporation provokes a genocidal backlash from its parent body, the Cartel, a Western multinational corporation. In a personal reprisal against Ofeyi, the Cartel's military thugs abduct his lover Iriyise as a personal prize for Zaki Amuri, the all-powerful feudal lord of Cross-River. Thus begins Ofeyi's journey into the self and history. From the lake of corpses at Shage dam (p. 173) through other grisly scenes of carnage (pp. 198–201, 220–8), the journey covers a landscape metaphorically transformed into Hell from which Ofeyi must rescue the life principle, Iriyise.

What Ofeyi immediately learns is the conspiracy between the indigenous ruling classes and multinational capitalism, which he connects to the self-betrayal involved in the African participation in the transatlantic slave trade and the role of religion in promoting imperialism. The trial of the peasant Salau is effectively a trial of the Cartel itself, as Salau's defence exposes the depredations caused by the Cartel through its Cocoa Corporation, The Mining Trust, and other subsidiaries (*SOA* pp. 121–3). The economics of neo-colonialism are further revealed in the connection established between the Cartel's reduction of the peasantry to beggary and the creation of inexhaustible pools of cheap labour. Salau's trial also exposes the treachery of the leadership who exploit ethnic and religious differences in order to secure the economic advantages of their collaboration with neo-colonialists, hence the feudal warlord Zaki Amuri's order at the end for the extermination of all non-indigenous residents of that part of the country (*SOA* p. 126). The mindless execution of this command by the populace constitutes another learning experience for Ofeyi, whose dream of Anubis offers some crucial insight into the psychology of mob violence (*SOA* p. 160).

There is considerable affinity between Soyinka's interpretation of history and his vision of the ideal society in *Season of Anomy* and those of Ngugi in *Petals of Blood*, *Devil on the Cross* and *Matigari*. As has been noted in Chapter 3, Ngugi wrote *Petals of Blood* to expose how a 'very huge tree prevents little flowers from reaching out into the light' and how 'the social system of capitalism acts to stifle life'.[40] This theme is effectively explored by a pervasive structure of metaphors: notably the chromatic imagery of golden flowers turned red by parasitic worms, the etiolation metaphor of shrubs dying from lack of sunlight, the ecological metaphor of drought and rain, and the physiological metaphor of maiming and sterility. The convergence between Soyinka and Ngugi (one may also include the later work of Armah) derives from the fact that the values which shape their world views are ultimately rooted in indigenous African culture.

Soyinka has compared his African Marxist opponents with adherents of an alien religion. They are, he writes in *Myth, Literature and the African World*, victims of 'externally induced fantasies of redemptive transformation in the image of alien masters' with their 'doctrine of self-negation, the first requirement for a transcendentalist (political or religious) fulfilment', and consequently fail to see that the 'universal verities' of their alien religion already exist from indigenous African world views and social structures.[41] The model for social reconstruction which he elicits from Yoruba cosmogony does indeed have remarkable resemblance to Ngugi's social theory despite the Marxist terminology of Ngugi's intellectual formulation of his own model. Soyinka's 'Aiyéró idea' which calls for 'the land to those who till it' and 'the sea to those who fish it' (*SOA* p. 111) becomes Ngugi's ideal of 'a human kingdom', 'a more humane world in which the inherited inventive genius of man in culture and science ... would not be the monopoly of a few but for the use of all' (*POB* p. 303; also pp. 246–7).

It is important to note, in this regard, that socialism in Ngugi's writing exists primarily in the rhetoric rather than the plot. There are invocations of Cuba, Mozambique, Guinea Bissau, Cambodia, and a few other societies that were officially Marxist at the time *Petals of Blood* and *Devil on the Cross* were written, but no incidents demonstrating the virtues of their social organization within the plot. Instead, models of resistance within the plot come from Gikuyu myth and legend, and the present militants are portrayed as successors to the long procession of resistance heroes stretching from the mythical past to the present, as revealed in Mugo wa Kibiro's blueprint. It is owing to their African origination that Ngugi's 'Marxist' arguments have retained their cogency in the wake of the disintegration of the Soviet Union and the haste with which its component republics (including Russia), erstwhile Eastern European satellites and Third World followers embraced the Western economic model.

Other superficial contrasts between Soyinka and Ngugi arise from the different focuses of their criticism. From a starting position that the institutional structures for achieving genuine independence already exist in indigenous African social organizations, Soyinka concentrates on the need to harness them, hence his emphasis on overthrowing a leadership which he considers a betrayal of African ideals. By contrast, Ngugi's Marxist orientation leads him to concentrate on the plight of the poor. In examining the society's plight in the context of humanity's struggle over millennia against 'the vagaries of nature and the uncontrollable actions of men' (*POB* p. 111; also p. 213), Ngugi is in effect highlighting the consequences of the leaders' apostasy, the betrayal of the promises of independence to foreign interests.

This is the meaning of the title, 'devil on the cross', taken from the heroine Jacinta Wariinga's recurrent nightmares in which after 'people in tattered clothes' have crucified the (capitalist) Devil he is promptly rescued and revived by 'people in dark suits and ties', the local stooges of the Europeans (pp. 139 and 239). The drought which ravages the village of Ilmorog in *Petals of Blood* is a natural disaster magnified by criminality in the leadership. The government's response to the community's appeal demonstrates the pitfalls of neocolonialist-sponsored 'development'. Ilmorog is opened up to Western businesses who, with their carnivorous ethics, quickly pauperize the peasant population, and destroy the family structures which have hitherto constituted the last bulwark against nature's vagaries and government's irresponsibility. The Trans-Africa Highway built ostensibly to unify Africa merely brings 'every corner of the continent... within easy reach of international capitalist robbery and exploitation' (*POB* p. 262). When the ancient shrine of Mwathi wa Mugo is finally erased with a bulldozer (pp. 265–6), the annihilation is symbolically completed. Ngugi's proletarian protagonist, Karega, sums up these forms of enslavement:

> In a world where a prince, a monarch, a business man can sit on billions while people starve... where a man who has never set foot on this land can sit in a New York or London Office and determine what I shall eat, read, think, do, only because he sits on a heap of billions taken from the world's poor, in such a world we are all prostituted. (*POB* p. 240)

Both writers also accompany their analyses with a decolonization programme which has three phases: mass education, mass mobilization (into such solid fronts as trade unions) and mass resistance. In *Season of Anomy*, Ofeyi's campaign begins with his conversion to Aiyéró ideals, and his working to educate the masses 'on a truly comprehensive scale'. Soyinka's imagery for the education and mobilization comes, with apocalyptic appropriateness, from the science of thermo-nuclear reactions: 'converting inertia into a mass momentum' (*SOA* pp. 117–18), an image that powerfully evokes Fanonian and biblical models of apocalypse. Ofeyi's grand vision aims to neutralize the 'conspiracy of power-besotted exploiters across national boundaries' (*SOA* p. 104) by cultivating 'a new concept of labouring hands across artificial frontiers, the concrete, affective presence of Aiyéró throughout the land, undermining the Cartel's superstructure of robbery, indignities and murder, ending a new phase of slavery' (p. 27; also pp. 90–2, 103–5).

Ideological education in Ngugi's novels is largely entrusted to such *raisonneurs* as Karega and the lawyer in *Petals of Blood*, Muturi, Wangari and Gatuiria in *Devil on the Cross*, and Matigari, Güthera and the trade unionist Ngarüro wa Kïrïo in *Matigari*. Like the author himself, all these characters emphasize the importance of what Karega in *Petals of Blood* defines as 'a vision of the future rooted in a critical awareness of the past' (pp. 198, 246–7). 'To understand the present', Karega explains, 'you must understand the past. To know where you are, you must know where you came from' (pp. 127–8). For Karega, history teaches the necessity of revolutionary praxis: 'the so-called victims, the poor, the downtrodden, the masses, had always struggled with spears and arrows, with their hands and songs of courage and hope, to end their oppression and exploitation: that they would continue struggling until a human kingdom came' (*POB* p. 303).

Through such education Ngugi stages a determined counterattack against neocolonialism's strategy of fomenting internal divisions among the oppressed in order to dissipate their energies and blur their common contradictions with the (neo)colonizer – a divide-and-conquer stratagem that informs much contemporary postmodernist and postcolonial cultural theory. Neocolonialism, the resistance leaders argue, does not distinguish between the victims' ethnic origins, religion, sex, or occupation, for 'the true house of Mumbi, Mumbi the mother creator, is all the black toiling masses carrying a jembe in one hand and three bullets in the other, struggling against centuries of drifting, sole witnesses of their own homecoming' (*POB* p. 237).

For both writers, the model of a functioning ideal society is also indigenous. In *Petals of Blood*, it is the original Ilmorog ideal that answers the question posed earlier in the novel: 'How did people produce and organize their wealth before colonialism?' (*POB* p. 199). Soyinka takes his own model Aiyéró from a real experiment by a similarly named Nigerian community in the 1960s, creatively modified to serve his purpose. Like its historical forebear, Soyinka's Aiyéró is a communalist utopia founded 'to seek truth, a better life, all the things that men run after' (*SOA* p. 9). Its other major purpose is to prepare the reader to accept the necessity of revolutionary violence in overthrowing the oppressive legacy of colonialism which perpetuates neocolonialism. Decolonization writers like V.S. Reid in *New Day* and Ayi Kwei Armah in *The Healers* have all confronted this grim imperative of liberation through violence, and in *Season of Anomy* Aiyéró's leader, Pa Ahime, calmly informs Ofeyi that 'The founding history of Aiyéró had its roots in violence' (p. 23).

Soyinka therefore uses Aiyéró to present revolutionary violence as a historical necessity. Historically, the commune's origination during the era of the transatlantic slave trade as a rebellion against an earlier commune, Aiyétómò, whose leaders had succumbed to the enervating message of European Christian missionaries, becomes a parable for the present. Aiyéró broke away from Aiyétómò because the parent society refused to abandon the teachings of the 'white god' whose members 'kill, burn, maim, loot and enslave our people' (*SOA* p. 10). Ofeyi's conversion finally comes about through a grim confrontation with scenes of carnage unleashed on Ghorolu or Curfew Town by the Cartel's military death squads (pp. 128–42). This experience constitutes his own death and descent into Hell, and he emerges enkindled with a revolutionary resolve to end such atrocities (p. 141). Ofeyi's conversion is ultimately shared by Ngugi's protagonists in *Petals of Blood*, *Devil on the Cross* and *Matigari*. Such acceptance of revolutionary violence is rooted partly in Kenya's own history of life-and-death guerrilla struggle against the British. *Petals of Blood* is specifically designed as a quest for the New Jerusalem which must be achieved through apocalyptic violence, a quest summarized through the sub-titles of the four divisions of the novel: 'Walking'/ 'Towards Bethlehem'/'To be born'/'Again . . . La Luta Continua'. The revolutionary slogan appended to the fourth sub-title proclaims an acceptance of struggle in whatever terms are demanded by the historical moment to break the vicious cycle of colonial and post-independence history. The apocalyptic process is initiated by the arrival of the school teacher Munira on his 'metal horse' at the wasteland, Ilmorog, like the biblical horsemen of the apocalypse (*POB* pp. 5–24). In *Matigari*, the eponymous guerrilla hero who discards his weapons of war following the attainment of independence is eventually forced by events to resort to armed resistance again.

Where Ngugi's work differs significantly from Soyinka's is the narrative form. Soyinka's *Season of Anomy* remains firmly within the realistic tradition of fiction, and the tone is consistently marked by high seriousness. Its tendentiousness is restrained within a very symbolic mode of exposition, and though a reader of average education can easily understand the novel at the level of narrative, considerable knowledge of Yoruba and Graeco-Asiatic myth and legend is required to really appreciate the symbolic and allegorical levels of its exploration of history. For its own part, Ngugi's writing from *Petals of Blood* is increasingly inclined towards explicit tendentiousness as the novel aims more and more at a proletarian audience who will translate the stories into social action in the real world. Tendentiousness frequently comes primarily through authorial voice-overs in the dialogue while the formal structure follows the conventions of the realistic novel. At the extreme pole of tendentiousness, *Devil on the Cross* and *Matigari* are designed as oral narratives within the tradition of Menippean satire, with staged debates in which the villains condemn themselves through naïve defences of their pernicious ideological positions and economic practices.

These differences play major roles in the dénouement of each plot. In the first of these three, *Petals of Blood*, the birth of a true liberation army – the 'Wakombozi' or 'society of one world liberation' – (pp. 343–4) bears the burden of future hopes after the portended apocalypse. From his torture cell in prison, Karega learns of these developments and derives consolation from contemplating 'tomorrow ... tomorrow' of struggle and eventual victory. In *Matigari*, the hero, seeker after truth and justice, is not just a character but also a role and a prophecy, an envisaged future in which the oppressed call the oppressors to account. In his role as an embodiment of the proletarian revolution, he calls the ruling class to account and defiantly tries to reclaim his house (the nation) from John Boy the descendant of traitors. The allegorical mode of the novel lends credibility to the plot, and Ngugi actually avoids any incidents that would strain belief. Failing to reclaim the house, Matigari burns it down and ignites an uprising in which the peasants unleash mayhem on other collaborators' property.

Between *Petals of Blood* and *Matigari*, *Devil on the Cross* stands as an illustration of a case in which a writer is seduced by the polemical denunciations and defiant speeches he assigns to his heroic peasant narrators and characters. In automotive-engineering symbolism which recalls Armah's *Why Are We So Blest?*, a lecture on the internal combustion engine becomes transformed into a lively propaganda on the generation and dynamics of revolutionary consciousness and movements. However, the *naïveté* of Wangari in her ordeal with the police (pp. 41–5, 105–8), the rash attack on the robber barons by a motley 'army of workers, and peasants, and petty traders, and students' (p. 203), and the idealized role of Jacinta Wariinga as ideal proletarian self-reliant heroine (pp. 216–23), all threaten to make these characters unintended butts of authorial irony. The shocking finale in which Jacinta Wariinga, meeting again the Rich Old Man who had ruined her youth, unflinchingly shoots him dead in his own house and wounds his three guests, despite knowing that he is the father of her fiancé's Gatuiria (pp. 246–54) raises human, social and legal questions which no revolutionary slogans can satisfactorily resolve. As Gatuiria stands petrified, 'Wariinga walked on, without once looking back. But she knew with all her heart that the hardest struggles of her life's journey lay ahead' (*DOC* p. 254). This folk-tale resolution is no more than a form of wish-fulfilment.

Soyinka's *Season of Anomy* does not climax in such Hollywood-style revolutionary pyrotechnics. The Dentist never even succeeds in executing Batoki, Chief Biga, or any of the other major villains. Nevertheless, undying hope is entwined in the plot which makes each defeat the prelude to another new beginning. The Cartel forces succeed in defeating the forces of revolution. But the cardinal quest to rescue Iriyise (Life) from the maws of Death or Hell (Temoko) is successfully accomplished. The title of this last section of the novel, 'Spores', with its biological symbolism of self-preserving encyst-ment, points to regeneration and future resistance. As Iriyise's inert form is borne homewards, 'in the forests, life began to stir' (*SOA* p. 320). 'The Aiyéró idea treks back to source', as the Dentist sum-med it up even earlier, 'but it marks the route for a more determined return' (p. 218). As the solid phalanx of questers merge with the night and the forest, the primeval womb, they carry the hopes of the future. They are the 'spores' of suspended lives, awaiting the resurrection.

The Novel as Cosmography

There is a sense in which every novel is a cosmographic document: a verbal structure that reflects, influences and enlarges upon a human society and individual experiences within that society. Accepted in its broad meaning, Philip Stevick's observation that 'almost everything one can say about Western culture from the beginning of the eighteenth century to the present can serve to characterise the [Western] novel'[1] is equally applicable to the relationship between ex-colonial societies and the decolonization novel. Unlike the Western novel, however, the decolonization novel did not simply 'emerge'. It arose primarily through conscious acts of nationalist (both political and cultural) assertion and quests for self-definition. It was *willed into being* in an origination context that does not in any way replicate the Englishman Daniel Defoe's serendipitous inauguration of the middle-class novel in Great Britain. Novelists in the (ex)colonial world made a conscious choice to harness the fictive mode as an auxiliary force in their societies' confrontations with colonialism and neocolonialism. One may go farther and assert that if the Western tradition had not existed, the imperatives of the decolonization struggle would nevertheless have led to a development of the genre, though its counter-discursive priorities and focus would have been somewhat different in the absence of whole generations of European novels which propagated the imperial ideology. The Australian Aboriginal writer Mudrooroo argues as much in his 'White Forms, Aboriginal Content'. Pre-European Aboriginals used prose 'in the telling of stories, tales and some historical events', he asserts, and 'this prose could easily be made to serve as a basis of a written tradition [as] has been done in the case of books of legends and stories'.[2]

The special circumstances of the decolonization novel's emergence, therefore, argue strongly against approaching it through theories and modes of critique which deny its material reference or subvert its agonistic purpose, such as the various postmodernisms (within which category one must include mainstream postcolonial discourse). For the same reasons, one must reject the brand of traditional criticism which assumes that the novel genre is a 'European' form to which non-European writers can only contribute 'content'. Early in the development of Maori europhone fiction the New Zealand critic Erik G. Schwimmer argued, 'the best of it resembles the type of work being done by African and West Indian authors writing in English; whilst the form is European, the subject matter arises out of the culture conflict to which the Maori intellectual is inevitably exposed'.[3] Nearly two decades later, the West African critic Eustace Palmer echoes the New Zealander, asserting that 'the novel' is a European form to which Africans could contribute only 'in the direction of themes, language, setting and point of view'.[4] 1990s postcolonial cultural theorists do not bother to assert such derivation any more, but this is only because it is now taken as axiomatic.

As a Western-originated, Western-defined theoretical practice and mode of critique, mainstream postcolonial discourse has no roots in the cultures or histories of the ex-colonial peoples, and its concerns are at polar variance from those of these societies. Its reference frames, cultural and historical landmarks, ideological orientation and anti-foundationalist posturing are rooted in European cultural experience rather than those of the (ex)colonial societies. Even the relatively simple issue of contradictions between 'art' and 'popular culture' is relevant primarily in a European context, where the commoditization of art creates a gap between what the rich collector can purchase and what the masses of people have access to. In most of the ex-colonial societies, art is merely one manifestation of popular culture, and ongoing changes to this relationship are best understood in terms of the class-aspirations of the local middle-class parvenus to locate themselves in what they perceive as a 'world culture' by mimicking the lifestyles of their European models. The Nigerian writer Cyprian Ekwensi unwittingly betrays this in his 1974 interview with Lee Nichols of the Voice of America. Introducing his 'technological' and 'electronic African', Ekwensi declares:

He's an executive and he's like his counterpart throughout the entire world except that he just happens to be an African. He's internationally travelled. He commutes to London or New York on a weekend and he's back at his desk the next morning. He's at an international conference. He purchases works of art for two thousand *naira*.[5]

What Ekwensi has noted, without recognizing it, is the indigenous elite's entanglement in the web of neocolonialism and its corruption of social relations. Postcolonial cultural theory is incapable of understanding the particular nature of this and allied cultural behaviours, but proceeds to subsume them within a universal movement of westernization in cultural tastes conditioned by Coca Cola and McDonalds burgers. Yet the spectacular success of Indian, Chinese, Japanese and other Oriental cuisine in many European/ American cities has not generated any corresponding universalist theory of orientalization in the domain of cultural tastes.

In more fundamental issues, such landmarks in the development of European civilization as the Dark Ages, the Renaissance, the Enlightenment, the Industrial Revolution, the 'post-capitalist' economy and the New World Order have a significance for Europeans that is different from their significance for the ex-colonial world. For Europe, the Renaissance represents rebirth, a reconnection of European cultures to their roots in classical Greece and Rome. For the rest of the world, however, the European Renaissance was the beginning of the descent into the Hell of imperialism and colonialism, and the New World Order is merely a climax of the historical processes inaugurated by the Renaissance. As a product of the same movement of history, the prevailing concept of postcoloniality is the academic obverse side of the political concept of 'international community', both serving the purpose of legitimizing dominance through semantic disruption of resistance. Just as the concept of 'international community' seeks to outlaw Third World resistance by anathematizing it as a threat to the New World Order, Western-defined 'postcoloniality' serves the purpose, presciently described by Walter Rodney, of keeping the colonized 'from dealing with their principal contradictions with the neocolonialist overlord'.[6] It is thus that decolonization discourse has been subversively infiltrated with social conflicts that more accurately reflect the West's cultural history, theories that propagate a Western view of the universe while blotting out the uniqueness of the Third World's colonial experience, and language that encodes and privileges Western social ideologies.

This is not to suggest a conscious complicity on the part of all scholars in this field, though one should not ignore the fact that many academics are part of the power structures and Think-Tanks that develop these political strategies. Most academics are, however, sucked into complicity by the fact of operating within a sphere of activity conceived as part of the grand schemes of geopolitical strategists and defined to channel all discourse into ready-made grooves. The natural instinct to excel in their fields, or, among the less serious, the desire to promote their careers, has ultimately resulted in unconscious collaboration with the structures of neocolonialist hegemony.

The subversion of academia by political interests through the packaging of political objectives as cultural discourse reached a triumphant climax in an aggressive reality-manipulation programme in the early 1990s, by which major international publishers were pressured by certain American interests to substitute 'postcolonial literatures in English' for 'Commonwealth Literatures' in the titles of readers, anthologies and encyclopaedias being prepared for publication.[7] Various 'innocent' explanations will no doubt be offered for this programme of renaming, but there can be no doubt about its relationship with the development of postcolonial cultural discourses in the preceding decade, and its practical effect on the development of the discourses during the succeeding period. At one level, the formulation of literary-cultural theories that reposition the triumphalist literature of imperialism and colonial conquest within the Western-defined 'postcolonial' domain, alongside the anti-imperialist literatures of the colonized, facilitates the erasure of the fundamental contradictions between the two traditions. Conceived as an existential, 'postmodern' condition in which colonizer and colonized are uniformly implicated, postcolonial discourses become no more than a branch of imperial or so-called 'metropolitan' discourse. At a second level, the infiltration of the discourse with alien paradigms of social conflict merely continues and perpetuates the divide-and-conquer stratagem whose potency has been proven in colonial wars of conquest. Thus did postcolonial 'gender discourse' emerge to neutralize the divisive effects of feminist scholarship in Western society while fragmenting ex-colonial societies with models of gender relationships constructed in the West from Western anthropological theses about non-Western cultures.

In effect, the colonialist criticism of the 1960s and 1970s is reasserting itself, after a brief retreat, as 'postcolonial discourse'. In *Mother Is Gold*, a typical work of the era, Adrian Roscoe had legislated that 'if an African writes in English his work must be considered as belonging to English letters as a whole, and it must be judged by the same critical standards as any other work written in English'.[8] African scholars, notably Chinweizu et al. in *Toward the Decolonisation of African Literature* (1980), promptly attacked Roscoe's inability to distinguish 'between English as a language used in literature by many outside the British nation, and English letters as a body of works of the British nation',[9] as well as the ideological implications of this distinction. The distinction forcefully but simply made by Chinweizu et al. has been ponderously reformulated in postcolonial discourse as a 'discontinuity' between 'English' and 'english' or various 'englishes'. Despite the word-game, however, postcolonial cultural discourse involves a hegemonic assimilation programme far more comprehensive than Roscoe's.

Indiscriminate amalgamation of all sorts of writing under the umbrella of cultural studies has also been demonstrated to militate against the development of a genuine postcolonial mode of discourse in other ways. To understand this issue properly, it is important to link it to another characteristic that Postcolonial Discourse has lifted from Postmodernist Discourse, and which Barbara Christian has properly denounced as 'the race for theory': an obsession with theory to the near exclusion of sustained, objective analysis of actual literary texts. Literature is a cultural artefact, but so are numerous products of science and technology. A theory of culture is therefore not necessarily a theory of literature. In the contest between colonizer and colonized, theories of culture have the advantage, from the (neo)colonialist viewpoint, of concentrating on issues of social organization and the internal relationships within a society, of which literary products are taken to be emblematic. In contrast, a theory of literature would sooner or later either confront the nationalistic embeddings in plot and theme or betray its own intellectual bankruptcy by a guilty silence. Consequently, a common phenomenon in academic cultural conferences is the smug dismissal of what is derisively called 'Literature with a capital L', by people who prefer to use literary texts in constructing cultural theories while manifesting a cynical disregard for serious literary criticism.

Among many Third World intellectuals, the generation of theory, or the demonstration of one's capability for doing so, represents the most visible proof of successful assimilation into the dominant order, even as the same intellectuals stake their claims as the vanguard of anti-colonialist resistance. A corollary to this is the demotion of serious criticism to a secondary level of intellectual activity. As many of the 'theories' are either mere adaptations of Western models or rehashes of the basic principles of traditional literary theory, all reformulated in the pompous jabberwocky language favoured in postmodernist discourse, they have proved dismally incapable of addressing the specific issues raised in the decolonization agonistics of the novels under study. They are therefore incapable of engendering a virile critical tradition, which demands probing beyond the surface of literary works to uncover, analyse and explicate a host of details as well as the pattern within which these are interrelated.

The discourse that purports to contest various hegemonies has itself become the site for frenzied quests for hegemony, and behind many practitioners' zeal for 'dismantling the Western canon' lies the desire to either join that canon or constitute oneself into a centre around which a new canon coalesces. For many, therefore, cultural theory has become the academic equivalent of racial 'passing'.

Decoupling postcolonial discourse from its unhealthy entanglement with imperial discourse has therefore been at the centre of the present study. In dealing with the decolonization novel as a cultural product responding to specific socio-historical forces, it has sought to refocus attention on the socio-historical, aesthetic and ideological determinations of this novel, hence the insistence on addressing the novelists' preoccupations with certain themes, the evolution of themes within the short historical span of the novel's existence, and the underlying patterns in form-content interactions. René Wellek and Austin Warren have rightly maintained that 'an artefact has the structure proper to the performance of its function, together with whatever accessories time and materials may make it possible, and taste may think it desirable, to add'.[10] 'All kinds of literature', Walter L. Reed observes in a similar vein, 'have felt and responded to the demands of representation, the need to modify or transform the inherited types and formulae the better to approximate the contemporary experience of author and audience.'[11] Ignoring these patterns has been largely responsible for the irrelevance of much Postcolonial cultural theory to the literature of the colonial experience created by writers from the ex-colonial societies.

The hypothetical evaluative model developed in Chapter 2 is offered as a rough guide towards understanding these interrelationships in a manner that a priori criticism rarely offers. Among the criss-cross of such interactions are those related to literary influences and aesthetic conventions, expository devices, structural devices, language and characterization. Of literary influences and conventions, the study has highlighted the proper role of oral literature in the development of the decolonization novel and the directions along which this literature exerts its influences. An understanding of the forms and functions of oral devices is indispensable to a deep appreciation of interrelationships among such constitutive elements of extended prose narratives as plot, setting, language and characterization, the modes of representing reality, time and space, and other culture-specific codes or conventions of aesthetic representation.

Of equal importance are the forms of affinity that exist among novels from various cultures which, though united by a common experience of European imperialism, colonialism and neocolonialism, are nevertheless as different from one another as human societies could be. Even within the same culture, writers retain individual distinctiveness going beyond mere personal style to more fundamental ideological perspectives that influence their representation of experience as art. For cross-cultural study to advance beyond both the facile universalism which elides difference by concentrating on trivia, and the quixotic assertiveness that creates the error it combats, it must be capable of isolating those ethno-aesthetic factors which constitute potential sites of convergence as well as divergence in the decolonization agonistic. Through the model developed in Chapter 2, it is possible to isolate such factors and their numerous gradations. Within that model, one may understand the decolonization novel as a composite whole, a quilt rather than a single piece, with certain major threads harmonizing and at the same time demarcating a host of individual and group practices. Applying that model to thematic analysis, for example, reveals a certain continuity from the first generation of novels usually classified as novels of cultural contact to the subsequent generations that comment on the failures of independence, or the failures of the promise of biculturalism in the case of Maori writing.

For European scholars in the humanities and social sciences, the antifoundationalist discourses of postmodernism may serve to assuage the anxiety of confronting the mind-boggling breakthroughs in the genuine sciences and technology where, ironically, the governing principle of language use is 'user-friendliness'. Third World scholars who pattern their discourse on the postmodernist template imagine that they are thereby participating in some grand intellectual phenomenon. Many have taken to heart Catherine Belsey's observation that 'new concepts, new theories, necessitate new, unfamiliar and therefore initially difficult discourses', but they ignore her timely reminder that 'the work of criticism is to release possible meanings'.[12] A genuine postcolonial mode of critique should promote the reader's appreciation of the literature in the fullness of its specific cultural and historical contexts, make accessible to the reader the codes and conventions of aesthetic composition which animate literary works, contribute to the development of the literary culture through intelligent analysis and evaluation that stimulate further interest in the literature, and reject the blandishments of a hegemonic ideological class which claims to be disestablishing the Western canon only to install itself as a new pantheon. It must therefore refocus its attention on the writer and the imaginative literature rather than the critic and his/her bloated ego, and this entails abandoning its sterile *in vacuo* theorizing in favour of developing theories rooted in actual cultural practice and literary texts.

A break from the baneful shadow of postmodernism and its derivatives need not entail a retreat from the currents of contemporary intellectual culture in the West or anywhere else; rather, it means the freedom to exploit the conceptual and methodological developments in fields of genuine cultural studies such as discourse analysis, psycholinguistics, sociolinguistics and literary stylistics, for the purpose of developing a critical culture that invigorates and enriches the imaginative literature. It also means a reconnection of academic practice with the political activism of writers who conceive their works as an extension of the anti-colonialist struggle. Adapting now the memorable words of Abiola Irele on the relationship between Western postmodernism and Africa's historical experience, Third World peoples have no use for 'the uncharted nihilism of this aspect of contemporary thought in the West' because, for them, 'history has not been ... a phantom play of mirrors, but rather a harrowing experience, vividly rendered in [their] imaginative expression and reflected in the general tenor of our discourse. This fact imposes on the [Third World] intellectual a certain moral responsibility'.[13]

Notes

1 CRISIS AND POLITICS IN POSTCOLONIAL DISCOURSE

1. Wole Soyinka, *Myth, Literature and the African World* (Cambridge: Cambridge University Press, 1976), p. x.
2. Rajeswari Mohan, 'Dodging the Crossfire: Questions for Postcolonial Pedagogy', *Teaching Postcolonial and Commonwealth Literatures*, special double issue of *College Literature*, 19.3/20.1 (October 1992/February 1993), 28–44.
3. Bill Ashcroft, Gareth Griffiths and Helen Tiffin, *The Empire Writes Back: Theory and Practice in Post-Colonial Literatures* (London and New York: Routledge, 1989), p. 2.
4. Ashcroft et al., *Empire Writes Back*, p. 2.
5. Ken Goodwin, 'Studying Commonwealth Literature', *Teaching Postcolonial and Commonwealth Literatures*, p. 149. Ashcroft et al. introduce this theory by referring to certain African-American, Canadian and West Indian writers who have supposedly 'drawn an analogy between the relationship of men and women and those of the imperial power and the colony, while critics like Gayatri Spivak have articulated the relationship between feminism, poststructuralism, and the discourse of post-coloniality', *Empire Writes Back*, pp. 31–2.
6. Ashcroft et al., *Empire Writes Back*, p. 2.
7. Edward Sapir, quoted in Roger Fowler, *Linguistic Criticism* (Oxford: Oxford University Press, 1986), p. 18.
8. Edward W. Said, *Culture & Imperialism* (London and New York: Routledge, 1993), p. 12.
9. See for example Elleke Boehmer, *Colonial & Postcolonial Literature* (Oxford: Oxford University Press, 1995), pp. 74–8.
10. Said, *Culture and Imperialism*, p. 62.
11. Pauline Hanson as reported by Sarah Ferguson, 'The Perils of Pauline', *Sunday Telegraph Magazine* (6 July 1997), 11 and 13, *passim*.
12. Bill Pearson, 'Attitudes to the Maori in Some Pakeha Fiction,' in *Fretful Sleepers and Other Essays* (London: Heinemann, 1974), pp. 54 and 55. See also Bill Pearson, *Rifled Sanctuaries: Some Views of the Pacific Islands in Western Literature to 1900* (Auckland: Auckland University Press and Oxford University Press, 1984).
13. Atareta Poananga, endorsed by Mana Wahine and Te Ahi Kaa, 'The Matriarch: Trample on Strong Women, Part II', *Broadsheet* (January/February, 1987), 25–9 (25).
14. Oodgeroo Noonaccal, Interview with Anna Rutherford, in Anna Rutherford, Lars Jensen and Shirley Chew, eds, *Into the Nineties: Post-Colonial Women's Writing* (Armidale, New South Wales: Dangaroo Press, 1994), p. 6.
15. Mudrooroo [Narogin], 'White Forms, Aboriginal Content', in Bill Ashcroft, Gareth Griffiths and Helen Tiffin, eds, *The Post-Colonial Studies Reader* (London and New York: Routledge, 1995), p. 231.

16. Derek Freeman, 'Derek Freeman: Reflections of a Heretic', address given at the Sydney Institute on 9 July 1996. Posted on the Internet at http://www.lse.ac.uk/depts/cpnss/evolutionist/evofeat2.htm. The full account of this hoax is given in Freeman's book, *Margaret Mead and the Heretic* (Harmondsworth: Penguin Books, 1996).

17. See Albert Wendt, 'Towards a New Oceania', in Guy Amirthanayagam, ed., *Writers in East–West Encounter: New Cultural Bearings* (London: Macmillan, 1982), pp. 202–15 (213). See also Wendt's introduction to *Lali: A Pacific Anthology* (Auckland: Longman Paul, 1980), p. xiv.

18. Freeman, 'Reflections of a Heretic'.

19. Chinua Achebe, 'An Image of Africa: Racism in Conrad's *Heart of Darkness*', reprinted in *Hopes and Impediments: Selected Essays 1965–1987* (London: Heinemann, 1988), pp. 1–13 (8).

20. Terry Collits, 'Theorising Racism', in Chris Tiffin and Alan Lawson, eds, *De-Scribing Empire: Post-colonialism and Textuality* (London and New York: Routledge, 1994), pp. 61–9 (67).

21. Bruce Fleming, 'Brothers under the Skin: Achebe on *Heart of Darkness*', *Teaching Postcolonial and Commonwealth Literatures*, 90–9 (94–5).

22. See Joseph McCabe, *The Lies and Fallacies of the Encyclopedia Britannica: How Powerful and Shameless Clerical Forces Castrated a Famous Work of Reference*, and his *The Columbia Encyclopedia's Crimes against the Truth: How a Popular Reference Work Is Being Used as a Weapon against Free Culture and Twisted to Fit the Purposes of Lying Obscurantists*. Both publications were available on McCabe's The Secular Web site, http://www.infidels.org as of 18 June 1997, when I accessed the site.

23. Oliver Bennett, 'Evolution of Man: Female Circumcision', *RX: the Sunday Telegraph Magazine* (22 June 1997), 36.

24. See Stanley K. Henshaw and Jennifer Van Vort, 'Abortion Services in the United States, 1991 and 1992', *Family Planning Perspectives*, Vol. 26 (May/June 1994), 101.

25. Atareta Poananga, Mana Wahine and Te Ahi Kaa, '*The Matriarch*: Trample on Strong Women, Part I', *Broadsheet* (December 1986), 23–8 (27).

26. Alison Donnell, 'Writing for Resistance: Nationalism and Narratives of Liberation,' in Joan Anim-Addo, ed. *Framing the Word: Gender and Genre in Caribbean Women's Writing*, (London: Whiting and Birch, 1996), pp. 28–36 (28).

27. Katherine Frank, 'Women without Men: the Feminist Novel in Africa', *African Literature Today*, No. 15 (1987), 14–34 (16).

28. Frank, 'Women without Men', 15 and 29, *passim*.

29. Anne McClintock, *Imperial Leather: Race, Gender and Sexuality in the Colonial Contest* (New York and London: Routledge, 1995), p. 254.

30. Mineke Schipper, 'Mother Africa on a Pedestal: the Male Heritage in African Literature and Criticism', *African Literature Today*, No. 15 (1987), 35–54 (35).

31. Florence Stratton, *Contemporary African Literature and the Politics of Gender* (London and New York: Routledge, 1994).

32. Stratton, *Contemporary African Literature*, pp. 16–17.

33. Fela's pidgin lyric could be re-rendered thus:

> Now listen to this one
> War Against Indiscipline
> And the Nigerian government's talk:
> 'My people are useless
> My people are senseless
> My people are undisciplined.'
> That's the Nigerian government speaking:
> . . . .
> I have never heard that kind of talk before
> . . . .
> What kind of talk is that?
> It is the talk of the insane
> It is the talk of beasts.

34. Barbara Christian, 'The Race for Theory', in JanMohamed and Lloyd, *Nature and Context of Minority Discourse*, pp. 37–49 (46).
35. Amos Tutuola, *The Palm-Wine Drinkard* (London: Faber and Faber, 1952), pp. 17, 25 and 59.
36. Stratton, *Contemporary African Literature*, p. 29.
37. James Olney, *Tell Me Africa: an Approach to African Literature* (Princeton, New Jersey: Princeton University Press, 1973), p. 167.
38. Maryse Condé, 'Three Female Writers in Modern Africa: Flora Nwapa, Ama Ata Aidoo and Grace Ogot', *Présence Africaine*, 82:2 (1972), 132–43 (142).
39. Chinua Achebe, 'The Education of a "British Protected" Child', *Cambridge Review*, Vol. 114, No. 2321 (June 1993), 51–7 (53).
40. Alice Walker, 'Letter from Alice Walker to President Clinton', 13 March 1996. Posted on the World Wide Web at http://www.igc.apc.org/cubasoli/.
41. Toni Morrison, *The Bluest Eye* (London: Pan Books, 1990), pp. 94–5.
42. Charlotte H. Bruner, ed., *The Heinemann Book of African Women's Writing* (London: Heinemann, 1993), pp. vii–viii.
43. Ibid.
44. Terence Hawkes, *Meaning by Shakespeare* (London and New York: Routledge, 1992), blurb.
45. Michel Foucault, 'What Is an Author?' in David Lodge, ed., *Modern Criticism and Theory* (Harlow, Essex: Longman, 1988), pp. 196–210 (209).
46. Linda Hutcheon, *A Poetics of Postmodernism: History, Theory, Fiction* (London and New York: Routledge, 1988), p. 55.
47. Dominic Strinati, *An Introduction to Theories of Popular Culture* (London and New York: Routledge, 1995), p. 242.
48. Jean-François Lyotard, *The Postmodern Condition: a Report on Knowledge*, trans. Geoff Bennington and Brian Massumi (Manchester: Manchester University Press, 1984), p. xxiii.
49. H.P. Grice, 'Logic and Conversation,' cited by Fowler, *Linguistic Criticism*, p. 106.
50. Christian, 'Race for Theory', p. 43.
51. See Albert Wendt, in Elizabeth Alley and Mark Williams, eds., *In the Same Room: Conversations with New Zealand Writers* (Auckland: Auck-

land University Press, 1992), pp. 109–10, and Witi Ihimaera, in ibid., p. 222.

52. Gayatri Spivak, 'Reflections on Cultural Studies in the Post-Colonial Conjuncture,' *Critical Studies*, Vol. 3, No. 1 (1991), 64–78 (65).
53. Abdul R. JanMohamed and David Lloyd, eds, *The Nature and Context of Minority Discourse* (New York and Oxford: Oxford University Press, 1990), p. ix.
54. Witi Ihimaera, 'Maori Life and Literature: a Sensory Perception', in *New Zealand through the Arts: Past and Present*, three lectures reprinted from the Turnbull Library record, May 1982 (Wellington: Friends of the Turnbull Library, 1982), pp. 45–55 (51–2).
55. Wendt, 'Towards a New Oceania', pp. 212–13.
56. The West Indies had, among others, *Forum Quarterly* (1931–4; as *The Forum Magazine*, 1943–5), *Bim* (founded 1942), *Trinidad* (1929–30), *The Beacon* (1931–3), *Kyk-over-al* (1945–61) and *Focus* (1943–60). In Africa, there were *Présence Africaine* (founded 1947), *Black Orpheus* (founded 1957) and *Transition* (founded 1961, became *Ch'Indaba* from No. 50), and *Nigeria Magazine* (established 1934). Several newspapers and commercial magazines also hosted literary works, while publications by higher educational institutions offered yet more outlet. In Polynesia, the South Pacific Creative Arts Society, established 1973 by some prominent Pacific Islanders and some University of the South Pacific staff, persuaded the *Pacific Islands Monthly* to allot four pages, called the 'Mana' section, in each issue to works by new local artists. From the setting up of Mana Publications in 1974 rose the society's own English-language literary biennial, *Mana*. Several New Zealand magazines like *Landfall, Islands, Pacific Quarterly Moana, Te Ao Hu* (published by the Department of Maori affairs) and the literary sections of the *New Zealand Herald* and *New Zealand Listener* provided ready outlets to the creative energies of Maori writers.
57. M.J.C. Echeruo, *Joyce Cary and the Novel of Africa* (London: Longman, 1973), pp. 1–18, *passim*.
58. Echeruo, *Joyce Cary and the Novel of Africa*, p. 5.
59. Albert Wendt, 'Towards a New Oceania', p. 213.
60. By Witi Ihimaera's account, his literary career began in response to his people's charge: 'You must work for the Maori people.' His first published work, the short story collection *Pounamu, Pounamu* was accordingly born of two cultural-nationalistic drives: 'to get out a novel by a Maori', and to reinvigorate Maoritanga, the Maori system of values, by imaginatively recreating it for Maori children who had been alienated from it by European settler domination. Rachel Nunns has also shown that Patricia Grace's *Wiariki* is a similar response to her Maori people's charge: 'Show others who we are.' See Ihimaera, 'Maori Life and Literature,' pp. 47–9, *passim*; also Ihimaera in 'The First Maori Novelist', private interview with Blanaid Fitzgerald, *New Zealand Listener*, October, 1972, p. 15; Rachel Nunns, 'Doing Her Job: Patricia Grace's Fiction', *Islands*, Vol. VII, No. 4 (August 1979), 416–21 (416–17). Albert Wendt scorns the fashionable Western image of the artist as a rebel isolated from a philistine society. He will not become 'a professional writer, making a living from writing', Interview with John and Rose

Marie Beston, *World Literatures Written in English*, Vol. XII, No. 1 (April 1977), 155. For Chinua Achebe, the task – 'to help my society regain its belief in itself and put away the complex of years of denigration and self-denigration' – is no less than 'a revolution'. See Achebe, 'The Novelist as Teacher', essay reprinted in *Morning Yet on Creation Day* (London: Heinemann, 1977), p. 44. *Things Fall Apart* was partly a response to European imperial-outpost novels like Joyce Cary's *Mister Johnson* and Joseph Conrad's *Heart of Darkness*, but also a counter to the missionary, Rev. G.T. Basden (Achebe, 'Named for Victoria, Queen of England', essay reprinted in *Morning Yet*, p. 70; also Robert Wren, *Achebe's World: the Historical and Cultural Context of the Novels of Chinua Achebe* (London: Longman, 1978), pp. 6–9). These positions had been anticipated by the West Indian writers. Roger Mais, for instance, insisted in 1942 that any Jamaican political nationalism must be invigorated by a corresponding cultural and literary nationalism. Mais's first collection of short stories, *Face*, was accordingly conceived in cultural nationalistic terms as the work 'of a hundred percent Jamaican writing about a hundred percent Jamaicans', quoted in Karina Williamson, 'Roger Mais: West Indian Novelist', *Journal of Commonwealth Literature*, No. 2 (December 1966), 138–47 (140). And V.S. Reid, in the Author's Note to his novel *New Day* (1949), proclaims such cultural nationalism to be his primary artistic motivation. George Lamming's boast about the political-psychological role of the West Indian novel has already been noted (*Pleasures of Exile*, p. 39), as has Witi Ihimaera's position about the sacredness of the Maori language as opposed to English which is profane (*In the Same Room*, p. 231).

61. See Wendt, 'Towards a New Oceania,' p. 204, and Aimé Césaire, quoted in Janheinz Jahn, *A History of Neo-African Literature* (London: Faber and Faber, 1966), pp. 243–4.

62. Wendt, in Alley and Williams, *In the Same Room*, pp. 111–12.

63. See Dennis Baron, 'Ebonics Is Not a Panacea for Students at Risk', *Chronicle of Higher Education* (24 January 1997), B4. The Colorado school board's action sparked off much debate, a sample of which may be found in the *Chronicle* of 17 and 24 January, 7 and 14 March, 11 and 18 April, and 9 May 1997.

64. Liz McMillen, 'Linguists Find the Debate Over "Ebonics" Uninformed', *Chronicle of Higher Education* (17 January 1997), A16.

65. Ketu H. Katrak, 'Decolonizing Culture: Toward a Theory for Postcolonial Women's Texts', *Modern Fiction Studies*, Vol. 35, No. 1 (Spring 1989), 157–79.

2 THE POLITICS OF FORM: IDEOLOGY, FORM AND TECHNIQUE

1. René Wellek and Austin Warren, *Theory of Literature* (Harmondsworth: Penguin, 1980), p. 22. Cf. Ruth Finnegan, *Oral Literature in Africa* (Nairobi: Oxford University Press, 1970), p. 17.

2. Roland Barthes, 'The Death of the Author', in David Lodge, ed., *Modern Criticism and Theory* (London and New York, 1988), pp. 166–95 (168).

3. Robert Te Kotahi Mahuta, 'Whaikoorero: a Study of Formal Maori Speech', Unpublished MA thesis, University of Auckland, 1974, pp. 6, 13 and 20, *passim*.

4. Soyinka, *Myth, Literature and the African World*, p. 2.

5. E.N. Obiechina, *Culture, Tradition and Society in the West African Novel* (Cambridge: Cambridge University Press, 1975), p. 156; cf. Mahuta, 'Whaikoorero', p. 25.

6. Walter J. Ong, *Orality and Literacy: the Technologizing of the Word* (London and New York: Methuen, 1982), pp. 37–8, *passim*.

7. See Jack Goody, *The Domestication of the Savage Mind* (Cambridge: Cambridge University Press, 1977), pp. 10–13, 36–7, *passim*; cf. Ong, *Orality and Literacy*, pp. 103–5, *passim*.

8. Robert Plant Armstrong, 'Narrative and Intensive Continuity: *The Palm-Wine Drinkard*', in Bernth Lindfors, ed., *Critical Perspectives on Amos Tutuola* (London: Heinemann, 1980), pp. 163–88 (174).

9. Robert Fraser, *The Novels of Ayi Kwei Armah* (London: Heinemann, 1980), p. x.

10. By Ngugi's own account, he abandoned English when he realized that continued use of the colonizer's language was to 'perpetuate the neocolonial vice, to identify with the language instrument of a foreign culture', 'The Writer of His World', Talk given at the Africa Centre, London, December 1980. Reported in *West Africa* (22–9 December 1980), 2606. In 'The Language of African Literature', his Robb's Series lecture given at the University of Auckland in August 1984, Ngugi revealed that this decision was the culmination of the crisis triggered by the 1960s debate on the language of African literature. This lecture was later incorporated in *Decolonising the Mind: the Politics of Language in African Literature* (London: James Currey, 1986).

11. Robert Young, *White Mythologies: Writing History and the West* (London and New York: Routledge, 1990), p. 2.

12. Ihimaera, 'Maori Life and Literature,' p. 50.

13. Witi Ihimaera, quoted in Richard Corballis, 'Witi Ihimaera: Literary Diplomacy,' *Landfall*, 129, Vol. XXXIII, No. 1 (March 1979), 64–71 (64); cf. Bill Pearson, 'Recent Maori Writers,' *Fretful Sleepers and Other Essays*, pp. 155–8, *passim*.

14. Mark Williams, *Leaving the Highway: Six Contemporary New Zealand Novelists* (Auckland: Auckland University Press, 1990), p. 131.

15. C.K. Stead, 'War Book: The Matriarch', review of *The Matriarch*, by Witi Ihimaera, *London Review of Books* (18 December 1986), 20–2 (20 and 21), *passim*.

16. See Albert Wendt, Interview with Michael Neill, in Alley and Williams, *In the Same Room*, pp. 102 and 106, *passim*.

17. Charles Larson, *The Emergence of African Fiction* (London: Macmillan, 1978), p. 102.

18. Charles Larson, *The Novel in the Third World* (Washington, DC: Inscape Publishers, 1976), pp. 45, 64–5, *passim*.

19. Goody, *Domestication of the Savage Mind*, p. 45.
20. Anthony Giddens, *Central Problems in Social Theory* (London: Macmillan, 1979), p. 201.
21. Ian Watt, *The Rise of the Novel: Studies in Defoe, Richardson and Fielding* (London: Chatto and Windus, 1957), pp. 22–4, *passim*.
22. Lewis Mumford, *Technique and Civilisation* (London: Routledge, 1947), pp. 15–16.
23. Thorleif Boman, *Hebrew Thought Compared with Greek*, trans. Jules L. Moreau (New York: W.W. Norton, 1960), p. 124.
24. Larson, *Emergence of African Fiction*, pp. 102 and 105. Both are footnotes in Larson's book.
25. Ihimaera, in Alley and Williams, *In the Same Room*, p. 231.
26. Soyinka, *Myth, Literature and the African World*, p. 10.
27. Obiechina, *Culture, Tradition and Society*, p. 125.
28. John J. White, *Mythology in the Modern Novel: a Study of Prefiguration Techniques* (Princeton, New Jersey: Princeton University Press, 1971), p. 7.
29. Mircea Eliade, *The Myth of the Eternal Return or, Cosmos and History*, trans. Willard R. Trask (Princeton, New Jersey: Princeton University Press, 1971), pp. 19 and 37.
30. Soyinka, *Myth, Literature, and the African World*, p. 1.
31. Ibid., p. 14.
32. See Wole Soyinka, *Idanre and Other Poems* (London: Methuen, 1967). I have treated this road symbolism and Ben Okri's debt to Soyinka for *The Famished Road* in my 'Modern African Literature: Quest for Order in a Changing Order,' *Cambridge Anthropology*, 15: 3 (1991), 41–51.
33. Wole Soyinka, *The Road* (London: Oxford University Press, 1965).
34. Patricia Grace, Interview with Jane McRae, in Alley and Williams, *In the Same Room*, p. 295.
35. Christopher Caudwell, *Illusion and Reality* (London: Lawrence and Wishart, 1946), pp. 41–2.
36. J.G. Frazer, *The Golden Bough: a Study in Magic and Religion*, abridged edition (London: Macmillan, 1987). See in particular Chapter 4: 'Magic and Religion,' and Chapter 7: 'Incarnate Human Gods'.
37. J.H. Nketia, *Funeral Dirges of the Akan People* (Achimota: University College of the Cape Coast, 1955), pp. 47–8, *passim*.

3 THE AGONISTIC OF TONGUES

1. Fowler, *Linguistic Criticism*, p. 31.
2. Lyotard, *Postmodern Condition*, p. 10.
3. Lyotard, *The Postmodern Condition*, p. 10.
4. B.L. Whorf, *Language, Thought and Reality*, quoted in Fowler, *Linguistic Criticism*, p. 32.
5. Fowler, *Linguistic Criticism*, p. 22.
6. O. Mannoni, *Prospero and Caliban: the Psychology of Colonization*, 2nd edition, trans. Pamela Powesland (New York: Frederick A. Praeger, 1964), p. 99.

7. George Lamming, in Jahn, *History of Neo-African Literature*, p. 240.
8. Dwight Bolinger, *Aspects of Language* (New York: Harcourt, Brace and World, 1968), p. 259.
9. Joseph Conrad, *Heart of Darkness*, ed. Robert Hampson (Harmondsworth: Penguin, 1995), p. 108.
10. David Spurr, *The Rhetoric of Empire: Colonial Discourse in Journalism, Travel Writing, and Imperial Administration* (Durham and London: Duke University Press, 1993), p. 102.
11. Spurr, *Rhetoric of Empire*, pp. 102–3.
12. Jamaica Kincaid, *A Small Place* (London: Virago Press, 1988), pp. 31–2.
13. Cyprian Ekwensi, 'African Literature', *Nigeria Magazine*, No. 83 (December 1964), 294–9, *passim*. See also his August 1974 interview with Lee Nichols, in which he describes 'the new African', a westernized middleclass academic or businessman who is just 'like his counterpart throughout the entire world except that he just happens to be an African'. In Lee Nichols, *Conversations with African Writers* (Washington, DC: Voice of America, 1981), p. 45.
14. Buchi Emecheta, Interview with Adeola James, in Adeola James, ed., *In Their Own Voices: African Women Writers Talk* (London: James Currey, 1990), pp. 34–45 (39).
15. Frank, 'Women without Men', pp. 27 and 28, *passim*.
16. Emecheta, Interview with Adeola James, p. 37.
17. Obiajunwa Wali, 'Dead End of African Literature?' *Transition*, No. 10 (September 1963), 13–15.
18. B. Rajan, 'Identity and Nationality', quoted in O.P. Joneja, 'Domesticated English: Symbiotic or Syncretic: the Language of African and Indian Fiction Novel' (sic), *ACLALS Bulletin*, 7th Series, No. 6 (1986), 20–8 (21).
19. Ngugi wa Thiong'o, *Decolonising the Mind*, p. xiv.
20. Chinua Achebe, 'English and the African Writer,' *Transition*, Vol. 4, No. 18 (1965), 17–30 (30). Ngugi reproduces this quotation from the reprint in Achebe's *Morning Yet on Creation Day*. See Ngugi, *Decolonising the Mind*, p. 7.
21. Wole Soyinka, 'Letter to the Editor', *Transition*, 10 (1963), 9.
22. Adewale Maja-Pearce, *A Mask Dancing: Nigerian Novelists of the Eighties* (London: Hans Zell, 1992), p. 2.
23. Ihimaera, in Alley and Williams, *In the Same Room*, p. 231.
24. Chinua Achebe, 'The Role of the Writer in a New Nation', *Nigeria Magazine*, No. 81 (June 1964), 157–60 (160).
25. Lewis Nkosi, quoted in Gerald Moore and Ulli Beier, eds, *Modern Poetry from Africa* (Harmondsworth: Penguin Books, 1963), p. 15.
26. Adewale Maja-Pearce, 'Just Another Sick Book', *Okike: an African Journal of New Writing*, No. 23 (February 1983), 133–6, *passim*.
27. Derek Wright, 'Love and Politics in the African Novel: Ayi Kwei Armah's *Why Are We So Blest?*' *ACLALS Bulletin*, 7th Series, No. 1 (1986), 13–27 (26).
28. W.J. Howard, 'Themes and Development in the Novels of Ngugi', in Edgar Wright, ed., *A Critical Evaluation of African Literature* (London: Heinemann, 1973), p. 111.
29. Stead, 'War Book: The Matriarch', p. 20.

30. See Collits, 'Theorising Racism', p. 67.
31. Raja Rao, *Kanthapura* (Bombay: Oxford University Press, 1963), p. vii; George Lamming, *The Pleasures of Exile* (London: Michael Joseph, 1960), p. 36; also p. 44.
32. See for example Barthes' 'The Death of the Author', p. 170.
33. M.A.K. Halliday, 'Linguistic Function and Literary Style', in Seymour Chatman, ed., *Literary Style: a Symposium* (London: Oxford University Press, 1971), pp. 332–4, *passim*.
34. Patricia Grace, Interview with Jane McRae, in Alley and Williams, *In the Same Room*, p. 294.
35. Keith Waterhouse, review of *No Longer at Ease*, by Chinua Achebe, *New Statesman*, LX (17 September 1960), 396.
36. Ann Banfield, 'Reflective and Non-Reflective Consciousness in the Language of Fiction', *Poetics Today*, Vol. 2:2 (1981), 62.
37. Peter Crisp, 'Albert Wendt: Pathways to Darkness', *Islands: a New Zealand Quarterly of Arts and Letters*, Vol. 7, No. 4 (August 1979), 376.
38. Roger Robinson, 'Albert Wendt: an Assessment', *Landfall*, 135, Vol. 34, No. 3 (September 1980), 275–89 (281–2).
39. Ashcroft et al., *Empire Writes Back*, pp. 67 and 68, *passim*.
40. Wole Soyinka, private interview with John Agetua, in John Agetua, *When the Man Died: Views, Reviews and Interview on Wole Soyinka's Controversial Book* (Benin City: John Agetua, 1975), p. 35.
41. T.S. Eliot, 'The Metaphysical Poets,' in *Selected Essays*, 3rd edition (London: Faber and Faber, 1951), p. 289.
42. Niyi Osundare, 'Words of Iron, Sentences of Thunder: Soyinka's Prose Style', *African Literature Today*, No. 13 (1983), 24–37 (33–4), *passim*.
43. Among Austin Shelton's more spectacular failures is the translation of the Igbo word 'utu' as 'penis' whereas it means a 'berry' in the context, without even a figurative connection with penis. From his error, Shelton proceeds to speculate philosophically on the penis, just as Chantal Zabus bases major language theories on poor translations. See Austin Shelton, 'The "Palm Oil" of Language: Proverbs in Chinua Achebe's Novels', *Modern Language Quarterly*, 30:1 (1969), 86–111. Zabus's efforts at independent 'translation', usually from contextual inference, also tend to have unfortunate results, as in her translation of 'Usa bulu okpili' as 'the moon kills little boys' whereas it means 'glutton'. See Chantal Zabus, *The African Palimpsest: Indigenization of Language in the West African Europhone Novel* (Amsterdam, Atlanta: Rodopi, 1991), p. 140.
44. Norman Simms, 'A Maori Literature in English, Part 1: Patricia Grace', *Pacific Quarterly Moana*, Vol. 3, No. 2 (April 1978), 186–99 (192).
45. Simms, 'Maori Literature in English, Part 1', 186.
46. Barbara Lalla, *Defining Jamaican Fiction: Marronage and the Discourse of Survival* (Tuscaloosa and London: The University of Alabama Press, 1996), p. 12.
47. Peter A. Roberts, *West Indians and Their Language* (Cambridge: Cambridge University Press, 1988), p. 5.
48. Merle Collins, 'Framing the Word: Caribbean Women's Writing', in Joan Anim-Addo, ed., *Framing the Word: Gender and Genre in Caribbean Women's Writing* (London: Whiting & Birch, 1996), pp. 4–11 (5).

49. R.B. Le Page, 'Dialect in West Indian Literature', in Edward Baugh, ed., *Critics on Caribbean Literature* (London: George Allen and Unwin, 1978), pp. 128–9.
50. Frederic G. Cassidy, *Jamaica Talk*, 2nd edition (London: Macmillan, 1971), pp. 2–3.
51. Le Page, 'Dialect in West Indian Literature,' p. 129.
52. Mervyn Morris, Introduction to V.S. Reid, *New Day* (London: Heinemann, 1949), n.p.
53. Roberts, *West Indians and Their Language*, p. 6.
54. Fowler, *Linguistic Criticism*, p. 18.
55. Quoted in Williamson, 'Roger Mais: West Indian Novelist', 140.
56. Lamming, *Pleasures of Exile*, p. 39.
57. 'Maori-go-Round,' anonymous review of *Tangi*, by Witi Ihimaera, in *Times Literary Supplement* (12 July 1974), 471.
58. Patricia Grace, Interview with Jane McRae, in Alley and Williams, *In the Same Room*, p. 295.
59. Chantal Zabus, 'Language, Orality, and Literature', in Bruce King, ed., *New National and Post-Colonial Literatures: an Introduction* (Oxford: Clarendon Press, 1996), p. 34.
60. Professor Bill Pearson, formerly of the University of Auckland, has translated this as 'What is the greatest thing in the world? People, people, people'.
61. J.H. Nketia, quoted in Finnegan, *Oral Literature in Africa*, pp. 389–90.
62. Vladimir Ivir, 'Formal Correspondence *Vs* Translation Equivalence Revisited', *Poetics Today*, Vol. 2:4 (1981), 56.
63. Chinua Achebe, 'English and the African Writer', *Transition*, Vol. 4: 18 (1965), 29–30.
64. E.N. Obiechina, 'The Problem of Language in African Writing: the Example of the Novel', *The Conch*, 5:1 & 2 (1972), 11–29 (17).
65. Shelton, 'The "Palm Oil" of Language', 103.
66. Susan Rubin Suleiman, 'Redundancy and the "Readable" Text', *Poetics Today*, Vol. 1:3 (1980), 119–20.
67. Achebe, 'Role of the Writer in a New Nation,' 160.
68. Frank K. Stanzel, 'Teller-Characters and Reflector Characters in Narrative Theory', *Poetics Today*, Vol. 2:2 (1981), 6–14, *passim*.
69. Quoted in Banfield, 'Reflective and Non-Reflective Consciousness', 61.
70. An extended discussion of this aspect of Achebe's language was presented in my 'Social Transition and Cultural Noetics in the Language of Chinua Achebe's Fiction', paper contributed to the 'Conference on Tradition and Transition in African Letters', Yale University, 19–21 April 1990.
71. Osundare, 'Words of Iron, Sentences of Thunder', 28–30.
72. Ashcroft et al., *Empire Writes Back*, p. 71.
73. Fowler, *Linguistic Criticism*, p. 32.
74. Homi Bhabha, 'Representation and the Colonial Text: a Critical Exploration of Some Forms of Mimeticism', in Frank Gloversmith, ed., *The Theory of Reading* (Brighton: Harvester Press, 1984), pp. 93–121 (99, 115, *passim*).
75. Bhabha, 'Representation and the Colonial Text', pp. 98–9.

76. Gérard Genette, *Narrative Discourse*, trans. Jane E. Lewin (Oxford: Blackwell, 1980), p. 164.
77. Umberto Eco, 'The Semantics of Metaphor', *The Role of the Reader: Explorations in the Semiotics of Texts* (London: Hutchinson, 1981), p. 68.
78. Jacques Lacan, 'The Insistence of the Letter in the Unconscious', in David Lodge, ed., *Modern Criticism and Theory* (Harlow, Essex: Longman, 1988), pp. 79–106 (89).
79. A.E. Darbyshire, *A Grammar of Style* (London: André Deutsch, 1971), pp. 162–5, *passim*.
80. Catherine Belsey, *Critical Practice* (London and New York: Routledge, 1980), p. 3.
81. Derek Walcott, 'The Swamp', *Selected Poems* (New York: Farrar, Strauss and Co., 1964), pp. 60–1.
82. G.D. Killam, 'A Note on the Title of *Petals of Blood*', *Journal of Commonwealth Literature*, Vol. XV, No. 1(August 1980), 125–32 (129–30).
83. Ngugi wa Thiong'o, Interview with Anita Shreve, *Vita* (July 1977), p. 35, quoted in Killam, 'Note on the Title of *Petals of Blood*,' p. 132.

4 CULTURAL AFFIRMATION AND RESISTANCE

1.   Maja-Pearce, *Mask Dancing*, p. 5.
2.   Ibid., p. 10.
3.   For Wendt's condemnation of such myth makers as Margaret Mead, Somerset Maugham and James Michener, see his Introduction to *Lali*, p. xvi; also 'Towards a New Oceania', p. 213. For the comment on culture, see 'Towards a New Oceania', p. 206.
4.   Chinua Achebe, Interview with Bill Moyers, in Betty Sue Flowers, ed., *Bill Moyers: a World of Ideas* (New York: Doubleday, 1989), p. 340.
5.   Carole Boyce Davies, 'Motherhood in the Works of Male and Female Igbo Writers: Achebe, Emecheta, Nwapa and Nzekwu', in Carole Boyce Davies and Anne Adams Graves, eds, *Ngambika: Studies of Women in African Literature* (Trenton, New Jersey: African World Press, 1986), pp. 241–56 (247).
6.   Stratton, *Contemporary African Literature*, pp. 30 and 31, *passim*.
7.   Patricia Grace, in Alley and Williams, *In the Same Room*, pp. 290 and 291, *passim*.
8.   I am indebted to Professor Bill Pearson of the University of Auckland for parts of this background.
9.   Richard Corballis and Simon Garrett, *Introducing Witi Ihimaera* (Auckland: Longman Paul, 1984), p. 29.
10. Williams, *Leaving the Highway*, p. 114.
11. Ihimaera, 'Maori Life and Literature', p. 47.
12. Ibid., p. 49.
13. Umelo Ojinmah, *Witi Ihimaera: a Changing Vision* (Dunedin: University of Otago Press, 1993), pp. 38–9.
14. V.S. Naipaul, *The Middle Passage* (Harmondsworth: Penguin, 1969), p. 73.

15. Michael Neill, 'Coming Home: Teaching the Post-Colonial Novel', *Islands* 35, New Series Vol. 2, No. 1 (April 1985), 38–53 (45).
16. Andrew Gurr, *Writers in Exile: the Creative Use of Home in Modern Literature* (Sussex: Harvester Press; and New Jersey: Humanities Press, 1981), p. 73.
17. Ngugi wa Thiong'o, 'A Kind of Homecoming', in Ngugi, *Homecoming: Essays on African and Caribbean Literature* (London: Heinemann, 1972), pp. 93 and 94, *passim*.
18. Gordon Rohlehr, 'Character and Rebellion in *A House for Mr Biswas,*' in Robert D. Hamner, ed., *Critical Perspectives on V.S. Naipaul* (Washington, DC: Three Continents Press, 1977), pp. 84–93 (91).
19. Michel Fabre, 'Samuel Selvon', in Bruce King, ed., *West Indian Literature* (London: Macmillan, 1979), pp. 111–25 (112).
20. Albert Wendt, Interview with Michael Neill, in Alley and Williams, *In the Same Room*, p. 108.
21. The representation of the West as 'Other-World' and 'Other-Worlders' is obviously a direct intervention in the current debate in cultural studies whose Eurocentric focus organizes reality through a binary opposition of the West and its 'Others'. Wendt adopts a Polynesian/ Third World self-focus by which the West is logically the Other.
22. Achebe, 'Education of a "British protected" Child', 52.
23. Mannoni, *Prospero and Caliban*, p. 106.
24. Gerald Moore, *Twelve African Writers* (London: Hutchinson, 1980), p. 268.
25. Gurr, *Writers in Exile*, p. 106.
26. Ngugi wa Thiong'o, cited in W.J. Howard, 'Themes and Development in the Novels of Ngugi', p. 137.
27. Ngugi, in ibid., p. 267.
28. See Jomo Kenyatta, *Facing Mount Kenya: the Traditional Life of the Gikuyu*, African Writers Series (London: Heinemann, 1979), p. xv.
29. Witi Ihimaera, quoted in Corballis, 'Witi Ihimaera: Literary Diplomacy', 64.
30. Ihimaera, 'Maori Life and Literature,' p. 50.
31. Ihimaera, Interview with Mark Williams, in Alley and Williams, *In the Same Room*, p. 224.
32. D.F. McKenzie, *Oral Culture, Literacy and Print in Early New Zealand* (Wellington: Victoria University Press, 1985), p. 33.
33. Ibid., p. 6.
34. Adam Shoemaker, 'Paper Tracks: Indigenous Literatures in Canada, Australia, and New Zealand', in Bruce King, ed., *New National and Post-Colonial Literatures: an Introduction* (Oxford: Clarendon Press, 1996), pp. 245–63 (251–2).

5   CASUALTIES OF FREEDOM

1. Wole Soyinka, 'The Writer in a Modern African State,' in Per Wastberg, ed., *The Writer in Modern Africa* (Uppsala: Scandinavia Institute for African Studies, 1968), pp. 14–21 (16 and 17, *passim*).

2. Albert Wendt has revealed to Michael Neill that the hero's disillusionment in *Sons for the Return Home* 'was also my own as a young writer'. Alley and Williams, *In the Same Room*, p. 107.

3. Young, *White Mythologies*, p. 14.

4. See T.S. Eliot, 'Journey of the Magi', *Selected Poems* (London: Faber and Faber, 1961), pp. 97–8.

5. See also Chidi Okonkwo, 'Chinua Achebe: the Wrestler and the Challenge of Chaos', in Michael Parker and Roger Starkey, eds, *Postcolonial Literatures: Achebe, Ngugi, Desai, Walcott* (London: Macmillan, 1995), pp. 83–100.

6. Cf. Okonkwo, 'Chinua Achebe'.

7. Arthur Ravenscroft, *Chinua Achebe* (London: Longman, 1969), p. 20.

8. Obiechina, *Culture, Tradition and Society* , pp. 136–7, 140–54, *passim*.

9. Frantz Fanon, *Black Skin, White Masks*, trans. Charles Lam Markmann (New York: Grove Press, 1967), p. 47.

10. Nketia, *Funeral Dirges of the Akan People*, pp. 47–8, *passim*.

11. Frantz Fanon, *The Wretched of the Earth*, trans. Constance Farrington (Harmondsworth: Penguin, 1967), p. 123.

12. Grace Ogot, Interview with Lee Nichols, in Nichols, *Conversations with African Writers*, p. 212.

13. See for example Stratton, *Contemporary African Literature and the Politics of Gender*, p. 60.

14. Buchi Emecheta, Interview with Adeola James, pp. 37 and 39, *passim*.

15. Fanon, *Wretched of the Earth*, p. 42.

16. Fanon, *Wretched of the Earth*, pp. 37–8.

17. Fanon, *Wretched of the Earth*, pp. 120–3, 123–41, *passim*.

18. Walter Rodney, *How Europe Underdeveloped Africa* (London: Bogle-L'Ouverture, 1972), p. 250.

19. James Ngugi, 'Satire in Nigeria,' in Cosmo Pieterse and Donald Munro, eds, *Protest and Conflict in African Literature* (London: Heinemann, 1969), pp. 56–69 (69).

20. Ngugi wa Thiong'o, 'Chinua Achebe: *A Man of the People*', in Ngugi, *Homecoming*, pp. 53–4.

21. Ngugi, *Homecoming*, p. xvi.

22. Ibid., p. xvii.

23. Wole Soyinka, Interview with John Agetua, in John Agetua, ed., *When the Man Died*, p. 41.

24. Soyinka, 'Writer in a Modern African State', p. 20.

25. Naipaul, *Middle Passage*, p. 130.

26. Ibid., pp. 71–3. See also p. 86 for Naipaul's exposition on racial attitudes and complexes.

27. H.B. Synge, 'V.S. Naipaul: a Spokesman for Neo-Colonialism,' *Literature and Ideology*, No. 2 (Summer 1969), 85, quoted in Robert D. Hamner, ed., *Critical Perspectives on V.S. Naipaul* (Washington, DC: Three Continents Press, 1977), p. xxvii; Chinua Achebe, quoted in Michael Neill, 'Guerrillas and Gangs: Frantz Fanon and V.S. Naipaul', *Ariel*, XIII, No. 4 (October 1982), 21–62 (21); Lamming, *Pleasures of Exile*, pp. 30 and 225; Ivan van Sertima, 'V.S. Naipaul', Foreword, *Caribbean Writers: Critical Essays* (London: New Beacon Books, 1968).

28. Fawzia Afzal-Khan, *Cultural Imperialism and the Indo-English Novel: Genre and Ideology in R.K. Narayan, Anita Desai, Kamala Markandaya, and Salman Rushdie* (Pennsylvania: Pennsylvania State University Press, 1993), pp. 9, 10–11, *passim*.

29. Gerald Moore, *The Chosen Tongue* (London: Longman, 1969), p. 26.

30. Moore, *Chosen Tongue*, pp. 6–7; Neill, 'Guerrillas and Gangs', p. 26.

31. Bruce King, *V.S. Naipaul* (London: Macmillan, 1993), p. 12.

32. V.S. Naipaul, quoted in Hamner, *Critical Perspectives on V.S. Naipaul*, p. 51.

33. V.S. Naipaul, 'London', *Times Literary Supplement* (15 August 1958). Reprinted in Hamner, *Critical Perspectives on V.S. Naipaul*, p. 12.

34. V.S. Naipaul, 'Without a Place', Interview with Ian Hamilton, reprinted in Hamner, *Critical Perspectives on V.S. Naipaul*, p. 40.

35. Karl Miller, 'V.S. Naipaul and the New Order', in Hamner, *Critical Perspectives on V.S. Naipaul*, pp. 111–26 (121).

36. Neill, 'Guerrillas and Gangs', p. 41.

37. Fanon, *Wretched of the Earth*, pp. 27–8.

38. A.C. Derrick, 'Naipaul's Technique as a Novelist', in Hamner, *Critical Perspectives on V.S. Naipaul*, pp. 194–207 (205).

39. Bill Pearson, 'Attitudes to the Maori in Some Pakeha Fiction', *Fretful Sleepers*, p. 57. See also pp. 54 and 63.

40. Ngugi wa Thiong'o, Interview with Anita Shreve, *Vita* (July 1977), p. 35, quoted in Killam, 'Note on the Title of *Petals of Blood*', p. 132.

41. Soyinka, *Myth, Literature and the African World*, p. xii.

THE NOVEL AS COSMOGRAPHY

1. Philip Stevick, *The Theory of the Novel* (New York: Free Press, 1967), p. 8.

2. Mudrooroo, 'White Forms, Aboriginal Content', in Ashcroft et al., *Post-Colonial Studies Reader*, pp. 228–31 (229).

3. E[rik] G. S[chwimmer], 'A Note on the Literature of the Modern Maori,' *Mate*, No. 4 (February 1960), 22–3 (23).

4. Eustace Palmer, *The Growth of the African Novel* (London: Heinemann, 1979), pp. 5–6.

5. Cyprian Ekwensi, Interview with Lee Nichols, in Nichols, *Conversations with African Writers*, p. 45.

6. Walter Rodney, *How Europe Underdeveloped Africa*, p. 250.

7. The present writer was involved in one such book project in which 'Postcolonial Literatures in English' was substituted for 'Commonwealth Literatures' under the described circumstances in 1992/93.

8. Adrian Roscoe, *Mother Is Gold: a Study in West African Literature* (Cambridge: Cambridge University Press, 1971), the blurb, also p. x.

9. Chinweizu, Onwuchekwa Jemie and Ihechukwu Madubuike, *Toward the Decolonization of African Literature*, Vol. 1: *African Fiction and Poetry and Their Critics* (Enugu: Fourth Dimension Publishers, 1980), p. 9.

10. Wellek and Warren, *Theory of Literature*, p. 29.

11. Walter L. Reed, 'The Problem with a Poetics of the Novel,' in Mark Spilka, ed., *Towards a Poetic of Fiction* (Bloomington and London: Indiana University Press, 1977), pp. 62–74 (64).
12. Belsey, *Critical Practice*, pp. 5 and 144, *passim*.
13. Abiola Irele, 'Dimensions of African Discourse', *Teaching Postcolonial and Commonwealth Literatures*, special double issue of *College Literature*, 19: 3/20:1 (October 1992/February 1993), 45–59 (56).

Bibliography

Achebe, Chinua, *Things Fall Apart*. London: Heinemann, 1958.
——, *No Longer at Ease*. London: Heinemann, 1963.
——,'The Role of the Writer in a New Nation', *Nigeria Magazine*, No. 81 (June 1964), 157–60.
——, 'English and the African Writer', *Transition*, Vol. 4, No. 18 (1965), 17–30.
——, *Arrow of God*. London: Heinemann, 1964, revised edition 1974.
——, *Morning Yet on Creation Day*. London: Heinemann, 1977.
——, *Anthills of the Savannah*. Ibadan: Heinemann, 1988.
——, *Hopes and Impediments: Selected Essays 1965–1987*. London: Heinemann, 1988.
——, 'The Education of a "British Protected" Child'. *Cambridge Review*, Vol. 114, No. 2321 (June 1993), 51–7.
Afzal-Khan, Fawzia, *Cultural Imperialism and the Indo-English Novel: Genre and Ideology in R.K. Narayan, Anita Desai, Kamala Markandaya, and Salman Rushdie*. Pennsylvania: Pennsylvania State University Press, 1993.
Agetua, John, ed., *When the Man Died: Views, Reviews and Interview on Wole Soyinka's Controversial Book*. Benin City: John Agetua, 1975.
Alley, Elizabeth, and Mark Williams, eds, *In the Same Room: Conversations with New Zealand Writers*. Auckland: Auckland University Press, 1992.
Anim-Addo, Joan, ed., *Framing the Word: Gender and Genre in Caribbean Women's Writing*. London: Whiting and Birch, 1996.
——, *Fragments* (1970). African Writers Series. London: Heinemann, 1974.
——, *Why Are We So Blest?* (1972). London: Heinemann, 1974.
Armah, Ayi Kwei, *The Beautyful Ones Are Not Yet Born*. London: Heinemann, 1975.
——, *The Healers* (1978). London: Heinemann, 1979.
——, *Two Thousand Seasons* (1973). London: Heinemann, 1979.
Armstrong, Robert Plant, 'Narrative and Intensive Continuity: *The Palm-Wine Drinkard*', in Bernth Lindfors, ed., *Critical Perspectives on Amos Tutuola*. London: Heinemann, 1980, pp. 163–88.
Ashcroft, Bill, Gareth Griffiths and Helen Tiffin, *The Empire Writes Back: Theory and Practice in Post-Colonial Literatures*. London and New York: Routledge, 1989.
Banfield, Ann, 'Reflective and Non-Reflective Consciousness in the Language of Fiction', *Poetics Today*, Vol. 2:2 (1981).
Baron, Dennis, 'Ebonics Is Not a Panacea for Students at Risk', *Chronicle of Higher Education* (24 January 1997), B4.
Barthes, Roland, 'The Death of the Author', in David Lodge, ed., *Modern Criticism and Theory*. London and New York: Longman, 1988, pp. 166–95.
Beach, Joseph Warren, *The Twentieth-Century Novel: Studies in Technique*. New York: D. Appleton Century, 1932.
Belsey, Catherine, *Critical Practice*. London and New York: Routledge, 1980.
Bennett, Oliver, 'Evolution of Man: Female Circumcision', *RX: The Sunday Telegraph Magazine* (22 June 1997), 36.

Bhabha, Homi, 'Representation and the Colonial Text: a Critical Exploration of Some Forms of Mimeticism', in Frank Gloversmith, ed., *The Theory of Reading*. Brighton: Harvester Press, 1984, pp. 93–121.

Boehmer, Elleke, *Colonial & Postcolonial Literature*. Oxford: Oxford University Press, 1995.

Bolinger, Dwight, *Aspects of Language*. New York: Harcourt, Brace and World, 1968.

Boman, Thorleif, *Hebrew Thought Compared with Greek*, trans. Jules L. Moreau. New York: W.W. Norton, 1960.

Brodber, Erna, *Myal*. London: New Beacon, 1988.

Bruner, Charlotte H., ed., *The Heinemann Book of African Women's Writing*. London: Heinemann, 1993.

Brydon, Diana, and Helen Tiffin, *Decolonising Fictions*. Sydney: Dangaroo Press, 1993.

Carroll, J.B., ed., *Language, Thought and Reality*. Cambridge, Massachusetts: MIT Press, 1956.

Cassidy, Frederic G., *Jamaica Talk*, 2nd edition. London: Macmillan, 1971.

Caudwell, Christopher, *Illusion and Reality*. London: Lawrence and Wishart, 1946.

Chinweizu, Onwuchekwa Jemie, and Ihechukwu Madubuike, *Towards the Decolonisation of African Literature*, Vol. 1: *African Fiction and Poetry and Their Critics*. Enugu: Fourth Dimension Publishers, 1980.

Christian, Barbara, 'The Race for Theory', in JanMohamed and Lloyd, *Nature and Context of Minority Discourse*, pp. 37–49.

Collins, Merle, *Angel*. London: Women's Press, 1987.

——, 'Framing the Word: Caribbean Women's Writing', in Anim-Ado, *Framing the Word*, pp. 4–11.

Collits, Terry, 'Theorising Racism', in Chris Tiffin and Alan Lawson, eds., *De-Scribing Empire: Post-colonialism and Textuality*. London and New York: Routledge, 1994, pp. 61–9.

Condé, Maryse, 'Three Female Writers in Modern Africa: Flora Nwapa, Ama Ata Aidoo and Grace Ogot', *Présence Africaine*, Vol. 82:2 (1972), 132–43.

Conrad, Joseph, *Heart of Darkness*, ed. Robert Hampson. Harmondsworth: Penguin, 1995.

Corballis, Richard, 'Witi Ihimaera: Literary Diplomacy', *Landfall*, 129, Vol. XXXIII, No. 1 (March 1979), 64–71.

Corballis, Richard, and Simon Garett, *Introducing Witi Ihimaera*. Auckland: Longman Paul, 1984.

Crisp, Peter, 'Albert Wendt: Pathways to Darkness', *Islands: a New Zealand Quarterly of Arts and Letters*, Vol. 7, No. 4 (August 1979), 374–85.

Darbyshire, A.E., *A Grammar of Style*. London: André Deutsch, 1971.

Davies, Carole Boyce, 'Motherhood in the Works of Male and Female Igbo Writers: Achebe, Emecheta, Nwapa and Nzekwu', in Carole Boyce Davies and Anne Adams Graves, eds, *Ngambika: Studies of Women in African Literature*, Trenton, New Jersey: African World Press, 1986, pp. 241–56.

Derrick, A.C., 'Naipaul's Technique as a Novelist', in Robert D. Hamner, ed., *Critical Perspectives on V.S. Naipaul*. Washington, DC: Three Continents Press, 1977, pp. 194–207.

Donnell, Alison, 'Writing for Resistance: Nationalism and Narratives of Liberation', in Anim-Addo, *Framing the Word*, pp. 28–36.

Echeruo, M.J.C., *Joyce Cary and the Novel of Africa*. London: Longman, 1973.

Eco, Umberto, 'The Semantics of Metaphor', *The Role of the Reader: Explorations in the Semiotics of Texts*. London: Hutchinson, 1981.

Ekwensi, Cyprian, *People of the City*. London: Andrew Dakers, 1954.

——, 'African Literature', *Nigeria Magazine*, No. 83 (December 1964), 294–9.

——, *Juju Rock*. Lagos: African Universities Press, 1966.

Eliade, Mircea, *The Myth of the Eternal Return or, Cosmos and History*, trans. Willard R. Trask. Princeton, New Jersey: Princeton University Press, 1971.

Eliot, T.S., *Selected Essays*, 3rd edition. London: Faber and Faber, 1951.

Emecheta, Buchi, Interview with Adeola James, in James, *In Their Own Voices*, pp. 34–45.

Fabre, Michel, 'Samuel Selvon', in Bruce King, ed., *West Indian Literature*. London: Macmillan, 1979, pp. 111–25.

Fanon, Frantz, *Black Skin, White Masks*, trans. Charles Lam Markmann. New York: Grove Press, 1967.

——, *The Wretched of the Earth*, trans. Constance Farrington. Harmondsworth: Penguin, 1967.

Finnegan, Ruth, *Oral Literature in Africa*. Nairobi: Oxford University Press, 1970.

Fleming, Bruce, 'Brothers under the Skin: Achebe on *Heart of Darkness*', *Teaching Postcolonial and Commonwealth Literatures*, 19.3/20.1 (October 1992/February 1993), 90–9.

Foucault, Michel, 'What is an Author?' in David Lodge, ed., *Modern Criticism and Theory*. Harlow, Essex: Longman, 1988.

Fowler, Roger, *Linguistic Criticism*. Oxford: Oxford University Press, 1986.

Frank, Katherine, 'Women without Men: the Feminist Novel in Africa', *African Literature Today*, No. 15 (1987), 14–34.

Fraser, Robert, *The Novels of Ayi Kwei Armah*. London: Heinemann, 1980.

Frazer, J.G., *The Golden Bough: a Study in Magic and Religion*, abridged edition. London: Macmillan, 1987.

Freeman, Derek, 'Recollections of a Heretic', Address given at the Sydney Institute on 9 July 1996.

Genette, Gérard, *Narrative Discourse*, trans. Jane E. Lewin. Oxford: Blackwell, 1980.

Giddens, Anthony, *Central Problems in Social Theory*. London: Macmillan, 1979.

Goodwin, Ken, 'Studying Commonwealth Literature', *Teaching Postcolonial and Commonwealth Literatures*, 19.3/20.1 (October 1992/February 1993), 142–51.

Goody, Jack, *The Domestication of the Savage Mind*. Cambridge: Cambridge University Press, 1977.

Grace, Patricia, *Mutuwhenua: the Moon Sleeps*. Auckland: Longman Paul, 1978.

——, *Potiki*. Auckland: Penguin, 1986.

——, *Cousins*. Harmondsworth: Penguin, 1992.

——, Interview with Jane McRae, in Alley and Williams, *In the Same Room*.

Gurr, Andrew, *Writers in Exile: the Creative Use of Home in Modern Literature*. Sussex: Harvester Press; and New Jersey: Humanities Press, 1981.

Halliday, M.A.K., 'Linguistic Functions and Literary Style', in Seymour Chatman, ed., *Literary Style: a Symposium*. London: Oxford University Press 1971, pp. 332–4.

Hamner, Robert D., ed., *Critical Perspectives on V.S. Naipaul*. Washington, DC: Three Continents Press, 1977.

Hawkes, Terence, *Meaning by Shakespeare*. London and New York: Routledge, 1992.

Henshaw, Stanley K., and Jennifer Van Vort, 'Abortion Services in the United States, 1991 and 1992', *Family Planning Perspectives*, Vol. 26 (May/June 1994), 101.

Hodge, Merle, *Crick Crack, Monkey*. London: Heinemann, 1970.

Howard, W.J., 'Themes and Development in the Novels of Ngugi', in Edgar Wright, ed., *A Critical Evaluation of African Literature*. London: Heinemann, 1973.

Hutcheon, Linda, *A Poetics of Postmodernism: History, Theory, Fiction*. London and New York: Routledge, 1988.

——, 'The First Maori Novelist', Interview with Blanaid Fitzgerald, *New Zealand Listener*, 71, No. 1718, October 1972, 15–16.

——, *Tangi*. Auckland: Heinemann, 1973.

——, *Whanau*. Auckland: Heinemann, 1974.

Ihimaera, Witi, 'Maori Life and Literature: a Sensory Perception', in *New Zealand through the Arts: Past and Present*. Three Lectures reprinted from the Turnbull Library record, May 1982. Wellington: Friends of the Turnbull Library, 1982.

——, Interview with Jane Wilkinson, Rome, September 1984, *Kunapipi*, Vol. III, No. 1 (1985), 98–110.

——, *The Matriarch*. Auckland: Heinemann, 1986.

——, Interview with Mark Williams, in Alley and Williams, *In the Same Room*.

Irele, Abiola, 'Dimensions of African Discourse', *Teaching Postcolonial and Commonwealth Literatures*, special double issue of *College Literature*, 19:3/20:1 (October 1992/February 1993), 45–59.

Ivir, Vladimir, 'Formal Correspondence Vs Translation Equivalence Revisited', *Poetics Today*, Vol. 2:4 (1981).

Jahn, Janheinz, *A History of Neo-African Literature*. London: Faber and Faber, 1966.

James, Adeola, ed., *In Their Own Voices: African Women Writers Talk*. London: James Currey, 1990.

JanMohammed, Abdul R., and David Lloyd, eds, *The Nature and Context of Minority Discourse*. New York and Oxford: Oxford University Press, 1990.

Joneja, O.P., 'Domesticated English: Symbiotic or Syncretic: the Language of African and Indian Fiction Novel' (sic), *ACLALS Bulletin*, 7th Series, No. 6 (1986), 20–8.

Katrak, Ketu H., 'Decolonizing Culture: Toward a Theory for Postcolonial Women's Texts', *Modern Fiction Studies*, Vol. 35, No. 1 (Spring 1989), 157–79.

Kenyatta, Jomo, *Facing Mount Kenya: the Traditional Life of the Gikuyu*. African Writers Series. London: Heinemann, 1979.

Killam, G.D., 'A Note on the Title of *Petals of Blood*', *Journal of Commonwealth Literature*, Vol. XV, No. 1 (August 1980), 125–132.

Kincaid, Jamaica, *A Small Place*. London: Virago Press, 1988.

King, Bruce, *V.S. Naipaul*. London: Macmillan, 1993.

Lacan, Jacques, 'The Insistence of the Letter in the Unconscious', in David Lodge, ed., *Modern Criticism and Theory*. Harlow, Essex: Longman, 1988, pp. 79–106.

Lalla, Barbara, *Defining Jamaican Fiction: Marronage and the Discourse of Survival*. Tuscaloosa and London: The University of Alabama Press, 1996.

Lamming, George, *The Pleasures of Exile*. London: Michael Joseph, 1960.

——, *In the Castle of My Skin*. London: Longman, 1979.

Larson, Charles, *The Novel in the Third World*. Washington, DC: Inscape Publishers, 1976.

——, *The Emergence of African Fiction*. London: Macmillan, 1978.

Le Page, R.B., 'Dialect in West Indian Literature', in Edward Baugh, ed., *Critics on Caribbean Literature*. London: George Allen and Unwin, 1978, pp. 128–9.

Lodge, David, ed., *Modern Criticism and Theory*. Harlow, Essex: Longman, 1988.

Lyotard, Jean-François, *The Postmodern Condition: a Report on Knowledge*, trans. Geoff Bennington and Brian Massumi. Manchester: Manchester University Press, 1984.

Mahuta, Robert Te Kotahi, 'Whaikoorero: a Study of Formal Maori Speech', Unpublished MA thesis, University of Auckland, 1974.

Mais, Roger, *Brother Man*. London: Heinemann, 1974.

Maja-Pearce, Adewale, 'Just Another Sick Book', *Okike: an African Journal of New Writing*, No. 23 (February 1983), 133–6.

——, *A Mask Dancing: Nigerian Novelists of the Eighties*. London: Hans Zell Publishers, 1992.

Mannoni, O., *Prospero and Caliban: the Psychology of Colonization*, 2nd edition, trans. Pamela Powesland. New York: Frederick A. Praeger, 1964.

Mazrui, Ali, *On Heroes and Uhuru Worship*. London: Longman, 1967.

McCabe, Joseph. *The Columbia Encyclopedia's Crimes against the Truth: How a Popular Reference Work is Being Used as a Weapon against Free Culture and Twisted to Fit the Purposes of Lying Obscurantists*. Full-length text posted on the World Wide Web in June 1997. http://www.infidels.org.

——, *The Lies and Fallacies of the Encyclopedia Britannica: How Powerful and Shameless Clerical Forces Castrated a Famous Work of Reference*. Full-length text posted on the World Wide Web in June 1997. http://www. infidels.org.

McClintock, Anne, *Imperial Leather: Race, Gender and Sexuality in the Colonial Context*. New York and London: Routledge, 1995.

McKenzie, D.F., *Oral Culture, Literacy and Print in Early New Zealand*. Wellington: Victoria University Press, 1985.

McMillen, Liz, 'Linguists Find the Debate Over "Ebonics" Uninformed', *Chronicle of Higher Education* (17 January 1997), A16.

Miller, Karl, 'V.S. Naipaul and the New Order', in Hamner, *Critical Perspectives on V.S. Naipaul*, pp. 111–26.

Mohan, Rajeswari, 'Dodging the Crossfire: Questions for Postcolonial Pedagogy', *Teaching Postcolonial and Commonwealth Literatures*, special double issue of *College Literature*, 19:3/20:1 (October 1992/February 1993), 28–44.

Moore, Gerald, *Modern Poetry from Africa*. Harmondsworth: Penguin, 1963.

——, *The Chosen Tongue*. London: Longman, 1969.

——, *Twelve African Writers*. London: Hutchinson, 1980.

Morrison, Toni, *The Bluest Eye*. London: Pan Books/Chatto & Windus, 1990.

Moyers, Bill, 'Chinua Achebe: Nigerian Novelist', in Betty Sue Flowers, ed., *A World of Ideas*. New York: Doubleday, 1989, pp. 333–44.

Mudrooroo [Narogin], 'White Forms, Aboriginal Content', in Bill Ashcroft, Gareth Williams and Helen Tiffin, eds, *The Post-Colonial Studies Reader*. London and New York: Routledge, 1995.

Mumford, Lewis, *Technique and Civilisation*. London: Routledge, 1947.

Naipaul, V.S., *The Mystic Masseur*. Harmondsworth: Penguin, 1964.

——, *A House for Mr Biswas*. Harmondsworth: Penguin, 1969.

——, *The Middle Passage*. Harmondsworth: Penguin, 1969.

——, *The Mimic Men*. Harmondsworth: Penguin, 1969.

——, *The Suffrage of Elvira*. Harmondsworth: Penguin, 1969.

——, *In a Free State*. Harmondsworth: Penguin, 1973.

——, *Guerrillas*. Harmondsworth: Penguin, 1976.

——, *A Bend in the River*. Harmondsworth: Penguin, 1980.

Neill, Michael, 'Guerrillas and Gangs: Frantz Fanon and V.S. Naipaul', *Ariel*, Vol. XIII, No. 4 (October 1982), 21–62.

——, 'Coming Home: Teaching the Post-Colonial Novel', *Islands*, 35, New Series Vol. 2, No. 1 (April 1985), 38–53.

Ngugi, James [Ngugi wa Thiong'o], 'Satire in Nigeria', in Cosmo Pieterse and Donald Munro, eds, *Protest and Conflict in African Literature*. London: Heinemann, 1969.

Ngugi wa Thiong'o, *Homecoming: Essays on African and Caribbean Literature*. London: Heinemann, 1972.

——, *A Grain of Wheat*. London: Heinemann, 1975.

——, *The River Between*. London: Heinemann, 1975.

——, *Weep Not, Child*. London: Heinemann, 1976.

——, *Petals of Blood*. London: Heinemann, 1977.

——, 'The Writer of His World', *West Africa* (22–9 December 1980), 2606.

——, *Devil on the Cross*. London: Heinemann, 1982.

——, *Decolonising the Mind: the Politics of Language in African Literature*. London: James Currey, 1986.

——, *Matigari*. London: Heinemann, 1987.

Nichols, Lee, *Conversations with African Writers*. Washington, DC: Voice of America, 1981.

Nketia, J.H., *Funeral Dirges of the Akan People*. Achimota: University College of the Cape Coast, 1955.

Nunns, Rachel, 'Doing Her Job: Patricia Grace's Fiction', *Islands*, Vol. VII, No. 4 (August 1979), 416–21.

Obiechina, E.N., 'The Problem of Language in African Writing: the Example of the Novel', *Conch*, Vol. 5:1 & 2 (1972), 11–29.

——, *Culture, Tradition and Society in the West African Novel*. Cambridge: Cambridge University Press, 1975.

Ogot, Grace, *The Graduate*. Nairobi: Uzima Press, 1980.

——, *The Promised Land*. Nairobi: Heinemann, 1990.

Ojinmah, Umelo, *Witi Ihimaera: a Changing Vision*. Dunedin: University of Otago Press, 1993.

Okonkwo, Chidi, 'Social Transition and Cultural Noetics in the Language of Chinua Achebe's Fiction', paper contributed to the 'Conference on Tradition and Transition in African Letters', Yale University, 19–21 April 1990.

——, 'Modern African Literature: Quest for Order in a Changing Order', *Cambridge Anthropology*, Vol. 15:3 (1991), 41–51.

——, 'Chinua Achebe: the Wrestler and the Challenge of Chaos', in Michael Parker and Roger Starkey, eds, *Postcolonial Literatures: Achebe, Ngugi, Desai, Walcott*. London: Macmillan, 1995, pp. 83–100.

Okri, Ben, *The Famished Road*. London: Vintage, 1991.

Olney, James, *Tell Me Africa: an Approach to African Literature*. Princeton, New Jersey: Princeton University Press, 1973.

Ong, Walter J., *Orality and Literacy: the Technologizing of the Word*. London and New York: Methuen, 1982.

Osundare, Niyi, 'Words of Iron, Sentences of Thunder: Soyinka's Prose Style', *African Literature Today*, No. 13 (1983), 24–37.

Palmer, Eustace, *The Growth of the African Novel*. London: Heinemann, 1979.

Pearson, Bill, *Fretful Sleepers and Other Essays*. London: Heinemann, 1974.

——, *Rifled Sanctuaries: Some Views of the Pacific Islands in Western Literature to 1900*. Auckland: Auckland University Press and Oxford University Press, 1984.

Poananga, Atareta, Mana Wahine and Te Ahi Kaa, '*The Matriarch*: Trample on Strong Women, Part I', *Broadsheet* (December 1986).

——, '*The Matriarch*: Trample on Strong Women, Part II', *Broadsheet* (January/February 1987), 25–9.

Rao, Raja, *Kanthapura*. Bombay: Oxford University Press, 1963.

Ravenscroft, Arthur, *Chinua Achebe*. London: Longman, 1969.

Reed, Walter L., 'The Problem with a Poetics of the Novel', in Mark Spilka, ed., *Towards a Poetic of Fiction*. Bloomington and London: Indiana University Press, 1977, pp. 62–74.

Reid, V.S., *New Day*. London: Heinemann, 1973.

Roberts, Peter A., *West Indians and Their Language*. Cambridge: Cambridge University Press, 1988.

Robinson, Roger, 'Albert Wendt: an Assessment', *Landfall*, 135, Vol. 34, No. 3 (September 1980), 275–89.

Rodney, Walter, *How Europe Underdeveloped Africa*. London: Bougle-L'Ouverture, 1972.

Rohlehr, Gordon, 'Character and Rebellion in *A House for Mr Biswas*', in Robert D. Hamner, ed., *Critical Perspectives on V.S. Naipaul*, pp. 84–93.

Roscoe, Adrian, *Mother is Gold: a Study in West African Literature*. Cambridge: Cambridge University Press, 1971.

Rutherford, Anna, Lars Jensen and Shirley Chew, eds, *Into the Nineties: Post-Colonial Women's Writing*. Armidale, New South Wales: Dangaroo Press, 1994.

Said, Edward W., *Culture & Imperialism*. London and New York: Routledge, 1993.

Schipper, Mineke, 'Mother Africa on a Pedestal: the Male Heritage in African Literature and Criticism', *African Literature Today*, No. 15 (1987), 35–54.

S[chwimmer], E[rik] G., 'A Note on the Literature of the Modern Maori', *Mate*, No. 4 (February 1960), 22–3.

Selvon, Samuel, *A Brighter Sun*. London: Longman, 1979.

Shelton, Austin, 'The "Palm Oil" of Language: Proverbs in Chinua Achebe's Novels', *Modern Language Quarterly*, Vol. 30:1 (1969), 86–111.

Shoemaker, Adam, 'Paper Tracks: Indigenous Literatures in Canada, Australia, and New Zealand', *New National and Post-Colonial Literatures: an Introduction*, ed. Bruce King. Oxford: Clarendon Press, 1996, pp. 245–63.

Simms, Norman, 'A Maori Literature in English, Part 1: Patricia Grace', *Pacific Quarterly Moana*, Vol. 3, No. 2 (April 1978), 186–99.

——, 'Maori Literature in English, Prose Writers, Part 2: Witi Ihimaera', *Pacific Quarterly Moana*, Vol. 3, No. 3 (July 1978), 336–48.

Soyinka, Wole, *The Road*. London: Oxford University Press, 1965.

——, *Idanre and Other Poems*. London: Methuen, 1967.

——, 'The Writer in a Modern African State', in Per Wastberg, ed., *The Writer in Modern Africa*. Uppsala: Scandinavia Institute for African Studies, 1968, pp. 14–21.

——, *The Interpreters*. London: Fontana/Collins, 1972.

——, *Season of Anomy*. London: Rex Collins, 1973.

——, *Myth, Literature and the African World*. Cambridge: Cambridge University Press, 1976.

Spivak, Gayatri, 'Reflections on Cultural Studies in the Post-Colonial Conjuncture', *Critical Studies*, Vol. 3, No. 1 (1991), 64–78.

Spurr, David, *The Rhetoric of Empire: Colonial Discourse in Journalism, Travel Writing, and Imperial Administration*. Durham and London: Duke University Press, 1993.

Stanzel, Frank K., 'Teller-Characters and Reflector Characters in Narrative Theory', *Poetics Today*, Vol. 2:2 (1981), 6–14.

Stead, C.K., 'War Book: The Matriarch', review of *The Matriarch*, by Witi Ihimaera, *London Review of Books* (18 December 1986), 20–2.

Stevick, Philip, *The Theory of the Novel*. New York: Free Press, 1967.

Stratton, Florence, *Contemporary African Literature and the Politics of Gender*. London and New York: Routledge, 1994.

Strinati, Dominic, *An Introduction to Theories of Popular Culture*. London and New York: Routledge, 1995.

Suleiman, Susan Rubin, 'Redundancy and the "Readable" Text', *Poetics Today*, Vol. 1:3 (1980), 119–20.

Thieme, John, ed., *The Arnold Anthology of Post-Colonial Literatures in English*. London: Arnold, 1996.

Tutuola, Amos, *The Palm-Wine Drinkard*. London: Faber and Faber, 1952.

Van Sertima, Ivan, 'V.S. Naipaul', Foreword, *Caribbean Writers: Critical Essays*. London: New Beacon Books, 1968.

Walcott, Derek, *Selected Poems*. New York: Farrar, Strauss and Co., 1964.

Wali, Obiajunwa, 'Dead End of African Literature?' *Transition*, No. 10 (September 1963), 13–15.

Waterhouse, Keith, Review of *No Longer at Ease*, by Chinua Achebe, *New Statesman*, Vol. LX (17 September 1960), 396.

Wellek, René, and Austin Warren, *Theory of Literature*. Harmondsworth: Penguin, 1980.

Wendt, Albert, *Sons for the Return Home*. Auckland: Longman Paul, 1973.

——, Interview with John and Rose Marie Beston, *World Literatures Written in English*, Vol. XII, No. 1 (April 1977), 152–62.

——, *Pouliuli*. Auckland: Longman Paul, 1977.

——, *Leaves of the Banyan Tree*. Auckland: Penguin, 1981.

——, 'Towards a New Oceania', in Guy Amirthanayagam, ed., *Writers in East–West Encounter: New Cultural Bearings*. London: Macmillan, 1982, pp. 202–15.

——, *Ola*. Auckland: Penguin Books, 1991.

——, *Black Rainbow*. Auckland: Penguin Books, 1992.

Wendt, Albert, ed., *Lali: a Pacific Anthology*. Auckland, Longman Paul, 1980.

White, John J., *Mythology in the Modern Novel: a Study of Prefiguration Techniques*. Princeton, New Jersey: Princeton University Press, 1971.

Williams, Mark, *Leaving the Highway: Six Contemporary New Zealand Novelists*. Auckland: Auckland University Press, 1990.

Williamson, Karina, 'Roger Mais: West Indian Novelist', *Journal of Commonwealth Literature*, No. 2 (December 1966), 138–47.

Wren, Robert, *Achebe's World: the Historical and Cultural Context of the Novels of Chinua Achebe*. London: Longman, 1978.

Wright, Derek, 'Love and Politics in the African Novel: Ayi Kwei Armah's *Why Are We So Blest?*' *ACLALS Bulletin*, 7th Series, No. 1 (1986), 13–27.

Young, Robert, *White Mythologies: Writing History and the West*. London and New York: Routledge, 1990.

Zabus, Chantal, *The African Palimpsest: Indigenization of Language in the West African Europhone Novel*. Amsterdam, Atlanta: Rodopi, 1991.

——, 'Language, Orality, and Literature', in King, *New National and Post-Colonial Literatures*, pp. 29–44.

Index